MW01392798

Got

Taming of the Wolf

Volume II

~

Shadow State

by Isabel Roman

Blood Moon

by Autumn Shelley

Raven's Shelter

by Dariel Raye

Marek's New World

by Renee Wildes

Werewolves in London

by Karilyn Bentley

This is a work of fiction. Names, characters, places, and incidents are either the product of the author's imagination or are used fictitiously, and any resemblance to actual persons living or dead, business establishments, events, or locales, is entirely coincidental.

Got Wolf Anthology: Taming of the Wolf, Volume II

COPYRIGHT ©2009 by The Wild Rose Press

COPYRIGHT ©2009 **Shadow State** by Isabel Roman
COPYRIGHT ©2009 **Blood Moon** by Autumn Shelley
COPYRIGHT ©2009 **Raven's Shelter** by Dariel Raye
COPYRIGHT ©2009 **Marek's New World** by Renee Wildes
COPYRIGHT ©2009 **Werewolves in London** by Karilyn Bentley

All rights reserved. No part of this book may be used or reproduced in any manner whatsoever without written permission of the author or The Wild Rose Press except in the case of brief quotations embodied in critical articles or reviews.
Contact Information: info@thewildrosepress.com

Cover Art by *Angela Anderson*

The Wild Rose Press
PO Box 706
Adams Basin, NY 14410-0706
Visit us at www.thewildrosepress.com

Publishing History
First Black Rose Anthology Edition, 2009
Print ISBN 1-60154-709-9

Published in the United States of America

Shadow State

by

Isabel Roman

Dedication

To my parents,
and all those who've helped along the way
and believed this was possible.
And to my co-patroness. You know who you are.

Chapter One

Near the Teutoburg Forest
Osnabrück, Lower Saxony, Germany
August 20, 1934

The darkness posed no challenge to Christoph von Berangar's eyes, he could see as clear as if the sun burned bright overhead. He gazed at the property through the glass-paned garden doors of his manor house. In the distance, he saw Peter. His friend and advisor ran near the riverbed, wild and free in his natural *wölfe* form. A part of Christoph envied the wildness Peter reveled in daily.

Yet for most of his twenty-seven years, he'd remained in human form, living as they did not as his ancestors had.

The clatter of dishes slamming onto his desk, an obvious attempt to disturb, did not faze him. Margaret always made her presence known when something bothered her. The scarred surface of his ancient mahogany desk was witness to her efforts. Another few mars wouldn't be noticed.

"Well?" The familiar sharp tone cut through his treasured silence.

"Did you make a decision? Are we going to Berlin?"

He said nothing, as he hadn't the last dozen times she'd cornered him.

"That's it!" Margaret stated in her usual dramatic fashion.

The reflection of her hands in the window flung into the air, one clutching a letter.

"I'm going to torch the nursery…No! I'm going to divest the entire house of its contents, linens, china, clothing. Why do we need it? I'll get rid of it all. That'll force you into the wild. Force you to become your *wölfe* again, so maybe, *maybe* you'll find some of your mating instincts. I'm tired of these games, Christoph!" She shouted now, her tone warned him of her seriousness.

"Enough is enough. Marriage is a serious prospect. We must plan for our future. The time has come to take action."

Expressionless, he turned to see the tall woman, her stark white hair peppered with black strands. Her hands crossed resolutely above the apron of her uniform, a frown creased her prematurely aged face, her glare fierce.

"I presume," he drawled, "the letter is for me?"

Without waiting for her answer, he strode the short distance between them. Leaning down, he took the letter and kissed her cheek. "Stop worrying so," he whispered.

"Meet the girl," she wheedled.

Margaret was correct, in that at least. The time had come to take action regarding his feelings for a woman he'd yet to lay eyes on. His only connections to her were the bimonthly Pack reports and more frequent personal correspondence. Through these mundane matters, a closeness had developed between them. A creature of instinct, he could not dismiss the intellectual aspect of her.

Alpha Females needed to be both strong and smart to lead their Clan.

Still, Christoph was impatient to explore their connection in person. Unbeknownst to Margaret, his initial plan stymied due to a medical conference. His woman traveled with her father for these past weeks. By the postmark on this letter, she'd returned to Berlin.

He hadn't questioned the letter was from Elsa. The intoxicating scent of her permeated his senses.

"I've never known you to hesitate when it's something you wanted....Until now," Margaret stated with a flat tone.

"I do not hesitate." He only just refrained from snapping at her. "As Alpha, I have too many responsibilities to leave the estate unattended. I shall meet her soon enough," he promised.

More from habit than any real need, he flicked on the desk lamp. Silver letter opener in hand, a sardonic gift from his father if ever there was one, he watched his housekeeper and one-time nurse bustle about the office. She ignored his pointed look.

"Do you think your mother would've approved of this?" she scolded. The pillow she plumped threatened to burst. "Breaks my heart I say, breaks my heart. This Alpha line will soon die out if you do not start procreating this century!"

Patiently, he watched her continue about the room. He didn't remember his mother, could recall her only through photos his father had lovingly preserved. It was a poor argument. He expected better from Margaret, who showed no signs of stopping her tirade or leaving him to his letter. He seriously worried for the pillow, too.

"No girl in Lower Saxony interests you. I don't care if this child has hooves and a snout...well she does have a snout when she transforms, I suppose. Doesn't matter! Marry her!"

Christoph gazed at her with warm chocolate eyes. She meant well despite her tendency to nag. That was Margaret, always consistent. "I gather," he said with a sly grin, tapping the letter on the desktop. "You have completed plans for a trip to Berlin?"

"Yes," she responded halfheartedly before his meaning sunk in. She dropped the plumped pillow in her haste to race to his desk. The pillow tilted drunkenly against the chair.

"Yes! Oh! I must finish the trunk. When are we leaving?"

"Two days." He grinned at her. With a whirl of excitement, she crushed his head to her bosom in undisguised glee and rushed through the door.

At last, he was left to his silence.

In one fluid movement, he opened the envelope. Her scent surrounded him. He took it in, savoring the sweetness of it, the strong undertone reminiscent of the forests that surrounded his estate. In reaction, he smiled.

His physical response to her scent, as strong now as it had been the first time he'd opened her letter, reinforced his belief that Elsa was for him.

As he withdrew the paper, he recalled the first report she'd sent in her father's stead. The business-like tone of the correspondence, the facts of her pack outlined in short, informative points.

Over time their writings changed, became more intimate. Christoph couldn't have said when, but over the months, his interest peaked for the woman behind the ink. His appetite whetted for more.

Margaret had taken notice of it, and, to his chagrin, so had the others on his estate.

"Pensive as usual, Christoph." Hans von Troschke stated, sauntering through the opened doorway. Margaret hadn't closed it in her rush to pack.

With a curse at this latest interruption, Christoph refolded the letter he hadn't even begun to read. His cousin, an unusually dour expression etched on his face, had a heightened air of tension around him. Lines bracketed his mouth, his stiff shoulders detracting from his languid grace.

Hans dropped a packet of sealed envelopes onto the desk. Suspicion colored his tone, and his nose wrinkled as he peered at the untouched plate.

"The thin slices of beef look edible enough, I suppose," he drawled. "But they're coated with that horrible mint sauce Margaret insists is the height of culinary fashion. We must put a stop to this," Hans mockingly announced in his customary tone.

The sentiment fell flat, since his eyes drifted to the envelopes he'd placed on the desk. The tension hadn't eased.

"Our kitchen should not be influenced by Berlin's latest peacock chef."

"Don't you ever knock?" Christoph growled. As Hans seemed in no rush to leave, with a quick move, he placed the letter back in its envelope and into a drawer. He was not going to read Elsa's letter in front of an audience.

A muscular grey *wölfe,* face and tail tipped with black, padded through the garden doors and jumped onto a cushioned mahogany chair. His form blackened, shifted and his body extended as bones and muscles reshaped and rearranged themselves. Within moments, a naked, light brown-haired man replaced the *wölfe* on the elegant black Rococo chair.

"I enjoy the mint sauce," Peter countered, lounging in the chair.

"You enjoy gnawing on tree bark," Hans scoffed.

"I'm sure mint sauce isn't our greatest crises right now." Christoph interjected before Hans and Peter got into another inane debate. Still seated, he nodded to the packet on his desk. "What's happened?"

"It's from the van Dietrich Pack of Berlin." Hans' voice wasn't light any longer. "Unscheduled communication."

Christoph's gut tightened at the mention of the unexpected letter. If something was wrong in Berlin, Elsa no doubt knew of it. Or would, soon enough. Things were too tenuous in Germany these days, even the slightest whiff of danger brought disastrous results. His fingers touched the drawer where her letter rested, and he wondered what it said.

"Messenger arrived this afternoon while you were out," Hans continued. "Along with some rather disturbing news."

Christoph took the envelope and sliced it open, but didn't read it yet. "What news?"

"What we heard on the wireless is true. The little Chancellor has gone and done it," Hans replied.

Christoph's attention now focused on his second in command, the letter forgotten.

"The intimidation he has wrought since…" Hans smoothed back his dark blonde hair. "What do they call it?"

Peter stood to slip into a black robe, one of many Margaret left for just this purpose. "*Nacht der langen Messer*—The Night of the Long Knives."

"Yes, of course. Their sanctimonious moniker to cover out and out murders," Hans spat. "They systematically killed any and all opposition to their seizure of power. They eliminated their own because it was politically advantageous."

"We do not have the option to live as *wölfes*, to live in the forests, anymore." Peter leaned against a side table, the plate of mint-covered beef in his hands. "They've hunted and killed every *wölfe* in the countryside."

Christoph glanced at Peter as he continued, well aware that not a single ordinary *wölfe* remained in Germany. "They've eradicated *wölfes* from the land. Our previous Alpha had to redefine the way we all live. Discovery is a constant threat, and with discovery inevitable eradication. Or worse."

"We must remain in human form, but even like this we're not safe," Hans added. "The Night of the Long Knives proved that. We lost two of our own. Now, *The Reichstag*, our own elected legislators," the tautness in Hans' voice increased, "has by its own vote, declared itself a puppet institution!"

"*Hitler*," Christoph said disgusted, "now has complete authority. This insignificant man from nowhere walked into *The Reichstag*, castrated them, and crowned himself like Napoleon."

"We must take precautions, Christoph." Hans said over his shoulder and paced to the large antique map of Germany on the far wall. Dark markers indicated the location of the Clan's twenty Packs.

Christoph didn't need to look at the markers. He knew where every Pack was located and where every family lived. No one moved without first informing him. During the past several years of turmoil and hardships, more members relocated to their Clan center in Lower Saxony, but thousands still lived as they had for generations.

Peter joined Hans by the map, but Christoph's attention was drawn to the missive.

"Stories of the Chancellor's—of the *Führer's*—interest in the unusual, the occult, are surfacing," Hans reminded. "Should just one of us be discovered–?"

Christoph looked up at his advisors, his closest friends. "We already have been."

****

Agitation consumed Elsa von Skyler, an emotion that reverberated in her every movement as she paced up and down the main salon of their Berlin townhouse. Impatient, she yanked pins from her hair, letting the blonde locks fall to her shoulders. Her stocking feet made no sound on the hardwood floor, or the Berber area rug her great-grandmother brought back from Morocco. Her shoes lay sprawled near the arched entrance where she'd flung them the moment they arrived.

The antiques scattered around the room blended oddly with the art deco furniture, many pieces handpicked straight from the Bauhaus School before its closure by the new regime. Silver accents highlighted the straight lines of the unique style. A representation of a forest, its trees elongated and stylized, hung framed on one wall. She'd never been able to make out the signature, but it drew her the moment she'd seen it. The image portrayed her sense of belonging to her Clan, even while so far from its center, all too well.

Her father, Gerard, sat stiffly on the last remaining brocade chair and watched. "*Liebling*, it's a terrible risk to undertake. I don't want you involved in this!"

"We have no choice!"

"Have you alerted Christoph?"

"Yes."

A warm sensation flooded her at his name despite the imperativeness of the situation. She ruthlessly squashed it under the urgency of the moment. In her letter to Christoph, sent this afternoon, she'd also clearly stated they were back in Germany. Still, now was not the time for fanciful thoughts of her Clan's Alpha.

"I dispatched one this afternoon."

"I've warned you. Twice you've skirted my warnings to assist those children. Now our worst fears are realized."

"Under these new policies they would've been euthanized!" she exclaimed.

"The policies are not our concern. We can no longer trouble ourselves with the humans. Understand that, Elsa." Gerard stood, his normally clear face florid with anger.

Her father had a formidable temper, one she'd inherited. Today she'd seen it directed fully at her.

"One of our Clan has been captured, something that has not happened in modern times. We've seen what horrors they do to twins," he waved in the general direction of *Charitéplatz 1* where their research hospital stood. "To those with the most common anomalies. With the leaps in science these past decades, I dare not think what they would do to us."

He pounded his chest, and she could see the fear in his eyes, the blue she'd inherited from him flashed darker. His *wölfe* was close to the surface.

"The one concern we have is the survival and safety of our Clan."

"I'm aware," she bit out through clenched teeth, her own fear making her temper sharper, her *wölfe* clawed to be released, "that because of these *policies* we're all in danger. The course they take with their eugenics studies at Kaiser Wilhelm is absurd. What they do to humans' effects us. You've seen it at *Charité*!"

"Your actions," he continued with more calm but no less fear, "brought the suspicion of the Department of Scientific Inquiries down on us. Now we're faced with one of our own in the clutches of that maniac Strasser. They'll watch us closer than ever."

"Erik is in mourning," she shot back.

"True. To see his mate torn apart by a looting mob is something I wish on no man, human or *wölfe*." Gerard agreed with a pain she knew stemmed from his own wife's death in the bloody aftermath of the war. She remembered her mother's scent but little else. On rare occasions, she could hear her voice, a distant melody of love.

"It doesn't change the fact—he's endangered us all."

"He's no longer a member of our Pack, but of Ursula's; that responsibility fell to the van Dietrich Pack when they mated. It's all our duty to protect him now."

"They know what he is," her father insisted.

"There were witnesses we'll never be able to find. The Nazi's know what Erik is and where his family is from. This will destroy everything we've worked for." He didn't look happy even as he said the words she dreaded all afternoon.

"We have two choices. We can help him escape, move him to Lower Saxony or elsewhere." He paused and took a deep breath. "Or we can kill him."

"Father," she began, but couldn't go on. She turned to stare at the forest painting.

The very thought of killing Erik made her ill. For years, her father worked to find a cure for their dwindling population, she alongside him once her schooling was completed. To kill a member of their Clan....She couldn't bear it, not when her instinct told her to protect the Clan at all costs.

More, she wasn't sure they could do it. The logistics of getting past the guards to Erik were hard enough, but with so few scientists working on his case, suspicion would instantly fall to them. And the Nazi's were not a forgiving group.

Gerard's unspoken words hung heavily between them. If they helped Erik escape, or worse were forced to do the unthinkable, there was a strong chance they'd have to leave Berlin, too. Part of Berlin's elite for centuries, the von Skylers had status, power, and connections. If they moved, all they'd worked so hard to achieve in the interest of their people would be destroyed.

In the end it didn't matter. They had to protect the secret. Whether they evacuated Berlin or not, they'd planned for that long before Germany was a unified country. They'd do what they had to in order to survive.

"The choice is unclear. Escape is what we all want but we may be forced," Elsa swallowed hard. "We may be forced to end Erik's suffering.

Chapter Two

"Christoph is due this afternoon," Gerard said while they walked along the corridor towards the hospital's main exit. "If you wish to still consult him."

"If an opportunity arises," she whispered back, "you need to take it. I'd prefer to discuss this directly with him, as well, but we may not have such luxury."

Since Scientific Inquiries brought Erik in, she'd considered various avenues of escape for the wounded *wölfe.* After two days of torture at the hands of so-called scientists interested merely in discovering his secrets, she understood how much of a blessing it might be to end his life.

Images that would never leave her mind now overwhelmed it. Electricity, starvation, beatings with rods and fists, they tried it all. They took so much blood it was a miracle he remained conscious. They bound him to a metal chair and didn't let him sleep. Bright lights blazed day and night, and the same song played incessantly, meant to drive him insane.

Elsa smashed all her Chopin recordings.

No longer recognizable as a human, the poor man hadn't allowed the change to his *wölfe*, either.

She was partly the reason for that, she and Gerard. Erik wasn't stupid; even through his delirium he knew what his change would cost the Clan. Seeing them with the other scientists confirmed his worse fears.

The Nazis knew of their species.

This morning, when she took another vial of

blood, he'd begged her to kill him. With four other scientists and two SS interrogators watching, all she could do was murmur that they would get him out.

Erik had laughed, a harsh, broken sound that made her skin crawl and the hair on the back of her neck stand straight.

"I've lost my mate," he'd said low enough for only her, with her enhanced *wölfe* senses, to hear. "I've endangered us all by changing before witnesses. I'm bound like a rabid beast. Tested like the anomaly they think I am. Kill me."

Now, Karl Strasser, Head of the Department of Scientific Inquiries—Special Interests Division, wanted the results of Erik's blood work. Gerard was on his way to meet with Strasser. Initially, Elsa wanted to see Erik again, but didn't wish to draw the suspicion of her colleagues. Instead, she decided to go home to await Christoph's arrival. She didn't envy her father.

Christoph.

Their relationship confused her. Well, no, she knew what she felt for him. A new tone snaked through his letters, one she knew wasn't present when her father handled the Pack's correspondence.

Elsa stopped midstride and shuddered at the very thought.

Finally meeting him had her stomach aflutter, and she wiped damp hands on her skirt. No, she knew how she felt for the Alpha. Whether the feelings in his letters would transfer when they met face-to-face, she didn't know. Instinct permeated her being, a powerful thing.

But is it enough?

"Insufferable man," Gerard continued. "Pompous ass who thinks he's a scientist. At least he's more interested in Erik than those children you helped."

"Greta told me this morning he's brought in more SS," Elsa whispered. "Now that they're the de facto army, you must be careful."

"I won't tell him what I really think," her father promised. "But I reserve the right to do so."

Elsa chuckled, and squeezed his hand. "Don't be long."

He looked down at her for several moments, eyes glinting. "I shall be the very soul of scientific savvy."

"It's not your scientific savvy I'm worried about," she kissed his cheek in farewell. "It's your temper."

With another light chuckle, she proceeded down the hallway, tracking Gerard's scent until he was deep into the office wing.

****

Christoph waited while Peter paid the taxi driver. Stepping out of the way, he looked about the neighborhood. Several people stared at him, but he knew it wasn't because he didn't fit in on *Brüderstraße*, with its grand architecture which once housed a variety of famous names.

If he remembered his history correctly, the von Skyler townhouse was by Karl Friedrich Schinkel, the neoclassic detail a clear indication.

He glanced at Peter, careful not to meet the eyes of those who continued to stare. Strangers needed to be treated warily these days; one never knew whom one could trust. Ignoring the interest they caused, Margaret bustled up next to him, directing a footman to unload the second taxi.

"I'll leave you to it, then," Peter said. He gazed about the streets like a wide-eyed farm boy on his first outing to the city.

"Don't get lost," Christoph warned, only partially joking.

Peter sniffed in indignation. It also served to memorize the area. "I doubt that'll happen."

With a final nod, he sauntered off. Christoph could all but see him sniffing the air as new scents crowded for recognition. Peter had visited Hannover several times, before his majority. By then he'd decided civilized life wasn't all that civilized.

Christoph, too, scented the air, searching for her heady signature. She was everywhere on the street, and for one blind moment he wanted to tear it apart, strike down everyone who'd ever laid eyes on her. The flash of possessiveness surprised him.

Not the best way to remain inconspicuous.

Margaret's commands came into sharp focus. Before she could pester him, he strode up the steps.

****

Elsa took a deep breath at hearing the party enter the townhouse. She waited in the drawing room just off the foyer, pacing like an expectant father and wondered what the reality of Christoph would be like. She didn't have too wait long.

An older woman barreled toward Elsa with a wide, toothy grin, arms outstretched. "Fräulein von Skyler, *liebling*, how wonderful it is to finally meet you!"

Stunned at the warmth of the greeting, Elsa allowed the woman to envelope her. When she pulled back, Elsa smiled, unable not to.

"Very nice to meet you, Frau…?"

"Margaret," a deep voice answered.

Her head jerked up at the newcomer. Elsa already knew him, his familiar scent reached her the moment their butler, Otto, let the party into the foyer. She felt flushed and wondered if the feeling reflected on her cheeks. She hoped not.

"Frau Margaret." Elsa squeezed the woman's hands.

She glanced at Christoph, who offered a small smile in greeting but otherwise gave nothing away. He wandered about the room, attention on her furnishings.

"What a lovely home you have, Fräulein. Such

modern taste."

Elsa looked at Margaret to thank her, and repressed a grin when she noticed the odd look the other woman gave her art deco furniture. Many, like her father, preferred the classic antiques of the previous centuries. After living so long with those antiques, she had to make the change.

"And you, child, you are an absolute vision, is she not Christoph?" Margaret continued.

"Thank you, Frau Margaret. I hope your journey to Berlin was pleasant?" Elsa directed the question to Christoph as Otto entered the room. She'd never been in the presence of the Clan's Alpha. Was there protocol she'd missed? Had she forgotten to bow or something?

"The journey was pleasant enough. There are many changes since the last time I ventured into Berlin." Christoph stepped around Margaret, effectively commanding Elsa's complete attention. "Tell me," he continued while Otto unobtrusively led Margaret out. "What is Erik's status?"

Taken aback by the very business-like tone, Elsa wondered if she would glimpse the man she knew from their letters or simply deal with the Alpha. In that same moment, she chided herself. Erik's situation was far too dire to bother with any other nonsense.

"I haven't been able to speak to him with any sort of privacy." She turned from the Alpha to pace a few steps. The space gave her more room to think, helped reign in her myriad feelings.

"Torture of the worst kind, Christoph. They *will* break him. It is simply a question of when."

"What do the Nazi's know?"

Elsa faced him. "For now they experiment. Testing the limits of his strength. They know of his dominance over other canines and the ability to dominate while remaining in human form." She delivered her statements with her usual scientific demeanor but her eyes told a different story, one she hoped Christoph would understand. "Erik has resisted. He—"

"What of the security around him?"

"There are four shifts—SS guards." She closed her eyes to better see the arrangement. "Two at his door, two others each at both entrances to the wing. Strasser, the head of the department in charge of this, two interrogators, and the six scientists approved by the department are allowed to study the subject."

Horrified at her slip, her gaze flew to his. "Erik."

He closed the distance between them. Taking her hand, he softly said, "What have you told this Strasser?"

"My father is meeting with him," she frowned at the clock on the mantle. "He's still there, but Strasser is a master at long boring meetings." She ran the fingers of her free hand down the front of her skirt. Christoph's hold felt large and reassuring around her other hand, and she tightened her grip.

"We altered the blood work. Strasser is paranoid but, for now, he trusts us. If anything unusual arises, he'll have another doctor test it. We are a close-knit group, many look up to and respect Gerard. Even so, there are those sympathetic to the new eugenics policies."

"Of those," he wondered, "how many would not think to hide the unusual properties of our blood should they be called upon to study the tests?"

"Exactly so."

"What are the chances this Strasser will become suspicious of you?"

"Unlikely, but with so much happening now…" she shrugged. "These are different times. I can't be sure who to trust."

"What else?" Christoph asked.

"I've looked at this from every angle, with an eye towards escape." She took a deep breath and admitted, "I don't know how we're going to manage it."

"It'll have to be something bold," Christoph agreed.

Chapter Three

Gerard waited while Karl Strasser studied the results. Again.

The office was utilitarian, a plain wooden desk, the single chair Strasser occupied, windows with a view of the back of the next building. Though Gerard knew the other man had family, no picture but that of the new *Führer* adorned his wall.

Squinting, he thought perhaps the *Führer* signed it. It wouldn't have surprised him. Strasser was a fanatical man. A Nazi flag stood upright on his desk, next to the phone.

He wondered how Elsa and their Alpha progressed. She thought he hadn't noticed her reaction every time the messenger arrived. From the sheer frequency of their correspondence, he could easily tell her attraction to Christoph. Her feelings for him.

It'd be nice to see her married. Away from the uncertainties of Berlin life. Married to Christoph would, indeed, be an honor to their family. The status their mating would add to the von Skyler Pack was one thing. The fact she'd move to Lower Saxony, far from the dangers of the city, another.

Gerard repressed an impatient cough and looked back at Strasser, who still read the pages of charts and explanations. Gerard detested men like Strasser, but if he had to play the game, he would gladly do so to see his only child in a secure future.

"There's nothing unusual about these results," Strasser said, jerking Gerard's attention back to the situation at hand. "What haven't you tested for?"

"We've run every test," Gerard said. "There's nothing there. Testosterone levels, blood cell count, it's all within normal parameters. Normal *human*," he emphasized, "parameters."

"You've missed something," Strasser snapped.

With effort, Gerard refrained from the urge to toss Strasser out the window. Temper, he reminded himself. He'd promised Elsa he'd reign in his emotions.

"I thought so myself," he lied. "I ran the tests three times, all the results produced consistent readings. If you'd like, Herr Doctor Strasser, I can fetch those papers?"

Strasser gave a curt shake of his head. "No, no, Gerard, that's unnecessary."

He put the papers on the immaculate desk, fingers splayed atop them. Gerard's gaze remained steady on the other doctor. Only when Strasser met his eyes did he remember to infuse his look with confusion.

"Based on what you've told me regarding the subject's reaction to the dogs you introduced, I can only assume he was raised around other rabid beasts. Tell me, Karl," he reverted to the familiar now that the interview was over. "Where did you find the…man?"

With an uncharacteristic huff, Strasser leaned back in the chair. "We picked him up in *Neukölln* after he attacked a mob. The details are unclear, but I understand it took four men to bring him in." He sat up and added, "Four men, even though the beast had taken two gunshot wounds."

"Hmm," Gerard said to cover his disgust at Erik's treatment. "*Neukölln*, I would have said in one of the outer provinces."

"I want you to set up a test," Strasser stood. "I'm going to have a subject brought in from the prisons. If the beast bites him, we can create more of these unusual creatures."

"You believe the legends of the *wehrwölfe*?" Gerard asked.

Strasser offered a smile that made him sick. "There's one way to find out."

Using that for a dismissal, Gerard turned to the door just as a knock sounded. He opened it to find Franz, Strasser's clerk.

"Franz," he greeted and allowed the younger man to enter.

Taking his time to close the door, he used every bit of his advanced senses to hear what the clerk reported.

"They've brought in the subject's property. Who shall I assign to go through it?"

****

Dinner was barely a half hour off, and Christoph hadn't seen Elsa since she'd told him of Erik. After putting the fate of their captured member into his hands, she'd waited for his response.

He had no answer for her, not until he learned from Gerard what Strasser believed. Though he wanted to speak with her of personal matters, he'd needed to get the business of the Clan out of the way first. She'd left him to see to the other guests, without his answer.

Now, he set out to find Elsa in the large townhouse. It was an eclectic mix of old and new, but the art deco suited her well. The unique style matched her personality. Efficient, sleek, sensual.

Following her scent to the library, he stumbled upon a far corner she'd clearly marked as hers. Lancet Medical Journal lay open on the window seat, with several more journals in various languages stacked in a corner. He sat by the window, letting the late afternoon sun warm him.

A fresh whiff of her reached him a heartbeat before the clatter of her rushed footsteps. Standing, he moved into one of the shadowed archways. Elsa scanned the shelves nearest her window, oblivious to his presence. Christoph took the opportunity to study her.

The sunlight glinted off her golden hair, neatly coiffed despite her rush. Her hands were delicate as they skimmed over the spines of her books, though he knew from her letters and the diplomas lining the walls that she was adept in her field of biochemistry. Her skirt accented her curved figure, and he wondered how she'd look with the material bunch around her hips as he took her.

Stealing out of the shadows, he stepped behind her with a growl. She startled, tried to turn, but he held her arms at her sides, trapping her between him and the wall. His lips tasted the side of her neck, the smooth, fragrant skin there. The feel of her body against his told him everything he needed to know.

My woman.

"We are creatures of instinct, are we not?" he asked in a low rumble. "Mine are very clear."

Her heart pounded, he could feel it jump where his fingers brushed the sensitive underside of her wrists. Her scent intensified, an added undercurrent of muskiness, and he knew she was as aroused as he.

Her head turned, but she didn't struggle. She leaned further into him, pressing her arse against his throbbing erection.

"I wondered what your instincts would tell you," she whispered. "You were inscrutable this afternoon."

"That was not the moment for *us*."

"Have you decided *this* is our moment?" she asked.

He pulled away just enough to see the eyebrow raised in amused question. But he could also see how her blue eyes darkened, could feel her breath coming in gasps. Could smell the change in her scent.

Trailing his lips along the back of her neck, he breathed her in. Another growl escaped him, louder and stronger, establishing his dominance over her. When Elsa growled back, his cock hardened further.

Yes, mine.

Nipping her shoulder, Christoph smiled in surprise when she entwined her fingers with his and moved them slowly up her body. Cupping her breasts through the thin silk of her blouse, he felt the harden peaks push through her clothing. Her entire body shuddered when he pinched her nipples.

"Christoph," she murmured.

Turning her, he slammed her against the bookcases. Mouth on hers in an instant, he took hold of her hands again, pinning them above her head. She tasted better than he imagined, and when she kissed him back, all thought fled.

He needed her.

A loud crash jerked his attention away from Elsa and back to their surroundings. Christoph spun to scan the library, Elsa secured behind him. He saw no one. The faint scent of Peter, however, lingered in the air.

He was going to kill his friend.

Dismissing the slight intrusion, he turned to Elsa. She rubbed the back of her head, and walked around him.

"We have dinner, Christoph," she said.

He took slim satisfaction in the quiver of her voice, none too pleased she tried to leave. Grabbing her hand, he yanked her flush against him. They needed to go to dinner. It'd be unspeakably rude not to, and he didn't want anyone interrupting their time together.

However, he wasn't letting her leave until he

made himself abundantly clear.

"You're mine. Dinner can only put this off so long."

"I know." Her fingers flitted along his cheek, and her lips pressed once more to his. Before he could pull her close, she stepped away and left the library.

****

Trying to steady her breath, she forced her legs to carry her from the room. Elsa hadn't realized how hard it'd be to walk away from him.

An unfamiliar scent caught her attention, but with several guests in the house, she ignored it. A quick glance at her watch confirmed dinner was about to be served. Had her father returned?

An unexpected knock on the front door startled her. Jumping, she cursed Christoph. He had her tied up in knots. As she crossed the foyer, waving Otto off, she wondered how rude it'd be to skip dinner, find Christoph, and finish what they'd started.

Spine straight, Elsa opened the door.

"Ah," a tall handsome man smiled, "you must be the fair Elsa."

He clicked his heels together and bowed over her hand. She stared at the lowered head, then at her hand and wondered how it had come to be in his possession.

"*Guten tag,* Herr…?" she asked, bemused. He still held her hand between his.

"I am Peter, Count Lungraf und Calvelage, eldest child of Emile, Count Lungraf and his beautiful wife, Greta, *seneschal* to our beloved Alpha. Protector of the Arminius—"

"He's my guard," Christoph interrupted, exasperated, from behind her.

Elsa shot him a look before returning her gaze to the man before her. "A pleasure, Count Lungraf."

"Ah, Christoph," the newcomer said. Christoph growled, and with a cocky grin, Lungraf dropped her hand.

"Now, now, old friend. Just saying hello."

Christoph growled again. If Elsa hadn't had an earlier conversation with him, she'd wonder if that was all he was capable of.

"Otto," she called, stepping back from the standoff, despite the excitement that spiked through her at Christoph's proximity. To Count Lungraf she said, "Otto will show you to your room so you can freshen up. Dinner is about to be served, but please do take your time."

"*Danke*, Fräulein Elsa." Lungraf bowed to her again, but didn't touch her again.

Elsa watched him follow Otto, and turned to Christoph. He took the hand Lungraf had kissed, studying it as if it'd somehow changed with the count's touch. Drawing it to his mouth, he swept his lips across the palm.

The erotic gesture had her swallowing, hard. A low purr escaped her lips, and she leaned closer. Torn between her primal instincts with her mate so close, and her duty as mistress of the house, Elsa let her fingers drop from his.

"Mine." His tone brooked no argument.

Not that she was inclined to argue with him.

****

Christoph watched Elsa until she disappeared down the hall. Margaret chose that moment to continue down the staircase. Her delighted grin and dancing eyes told him she'd seen enough.

"Contain yourself, Margaret."

She didn't say a word about the incident, though he could see she burst to do so.

Chapter Four

"Wonderful lamb," Peter remarked. "Remind me to ask Margaret to get the recipe."

"You think of nothing save your stomach, Peter," Christoph chided.

His cock throbbed throughout dinner with a nearly irresistible need to mate with Elsa. She sat too far from him, but in retrospect the seating arrangement worked for the best. No need to give the diners a display they'd not soon forget.

Images of her spread across the long table had him grinding his teeth and fighting for command of his urges. Unused to this lack of control made him want Elsa more. Just to have her, to taste her, to feel her under him as he moved within her. He fought to check his desire.

Unfortunately, he knew that to be a precarious hold until he had her. He hoped, once he marked her, some semblance of his precious control would return. Doubted it, but hoped nonetheless.

"That's not true," Peter countered.

Christoph prayed he meant their conversation and not his need for Elsa. They entered the study Gerard directed them to; where he and Elsa would join them shortly.

"I also wonder if the fair Elsa will bring her impressive chef when we return home."

Christoph's jaw clenched. Not at the implication, for he had every intention of returning to his estate with his mate. At Peter's assumptions, though he knew his friend meant it as an innocent gesture to irritate him, he couldn't put aside Peter's touching of his woman.

"You push too far," he snapped.

"No, Christoph," Peter said in all seriousness, a rare trait. "I observe what's between the two of you. I'm happy for you. It's about time you found your woman. The Clan needs an Alpha Female; we've been too long without one."

Christoph nodded his thanks, and a coil of tension unraveled at the sincerity in Peter's voice. He didn't need his Clan's approval for his mate, but he wanted his friend's. Hans would be annoyed Peter met her first, but there was no help for it. Idly, he speculated how much money had been bet on this meeting.

Hans prepared for the possible arrival of the van Dietrich Pack among those already in Lower Saxony. Christoph wondered how his friend fared with the forged papers. They were becoming impossible to find and damned expensive.

"I'm truly sorry old friend," Peter continued, strain evident in his voice, "your mating is marred by Erik's capture. Now tell me, what happened?"

Gerard and Elsa entered the room as he finished recapping the situation with Erik.

When Christoph saw her, he wanted to ignore the other men and take her. He ached for her, and his primal instincts surfaced, near impossible to control. The *wölfe* within knew this woman. It wouldn't be deterred.

With effort, he restrained himself. Clenching his fists, he remembered Erik. The scent of Elsa drifted along the room until it surrounded him. He had doubts a single mating would quell this insatiable need or reassert his focus.

They had urgent matters to discuss, more he needed to retain a modicum of civility.

He'd yet to ask Gerard for her hand.

"I've seen quite a number of experiments,"

Gerard said the moment he closed the doors. An unnecessary move since the entire household knew of Erik. "What they do to that young man is beyond anything, even beyond medical experimentation. It's sadistic."

"What did Strasser say?" Elsa asked.

"He believed the forged tests," Gerard affirmed. He ran a hand through his graying hair, thin lips pressed together, his cheeks sunken. Unsure of Gerard's normal appearance, Christoph thought he looked exhausted and haggard. "I have to return to the hospital within the hour," he added. "Strasser ordered more tests."

The eyes that looked into Christoph's were haunted. "He wants to provoke Erik into biting a prisoner."

"The legends," Peter spat, disgusted. "He believes the legends about a *wehrwölfe's* bite."

"He *tests* the legends," Gerard corrected. "It's the first in a new round the good doctor wants preformed."

"He hasn't changed?" Peter inquired.

"No," Gerard shook his head. "I don't know all Strasser has planned, but it'll be much worse than they've already done."

"Given what I saw this morning," Elsa said, "I don't know how much more Erik can take before he breaks."

"We must act quickly," Peter agreed.

"At any interval it would pain me to sanction the death of one of our own," Christoph said. He kept his voice even despite the grief this decision brought him. "However, should we fail to free him, there is no other option."

This was the first time he'd had to order the death of anyone. In fact, he believed it to be the first time in over three hundred years that one of their Clan needed to be disposed of. His gaze locked with

Elsa's. She seemed to understand what he wanted, and moved closer to him. Just barely touching his arm, she stood by his side.

"We can not permit additional experimentations. We must end his suffering, not merely for him, but for the good of the Clan. I worry about putting you and Elsa in harm's way, Gerard. However, you are the only ones who can do it."

"It has to be me," Elsa interrupted.

Christoph's hands, already stiff, tightened further at the thought of her in danger, but he stopped his automatic objection.

"Father's movements are more scrutinized than my own."

"It's a terrible risk to take, Fräulein Elsa," Peter said. "Perhaps I can step in?"

"No." Elsa and Gerard spoke at the same time.

"There's no way to bring you in without notice," Elsa said. "Papers are checked at all entrances every morning, and only six scientists have access to Erik's room. Strasser trusts no one else."

"Can you do it tonight?" Christoph asked.

He hated letting her go before he mated with her. Wasn't certain he could. The *wölfe* clawed for release, to mate. Duty first.

"No, the guards around Erik's room know I'll be gone all evening. They'll let Gerard in," she nodded to her father, "because Strasser ordered it. They'll expect me tomorrow."

Christoph nodded. He had the evening with her. He did not intend to squander it.

"There's nothing to be done until then. If something changes," he looked to Gerard. "You'll let us know?"

****

Peter always could be counted on in sensitive times. He'd read Christoph's desire to have a moment alone with Gerard without a word between them. With a sly grin, he'd taken Elsa's hand and asked for a tour of the townhouse. On their way out, he'd heard Peter refining the more delicate points of their plan. The moment they left the room, Christoph took the opportunity to approach Gerard.

"Herr von Skyler," Christoph begun formally. "I must apologize for pressing you with this question at such a time, but I want my position firmly established."

Gerard nodded. "This regards my daughter, does it not?"

"Yes. It is my intention to declare her my mate."

"Christoph, nothing would please me more. Elsa is a fine, intelligent woman who shall match you beautifully. Though," he offered a wistful grin, "I admit I shall miss her deeply."

"As her father, you are more than welcomed to join us in Osnabrück."

"Thank you, Christoph," he shook his head. "That is a kind offer to an old man. But I must remain in Berlin. There is still much work for me."

"I understand, but the offer remains open."

****

Elsa stood in her garden. A small affair, barely twelve feet long, it had always been her favorite spot in or out of the house. Treasuring her patch of grass within the city confines of Berlin, she wondered if Erik would see such beauty again.

Her last encounter with the imprisoned *wölfe* laid heavily on her thoughts. Another scientist stood in the room with her, watching him struggle against his leather restraints. Erik's eyes were wild. He begged, though not directed towards her as she first feared, more in a repetitive mumble. "Let me die. I have failed."

Wandering among the remnants of the late summer flowers, she tried to calm her stormy thoughts. Her feet were bare and she hadn't changed from her day clothes, the hour grew late and the house darkened. Thoughts of tomorrow would not let her rest.

She stared at the Luger in her hand. Unloaded, its weight was still significant.

Would she be able to fire it? Never did she wrestle with such a question. The thought, ludicrous until now, unsettled her.

Then there was Christoph. No wonder she could not rest, a war of emotions raged through her. Instinct urged her to seek Christoph out. Logic kept her rooted.

She stiffened when a change in the breeze alerted her to Christoph's presence. His large hand moved around her body and rested over the pistol.

"I don't want it to be you." He encircled her waist with his other arm. "I'll find another way."

"There is no other way, however much I wish there was," she whispered. "I am prepared, Christoph."

Relinquishing the pistol to his grasp, Elsa turned in his embrace. The nearly full moon illuminated the area more than enough for her enhanced eyesight to see him clearly. His eyes captured her own with their intensity, and she could feel the tension within him, the need for her. She could all but hear his *wölfe* call to hers. Her hand swept across his cheek. Despite the late hour, it was still smooth.

"Fate is a cruel crone." His low, deep tone didn't mask his barely tempered anger.

A visceral rumble coursed through him. The vibration of it made her shiver, in comfort, in need. She reacted to his growl like nothing else. Heat rose within her. Want of Christoph ignited her skin, her entire being.

She'd never needed anything as she did him. Elsa brought her hand up to rest on his chest. She brushed her fingers against the fine linen of his shirt, almost as if she could feel the growl within.

The change in Christoph, the urgency that took hold of him arced between them, and she growled her own need. He took possession of her mouth, a hard kiss meant to take and brand. They kissed hungrily, their need blocking all else, driving their actions into a frenzy.

Elsa broke off, afraid of her own reaction to that one kiss. Her eyes met his, black with desire. Unable to look away, unable to ignore her feelings, she kissed him again. And stumbled against Christoph as he moved backwards into the study, lifting her to keep her steady against him.

She heard the clatter of something hitting the floor, but she didn't care as he laid her on the rug. He didn't hesitate, fingers already untucking her shirt.

The instant his skin touched hers, Elsa lost whatever coherency remained. Who knew his mere touch could ignite her so? Could feel like this?

Within moments, their clothes lay scattered across the room. Christoph suckled her tender breast. His tongue teased her taut, responsive nipple. A small moan escaped her, and she arched into his mouth, running her hands through his hair, holding him closer. Her heart pounded, her skin burned wherever he touched her. Their scents intensified, combined, filled her.

Christoph nibbled small patches of skin as he moved down her body. Her breath came in short, heated puffs and then stopped altogether. Dear God, Christoph *blew* on her moist center, his mouth hovering over her slick core. She tried to take in air, but couldn't. Tried to anchor herself, but couldn't.

He moved her legs apart, spreading her wider for him.

Vulnerable, open, exposed. Sensuous.

In the instant before his head descended between her spread thighs, she felt wanton, the eroticism of the move unimaginable until now. Elsa wanted more.

His fingers smoothed along her nether lips, spread them, teased their slick folds. Cool night air glided along her hot flesh, a tantalizing counterpoint to his fingers. One finger entered her, and she bucked her hips at the intrusion.

And then his tongue tasted her, licking along her slit until he found the plump nub. The rough surface circled it, further stimulating the already sensitive clit.

Elsa' back bowed, she pushing against his mouth. Her fingers clawed the rug, entire body tense as waves of sensations traveled through her. A noise, half moan half growl, burst from her. She reached for Christoph, wanting him closer, needing him inside of her, desperate. An all-consuming instinct to mate.

Christoph moved up her body with natural predatory grace. Moisture flooded her already wet core at the sight. He was hers.

His cock stood long and hard, a beautiful sight in a graceful predator. Wrapping her legs about him, she cradled his hips, rocked against his erection. With every movement her breath caught.

Their eyes met, his dark ones clouded with desire for her. She could see his *wölfe* beneath the surface, felt it call to her own.

Under her fingers, the muscles of his back bunched. Another growl danced along her skin, shooting straight through her. Her core tingled at the sound, throbbing in time to her racing pulse.

He kissed her softly, then, with a deep tenderness as he positioned himself at her entrance.

Elsa held onto his arms and spread her legs wider. Hovering over her, eyes inscrutable, he pushed into her. She felt the connection of more than just their bodies. The sensation hammered through her, and she reveled in it. It moved through her in waves of love and pleasure.

He entered her painfully slow. Too slow. She wanted him within her, assuaging this ache. Needed him, had to have him deep within, completely joined to her. She angled her hips higher. With one hard thrust, he pierced her virginity. Laid claim to her as his mate, marked her as eternally his.

Christoph remained unmoving for a long, excruciatingly erotic moment. Then his teeth scraped along her neck, clamped on her jugular. Elsa shuddered, gasped, arched further into him. His hips moved again in a steady, intense pace. Pressure built as he pumped in and out of her body. Her legs quivered, her nails dug into his arms. The power behind his thrusts increased, as did their speed.

With primal force, she climaxed, biting his neck. Placing her own mark, that of the Alpha Female's. He was hers.

"Mine."

Spots danced behind her eyes as desire peaked and exploded. Elsa felt as well as heard him roar his own completion.

His.

Christoph withdrew from her, and she was left with a pang of emptiness. Her need for him seemed endless, even now it washed through her. He rolled onto his back, pulling her atop his chest.

"You feel it, don't you?" he panted. His fingers grazed the mark he'd just placed on her neck.

His mark.

His mate.

Elsa kissed his neck, licked the mark she'd just placed, and nipped at his jaw. That action took all the strength she had, and she settled her head on his smooth chest.

"It's the strongest thing I've ever felt. You are my mate, there is no question. There is only need."

A loud growl erupted from Christoph, startling Elsa. He sat up, arms tight about her. Despite the severity of his expression, she settled comfortably, intimately over him, aroused. Exhaustion forgotten, she wanted him once more.

"I don't want you to proceed with Erik's rescue."

"There is no other way, Christoph," she replied, hands entwined with his.

"I can't risk you, Elsa."

His words heated her blood and warmed her heart. She cupped his cheek and brought his mouth to hers, leisurely exploring him.

When she pulled back, it was to whisper, "Isn't that part of being your mate? Of being the Clan's Alpha Female? To protect the Clan from harm?"

With an angry rumble of reluctant assent at what they could not change, he captured her mouth. The fervor of his kiss marked her as his, as surely as their mating branded her his mate.

Chapter Five

Elsa watched the familiar streets race past, the everyday bustle she was accustomed to. She held Christoph's hand in silence as Otto maneuvered the car through the busy streets.

Berlin today was different than of her youth. Now, people prowled the streets in search of food or work. Or life. She wondered if they found what they searched for in the morass of humanity and the disorder of political disarray Hitler and his regime declared.

Before she and Christoph extricated themselves from each others' arms this morning, Otto took Peter to his position for Erik's escape. The butler mapped out a short path through the sewer tunnels leading from the alley behind the hospital to an alley two blocks away where he'd wait with a car. Peter didn't want Christoph near the hospital, but Christoph refused to stay away. He'd decided to observe from a nearby roof, ready to intervene if necessary.

Elsa also would rather their Alpha stay away, yet understood his need. He wasn't just concerned for Erik but for her and Gerard. Most especially for her.

Squeezing his hand, she turned to him. "Allow us to complete this, Christoph."

He rubbed her knuckles with his thumb. The touch sent shivers down her spine. It had been the discrete clatter of a household waking that finally roused them. Rather, roused them enough to make love again. Sore and sated, Elsa wouldn't change anything about their night together.

"I'm not the one in jeopardy today. I want you to think only of the plan."

Elsa patted her purse. The pistol, which had fallen to the floor last night, was now loaded and stowed in her bag. She didn't respond, except to tighten her fingers around his. Rubbing her thumb over his knuckles, she kissed his cheek. An instant intimacy developed between them since they'd marked each other.

Otto pulled to a stop at the side entrance Elsa used everyday. He opened her door then stared stoically ahead. Elsa was sure he still smarted from his trip through the sewers. Not once, when they realized whom the Nazi's had captured and planned this escape, but twice when he had shown Peter the route. It impinged upon his butlery dignity, and Otto was nothing if not the consummate butler.

She gave Christoph a quick kiss, and moved to exit the car when he stopped her, pulled her back.

"It isn't too late to find another way, Elsa." Even as his *wölfe* rumbled its displeasure, the concern showed on his face.

"I will return to you, Christoph."

Gazed locked with hers, he turned her palm over and kissed the inside, tongue flicking over the sensitive skin. She shuddered, closed her eyes against the sensation. With one final look, she exited the car.

She knew he wasn't happy with her role in this but they could do nothing else. No matter how he hated it, neither Christoph nor Peter could enter the *Charité*, let alone Erik's room.

Her heart pounded part in arousal from his last kiss, part in nervousness. No other way, and the risk they took was great. Much depended on Erik cognizant enough to follow her instructions, but she couldn't be certain of that.

Elsa smiled at Paul, the guard she'd befriended

years ago. She clutched her handbag tighter until her fingers felt as if they would break. True to his habit, he waved her through the entrance checkpoint with his usual warm greeting.

"Fräulein von Skyler, guten Tag."

Responding with a smile and a small wave, she tucked her purse under her arm and strolled to the elevators. Her first order of business, find her father and make sure everything was still going to plan.

****

Any other morning Gerard would complain about his stiff and sore back. A night on his office's sofa was no way to spend an evening. Especially not with a house full of guests he'd rather entertain. This morning, however, only one thing occupied his thoughts.

Seeing their plan executed without incident.

More lay at stake than a captured *wölfe*; his daughter would be in harm's way. He would not allow anything to go wrong.

One of Gerard's many regrets over this plan was that his attempt to secure the ephedrine stimulant hadn't come through earlier. He'd wanted to inject Erik last night and prepare him for today. As it was, Gerard managed to inject the *wölfe* an hour ago. The guards never paid attention to his ministrations. As far as he knew, were unaware who inhabited the room.

"Father," Elsa called from the outer office.

"In the lab, *liebling*."

Glancing about she asked, "Are we alone?"

"Yes." He finished washing Erik's blood samples down the sink. "We're nearly ready. All of Erik's blood vials have been replaced with human samples. I have a report ready for Strasser. I've injected Erik with the stimulant, though I'm not sure how quickly it will take effect."

Elsa nodded. "Did you manage to speak with

Erik?"

"No." Gerard shook his head. "I should go back and do so before I leave the hospital."

"No, I can handle it. I don't want you on the premises when this happens."

"Elsa, I'll stay nearby in the event you need me. I know we spoke of my leaving, but I'm too concerned—"

"Father, please." Gerard heard the plea in her voice, the anxiety. "I don't want to worry about your safety at the same time. If something went wrong…I need to know you're safe."

"It should be the other way, *liebling.* I should be the one in there, not you."

"If you were there, Strasser would sacrifice you to the SS without blinking."

"And you?" he shot back. "Strasser will sacrifice anyone to save his own neck."

"I know." She shook her head. Lines tightened around her mouth and eyes. "At least with me, a mere woman," sarcasm colored the word like a paintbrush, "he has less of a chance of getting away with it."

"There's nothing else to do. You're right, Elsa." Anxiety hitched his voice. Knowing so did not ease his apprehension about his child's safety.

"Take the report to Strasser." She handed him the file on the side table. "Everyone's ready."

****

Elsa stared out the lab window and watched her father walk down the street. The sight gave her a sense of relief. If something did go wrong, her father would be secure, Christoph would see to it.

She glanced to the adjoining rooftop, but Christoph wasn't there. He waited on the other side of the building, nearer where Erik's cell sat. Still, she could feel him as if he stood next to her, a strong presence, a concerned lover.

Holding his presence close, she fortified herself for the next move in their plan.

Luger hidden under a towel in her lab coat pocket, Elsa walked down the corridor. The click of her black heels against the wooden plank floor echoed around her, and the feel of the steel tray she carried weighed heavier than it should.

She approached the two SS guards. Both armed with pistols at their hips. They flanked the heavy metal door as they had for days, unmoving save for changes of the guard every six hours. For a moment, she wondered what they thought of the sounds reverberating from the room. They could hardly help but hear them. Rumor ran ripe around the entire hospital.

Issued strict orders never to enter except under extreme emergency, she wondered if they were tempted to look. Had they heard the stories about Erik? She could only hope that with Erik's escape, the belief in *wehrwölfes* would fall back into legend.

The taller, blonde guard nodded at her. He'd attempted to engage her in conversation since they'd met three days ago. Other than polite greeting, Elsa ignored him. The uniforms they wore made her ill.

"Fraulein von Skyler, you were missed yesterday. I saw much of your father but not you. I was afraid you'd been reassigned."

Elsa forced a grin. "No, no, I had to attend to guests while Father continued his work."

"He was here all night," the guard stated.

"Yes, I finally convinced him to return home for a proper rest. I'll be handling all the blood work today." She gestured to the door, and the other guard immediately opened it.

"I'll be a few minutes." She lifted her tray. "I've several vials to fill."

With a final smile at the flirtatious guard, Elsa strode through the door and waited for it to clang shut behind her.

Grateful no window adorned the room, she put the tray on the lone table a foot from where Erik sat, restrained.

"Erik," she placed her hand on his. "Erik!" she hissed as loud as she dared. "I need you to understand me. We're going to get you out now."

Erik craned his head to face her. "Elsa." His voice sounded hoarse from too many hours of screaming. "You must leave. They'll capture you, too."

"Erik, please," she begged him and wondered if the ephedrine was enough. "I have a pistol. The guards must be shot in order for your escape to be successful."

She slipped her fingers through both sides of the leather restraint on Erik's right wrist. With a hard yank, she tried to break it. Snarling, Erik yanked his hand with her, and through their combined force, the bindings broke.

Glancing at the door to see if the guards heard, she removed the towel from her pocket and unwrapped the Luger.

"Erik, can you do this?" She took his now freed hand before he reached across to release his other wrist. "Erik, both our lives are at stake. The others must believe you took *this* pistol," she raised it so he could see it, "from one of the guards. If they do not, I will surely be put to death." He didn't respond.

Heart pounding, she took his face between her hands. Her voice cracked and nerves knotted her stomach. "*Erik!*" She shook his face. "*Do you understand?*"

His eyes shone clear as glass, glazed over in grief, focused in fury. He looked straight at her and gave her a slow nod.

Elsa released his face so he could undo his straps. She crossed to the tray and retrieved the syringe and a vial. Once more in front of him, pistol in her other hand, she waited. Her hands trembled slightly.

"Erik," she whispered, insistent. Not much time had passed but she could take no chance. The guards weren't the only danger. Another scientist or Strasser could enter.

"Push me against the wall."

Erik took the Luger. His unsteady fingers, damaged from days of torture, closed tight over the handle. It shook, as her own hands still did.

"Push me against the wall." She repeated.

"Elsa, you must forgive me." His eyes raised to hers, steadier now. Voice harsh and heated with pain he rasped, "Madness overtook me when I saw Ursula die. My actions endangered us all."

"I know, Erik." She softly and squeezed his hand in sympathy, ignoring the blood. Though they'd been together only a day, she didn't know what she'd do should anything happen to Christoph.

Yes she did. Erik did what he had to. Elsa didn't think she'd have done any differently.

"What's important now is freeing you from this hell."

Elsa glanced back at the door. Her heart raced in expectation. "Once they're dead, run straight across the hall to the very last door. The window is open, climb down the sewage pipe to the left. There's someone in the alley who will lead you to safety. Understand?"

"Yes, Elsa." His voice steadied, grew stronger. She feared he'd be too beaten to do this himself. "Thank you."

Erik adjusted the pistol in his grasp. "Scream."

"Erik, wait."

"*Scream!*" he roared.

The metal chair he'd been strapped to crashed into the table, causing a tumult of sound. Elsa screamed as Erik shoved her into the corner. The door slammed opened.

Erik shot the first guard squarely in the chest. She jolted at the sound, piercing in the confines of the room.

The second, the tall blonde who'd flirted with her, Erik grabbed in a blur of motion. One yank brought the guard's neck within easy reach. Controlling his change just enough to transform his teeth from the relatively flat ones of a human to the vicious points of a *wölfe*, Erik ripped open the man's throat.

Blood spurted over him and along the once pristine tiles of the floor. Elsa watched in stunned detachment, still crouched in the corner. With definite movements, Erik released the guard, who collapsed to the floor, blood gushing from his throat. He bent, tore the guard's gun from his hand, and slid it to her.

Elsa caught the gun and shoved it into her pocket. The trembling, once restricted to her hands, spread. Still, she watched Erik, willed him to escape.

Now.

Clattering footsteps sounded before the alarmed shouts. It'd been seconds, but the gunshots echoed through the hallways, bringing everyone in the vicinity to the room.

"Go!"

Erik didn't move. Dread settled in her belly, her heart contracted. She tried to stand, to stop him. Her legs wouldn't work. And then, it was too late.

"Please forgive me."

He brought the pistol to his head and fired.

Chapter Six

Christoph watched the window. He'd spotted Peter, or the silhouette of Peter, in the alley below, just inside the hospital's shadow. Everything hinged upon Elsa's and Erik's actions now.

Tension wound through him until he was as taut as a bowstring. To find his mate and risk losing her seemed unimaginable mere days ago. Now it appeared all too real. If she didn't make it out alive, Erik better hope he didn't either. Christoph would see the pain the SS performed paled in comparison.

Erik's uncontrolled rage changed things. Not just in the confines of his Pack, but for the entire Clan. They could no longer go on as before.

Even if Strasser discovered nothing, they knew of the existence of *wölfes*. It was only a matter of time before Strasser and his Nazis expanded their search and the old legends resurfaced. Before everyone fell under suspicion, before everyone was tested. Before Gerard's deception was discovered and they were all condemned.

He'd have to assess the damage Erik's capture caused before deciding on how to properly protect the Clan.

Where was he? Erik should've been out the window by now. Something was wrong.

****

Erik was dead. He'd killed himself rather than...than what? Face the judgment of the Alpha? Live without Ursula? Elsa wished she knew, though somehow it didn't matter. Not anymore.

Three men were dead, their blood painted half

the room red in razor—sharp relief to her white lab coat. Except, no, there was blood on her coat. She didn't know where it came from, or if her own blood colored the sleeve.

Heavy footfalls raced toward her. She snapped her attention from the carnage. Improvising now, Elsa pushed the pocketed side of her coat behind her and made sure the pistol stayed well-hidden. It'd be disastrous to be revealed now.

The SS guards arrived first from the two far wings of the floor.

As their footsteps neared, Elsa panted, her heart pounded, stomach churned. Unmoving, seated on the floor with one leg under her, she tried to concentrate.

Three dead.

Erik's suicide.

The men stood in the doorway, mouths wide at the gruesome scene.

"He broke free!" Elsa exclaimed when they didn't move. She couldn't either, the shaking worsened. "He..." she swallowed. "He did this."

One guard entered the room and stared at her. He looked as if he'd never seen her before, as if the scene he walked into overwhelmed him.

"Help me up," she ordered. Her voice wobbled. Stronger, she said, "Get me out of this room!"

The guard hesitated until Elsa repeated, "Get me out *now*!"

He stepped around the blood, careful to avoid the spreading stains, and extended his hands. She took them, unsteady. In a move too real to simulate, she held the wall for additional support before she managed to get her bearings.

"Out," she insisted. "Get me out of here!"

The guard helped her move around the bodies and blood. Once she exited, she stepped to the far wall. Leaning against it, she surveyed the area. Four guards still gaped in astonishment at the scene.

Still time then.

"Quickly, go find Strasser." Elsa started down the hall, down the very path Erik should have followed. One step, then another. *Don't think about it. Don't look back.*

"Find Strasser! Bring him here!" Her command was forceful and two of the guards jumped to do her bidding. "I need air."

The guard who'd helped her stand ran to her but she shooed him away. "Stay at the door, let no one else near the room until Strasser arrives."

Again, her hand fell on the wall, a steady and solid connection. She picked up her pace, until she nearly sprinted to reach the window.

With a quick look around the office, confident no one watched her, she peered outside. A lone figure stood in the shadows. Removing the pistol from her pocket, she released it. The black piece plummeted to where Peter hid.

He'd know what to do with it. They hadn't discussed this, but when only a gun dropped and no Erik, he'd know what happened. He'd have to know, she relied on him to keep her safe.

Elsa took a breath, one she didn't realize she needed until her lungs burned. Surprised at the cleanness of the air compared to that small room, she took another.

Christoph hid just across the way, she could sense him if not see him. She waved a hand out the window, a quick signal she hoped he understood. God, she wanted to see him.

Back in the hall, a commotion commanded her attention.

Not now.

Not until she settled this. She couldn't risk him.

Wouldn't risk him.

"***Dammit!***" came Strasser's voice. "How the hell

did this happen?"

"Sir," one of the guards answered. "This is what we found when we arrived."

Elsa moved to the doorway, not wanting Strasser to believe she hid. If he suspected her, she was lost. He'd never let her leave the hospital. Not alive. The guard pointed, and Strasser marched toward her.

"*von Skyler!*" Strasser bellowed. "You were in there when this happened."

Upon reaching her, Strasser grabbed her arm and dragged her into the office she'd just exited. With brisk actions, he closed the window and snapped the shades shut.

She felt clammy, cold. The shaking had lessened but had not subsided. With luck, he'd presume she suffered from shock and not fear.

He pushed her onto a chair then squinted at her, examining her face and coat.

"The subject broke free of his restraints," she offered before Strasser questioned her, surprised and satisfied with the steadiness of her speech. "I was preparing to take additional blood samples when he stood, threw his chair aside like a toy, and attacked me!"

"How did you escape with your life?"

She frowned. So much for relief that someone had lived to tell the tale.

"He pushed me," she whispered. She knew what happened, could see it clearly in her mind's eye as if it happened before her now.

"I screamed and fell against the wall. The guards rushed in...he killed them. Shot them."

"You're bleeding."

Yes, she knew, and gingerly dabbed the general area where Strasser stared.

"Ow," she hissed. "I fell against the wall. Hit my head. When he attacked the guards, I didn't move.

Didn't want him coming after me."

"What happened to my guards?"

His guards? They were Himmler's guards, loyal to their commander and the *Führer*. Taking a moment to dab at her scalp, hands slightly steadier, she did her best to craft her story. Erik had done as she'd asked. No one could connect her to this.

"They rushed in," she began. She was going to be there for a while.

****

"It's been hours!"

Christoph prowled the room. Elsa still hadn't returned. Nor had she called or sent word. Instinct bade him ignore the danger to his people, to himself, and get his woman. He'd snarled at Peter and Gerard when they suggested restraint. After this, she'd be lucky if he ever let her out of his sight again.

He might tie her to their bed, just to avoid such a reoccurrence.

He'd raged against Peter when the other intercepted his attempt to enter the hospital. Somehow, Peter had gone from the street to the rooftop, the instant Christoph changed. He'd sensed his mate in danger. That was all that mattered.

He still hadn't forgiven his friend, who now sported four claw marks on his chest. It was, as Peter reminded him, what a good advisor did.

"Strasser is interrogating her," Gerard said from his place by the window, the heavy curtains bracketed the light. "I'm certain of it. I'm afraid that by going to the hospital, so soon afterwards, I'll jeopardize her."

"She dropped the gun," Peter said. "She was safe when she did so."

"You *believe* she was safe," Christoph barked. "You don't know the context of her appearance. Is Erik alive or dead? Is he wounded?" He swallowed and voiced what he dreaded for hours. "Did he wound *her*?"

"My contacts at the hospital said there was a commotion," Gerard offered. Christoph heard the apprehension in his voice, which mirrored his own. "They don't know what. Strasser is covering this up."

They'd repeated the same conversation since their return to the townhouse. In an effort to do something, he'd sent for the leader of the van Dietrich Pack. The man would arrive momentarily, and Christoph wondered if he could restrain from tearing his Pack leader apart with teeth and claws.

He'd never felt so close to his *wölfe* as he did now. He longed for the days when he could rip into any who threatened his mate. Times had changed, with it the Clan. He'd never regretted that as much as he did today.

"Herr van Dietrich," Otto said in his stoic voice.

Christoph had seen another side of the butler when Otto had helped Peter all but drag him off the rooftop and back to the townhouse. Strong despite his years, Otto proved fierce in the protection of him and Elsa.

Looking at the butler's retreating form, Christoph now wondered how he'd gone from two blocks away to the rooftop. Wölfes moved fast, even in human form, but two blocks in the time it took Christoph to change? A feat. However, that time blurred into *wölfe* and worry.

Elsa's scent had drifted along the wind from the hospital to him. She'd been unharmed when they dragged him, human form again, away.

"Helmut," Gerard greeted the van Dietrich Pack leader, but made no move to welcome him.

"What do you know?" Christoph demanded.

"Aside from the SS seizing all of Erik's and Ursula's possessions," Helmut shook his head. "Nothing."

With an impatient wave, Christoph snapped, "I'm aware of that. What else?"

"I've made a list of all their closest friends and of any outsiders I could identify as knowing them. I've just come from making arrangements to have the last of them leave Berlin. They're to leave Germany."

Christoph nodded. He'd have to contact Hans, too, ensure all ran smoothly on his end.

"Christoph," Helmut continued in a contrite voice, "my Alpha, Erik was foolish. He witnessed his mate's murder. When he's rescued, I'm prepared to speak on his behalf."

"If he doesn't take my mate with him!" he roared.

Helmut closed his mouth on whatever else he planned to say. Dimly, Christoph heard Peter rumble a warning, but he didn't heed it, long past warnings. He needed action, needed to find Elsa, needed to keep her safe.

He needed to control his beast before he turned in the open parlor and destroyed one of his own. The *wölfe* wailed within, crying out for its mate. The mark Elsa made on his neck throbbed, and he brushed his fingers over it. The move served to calm him, marginally, but his rage lessened.

"Your mate?"

"I've taken Elsa as my mate."

Helmut shook himself and glanced at Gerard. No help came from that quarter. Christoph noticed the older man looked ready to pounce on Helmut, too.

"Congratulations, my Alpha," he said in a reverent tone.

With a curt nod, Christoph waited. Helmut looked uncomfortable, but he knew it couldn't be from the announcement of his mating.

"Ursula was with child," he added in regret. "They told me the day she died."

His admission took Christoph aback. Some of his rage softened further. Until he'd mated, he couldn't have understood. Now he did—he'd do anything to protect Elsa. A mate was reason enough to change, to protect. A mate and child? No, he couldn't blame the *wölfe*.

Unless Erik hurt Elsa in the process.

"Gerard." He turned to the other man. "Is it possible you can return to the hospital now?"

"Yes," he nodded. "It's still earlier than ordered, but they're used to my erratic hours."

"Good. Go. Report back as soon as you can."

Without another word, the scientist left the room. Despite his sympathy for Helmut and now Erik, Christoph whirled on the Pack leader.

"Pray she isn't hurt."

****

Closing the parlor doors behind him, he left Peter and Helmut alone. Peter wouldn't physically harm the Pack leader, Christoph surmised. If he did, at least one of them would get to take out their frustrations.

Christoph awaited Otto's return. Elsa served as the de facto leader of the Pack and, with Gerard back at the hospital that left Otto to answer his questions.

He headed for the kitchens, only to discover Margaret. She sat at a small wooden table near the fire, though the embers had been banked. The room smelled of the afternoon's untouched meal, tempered by the open back door where a breeze wafted in from the gardens.

Several sketches hung along the wall opposite the fireplace, various scenes of a very different Berlin.

"Why don't you eat?" She pushed a tray of sausage and bread towards him.

"No thank you," he shook his head.

"Christoph—"

"No, Margaret. Don't...please just don't."

She poured him a glass of beer but left him to his silence. They sat together until Otto arrived, when Christoph asked Margate to leave.

"Otto," he began, "I take it you know fully the operations of the von Skyler Pack?" Otto offered him a look that indicated him an ass for even asking. "I cannot wait for the return of Gerard or Elsa. I need the Pack to prepare for a possible departure."

Otto stiffened but nodded. Christoph wondered about the butler. Nothing he'd seen so far of the man specified *butler* was his first profession.

"The official decree will, of course, come from Gerard. But I fear there isn't enough time."

"We'll be prepared." Otto nodded. "Our evacuation plans have been in standby for centuries."

Chapter Seven

"Herr Strasser, I cannot recall additional details. The beast tore his restraints. I had no way of averting his escape."

The blood on her hand had dried, and her head throbbed. Thankfully, the trembling ended and her stomach settled. Elsa didn't know how many hours Strasser kept her prisoner in his office, but she did know Christoph would be beside himself.

Tired and hungry, all she wanted was his arms around her.

Still, Elsa inwardly admitted her relief he hadn't entered the building. Peter had something to do with that, though how Count Lungraf had managed, she didn't know. She couldn't take chances with Christoph's safety not with Strasser enraged and the hospital on high alert. Praying he showed restraint and remained at the townhouse, she continued to listen to Strasser.

"You were the last to see my specimen alive," he said. "Elsa, I'm sympathetic to your plight, but I must know all you do before the details are no longer fresh in your memory."

He changed his tactic to a new line of questioning. No more demands, no more *'repeat from the time you arrived at the Charité'*, at least.

"You alone escaped his rage. Why? Did you do *anything*? A kindness?"

"I did nothing," she insisted. Erik's voice drifted back to her. *"Kill me...Let me die. I have failed."*

"I hadn't even managed to take his blood."

"You must know I'll have his body examined. I

want his secrets, Fräulein, and anything you did to him will be discovered."

"*I did nothing*," she spat. "I know the importance of the subject as well as you do, Herr Doctor. Do you think I would deliberately sabotage this project?"

Silent, he studied her with a quizzical look as if he contemplated her question all too seriously. Before he could come up with a reason to keep her further, she stood.

"Very well, Elsa." Strasser nodded. "Shall I have one of the doctors see to your injury?"

"No, thank you, Herr Strasser, I'll see to it myself." Elsa smoothed the black linen of her skirt. "Should I remember anything else, you may be assured I'll contact you directly."

The door crashed open.

Even though she scented her father, for an unrealistic instant, she hoped for Christoph. Danger aside, she needed him.

"What's going on?" Gerard's voice echoed around the room.

Elsa turned, relieved to see Gerard, but concerned his appearance might mean more badgering from Strasser.

"Elsa," Gerard looked over his daughter with a furrowed brow, lines bracketing his mouth. "You're hurt." To Strasser he demanded, "What have you done to my child? Have you dared touch her?"

"Gerard, Elsa was present when the specimen attempted escape. I was questioning her on the series of events. Her injuries are a result of what happened in that room." Strasser seemed tired, just as tired as she felt, though she held no sympathy for him.

"The subject escaped?" Gerard questioned as he took Elsa's hand. She saw his nose wrinkle at the smell of her blood—not in disgust, in concern. His hand tightened around hers.

"It did this to my daughter? What of the guards? What kind of incompetence is this!"

"The subject is dead."

Gerard looked between Elsa and Strasser. "How…?"

"I'll fill you in later, father. I just want to go home and clean up." Elsa tried not to look at Strasser, she didn't want to give him an opening for further questions.

"Elsa, Gerard, before you leave." Strasser stood the tips of his fingers atop his desk. "As far as I can tell, the subject was shot by one of my guards. Do you understand?"

"Yes, Herr Strasser," Elsa replied.

****

Dried were the hot tears that streamed down her cheeks and spilled onto Christoph's neck. Exhausted from both the grief she felt over Erik and the release of strain, and too content to move from his arms, they sat tucked away in a corner of the garden. The stars shone brightly overhead.

He cradled her in his lap. His large frame shielded her from the outside world, protecting her. His lips brushed her temple, achy from where she'd hit her head.

When he saw her injuries, he'd gone wild with rage. His growl told her all he couldn't put into words, the fear, the hopelessness. Unable to do more, Elsa had wrapped his arms around her, pressed her body to his. They fit perfectly.

He'd then picked her up and taken her outdoors.

"I love you," he stated now jarring her back to the present.

She scraped her teeth along his neck, over the mark she'd made. "I could feel you. I knew you were with me every moment."

"Always," his hand smoothed up her back,

grasped her neck. "You die, I die. There is nothing else."

****

"You want me to leave you now?"

Christoph grabbed her elbows, pulling her to him, and shook her once. Since finding her, his *wölfe* clawed so close to the surface as to be almost one with his human side. He'd nearly gone berserk when he couldn't get to her yesterday morning after Erik's botched rescue.

Last night, after she'd told him what happened, he hadn't let her go. They sat in the gardens long into the night before he carried her to her room. He'd lain next to her, unable to leave her.

Though he tried, he hadn't been gentle making love to her. He needn't have worried. Elsa had been as needy, as insatiable, as he. Only when the midmorning sun shone through the windows had he stirred.

Their argument began after a late breakfast. No one disturbed them in the closed room.

"You stubborn man!" Elsa shouted. "Strasser is watching us. If not now, he soon will be. He lost his precious subject." She said the words in disgust but he could hear the edge of worry in her voice. Not for Strasser, certainly not. For him.

"Do you think I can let you stay here, knowing he *does* watch you? You're mine," he growled with another shake. "I protect you."

She let out a breath and her eyes shifted, lightened from her impressive anger. Christoph loosened his hold on her, wary. She raised a hand to cup his cheek.

"I know you do. When I'm with you I feel protected."

Her lips were warm against his, a light probing kiss. His reaction was immediate; at her merest touch, he lost control.

Deepening the kiss, he walked forward until her back hit the wall. Undoing the buttons of her shirt, he slipped his hand beneath the camisole. Her response intoxicated him. She opened her mouth, wrapped arms and legs around him, and rocked against him.

Christoph caught her moan with another kiss, felt her nipple raise and harden under his fingers.

"I can't live without you, Elsa. I have to protect you, don't you understand? You're my mate, nothing else matters."

She rested her forehead against his, and he felt her fingers beneath his shirt, stroking his back.

"I know, love, but I can't let anything happen to you, either. Strasser is obsessed with this. Father thinks he's even contacted someone higher up, someone as interested in the old legends as he."

"All the more reason for you to leave now and return to Lower Saxony with me."

Instead of shouting more insults about his stubbornness, she chuckled.

"What did Helmut van Dietrich say?"

Undeterred from her body, Christoph carried her to a settee. Settling her so she straddled his lap, he unbuttoned the rest of her shirt.

"He evacuates his entire Pack."

She pulled back, clearly surprised, but he nipped her mark. Shuddering she leaned into his bite. Smiling against her skin, he guided her back to his mouth. Tossing the shirt to the floor, he left her camisole on. The thin material outlined her body, revealing bare hints of the curves he knew lay beneath the silk.

"I don't want Erik's papers to lead to them. They can't go to Lower Saxony," he said against the side of her neck. Her skin fragrant with her own scent, and he could smell himself there, mixing with her. Bonding them.

“Within two days they should be gone, the only trace they lived in Berlin empty apartments and abandoned jobs.”

“Strasser will be furious,” she panted. Her back arched, granting him further access to her luscious breasts. He suckled her nipple, wetting the fabric so it clung to her.

“That is my intention.” He switched to her other breast. “I want him angry. Angry, he’ll make more mistakes. I don’t want him finding anything. The new regime is vicious with failures. Strasser’s will make him a target.”

With the same attention he lavished on the first, he paid homage to her other breast. The wet silk clung to the engorged peak. He made a mental note to buy her all the silk she wanted.

“Please, Christoph,” she begged.

“Please what?”

“It’s not safe for you here,” she gasped. “You have to leave. *Please*.”

He bit her neck, harder than he intended. She didn’t shy away, but growled at the feel and tightened her thighs around his waist. The move brought her against his cock, already hard and throbbing. Christoph wanted nothing more than to bury himself deep within her.

“Not without you.”

Her eyes were heavy when she brought her head up to look at him. The skin of her neck reddened from his teeth but he wasn’t sorry. His mark, visible upon her.

“I’ll be with you again in a day.” Her breathless promise wasn’t enough. She meant it, Christoph didn’t doubt that. He needed her safe. With him. His.

“Two at most,” she gasped as his teeth scrapped over her nipple. “I’ll resign my position at the hospital. Strasser will have no choice but to accept it."

"Elsa," he said seriously, "though the van Dietrich Pack is leaving, it doesn't mean the danger is over for you, either. Strasser isn't the type to take blame. If he can, he'll blame Erik's death on you."

"I know," her voice quieted with the gravity of the situation.

"I fear," he began. Her hips rocked slowly against his, the motion almost unconscious on her part, for he could tell she gave her full attention to his next words.

"I fear this is only the beginning. I'll need to meet with my other Pack leaders. Otto tells me your evacuation plans are in place?"

She nodded. "It was created centuries ago. We've paid for the upkeep on the houses through a broker in Switzerland."

"Good. All my Packs in Osnabrück are prepared. Margaret will have the house packed in a day, if she has any say. I'm uncomfortable," he confessed, a first for him, admitting a fear, a failing. Even to Hans and Peter, he presented a decisive demeanor. The Alpha never admitted to indecisiveness.

"I'm uncomfortable with one of my Packs out of Germany."

"Can they ever return?"

The sadness in her eyes told him she already knew the answer. He shook his head, and she nodded. He thought she nodded in understanding to more than the van Dietrich's.

"Christoph, two days is all I ask. I must assist in our own Pack's evacuation. Father would be lost without me." Elsa stroked his lips with her fingertips. "Just two days."

"One day." His mouth met hers in a hard kiss. "No more."

Tearing away the bit of silk covering her, Christoph quickly unbuttoned his pants. In one decisive move, he entered her. She clenched around him, the feel of her heat heaven. Gripping her hips, he lifted her slightly, only to slam up, deep within her.

"Mine," he growled against her mouth.

He wanted to say more. Wanted to express his need of her, his possession of her. Every time they were together he felt closer to her, wanted more of her. Everything he was blended with Elsa.

He'd destroy anyone before he lost her.

Elsa screamed his name, her orgasm shuddering through them both. Her beauty was unmatched, her body his.

Reaching his own climax, Christoph clamped his teeth on her mark. She shuddered again in orgasm, tightening around him as he came.

"Mine."

Chapter Eight

"You're in earlier than I expected, Gerard." Strasser halted near an empty gurney in the cadaver wing.

"Do you expect me to sleep after learning my daughter was attacked by a beast?" Gerard slipped his clenched hands into his pockets; loathe to refer to Erik as a beast when Strasser was the real animal.

"I've barely closed my eyes. I told Elsa not to come in today, but does she listen to her father?"

Strasser nodded. "I want you to redo every test already performed on the specimen."

"I won't have enough blood samples, Karl. Elsa was unable to retrieve the last round. The body will no longer yield fresh samples. We could," he said pensively, glad he hadn't anything to eat that morning, "perform muscle and tissue studies now that we can cut into the subject."

"I'm still interested in proceeding with the experiment from yesterday," Strasser continued. "I want to see what happens to the prisoner, a full-blooded human, when introduced to our specimen's blood. Perhaps it will produce our desired result."

"With a dead specimen? What kind of results are you imagining?"

"We've retrieved what blood we could from the corpse," Strasser informed him. Gerard already planned for this eventuality. "We'll use the preserved blood and what other samples can still be harvested."

"I'll conduct the tests, but I must empathize the potential harm to the test subject is great. Possibly lethal." Gerard stepped away from Strasser to stare at the scuffmarks made by the gurneys. He had no intention of harming this prisoner, or of fouling Erik's body further.

"That does not concern me," Strasser barked. Then his voice lowered in case others listened. "I want another *wehrwölfe*. We had one in our hands, Gerard, a living man-*wölfe*. The honor and prestige we lost, the resource for a stronger Germany." He shook his head at the imagined loss. "It is unthinkable."

Gerard half turned toward Strasser with a nod.

"The corpse is in the large lab in Wing C. I want the experiments begun this afternoon."

Time to implement part one of our plan.

****

"Elsa, has Otto sent word?" Gerard stepped around one of two leather visitor chairs to stop in front of Elsa's desk.

"Yes," she rose. "Where have you been for the last two hours? I was about to search for you."

"I'm glad you didn't. I want us both to be as visible as possible, preferably with Strasser to discuss the upcoming," he scowled, "tests."

"Father, what have you done?" She stepped around her desk.

"Never mind now, what did Otto report?" Gerard rubbed his face and realized he'd forgotten to shave this morning.

"The entire Pack has been alerted. Word has been given to evacuate, today if possible. Otto has our valuables packed. First we must see Anton and sign the transfer authorizations."

"Excellent." Gerard picked up Elsa's lab coat from a chair and held it out for her. "Let's find Strasser."

****

Strasser hovered over Franz, his clerk, in an

office down the hall from Erik's body.

"Karl," Gerard called as they entered the cluttered room.

Boxes stacked against two walls were marked with Erik's subject number. A pang of sadness for the lost *wölfe* constricted her heart. Knowing first hand the connection she had with Christoph, she couldn't imagine the horror Erik experienced when he witnessed Ursula's death.

"We've prepared a list of tests." Gerard opened the folder containing the barbaric experiments Elsa constructed while waiting on word from Otto.

"Good. Good." Strasser approached them. Elsa detested the man, more now than before Erik's capture.

"The first few should be relatively harmless but the last several may cause death," Gerard stated with his usual even tone. "I recommend observing the subject for a minimum of twenty hours between procedures."

"Too long," Strasser countered. "I want to know the viability of each method before the material is unusable. One hour is all you have between procedures."

"Herr Doctor," Elsa interjected. "An hour is barely enough time for a reaction much less full analysis of the results."

"An hour." Strasser took the folder from Gerard. "I won't allow an opportunity—"

A scream interrupted him. Seconds later, the sound of pounding boots raced past the doorway.

"Hell, what now!" Strasser pushed past them and followed a set of SS guards down the hall. Elsa followed, Gerard close behind.

A bright yellow-orange glow emanated from one of the small windows centered in a lab door. Flames roared on the other side of the door. The room burned.

The guards and several scientists and nurses stood outside the lab in a half circle.

"No!" Strasser screamed. "My specimen! Open the door! Retrieve my specimen!"

"The lab is sealed," one of the scientists offered. "If we open it before the fire suffocates, we risk the entire wing."

"Get the body out, now!" Strasser ordered.

Two SS officers grabbed sheets off nearby gurneys, while a third dragged the thin mattress off. The spectators dispersed to allow them room.

Elsa pulled her father back as they kicked open the door. As predicted, the fire accelerated. The body was lost. Understanding the implications, she slowly glanced at Gerard.

****

"I'm not the only one who takes risks in this family." Elsa made sure the door to their office shut tight behind her. "I can't believe you managed it. *How* did you manage it?" She took off her lab coat and hung it on the rack.

"Miracles of modern science—the right combinations form a surprising number of untraceable combustibles."

"I don't want to know. Strasser is screaming sabotage; he'll question every person in the hospital. It was a stroke of brilliance to find him. We're above suspicion."

"We either had to be surrounded by many or in his presence. In his presence worked best." Gerard removed his own lab coat and hung it beside hers. "Our research files are secure?"

"Yes." She opened a false drawer in her desk to show him. "I sent those few we had left with Otto. The neighbors were curious about the loaded truck, so the servants informed them of my imminent marriage."

"Elsa," Gerard started, "I want you to head to

the bank and sign out your accounts. I'll call Anton, give him the same story about your marriage. I'll follow behind. First, I want to talk to Karl. Tell him we're taking a few days to recover from this turmoil."

"Don't delay, Father." Elsa didn't want to leave his side, but had promised Christoph she'd be at his house by tonight. She grabbed her purse and kissed his cheek. "We'll be ready."

****

Gerard peered into Strasser's office.

It appeared mysteriously empty. He expected lines of people awaiting interrogation. Last he'd seen, Karl looked livid over the loss of Erik's body.

Perplexed, he walked through the empty room. Just as he turned to go, he heard voices from the office across the hall. Franz rummaged through Erik's things.

"I wasn't certain I understood it correctly, Herr Doctor," Gerard overheard as he crept to the office door. "But—"

"Give it here," Strasser demanded.

After a moment of silence, Strasser said, "*A new child in our Clan…wanted your blessing, Alpha…*" he paused and Gerard, frozen in fear, felt sick. "It's addressed to Christoph von Berangar."

With all the stealth with which he entered, he left, things now immeasurably worse.

Gerard raced to the car. One of his footmen held open the door and before the man closed his own, Gerard snapped directions. Their possessions could wait. He needed to see Anton about the money transfer, warn Elsa. Warn Christoph.

"No," he changed his mind. "Head home first."

The second the car halted on the street, Gerard jumped out.

"Otto! Elsa!"

"You're back early—"

"Strasser knows about Christoph."

He could see the blood drain from his daughter's face, hoped she wouldn't faint. But no, not his daughter, not the Alpha Female. She straightened and snapped questions as he entered his study.

"Erik's papers?"

"Otto," Gerard nodded to her. "Leave the rest of the belongings. Take what we have."

"I'll see to everything, sir," his loyal butler and friend said. They'd survived the trenches of Flanders together; he had the utmost faith in the other man.

"What else did he say?" she demanded.

"I returned here immediately. I need to call Anton, see to the rest of the Pack, but Christoph needs to be warned."

She already held the phone, no doubt dialing the Dungraf Pack leader. Christoph was meeting with Oskar Dungraf, going over evacuation plans and Pack security. On his way from Berlin to Lower Saxony, and at the time, the stopover had made sense.

Now, Gerard wished he'd gone straight to Osnabrück.

Opening his desk drawer, he stuffed papers into a briefcase. Moments later, Elsa slammed down the phone.

"No answer. Keep calling Oskar. Try to catch Christoph before he leaves. I'm taking the 500K."

Yes, good, the Mercedes 500K was fastest. Nodding, he said, "Strasser will need time to gather his forces. I don't know if he'll contact anyone higher up—he's mad, in disgrace. But he'll need men."

Gerard rounded the desk and took her by the shoulders. Kissing her forehead he said, "Be careful child."

"I can't let anything happen to him. I won't."

She embraced him tightly. "Be safe. Don't tardy, we have to get out before Strasser realizes our connection."

He watched her consult with Otto before leaving. Listening for the car, he dialed Oskar Dungraf's number.

Still no answer.

For the rest of the afternoon he tried, panic increasing. When he left to see Anton about the transfers, he took a footman and left Otto to continue trying to reach Christoph.

Nothing.

The sun hid behind the city when he finally reached the other Pack leader.

"Oskar," he said without preamble. "Is Christoph still there?"

"Gerard?" the other man asked. "No, he left not thirty minutes—"

"Can you intercept him?" he interrupted.

"With some effort, yes. Why?"

"There's been a discovery. I fear his door may be vulnerable."

"I'll see to it myself," Oskar said.

Gerard hung up and called to Otto. He didn't want Elsa to experience what he had when his wife died. More he couldn't bear losing his child.

"Otto," he said the moment the butler entered. "We must hasten to Dungraf's Pack."

Chapter Nine

Elsa's hands gripped the polished steering wheel until her knuckles whitened. The needles on the maroon Mercedes Benz 500K jumped with her speed, and yet the car didn't go nearly as fast as she needed. In the distance she could hear the train, but couldn't see the tracks, had no way of cutting over.

Only one direct route to Osnabrück existed. The road, not the best kept, was mercifully empty. On the occasion she came upon another car, she passed without slowing.

One thing they hadn't planned. Until her father returned, white and scared, she'd have said they took everything into account. Erik's friends, family, bare acquaintances, even his body.

Betrayed by a letter none could have foreseen.

"Damn it, Erik," she muttered. "How could you have been so stupid?"

It wasn't his fault. Telling the Alpha of an impending birth was to be expected, required even. Children were so rare in their Clan each one was celebrated.

Erik had possibly the worst timing in history. Now Strasser knew and headed to Lower Saxony.

To Christoph.

She had to get there first. She had to. It wasn't just her mate she protected, but her Alpha.

The trees hid the sun, nearly set now, making it harder to see the road despite her headlights. The manor house should be close. She'd passed a sign for the town ten minutes ago, after one wrong turn had taken her too far out of her way.

"Please let me arrive in time," she breathed. "Please, God, don't let me be too late."

****

"I'll see Herr Röhm the end of the week," Hans murmured, noting it in his calendar.

Röhm would be thrilled to finally get the chance to purchase their land. It grated on the nerves to sell something that had been in the Clan since the beginning but desperate times and all.

The house blazed with light, people came from deep within Lower Saxony. More were expected to arrive in the next days, the rest by month's end. The household, itself, bustled in a minor uproar. Quiet preparations had begun to move centuries of possessions, no small feat. The other Pack leaders had just left. Everything was in place for the evacuation.

Still not certain of this course of action, and not one to second guess his Alpha's decisions, he followed Christoph's instructions. But to leave all they were, all they knew…

Frantic pounding interrupted his thoughts.

He stalked into the foyer before the butler could open the door. Her scent caught him first, the distinctiveness of it. Deeper, now a part of her, lay Christoph's scent.

"Is Christoph here?"

Beautiful, tall, authoritative, the mark on her neck told him all he needed to know. She was their Alpha Female.

Frowning at the alarm that surrounded her, he waved the butler off.

"He hasn't arrived yet, Fräulein von Skyler. What's wrong?"

Startled at the familiar greeting, Elsa looked at the man. He was tall, lean. Christoph had told her of his friend, Hans. This had to be him. The heavy door closed behind her as she stepped forward.

"Not here yet," she sighed in frustration. "I need to speak with Herr von Troschke."

"I'm von Troschke, Fräulein."

She nodded, still trying to catch her breath. Her fingers ached, and her heart had yet to slow its mad pace. No Christoph and no Strasser, either, a fear she'd fought on the long drive up the driveway.

"Gather everyone. It's imperative we leave. We must warn Christoph."

"Slow down, Fräulein." He took her arm and led her into a room off the foyer. It was the study. Christoph's. Elsa took a moment to inhale his scent. Given the situation, it did little to calm her.

"What's the problem?"

"The Nazi, Strasser," she said, rushed. "He knows Christoph is a *wehrwölfe*. There isn't time to explain. He's on his way here. I don't know how long we have."

For a heartbeat, Hans stared at her, and she wanted to scream at him to go, abandon the manor. With no time for contemplation and delay she growled a warning, a command at him. Startled, he automatically bowed his head at the Alpha Female's command. He nodded and crossed to the phone.

"I'll have someone meet Christoph at the train. The moment he disembarks he'll know."

He dialed even while bellowing orders to the staff. She admired his composure, but then it wasn't his mate in danger. No, that wasn't fair. From what Christoph had said, the three of them—he, Hans, and Peter—had grown up together.

The phone trembled slightly in Hans' hand. He feared for Christoph as much as she.

"Jörg," he barked into the phone.

When he said nothing more, she strode to the desk. "What is it?"

"The line's dead."

Her stomach clenched. "Strasser's here."

"Fräulein," he rounded the desk, urgency in every movement. Once more, he took her elbow and maneuvered her out of the room. "I must get you out of here. We'll meet Christoph in the countryside. He'll know where."

This was worse than she imagined. On her drive here, she believed—no hoped—Strasser to be at least half a day behind her. He'd need to gather men, armaments, prepare the *Charité* for his precious subjects.

He must have left without any preparations in his haste to find a new specimen.

The trees half obscured the full moon, the lawn before the thick Teutoburg Forest glowed like something out of a fairytale. Hans led her through the glass doors and into that eerie glow.

Three men attacked Hans. He pushed her away, and she stumbled to the ground. He growled, and Elsa knew he was going to change.

"Don't!" She screamed. She refused to allow him to give the SS what they wanted.

"Go!" Hans snarled. In the bright light she could see his teeth elongate.

"Don't," she repeated, pushing off the ground. A burly arm encircled her chest, holding her captive, the black of the SS uniform unmistakable. Her hand struck backwards, hitting the man in the face. He cried out, but didn't release her.

The *wölfe* within struggled for dominance. Even knowing the risk, it needed to break free and attack. Elsa couldn't allow that. She'd be faster, stronger, but it was what Strasser wanted, what he'd come to Lower Saxony to search for.

Still fighting the officer, another caught her legs. She saw Hans throw off two of the men, and lunge for her. He clawed at the man holding her legs, who screamed in pain and released her.

"Don't turn," she ordered.

Caught in the change, she could see his face partially morph, claws extend. Stronger now, he snapped at his assailants, catching one's arm in the steel grip of his jaw. The scent of blood mingled with the screams of the man. Hans released his hold, and the man crumpled to the ground in agony.

Metal glinted in the moonlight. Before she could scream a warning, the officer holding her struck her head, once, twice. The SS officer snarled in hatred and fear when she stayed upright. With a low growl, she partially shifted, turning her hands into claws, and dug them into the arms holding her. He released her with a surprised grunt of pain.

"Hans!" she warned, too late.

The knife plunged into him. Hans wailed and threw back his arms. The knife struck again, then a third time before the move knocked those trying to hold him off balance. Turning, he swiped claws at the one who stabbed him, gutting him from chin to chest.

Shaking her head from the blows, Elsa stumbled forward. The ground swayed, her stomach with it, and she stopped.

Hans turned on the remaining guard just as the SS officer took his pistol and whacked it on the side of Hans' head. Instantly, he crumpled to the ground. The officer struck him again when Hans struggled upright.

The guard who accosted her unsheathed his own Luger and pointed it at her head.

"I wouldn't."

With a final glance at Hans, Elsa allowed herself to be hauled into the house. She couldn't heed Hans' shout and go, she was the Alpha Female. The safety of her Clan came first. If Strasser dealt with her, he'd leave the rest of them alone. And deal with her he would—when he discovered her deception, nothing in this world would stop him from his interrogation.

Grunts echoed behind her. She could hear the officers beat Hans while he lay unconscious.

Hans wouldn't agree with her, but with Christoph's whereabouts unknown, she had to remain.

Jerking her arm from the guard's meaty grip, she walked as proudly as she could into the foyer. Why he led her into the house and not a waiting car, she didn't know.

And then the door opened.

Karl Strasser, Head of the Department of Scientific Inquiries, Special Interests Division, entered. He slowly pulled off his traveling gloves and gazed about as if he owned the manor.

Still in the shadows, Elsa watched him scan the area. In the distance, she could hear the howls of *wölfes*. Some retreated into the forest, some warned of the danger. Closer, she could hear whimpers of those caught, beaten, stabbed, but not shot. No scent of gunpowder filled the air.

He wanted them all alive then. The better to experiment with.

The guard dug the Luger into her neck. "Move."

She stepped into the light as the guard called, "Herr Doctor!"

The look on Strasser's face was priceless. Grim amusement warred with fear. Here he stood, in the middle of a forest, hunting *wehrwölfes*, and it was her appearance which astounded him most.

"Fräulein von Skyler?"

Chapter Ten

Rage.
Hatred.
Fear.
Find Elsa. Rescue Elsa.

His need was clear, his mate endangered. Nothing else mattered. He would disembowel the man who held his mate.

Oskar Dungraf warned him of the danger the moment he disembarked the train. Gerard had not been far behind with the complete tale. It hadn't taken him long to discover the situation at the estate. Hans and several of Christoph's staff had been captured by the repugnant Strasser. Worse, his Elsa was also a hostage.

Attack the house. Kill those who endangered his woman.

"Christoph!"

Peter's voice barely penetrated the *wölfe's* instinctual reaction. Christoph paced within the confines of the circle, snarling, snapping at those around him.

"Christoph!"

Christoph snapped his head toward Peter, his face changing to his *wölfe* visage then back to his human form again. A deep, hissing snarl all he was capable of . The others surrounded him, encircling their Alpha in a protective and respectful manner.

He paced, ready to leap and tear the throat of any who opposed him. He stood to his full human height, face a contorted mixture of anger and hatred.

"We are all with you, Christoph." Gerard's voice

registered.

Christoph's pace slowed. His anger remained, but reason reappeared. They would not let him do as he must. There were not enough of them left to risk the Alpha. Protected and coddled when it was he who led their warriors.

"Assess their forces. Kill the guards. Strasser is mine."

He discarded his human vestments. Dozens beside him did the same. Margaret stood a short distance off, and would see to their clothes as she awaited their return. In a fluid move he turned, fingers growing into claws, muscle and bone bunching as he shifted to his *wölfe*.

Eyes already accustomed to the night sharpened with his transformation. He howled in anguish and anger, a call to the manor.

To war.

With his *wölfes* beside him, he raced for his mate.

****

Surrounded by Christoph's scent, the room spoke of him. It grounded and comforted her.

Strasser backhanded her again, splitting her lip wider. The blow did nothing to help her already aching head, nor stop her vision from swimming.

"The magnitude of your betrayal is beyond comprehension!"

Elsa heard Hans behind her. He'd been chained to one of the stone pillars flanking the room's fireplace. Silver chains, which did nothing but hold him securely in place. He raged each and every time Strasser struck her.

He could easily break free, he only had to fully change. But she'd given him a direct order not to, and he obeyed.

"Tell me of your kind, *wölfe*. Spare her further injury." Strasser smeared blood from Elsa's face onto his hand and shoved it at Hans. "I have taken a small amount of her blood. I can take it all. Now ***tell me***. This map what does it represent?"

Hans hissed and bared his teeth.

"Are these the locations of other *wehrwölfes*? How many are out there? A hundred? A thousand?" For an instant, she thought she saw fear on Strasser's face. She certainly scented it on him despite his bluster. "How do you add to your numbers?"

She said nothing. If this was where her life ended then she would end it in the protection of her Clan.

Had there been anything to regret, it would be mating with the Alpha. She wanted to think Christoph would go on, find another. Elsa knew better. Try as she might, she couldn't regret her connection to Christoph. For the briefest time, she knew the passion only a lover, her true mate, could share.

Another strike and blood slipped down her forehead and pooled into her left eye. Another and her breathing began to suffer.

****

"You are to go directly to *Reichsführer* Himmler with this note. Do not divert from your destination."

Strasser watched the two men he appointed to return to Berlin exit the house. This evening's events would go down in their history books. Children would tell tales of how he captured the legendary *wehrwölfes*.

Karl envisioned his future at the left hand of the *Führer*, commander of the *wehrwölfes* for the glory of the Reich. All that marred this grand evening was his incredulity at the discovery of Elsa von Skyler in this house. It had shaken his unfathomable belief in his own intuition. He'd respected the von Skylers, considered them among the best the *Charité* had to offer. To discover they were beasts had him doubting all he knew.

He stared at his hand. Elsa's blood covered it and stained his clothing. He left the room, a single officer guarding the two beasts, to find a sink. No sense in taking chances. He wanted to lead the *wölfes*. Not be one of them.

The other *wölfe* reacted violently to his abuse of the female. Karl wondered if they protected all the females among them so fiercely.

What would happen if a pure blood German mated with one of their females? Would it produce a superior species? How difficult would it be to train these animals? They could corral all the females, use them to threaten the males. Use them to have the males do the *Führer's* bidding.

Females. He suddenly realized Elsa was the sole one. There were two other males, household staff, but no additional women. His guards reported several forms raced to the woods, but Karl waited for reinforcements before searching for them.

Perhaps the lack of females caused the male to react with such savagery. He couldn't wait to find out.

****

Two grey *wölfes* stood guard over the crash site. They waited at the end of the long driveway for more SS, the alert sentries. Behind them, a black Mercedes tilted on its side. In the tree-filtered moonlight, two bodies, their black uniforms mangled and bloodied, lay ripped through the broken windshield. Mere yards away, its lights the sole illumination for miles, the estate waited for its master.

****

The darkness was their domain. Humans were arrogant creatures to think they could hold off destruction. Christoph awaited Otto's single short howl that he'd dispatched the perimeter guards.

Rage burned coldly within him. Mind cleared of everything save Elsa, he stood silently in the shadow of the trees. Both Peter and Otto refused to let him take part in the initial attack. Their arguments had been feeble at best, considering he was Alpha and stronger than either of them. However, he didn't wish to waste any more time. He agreed faster then normal to stave off a prolonged disagreement and get to Elsa.

Elsa.

His blood boiled through him, lethal teeth bared at the night.

Attack.

Peter hunted with Otto, and though Christoph had sent a dozen *wölfes* with them, he knew the two could take whatever SS Strasser had.

He'd deal with Strasser himself.

What unspeakable things the Nazi scientist did to his woman, Christoph refused to dwell on. No matter, he'd die tonight. The look in Gerard's eyes when he'd left the older man deep in the woods, held the same fear for Elsa.

With a small flash, the house lights extinguished, leaving only the moon to illuminate their way. Peter had done his job and would join him in the manor. A scant heartbeat later, Otto's sharp howl signaled the SS guards were dispatched.

Snarling, he leapt out of the woods, four additional *wölfes* beside him. They looped across the moonlit grounds. Peter, his grey fur splattered with red, and Otto's grey-black form joined him.

He knew where Strasser held Elsa, and circled the manor to the study. With a graceful leap, he crashed through the window. The sound of breaking glass echoed throughout the house as his force entered their assigned areas. Peter and Otto followed him.

Glass littered the marbled floor, but he ignored its sharp cut into his paws and fur. He could hear human shouts, gunshots, a *wölfe's* howl as the bullet hit home.

To his left, Hans growled. A quick glance confirmed him chained to the stone pillar, just now changing form.

Attention focused on Elsa, he roared. The fragrance of her blood filled the room. Her head rose, bloodied, bruised. Once blue eyes were coated red but when they met his gaze, fire burned within them.

Though she must be weakened, her form shifted, morphed. Strasser, or the man Christoph assumed to be Strasser, stood before her, fascinated by the transformation. Petrified of the commotion around him.

Barely registering his lieutenants as they took out the terrified guard, Christoph pounced. Elsa's blood stained Strasser's hands and clothes, fear clung to him like a rotting stench. The human had no time to unsheathe his weapon. A cry of horror whimpered past his lips.

He took a breath to savor Strasser's terror. This was the man who tried to take control of the uncontrollable—of them. Who worked to expose their secret and enslave their Clan. He would not leave the room alive.

Letting lose all his fury and fear, he tore into Strasser's throat. Christoph's teeth sank into his neck, crushing his spine. Another whimper died with the human's death.

Without another thought, Christoph turned to his mate. She hadn't changed, and he realized her earlier shift was more to distract Strasser from his weapon than to escape.

Jumping two paws atop the arms of Elsa's chair, Christoph moved his face into the crook of her neck.

Nuzzling his mark, he laved his tongue along it. Elsa leaned into him, weak yet he could scent her arousal.

Transforming back to his human form, the soft black fur of his *wölfe* state retreated to reveal his smooth skin. Before his claws completely retracted, he slashed through her ties.

"Christoph," she murmured her breath labored, lips cut and swollen.

"Elsa," he whispered.

Gathered in his arms, she felt slight, weak. Lifting her, he held her as close as he dared against his naked form.

Her arms, red from the tightness of her bonds, wound around his neck. Despite her bloodied lips, he kissed her. She was safe. His.

Christoph turned with her in his arms to assess the room. Peter had gone to Hans and snapped the chains.

"I am Peter, Count Lungraf und Calvelage, eldest child of Emile, Count Lungraf und Calvelage and his beautiful wife, Greta, seneschal to our beloved Alpha, Protector of the Arminius Clan. And rescuer of Hans von Troschke!"

Hans said nothing to Peter, but glared at him with a look of abject horror and disbelief.

Mate in his arms, Christoph studied his friends. Hans, leaning heavily on Peter, looked far the worse for wear. Several prominent bruises and a couple deep gashes marred his bare chest, and Otto pressed a cloth to what looked like a trio of knife wounds on his side and back.

"Otto, see to Hans. Peter, fetch Margaret and Gerard. Send word—the Clan leaves by dawn."

He carried Elsa to his room. He had much to do, too much for him to properly see to her injuries. Christoph didn't care and laid her on the bed.

He could tell she put up a strong front, he could

see her fierce will despite the obvious pain.

"The others, get them away, Christoph!" She sat up and held onto his arms. She wheezed, a hand clutching her side. "Strasser sent word to Himmler."

He caressed her cheek with soft, long strokes. "We stopped his messengers. We're safe for now."

"Will we ever be safe again?"

"Yes," he whispered fiercely, forehead touching hers. "I can not lose you. You die, I die, remember?"

She squeezed his hand, touched her lips to his. "I remember."

"I'm never letting you out of my sight again."

Epilogue

Dawn lingered on the horizon. Christoph stood outside the house he'd called home all his life, Elsa's warm hand in his.

Oskar and his men had left an hour earlier, along with Margaret and the remaining Clan members. Christoph remained with Peter, Hans, Gerard and his Elsa.

Peter had no interest in watching what they were about to do, and sat in the last car facing away from the house. Hans and Gerard stood behind them. This house had been the Arminius Clan seat for over eight hundred years. Inside lay the bodies of seventeen SS officers. Christoph did not doubt Himmler would stop at nothing to track down their killers. To discover their secrets.

He'd found the letter Erik wrote, exposing him as Alpha, on Strasser. It was a small relief; he had no way of being certain they'd gotten all the reports and files.

Christoph regretted not seeing Elsa as head of this household. Not playing with what children they'd have near the same river he once raced along. They could not risk remaining.

"It's time." he said simply. "We have a new life to carve out."

He entered his doorway one last time. Picking up a long fireplace match, he struck it alongside its wooden box.

Christoph tossed the lit match onto the bodies. The petrol they'd spilled caught fire in a funeral pyre for the dead officers and his ancestral home.

Ignoring the SS, he watched the flames lick along the floor, up the walls. Elsa touched his back. It was time. Together they left.

Only the legends remained.

****

Reichsführer Heinrich Himmler surveyed the charred ruins. The walls, dull black in the noon sun were all that remained. Any proof Karl Strasser gathered on the *wehrwölfes* burned days ago, destroyed along with him and seventeen of Himmler's guards.

No trace of anything remained in a fifteen-mile radius. Cottages abandoned, houses burnt, the ashes still warm to the touch.

Germany's army of *wölfes* would not see fruition.

"Go through the ashes," he ordered. "I want no trace of this to survive."

About the author...

I've been writing for 4 years, and love just about every second of it. I say just about because there are seconds of writing that make me want to pull out my hair. Historical paranormals caught my eye (and ear) when I realized the vast conflicts inherent in historicals, and my deep and abiding love for all things paranormal. Nurturing a love of all time periods, I plan to explore as many as I can with as many couples as I can.

Visit her at http://www.isabelroman.com

Blood Moon

by

Autumn Shelley

Dedication

For Bill

Prologue

The shadowed figure scaled the last chain fence separating him from freedom. He hit the ground, rolled, and came up on all fours, sniffing the air. The crisp night air helped to clear his brain. He wasn't sure how many weeks he'd been held prisoner in the compound, everything was so foggy. All the drugs, all the injections, all the beatings. Logan turned his head when he heard pursuers behind him. It didn't matter—he was beyond their boundaries and their capabilities.

Logan lowered his head and allowed his wolf to come forward. The transformation wasn't painful but it took a certain amount of energy and his energy supply was currently short. He waited patiently as his head widened and his face elongated. His musculature shifted and lengthened as his bone structure re-arranged itself completely. Hair began to emerge from every pore on his body. Logan shivered at the sensation. It made him want to lie on his back and roll until the itching subsided. Instead he lay on his side, panting, taking precious moments to rest before the run he knew was ahead of him.

He had to find her. Had to get to the woman before the others found her. He only hoped once he did, she would be willing to help. So many lives depended on it.

Chapter One

Kate Barrister locked the vet clinic and dashed to her car in the pouring rain. Whoever said summer thunderstorms were the worst must never have lived through autumn showers in the Ozark Mountains. Cold rain pelted her all the way, running down the back of her neck and into her shirt. *Certainly wasn't going to be an enjoyable drive home*. She gave a sigh as she turned the ignition and pulled onto the highway. She looked forward to getting home, making some soup and settling in for the night.

As she thought about the things she needed to do at home, Kate chastised herself. She could not put off looking over the papers any longer. Her parents died in a car accident nearly a month ago and Kate had been neglecting to sign the documents needed to legally put things in her name. Would she ever be able to move on from her parents' death? Every time she turned around there was a paper that needed to be signed or something to be done at the courthouse. She was an only child for heaven's sake, and there was a will that clearly stated the business and the homes were to go to her. So, why did there have to be so much paperwork?

The unfairness of it all lingered in her mind as she rounded a curve and noticed something lying in the road. In the headlights, it was only an outline. For a moment she thought it was a person. As she slowed, she realized it was a large canine of some kind. Coyote? Dog?

Kate stopped the car, turned on the hazards, and got out. The rain wasn't pelting now; instead it was a steady pour. *God, it's huge, whatever it is.* She approached cautiously. As a vet she knew very well there was nothing more dangerous than an animal in pain. Any animal, even a rabbit could inflict damage, but a predator-type animal could be lethal. Too often, people forgot their canines were nothing more than domesticated predators.

Kate spoke quietly to see if there was any reaction at all. "Hey big guy, what's happened to you, hmm? How did you get out here, in the rain no less? Not a good time or place to be taking a nap, buddy."

It looked like a wolf, but that couldn't be right. There hadn't been wolves in the Ozarks for a hundred years or more. Maybe it was some kind of cross? There were fools out there who thought it looked bad-ass to cross wolves with domestic dogs then pass them off as pets. She had euthanized her share of *pets* because their primal instincts were so strong they were a danger to the public.

Ears flicked and a low growl sounded. Kate continued to talk and moved slowly closer. She didn't want the dog to hurt itself more by attempting to run away. Wounded animals could be aggressive because of their inability to defend themselves. Right now this creature would see Kate as a bigger, stronger predator, one higher up on the food chain.

Kate moved in closer and the growl continued. The dog attempted to raise its head. As it did, it yipped before dropping its head back onto the pavement. Kate kneeled by the dog's head and offered her hand for it to smell before she touched him. Pain and fear hung like a cloud around the dog and Kate's heart went out to it.

She was surprised when the growling didn't change once she began to run her hand behind its ears. It didn't try to nip or bite, but lay there, the growl a constant grinding sound coming from deep within its chest. Just below the shoulder she felt blood. It was warm, wet, and already matting the dog's hair.

Kate muttered a curse under her breath. A gunshot wound, though she would need to get the dog on the table to be certain. She continued her examination, gently running her hand along the spine, ribs, and hips. She noticed that although the hair was damp with rain, it was rough to her touch. The dog had not been receiving proper nutrition. She moved back along the ribs once more and it whimpered. The ribs didn't feel broken but if the dog had been hit, the ribs would certainly be sore from the impact. She looked up and down the highway. The road was deserted.

"Yep, nobody out tonight but you and me, Rover. Figures."

She looked back toward her car—nothing. Thunder grumbled and the trees were dark, damp shadows all around her. The dog was enormous, easily weighing over 150 pounds. Kate wasn't sure how she was going to get it into her car and back to her clinic without getting bitten.

"Hope you had your rabies shot there, Rover."

She let her fingers caress the head once more before she left him to get a blanket from her vehicle. Careful to move the dog as little as possible, Kate worked the blanket under it to form a body sling. She pulled the car up as close as she could and, lifting first one end, then the other, got the dog into her SUV. Throughout the process, the dog continued to growl but didn't attempt to bite. She took that as a good sign.

Kate returned to the clinic and pulled next to the emergency door. She wheeled a gurney out to the car and using the blanket sling, managed to get the dog onto the gurney and into the surgery.

Under the harsh light the dog looked even

worse. In addition to obvious signs of near starvation and an apparent gunshot, it appeared he had been beaten. There were welts under the hair across the dog's back and shoulders. Hair was missing in patches. Older wounds were in various stages of healing. This was more than just neglect.

Her hands shook as she searched for more injuries. How could someone do this? She detested people who didn't care for their pets, but to deliberately inflict harm on an animal was unforgivable. Nothing deserved to be treated this way, then cast aside, much less shot at.

As a professional, Kate was trained not to assign human characteristics to animals. She and her father had many a discussion about the amount of feeling and understanding animals were capable of. Both believed there were things that went beyond science. This animal had suffered physically as well as emotionally.

As Kate looked in the dog's eyes something clicked in the back of her brain. For a victim of severe trauma, the pupils weren't dilated as much as she would have expected. *Odd.* She glanced at the forelegs and noticed the toes were long, almost like fingers. Closer inspection showed her that the dewclaw was placed differently. It was almost...*opposable? Impossible!* Her mind rejected the idea before it could fully form. *I'm tired and under a lot of stress. It's just a dog.*

Kate's mind refused to acknowledge the truth; instead she allowed the clinical part of her brain to take over. She had more important things to do than consider this some kind of supernatural anomaly. Her immediate concern was evaluating the dog's condition and his chances of recovery if she had to operate. The bullet had to come out, and she suspected at least one broken leg.

Her decision made, Kate prepared surgery, then

wheeled her charge in for x-rays. While she waited for the x-rays to develop, she gave the dog an IV containing a glucose solution and a sedative.

The x-rays confirmed her suspicions. The bullet was lodged in the shoulder and would need to come out, although it wasn't life threatening. The dog also had a broken hind leg that would have to be set. The x-rays showed one other interesting bit of information—a microchip.

When Kate noticed the chip she gazed down at the dog. "So somebody thought enough of you at one time to chip you, but recently decided to starve you, shoot you, and leave you for dead on the highway? I bet you have some story, Rover."

The dog's ears flicked and he looked her askance.

"Seriously, please tell me someone did not really name you Rover?"

Another look.

"Okay, Rover it is." She shook her head. "You are going to sleep for awhile."

Chapter Two

An hour later, Kate tilted her head back to stretch tired muscles in her neck, back and shoulders. She had retrieved the bullet that, after impact, was a twisted, flattened lump. She set the broken bone and stitched open wounds.

Kate looked at him lying on her surgery table. He was spectacular. Dark colored over his body and back with a silver mask and amazing blue eyes. Definitely some type of Husky or Malamute. Kate was certain there was also a high percentage of wolf as well. Again that small ping at the back of her brain as though she should be putting something together. Kate shook her head. She was tired. Whatever it was would have to wait.

Kate made him as comfortable as she could. She had given him enough medication he should sleep through until morning. She wanted him to rest quietly as long as possible in order to give his battered body a chance to heal. She put off checking the microchip. *Plenty of time to contact the owners tomorrow, if he makes it through the night.*

She was not pessimistic by nature, but it was up to him if he wanted to live or not. Kate sighed and let down her long brown hair. She needed to stay nearby and monitor his condition through the night. It looked like it was the couch in Dad's office for her. She smiled at the memory of all the nights he had done the same thing. Kate and her dad were definitely alike in the fact neither believed any one life was more valuable than another. Human or animal, it didn't matter. Life was life.

Kate wheeled Rover to an end run in her small kennel. She wanted to give him as much space as possible. It was always easier for an animal to recuperate in a safe, quiet environment. Kate doubted Rover had felt safe in a long time.

She let herself into the office, turned on the light and tried not to look at the things that reminded her of Dad. His jacket hung on the hat tree in the corner. One wall was filled with his old college textbooks and various other books and research materials that were part of his everyday life. His desk was littered with papers he never had enough time to get through. The scent of his cologne still hung faintly in the air. His old leather couch was scarred and worn from use, but comfortable. Kate settled on it and wrapped herself in the flannel throw. She'd allow herself a few hours to nap before it would be time to check on her patient.

Kate came awake to an anguished howl as her kennel exploded in frantic barks and howls. She stumbled as the throw wrapped around her legs when she tried to bolt for the kennel. Kate cursed as she grabbed furiously at the throw.

When she entered the kennel, pandemonium was in full swing. Dogs barked and paced their runs. Some howled while others frantically threw themselves on the panels that divided them. Kate attempted to soothe them. It was impossible to speak in a calm voice when she had to project so hard to be heard above the din.

"Hey, hey…settle down in here. C'mon guys, it's okay. What's up with everybody? You guys sound like a dog pound in here." Kate continued talking as she made her way down the aisle to Rover's kennel.

When she got there, she stopped dead.

"What the he…?" she breathed as she reached for the chain mesh to steady herself.

There on the kennel floor, was not the large

Husky that had been the victim of a hit and run. Instead, lying on the same kennel floor, with the same IV, in what would have been the same arm—or would that be paw—was a naked man. A very gorgeous, muscled naked man.

She stared. Her brain finally made the connection she hadn't earlier. A naked man slept…in her kennel…where she left a hit and run Husky a few hours ago. Or, what she *thought* was a Husky, she corrected. The IV was in the same place in this guy as it had been in the dog. She noted the stitched skin near the hip where she had set the bone. She knew if she looked at the shoulder, the stitched up bullet wound would be there as well.

Lycanthropes were not common in this area since Missouri outlawed them two years ago. For that matter, they were no longer common in the forty-eight continental states. Ever since the supernatural community *emerged* twenty years ago they had become the new minority. Instead of tolerance they were met with angry mobs and pitchforks, literally. Most states not only passed laws to make supes illegal, it was also against the law to house them, employ them, or provide medical care. A special task force known as Supe Authorities was created to register all supernaturals. The rumors about registration were grim. No one seemed to notice there were no registered supes living.

Kate and her dad knew the supes had been around as long as humans and they adapted quickly. Most migrated to the few northern states and Canada where such drastic measures had yet to be enacted. Her father hadn't mentioned the weres in years. Yet, now she had one in her kennel.

Rover, if she could still call a guy that, continued to sleep despite the noise. His brow creased in pain and his limbs twitched from time to time. She wondered if werewolves chased bunnies.

Her rational brain was screaming that this wasn't happening while her more basic mind was busy running her gaze over muscled shoulders, a wide chest, and the most incredibly sexy thigh she had ever seen on a man.

Snap out of it! How the hell was she going to explain this? She couldn't leave him here, but what exactly was she supposed to do now, call an ambulance? Turn him over to the Supe Authorities? No, that was out of the question. She didn't know why after all this time a were suddenly showed up in her kennel, but she would not turn him over to the Supe Authorities. She heard stories of what happened in the early years when some supes, attempting to assimilate, had readily volunteered for registration. To this day there were many families with no idea what happened to their loved ones.

Kate's mind was fast-forwarding to panic mode when she realized the pounding she heard wasn't her blood pressure. Someone was beating on her office door and it sounded like they were about to break it down.

She made sure the kennel door was closed and stalked to the front door about to fracture into a million pieces. Kate must have looked as annoyed as she felt because the man stopped beating on the door when he saw her walk through the reception area.

"Do you have an emergency?" she asked crossly.

Even annoyed, Kate was sensible enough to notice a couple of things. Whoever the door beater was, he didn't have a pet anywhere near him. No bloody cat, no howling dog, not even a weak parakeet.

Instead, he was accompanied by what could only be described as three goons. A trio of large men dressed all in black like a swat team, stood in front of a suspicious looking black van. Kate turned her attention back to door-beater. He was an older man, mid-fifties, with thinning gray hair tufting around his ears to give him an odd feral look. He had tiny pig-like eyes and no neck. He was broad through the chest and shoulders. In his younger days he may have been intimidating, now he looked like an old bridge troll. At her words, he took a step back and his eyes narrowed into slits. It didn't help the bridge troll look any.

Kate considered that perhaps English wasn't his first language. She asked him again, slower this time, careful to enunciate the important words, "Sir, do-you-have-an-emergency?"

His response was short and fired from his mouth like a machine gun. "No! Young lady, I do not have an emergency! I am here to pick up some documents your father left for me."

Kate raised a brow and looked pointedly at her watch. 5:30 a.m. "And you are?"

He looked insulted. "Hansen. Dr. Sig Hansen. I'm a colleague of your father's. We share similar, ah, interests, you could say. I believe he left some research work for me, so if you would be so kind as to let me in, I can retrieve my documents and be on my way."

Kate narrowed her eyes. She had no idea what this was about, and quite frankly didn't care. Her parents had been dead for less than a month, there was a werewolf lying on her kennel floor, and a bad version of Dr. Who was demanding secret documents? Enough!

"Look mister. I don't know who the hell you are, but I assure you my father didn't know you, nor did he leave anything for you. I don't know anything about any papers or documents and even if I did, they are mine now, not yours, so take your goons and get lost!"

Kate was shocked at how rude and angry she sounded. She didn't care. Very few people, if any, knew about her father's work with the were community, so what could this man possibly be after? Kate did not believe in coincidences. She suspected there was some connection between the man outside her door and the one sleeping in her kennel. Her eyes narrowed as she considered the man standing in front of her and what he might possibly have to do with the condition of the man in her kennel. A protective instinct she didn't know she possessed suddenly consumed her.

One of Hansen's goons ran over and said something in his ear. Hansen looked at the goon incredulously. "Are you quite sure?"

The goon nodded affirmatively.

"Well, well," Hansen narrowed his eyes and turned to Kate. "Dr. Barrister, it seems you have more than one thing that belongs to me. I believe you have a wolf somewhere in your facility. He belongs to me. I want him. Now."

Her suspicions were correct. "I told you once already, I have nothing for you. Any patient in my clinic is my responsibility and doesn't get released until I say so. There is nothing here for you and visiting hours aren't until 8 a.m. so I'm going to ask you to leave before I call the sheriff."

Hansen's piggy eyes narrowed. He considered a moment, and then a slow smile stretched across his face. It made him look even more sinister.

"All right Dr. Barrister, have it your way. I'll let you find out for yourself what you have locked up in your clinic. Here's my card, call me if you live long enough to make it to your phone."

He dropped his card through the mail slot and Kate noticed a familiar logo. Pro-Gen was a pharmaceutical company reportedly working on a *cure* for lycanthropy. The majority of the medical community seemed of the opinion that werewolf-ism was some type of disease requiring a cure.

Without a word, he turned and stalked back to the van. The goons slid the side door back and got in. As they did, Kate noticed the back of the van was a cage, complete with heavy bars and mesh separating the rear half of the van from regular seating at the front.

Kate's eyes grew large. She wasn't sure who this man was, but she knew about him, or at least his kind. For years her father worked with and treated the weres. He never advertised it, never solicited the business, but from time to time one would show up at his door, in either form. Her father would do what he could. Since the supernaturals had become the minorities of the twenty-first century, they were often refused service by the human medical community.

Kate didn't know how this man knew about her father's work, but it was clear she was at the center of something. Something that wasn't good for her or the naked were-man lying in her dog kennel. Kate wasn't sure what Mr. Bridge-troll Hansen wanted with her patient, but from the assorted cuts and bruises in different stages of healing on his body, she doubted it was civilized. She had to get her father's papers and this guy someplace safe until she could sort things out.

Her brow furrowed as she wondered how Hansen had known about her patient. Then, she really did slap herself on the forehead.

"Of course, bonehead!" she rolled her eyes. Then again, why would she have considered it before the events of the last few minutes?

She passed through her surgery, grabbed a scalpel and stitches from her supply, and ran to the kennel. Until she got some answers, Rover was under her care. He was her patient and would remain so until she was satisfied he was no longer in danger.

Chapter Three

The kennel was quieter than before though some of the dogs were still pacing their runs, hackles raised. Kate approached the end kennel slowly. The guy was still there. His brow was creased and he was moaning while reaching for the back of his neck. She looked closely. On some level, he was aware of the microchip. Usually people micro-chipped their pets for identification purposes—basic information like the animal's name, owner's name, contact info, etc. Since her encounter with Dr. Hansen, Kate knew her suspicions about this chip were true. It had been purposefully inserted as a tracking device. They didn't want this one to get away.

She spoke quietly and let herself into the kennel. She must be nuts. The only thing more dangerous than a werewolf was a wounded one. They tended to be aggressive by nature. Compound that with pain and fear, and they could be downright deadly. Kate was relying on the drugs and his condition to keep him quiet.

Removing a microchip was a quick procedure. Chips were usually placed at the base of the neck between the skin wall and muscle. Kate hoped Rover would sleep through the entire process. She knelt next to the man and held her hand in front of his nose, letting him breathe in her scent. She tentatively reached out a hand to gently rub it through the too long brown hair. His breathing remained even and he slept.

Kate worked quickly, injecting a local at the base of his neck where the chip had been placed. A small incision, less than half an inch, and the skin separated to reveal what looked like a small black circuit board about the size of a fingernail. Using a clamp, Kate fished the chip out, cleaned the wound, and closed it up with a couple of stitches.

She slipped the chip into her pocket before she covered the man with a blanket. The floor wasn't cold, but it was by no means warm either. She checked her watch. Her staff would start to arrive in another half hour. She had to make some decisions, and make them fast.

Kate looked down at the man sleeping on her kennel floor. She couldn't stop herself; she reached out and stroked his head. His hair was soft and curled slightly around a face that was chiseled, even in sleep. High, strong cheekbones were covered by a short beard. He probably hadn't shaved in weeks. Dark circles under his eyes confirmed he hadn't slept in some time. A long jagged scar twisted its way across his left ribs and several smaller scars dotted his back and torso.

His lips were thin and set in a firm, hard line. Even in sleep he was intimidating, and gorgeous. She couldn't stop staring. He was so good to look at. Wide shoulders tapered to powerful arms and hands that were large and strong. What it would be like to feel those hands roaming over her body? She shook her head. Now was *not* the time to get lustful over some guy who would in all probability turn out to be a crazed lunatic. She hoped he wouldn't kill her.

She rose and closed the kennel door. It felt odd to close the door on a person. Practical Kate won out. Better safe than sorry.

Now, how to get him away from her clinic and where she could take him? Rover posed too much of a threat to stay here, not to mention that by protecting him she was breaking the law. Kate was glad the only person she really had to worry about was Margaret, her bookkeeper. Margaret had been with her family for 15 years and was considered part of the family. When her parents were killed, it was Margaret who made sure the business stayed running and helped Kate make the arrangements. She would never put Margaret in harm's way.

Suddenly it came to her—her parent's cabin. She hadn't been there in over a year. She could get groceries on the way and nurse Rover back to health in complete seclusion.

The cabin sat on a lake, surrounded by forest and bordered over ten thousand acres of land controlled by the state forestry department. At least if Rover was a mad dog, no pun intended, if he didn't kill her, he might run into the forest instead of murdering innocent people.

Once the decision was made, she had to act fast. Margaret would be here soon. How was she to get a 180-pound unconscious man off her kennel floor and into her car? The gurney was waist high and didn't lower. What she needed was one of those devices she'd seen mechanics use when they fixed her car. Kate snapped her fingers. Dad left one of those in the storage area. He often brought Mom's car to the clinic to change oil and do minor repairs.

Kate nearly danced a jig when she found the creeper stowed in a dusty corner of the storage area. Pulling the cobwebs off, she ran back to the kennel and thought how insane she must be. She didn't even know this guy and she was whisking him off to the middle of nowhere to allow him to recover. *He might be some kind of mass murderer for crying out loud!* The logical part of her brain reasoned if he was running from the law, then law enforcement would have been after him, not some maniacal bridge troll who demanded documents and wolves.

She was nearly to the kennel door when an explosion of sound hit her. A guttural bellow rose above the din of barking canines. A crash echoed as something very large was thrown against the kennel panels.

Kate checked her watch. “Time’s up, kid.” Her patient was awake and angry.

Kate approached the far kennel door with caution. It probably wasn’t in her best interest to sneak up on him. She began talking as she reached for the door.

“Hey. Hi. I, uh, I don’t know if you can hear me in there, or if you are in any shape to understand me, but I’m coming in, okay? My name is Dr. Barrister and you have been injured. I’m trying to help. I’m going to take you someplace safe so we can get you healed up and on your way.” To herself she muttered, “God, I hope you can understand some of this…” She tensed as she pushed the door inward.

Her other patients barked and paced in their kennels once again. She couldn’t make out what was going on at Rover’s end of the room. Realizing she couldn’t see a guy standing up, much less letting himself out, she took a breath and walked into the aisle.

Softly, she said, “Hey, quiet down now. Nothing to see here, everybody just take a breath…” She carefully placed one foot in front of the other, ready to run in case her patient attempted to escape.

The dogs continued to sound the alarm and she gave up trying to calm them. She proceeded down the alley way, craning her neck to see what was going on in Rover’s kennel. The first thing Kate saw was the blanket, still on the kennel floor. She took a step further and stopped.

There, curled in a crouch as far back into the kennel as he could get, was her patient, once again in wolf form. The sight of him brought tears to her eyes. Injured and in pain, his body swayed back and forth, He was in protection mode: ears back, teeth bared, a low growl in his chest. His eyes were glazed from the medication and she knew he was trying desperately to focus. All mammals are equipped with two protection mechanisms to deal with stressful situations. It is called fight or flight. It enables them to know when to flee danger or use their teeth, claws or jaws to fight to protect themselves, their young, their territories or their mates. Kate knew that right now his muscles trembled because he was trying to obey his brain's message to run. The self preservation instinct was on high alert and battling panic.

She spoke quietly. Seeing her as a threat, he was likely to throw himself against the kennel door. "Easy boy, easy. I'm not going to hurt you, as long as you don't hurt me. I have to get you out of here and I'm going to need you to cooperate with me. I'm trying to help you but I doubt you get that right now. From the looks of things, you haven't been getting much help lately, but you have to trust me, I'm one of the good guys."

The wolf flattened his ears against his head and growled louder. He sensed only danger. Wolf didn't like this place, didn't like the smells or the sounds or the cold concrete beneath his feet. It smelled like the prison he had just come from with men and sticks and clubs. His heart raced and he wanted to be free. Alone. He wanted to lick his wounds and heal. Wolf's instinct was self preservation at all costs.

Logan came forward and held his wolf at bay. The woman's voice was soft, soothing and her smell was somehow familiar. She was doing her best to reassure the beast. Logan shook his head. Why was it full of cobwebs? He couldn't focus, he couldn't think! What the hell had she given him?

He remembered escaping and running. A bright light and pain. Intense, abrupt pain, worse even than the gunshot. He thought he was dead.

It was all Logan could do to keep the wolf from lunging, twisting the metal and wreaking havoc until he found a way out. He realized that if the wolf bolted, it would be directly at the woman in front of him. Logan gazed at the woman from the wolf's cold blue eyes. His stare was intense. *Did she say she was one of the good guys*?

The wolf fought. He wanted control. Logan breathed deeply and applied all of his focus to subduing his animal nature. In another moment, the drugs would take over. He had to keep her safe from his wolf's instincts until he could reason this out, she might be his only chance.

Kate watched the struggle going on behind the wolf's eyes. She could have sworn the animal was debating with itself whether to attack her or not. She didn't really understand the whole wolf/human transformation. She wasn't sure how much, if any, human remained when he was in wolf form. For that matter, she didn't know how much control the wolf mind had when he was in human form. What she did know was that even true wolves in the wild would care for their pack members. Females were known to nearly starve in order to feed their young. Kate realized she wasn't a pup and she wasn't pack, but she could show this wolf that she was a submissive who needed looking after. She decided to take a chance.

Kate lowered her eyes and then her body down to the floor. The wolf's growl raised a notch at her movement. She turned her back to the kennel gate keeping her head turned so she could see him out of the corner of her eye. She assumed the least threatening pose she could muster and did her best to make herself lower than the wolf. The growling stopped. Kate could hear curious snuffing as she assumed he was getting her scent.

Moments later she heard a soft thud as the wolf

dropped to the floor. Kate let out the breath she didn't realize she was holding. His size was intimidating but knowing what he was, and what he was capable of, was overwhelming. She turned slowly to gaze at Rover. She would have to sedate him again before getting him into the car. The last thing she needed was for him to wake up halfway there. Somehow she doubted she would stand much of a chance if nothing were between them.

Chapter Four

Kate retrieved a syringe of Acepromazine and entered the kennel after assuring herself that her patient was out again. She administered a double dose of the sedative and pulled the creeper into the kennel. It was difficult to shift his body weight, one part at a time, onto the creeper. Even more difficult to move him without causing pain. The last thing she needed would be for him to wake up from a pain response. Animals that woke up from pain stimuli tended to be cranky. She didn't need this one cranky, she needed him sleepy. She took her time and got him onto the creeper then wheeled him to her car.

The car was still parked in the emergency entrance. She took advantage of the extra dose of sedative and his near comatose state, carefully maneuvering him into the back of her SUV. She was putting in additional sedative, pain killers, and assorted supplies she might need when she heard car tires on gravel. She closed the rear hatch not a moment too soon as Margaret pulled into the parking area.

She had to think fast to come up with something plausible. Hating herself for using her parents' death to hide a lie, Kate fabricated her story. "Good morning," Kate called. She tried not to look too nervous.

Margaret smiled as she came toward her. "Good morning dear, how are you?"

Kate resisted the urge to look over her shoulder back at her waiting SUV. "Well..."

Margaret cocked a brow and looked at her

expectantly.

"You know how with everything that's happened, with Mom and Dad, and I, well, I..."

Margaret placed her hand on Kate's arm. "Are you going to take some time off?" she asked quietly.

Kate was surprised as her eyes filled with tears, "Yeah, I think it would be best." She sniffed.

Margaret reached up to give Kate a warm embrace. "I think that's a wonderful idea. Everyone will. Don't worry about the clinic, it'll be just fine, but you need some time to deal with this."

It was Margaret who guided Kate into the clinic, handed her a tissue and told her to get her things in order. Kate smiled and hugged the older woman. She hated lying to Margaret like this but she didn't think she would be able to live with herself if she allowed a rogue werewolf to harm the older woman.

"Thank you," she said. "Thank you for understanding."

"It's nothing." Margaret waved a hand at Kate. "Honey, you've been through a terrible ordeal. Nobody is going to begrudge you a little time off to get yourself together. Now get on with you."

Kate put her hand in her pocket as she headed for her dad's office. The chip was still there. She took it out and studied it.

"Margaret," she called from the office. "What time will Mr. Turnbull be here to pick up our deceased patients?"

There was a pause. "He was supposed to come yesterday but Norma Jean got sick so he said he would be here in the morning. I expect him in the next hour or so, why?"

"Oh, no reason," Kate said, a plan taking form in her mind. "I just wondered when he was coming by. I'll try to have things ready for him."

Margaret gave a satisfied "Mhmmm." And went to make coffee.

Kate thought a moment about who could potentially be impacted by her actions. Then she made a decision.

Kate performed a service for the county dog pound. When it came time to euthanize unadoptable animals or animals that were too ill, she did it at no charge. It was her least favorite part of her job but one that had to be done. The euthanized animals were stored in a cooler until Homer Turnbull came to collect them for the city dump where the bodies were buried. Kate recalled she euthanized a malnourished stray Husky last week. At least she assumed it was a husky, until now. The skin on her neck and arms crawled and her stomach lurched as she considered how many other euthanizations could have been supes in their animal form. She resisted the bile rising in her throat. She would have to re-think her community service contributions after this.

Kate pushed the thought aside. There was nothing she could do about it now. She stepped into the walk-in refrigerator and located the bag with the tag Husky/Stray/County on it. She quickly made a small incision in the cold flesh and deposited the chip. *Let them chase that for awhile.*

In her father's office she retrieved his notebooks and laptop. She looked around the office for anything else that might help her understand what she was in the middle of. She retrieved his files from the cabinet and was about to leave when she noticed a photo on her father's desk. It was her favorite. The photo had been taken when she was about eight and showed her and her family, with several other families, in the mountains of Northern Montana. On that trip she experienced her first kiss with a boy named Logan. He was all of twelve and she had been hopelessly in love. Although the boy wasn't in this particular photo, it always reminded her of him and the kiss. She put the photo in the computer bag and walked out.

Kate was surprised at how easy it was. She gave Margaret another quick hug, and went to her car. Rover was sleeping soundly in the back so she drove home where she threw some clothes in a bag, grabbed her toothbrush, and left.

On the way through town she stopped at the grocery store for additional supplies. As she was leaving she noticed Mr. Turnbull's truck coming from her office. She watched him go past and moments later a black panel van slipped off of a side street and pulled in behind him. Kate sent up a quick prayer for Mr. Turnbull's safety as she pulled onto the highway.

She barely registered the trip to the cabin. Her mind kept looping around to how nuts she must be for not handing the guy over to Dr. Hansen and how she would probably get herself killed. She wondered if wolf-boy would leave enough of her bloody carcass for someone to eventually find.

Chapter Five

She pulled into the cabin drive in the early afternoon. The weak golden light sifted through the trees to cast long shadows. The cabin stood as always, nestled in a small meadow, its back to the lake. The windows looked in need of a good cleaning but everything looked intact. She inserted her key into the lock and opened the door.

A year's worth of dust hung suspended in the air illuminated by the sunlight slanting through the windows. The cabin had a lonely, forlorn feel. Kate looked around cautiously for any signs of a break in, storm damage, or critter infestation. When she found nothing, she began opening windows to give it a chance to air out.

The cabin was luxurious by most vacation standards. Because her dad planned to retire here he built the cabin like a full size second home. It was two stories with a master suite and study on the second floor as well as a deck that looked out over the lake. Downstairs the cabin consisted of a great room, a kitchen, and a second bedroom and bath that belonged to Kate. Warm wood floors, a stone fireplace, and rustic pine cabinets in the kitchen gave the cabin a friendly glow. Her mom had decorated the walls with assorted flea market finds. The plaid curtains depicted lodge scenes of bears and trout. It was cozy and inviting. She thought she might cry as happy memories began to seep from the woodwork.

She paused when she realized the master suite now belonged to her. This begged another question.

Where was she going to keep her patient? She couldn't exactly give him the run of the house? How did one go about knowing if a werewolf was even housebroken for that matter? Kate groaned. She didn't want to put him in a cage, which was good since there wasn't one here anyway. All she could do was lock him in her old room and hope for the best.

She returned to her car and registered only mild shock to find he had changed back into a guy. She wasn't sure if this was normal or some kind of reaction to the drugs. Since he was still sleeping, she filed it away as something not to worry about right now. Glad she remembered to bring the creeper from the office, Kate began the task of moving a mountain.

"Okay, big boy. We're here, and we're going to be moving again so I need you to help me by staying asleep okay?" She lowered his torso gently to the ground. He groaned and mumbled but she didn't feel his muscles tighten in alarm so she continued.

"I know it hurts, fella, I really am trying to help. I just hope you tell your dark half that. For that matter I hope this half gets it as well. Okay, buddy? Seriously? I really am trying to help you, so please, please, please don't eat me, okay? Is it a deal?"

She continued talking as she worked his torso onto the low platform. Damn. He was all muscle. His skin was great with a light dusting of dark chest hair. She tried to keep her eyes from roving over his flat stomach. Oh hell, she quit bothering to even try. She drank in the sight of his flat belly and the trail of hair that led her eyes directly to his manhood. His muscled thighs looked like they were carved of stone and his hips were lean and long. Kate was tempted to run her hand along a hip and thigh, and maybe even give him a friendly squeeze to see if *that* area felt as warm and inviting as it looked. She shook her head. She must have really lost her mind.

His feet drug the ground as she took the loop of rope that served as a handle and hauled him to the cabin door. Once inside, it was an easier trip across the hardwood floor to the bedroom. She forgot to bring any clean bed linens, so the dusty ones would have to do. She thought about getting him onto the bed and gave the idea up immediately. He would have to do with a blanket on the floor.

She piled some pillows and a couple of heavy quilts on the floor and eased him onto the patchwork pallet. She covered him with a blanket and stopped to look at his face. Dark brown hair, just a bit too long, curled around his forehead. Dark brows and lashes that she already knew framed mesmerizing blue eyes. High cheekbones rose above a beard long enough to be soft without being unruly. Kate wasn't normally attracted to men with beards but there was something about this guy. He would probably look good bald, she thought wryly. Hell, she already knew he looked fabulous naked. Without thinking she reached down and stroked his cheek.

She never saw his hand move, only felt the vise-like grip as he captured her hand. At the same moment, his eyes flew open and he looked at her, his lips lifting into a snarl.

Kate gasped and attempted to draw back, to flee. The grip was too strong.

He looked her in the eye. "Who..." his voice ended in a croak.

Against her better judgment, Kate leaned forward slightly. "I'm sorry; I didn't mean to scare you. You've been injured. I'm trying to help. You're safe."

His gaze darted around the room.

"You're safe," she repeated. "This is my place."

His gaze shifted back to her. Already he appeared to be losing the battle with the drugs. "Not safe," he said, as his grip loosened. "Chip..."

"I know. I know about the chip. It's gone. I took it out. Just sleep, it's okay." Her tone softened as he succumbed to the sedative. She moved him to a more comfortable position, and sat there awhile, stroking his head and listening to him sleep.

She rubbed her wrist where he had held it. She'd have to remember not to give in to moments of weakness. She could get hurt, or even worse, killed. As much as she wanted to offer comfort and protect him, it wouldn't do either of them any good if he killed her.

Kate needed to acclimate him to her, or at least let him know she wasn't a threat. She couldn't have him being reactionary every time he woke. She knew nothing about making friends with lycanthropes or if it were even possible. She couldn't exactly stick out her hand and introduce herself so the human method was out. Should she try the canine method?

When she was a girl, her dad taught her to bond with canines by surrounding them with her scent. He told her to sleep with the pup and to let the pup sleep on her worn underwear. As a kid it grossed her out but as a vet she understood that a human's strongest scent glands are located around their sexual organs. It made sense if she wanted to teach something her scent, to let it sleep on her underpants.

Kate paused, grimacing. She absolutely was not going to put her worn underwear in this guy's pillowcase. But, scent glands were also located in the armpits, right? That she could handle. Kate stripped off her shirt and tucked it in the pillow under Rover's head. She didn't know if it would work. It was worth a try. She wanted him to associate her with safety and friendship, not pain or torture.

Chapter Six

Thunder rumbled. Outside the skies darkened as the storms rolled in. Kate closed the door to Rover's room and then went to the kitchen. She wanted comfort food. She went to the old stereo, found some music to put on, and went to the kitchen to make her favorite dish for cold, stormy nights. Her mom's minestrone had always been her favorite and as she began the soothing process of choosing and chopping vegetables her frazzled nerves began to take a break.

Kate was completely in the zone as she chopped, peeled and diced. There was a meditative aspect to working in the kitchen. Perhaps it was the comfort of being able to do something that didn't require thought. She could go about the tasks of making the soup and bread and let her weary mind take a rest. She often cooked when she was stressed.

She didn't hear the door open or the footsteps approach. All she knew was when she looked up, he stood before her, wrapped in a blanket. He didn't look happy.

They stared at one another for a full minute. Kate began to wonder if he could talk, if maybe he was more canine than human. She looked down and realized she gripped the paring knife in her hand. She looked back up at him, and slowly lowered the knife.

He continued to assess her with the most penetrating blue eyes she had ever seen on a man.

"Uh, hi. I'm Kate. Kate Barrister. I, uh, found you last night. You really shouldn't be up, ah, eww, this is awkward." She looked away.

His penetrating gaze made her tongue tied and more than a little concerned she had done a really dumb thing. He continued to stand silently in front of her. Kate was beginning to get nervous as well as embarrassed. A million thoughts rushed through her head, all some sort of variation on *he really is a killer and I should have let the bad guys have him.*

He cocked an eyebrow as though she had spoken out loud. Oh great, now he's a mind reader? "Uh, do you, I mean can you talk? Do you…?"

"Understand the words comin' outta my mouth? Yeah, I saw that one." His face was impassive, his tone sarcastic.

"Okay, well, you can talk. That will certainly make things easier. I'm Kate Barrister."

"You've said that once already. I got it. We'll get to the formalities in a minute. What I want to know right now is, do I have any pants?"

Kate paused as she wondered if her naughty subconscious had done this on purpose, and then gave a nervous laugh. "Sorry. I didn't think. I've got some clothes I can give you. Some of Dad's old stuff is here. I guess I left a little fast and you, uh, weren't really in a shape for pants, literally, well, I mean at one point you were, but then..."

She was running at the mouth so she snapped it closed. She mumbled something to him about being back in a minute and went upstairs. She found a denim shirt and jeans in her dad's closet. She wasn't sure they would fit. Her dad had not been a small man but this guy redefined large.

"I'm not sure these will fit but it's something." As she came down the stairs she saw him standing at the stove, stirring her soup. He turned to face her, his expression blank, like he stirred soup everyday.

"Soup was getting hot. I turned it down." A conversationalist he was not.

“Thanks.” She breathed, staring at him again. There was something incredibly sexy about a man in a kitchen, even one wrapped in an old patchwork quilt. It hung over one shoulder. One very nice, well rounded, muscled shoulder. He turned to set the spoon on the stove and afforded her a delicious view of an equally muscled neck and back. The blanket hung dangerously low over one hip. Made her hungry, and not for soup. Where was her head?

When she made no move to hand him the clothes he reached for them. “Thanks, I’ll be out in a second.”

Kate felt like a fourteen-year-old girl. Speechless. Confused. Nervous as hell. She watched him all the way to the bedroom. She sneaked another peek at that backside. He walked like a predator. Not fast, not slow, but deliberate. A fluid grace that was elegant and dangerous. He was tall, probably six two or six three. It was the span of his chest and shoulders, the narrowness of his hips, and the length of his legs that made the whole package larger than life. This was a guy who couldn’t walk into a room without all heads turning. Kate licked her lips.

She returned to the dinner preparations. Her soup was bubbling and she had bread in the oven. She busied herself with what clean-up she could do and set out bowls, spoons, and plates. This time she heard the door click as he returned to the kitchen. He took a seat on one of the bar stools and leaned forward on the bar, clasping his hands. His expression had not changed. His eyes followed her but he said nothing. Kate gave him a nervous half-smile and returned to what she was doing. Damned if she was going to speak first this time. Let him start the conversation.

Kate busied herself with the soup, stirring, adding a pinch of salt, stirring some more, checking the bread, stirring again.

"You're going to ruin that soup if you keep stirring it like that."

His voice caused her to jump so violently she dropped the spoon. Soup splattered all over the range and floor. "Crap," she muttered, grabbing a towel. She bent down to wipe the soup off the floor.

The wolf watched as she lowered herself onto hands and knees, presenting him a tantalizing view of her backside. His groin tightened as he enjoyed the view. She had a great ass. Round. Firm. He had a flash of his hands grabbing that ass firmly as he sank himself deep into her. In his fantasy he could hear her moan of ecstasy as he filled her.

She stopped what she was doing. Without turning or looking up, she asked, "Are you enjoying the view?"

This time he did smile. He was caught and there was no sense denying it. "Yeah, actually, I am."

"So, you are capable of smiling. Good to know. I was beginning to think you had no emotion."

As quickly as the smile came, it left. He leveled his gaze at her. "Not a lot to smile about where I just came from, cupcake."

"Cupcake?" she arched a brow at him, "My name is Kate." She turned back to the stove. Her hand trembled. This was not going well.

"You should be, you know. Afraid."

"So you're a mind reader too?"

He paused, how to answer that one? "Not so much a mind reader. Your face is a dead giveaway. You'll never make it at poker." *Maybe not all the truth, but enough for now.*

"Well hell, now my whole life's ambitions have gone down the drain" she replied caustically. "Any other sage advice for me, mister?"

No response. He stared.

Kate had enough. "Let's get something straight

here, Rover. Last night I pick up a beat-up wounded dog from the side of the road. I take him…"

"I am not a dog," he ground out.

Kate ignored him and continued. "Back to my surgery where I do the best I can to fix what was broken. A few hours later, my whole kennel goes to hell because suddenly I have a guy sleeping where there was a dog before. I've got a deranged bridge troll demanding documents and threatening to beat my door down. Then, he figures out you are in my clinic and demands I turn you over to him like you were a rug."

He looked up with a startled expression. "What did they look like?"

"Oh, I'm not done yet!" she said as she advanced toward him, spoon held like a weapon. "So, I keep my little secrets, one of which happens to be you, run off the bad guys, take a chip out of your head, take you some place relatively safe and now you have the nerve not to even tell me your name. For crying out loud stop smiling at me like I'm a piece of meat!"

His smile stopped. "Did you just call me Rover?"

Kate paused, did she? *Crap.*

"Maybe I did. But you know what? Oh…never mind. I could care less. But just a heads up buddy, I think those bad guys wanted you pretty badly, and considering they looked like they were loaded for bear, I would suggest you find some buddies or some herd, or pack, or whatever it is you have to help you. You didn't seem to do so great the first time!" Kate's frustration level was turning up a notch.

"Rover." He crossed his arms and the look he gave her made her nearly pee her pants.

Kate dropped her eyes, embarrassed. "Yes, Rover. I didn't mean it as a slight. I just…I had to call you something. With dogs, I don't know, I give them a name. You said your name was Rover." She finished lamely.

He looked at her intently. “I am not a dog. And how could I possibly have told you *that*?”

“Well you were when I found you,” Kate snapped back. “And pardon me for not looking closer and making a better ID the first time. I was a little busy trying to save your life.”

Thinking, she answered his other question. “Your ears flicked okay? Every time I called you Rover your ears twitched. I was just making conversation.” Kate realized she was talking herself deeper into a hole.

He rolled his eyes. “Great. So because I respond with ear flicking, you decide to assign me a generic dog label? Why not Spot or Fido?”

Kate refused to meet his eyes. She turned her head as tears welled in her eyes. Great. Now he was making her so mad she was going to cry. So much for the strong veterinarian swooping in to save the day.

Softly this time, he said, “For the record, my name is Logan. Logan Turner. Thank you for what you did, and what you have done. And don’t call me Rover.”

Kate looked up at him trying to place the familiar name. She gave up as the dam burst and tears spilled onto her cheeks.

“Logan,” she whispered. “No one should have done what was done to you. I don’t care who you are, or what you did.” She reached for the towel before the sniffles she knew were coming could make her embarrassment complete.

“You’ll have to excuse me. I’ve had a bad time lately. My folks died in a car crash a month ago, and I’m dealing with that. Then I find you on the road, then this guy is demanding…stuff, and I probably shouldn’t be telling you any of this, but somehow I guess I thought you were part of it or something, that it was maybe all connected and, and oh, I don’t know, now it just all sounds crazy.” She blew her nose.

Quietly from behind her, he said, “You aren’t crazy, Kate. And some of it, hell, I don’t know, maybe all of it, is connected.”

Kate turned to face him. She noticed shadows under his eyes, and how his cheeks were hollow. He looked tired and beat.

“I’m sorry,” she sniffed. “You look terrible. Why don’t you eat something and then we can talk?”

Logan nodded and she turned back to the stove to ladle the soup into bowls and place the bread on plates. He watched her wordlessly. He wasn’t sure how to respond, or react around her. When she said his name just now his chest tightened and his gut did some kind of flip-flop. What he really wanted to do was take her in his arms and hold her, make her pain go away. He’d never reacted to a woman that way. Maybe it was some kind of reaction to the medications she had given him? He had things to tell her, but he wasn’t sure if that would make it better or worse.

Little Katie Barrister had grown up into a strong, capable woman. She was beautiful, smart, and braver than most. He couldn’t imagine what it must have taken for her to stand up to Hansen. And, damned if she wasn’t amazing when she was mad, all snapping eyes and swirling dark hair. He wanted to bury his hands in that hair, breathe in her scent. Strip her bare. He stopped his thoughts before they could go any further. He was acting like he was attracted to her or something. What the hell was this?

Logan had little experience with women, human or supe. He tended to avoid them if possible. They seemed like a lot of trouble. He had certainly never felt protective of one, but damned if he didn’t feel protective of this one. And even worse, as he considered this new sensation coursing through his veins, he realized he wanted to please her. He wanted to see her smile, at him. Logan snuck a glance at Kate as he tried to get a handle on his confusion. He wasn't sure how to respond to her, so he took his bowl and ate.

Silence hung between them. Logan ate like a man who hadn't seen food in a month. For all Kate knew, he may not have. She waited for him to finish and when he did, she asked, "Are you still hungry? There are plenty of groceries, I can make something else."

"No, thank you. It was good. I haven't eaten like that since…well, in quite a long time. You're quite a cook, for a vet." He smiled.

Kate couldn't help it, she smiled back. "I figured you wouldn't be too impressed if I tried to feed you kibble."

He tipped his head back and laughed.

Thank God he wasn't offended. Kate pushed her plate away and sat with her hands in front of her. "I'm not sure what happens next. I think some rather bad characters are after you, and while I think you're relatively safe here, I don't know how long."

He stopped her with a hand. "I'm sorry to get you into this. I never meant for it to happen this way."

She looked at him, "What do you mean?"

Logan sighed. "You know what I am. What you don't know, is that I was on my way to find you." At her look of surprise he went on. "What do you know about your father's work?"

Kate was taken off guard. She answered carefully. "I know he was a vet, I know he cared for weres. It was kind of his pet subject, pardon the pun." She looked at him from lowered eyes.

He motioned for her to continue.

"I don't know anything specific about what he

did or what he studied. I was away at school for the last few years. I know he helped the weres, treated them, that kind of thing. I guess I thought recent events had separated him from the were community." She looked at Logan, halfway expecting an affirmative answer.

"Somewhat, but not exactly," he began. "We, as in my father's pack, feared for your dad's safety. Humans who helped us were becoming targets just as we were. Your dad and my dad were friends. You don't remember me do you?" he asked.

Kate looked startled. "Why would I…Oh, my god!" Realization flooded her. The photo on her father's desk! Her first kiss. A boy named Logan!

"You're *that* Logan?" she asked incredulously.

He smiled.

"But that means that, that…" Kate was now very confused. "What exactly was that? Dad just said it was a seminar."

"Sort of," he answered. "More like a rendezvous. It was a meeting my father organized as the alpha of the Northern Territories. Think of it as a professional gathering. Your dad was there to share info with other people like him. Some packs were fortunate enough to have MD's. Some had veterinarians. Some had nothing. It was a way to share information in a relatively safe environment. Our fathers have maintained communication over the years."

Kate's head was spinning. "Wait. I still don't get what any of that has to do with why we are here." She motioned to the two of them.

"Your dad's specialty was genetic research, right?"

Kate replied with a long, "Yeeesss…" Still not comprehending.

"Kate, you know there are certain groups who would like nothing better than to see supes of all kinds eradicated from the planet, right?"

Kate nodded. She did know about such groups. Foremost among them was Eden's Children, a quasi-religious group based in the Midwest and led by a fire and brimstone purist named Malcolm Pearson. He and his followers lobbied the government heavily, and often successfully, for laws to eradicate werewolves.

They had been the driving force in most states under the banner *Human Rights are only for humans*! Kate viewed them as extremists. Eden's Children did such an effective job of spreading their malicious propaganda that it resulted in some ridiculous laws that de-humanized the supernatural community in every possible way.

Logan continued. "My family believes there is a connection between Eden's Children and a company called Pro-Gen."

Kate stopped him. "You mean the company that is working on a cure for things such as vampirism, lycanthropy and the like?"

Logan looked at her levelly. "They aren't developing a cure, Kate. They're developing an epidemic."

Kate gaped. "Are you talking about biological warfare? That's insane!"

Logan's gaze bore into hers. "More like a genetic epidemic. I think it's insane, but then I'm one of the bad guys."

"You are not a bad guy, Logan," she said quietly.

Silence hung between them. Kate's brain was working overtime. Maybe he was crazy? Secret labs? Conspiracies? "Do you have any idea how all of this sounds?" she finally asked.

"Yes." He didn't elaborate, and given previous conversation, she didn't expect him to. Logan wasn't there to convince her. He would let her make up her own mind.

"Okay, enough. I can't handle anything else. I don't know about any of this." She looked at Logan. "I'm not trying to call you a liar, but this all seems so far-fetched. I have Dad's notes and his laptop. I'll go through them tonight and..."

"See if my story checks out?" he finished wryly.

Kate was embarrassed. "I'm not questioning your honesty. I have to make sense of all this."

"Fair enough. Why don't we call it a night and we can take another look in the morning?"

Kate smiled gratefully. "Thank you."

As he stood up to leave, he winced slightly, but Kate saw it. "I ought to look at that," she said and moved toward him.

Instinctively he stepped away from her, "It's fine. Really. You did a nice job. We heal faster than most."

There was a moment of uncomfortable silence that Logan broke. "You sit, I'll do these." He indicated the remaining dishes.

Kate smiled. Wow. He was housebroken and did chores. Maybe she should get one of these. She took her seat at the counter. Her curiosity was getting the better of her. Shyly, she asked, "So, is it true, that you have magical abilities?"

He looked at her like she had grown a second head. "What have you been reading for crying out loud? Tabloids?"

"Sorry, I'm just curious."

Logan sighed "Some weres have certain—abilities. It's stronger in those of us who are born as opposed to the ones who are made. I wouldn't call it magic. Some have limited telepathy, some send, some receive, a few of us do both. Some have what the old timers called glamour which is more about charm than magic." He shrugged. "And, some do other things."

It was obvious he had no intention of explaining

what those *other things* might be.

Kate tried a different route. "So, what do you like to eat?"

"Organic. Mostly."

Kate had to stifle a laugh as she imagined wolf-boy here shopping at the local organic produce market, handling the melons, poking the peaches, a basket full of leafy greens over his arm.

"Now what?" he asked, his back to her as he put the dishes away.

"Nothing," she giggled.

He turned to face her, leaning against the sink, his long muscular legs crossed. He casually wiped the plate in his hand, staring at her. "Mmm-hmm?"

Kate couldn't help it, she burst out laughing. "I'm sorry. It's the organic part that got me. I was trying to picture you at the supermarket, loading up on veggies and, and…" she left off as another peal of laughter nearly doubled her over.

His mouth quirked slightly. "I said organic, cupcake, not vegetarian. They are two completely separate things."

Her mouth formed a small *oh* of shocked surprise as the realization of what he meant hit. His stoic façade nearly cracked before he turned to the sink.

Kate fled the room.

Chapter Seven

He finished the dishes and turned out the light. The hairs on the back of his neck rose. He tensed, senses on full alert. He backed away from the window, knowing he wouldn't be able to see anything and was a perfect target in the light. He crossed silently to the back door and stepped out into the rain, barefoot.

He lifted his head, tasting the night. Scent was impossible to pick up with all this rain. He crept forward, testing the air. His nervous system crackled and his wolf stirred, wanting to be set free. The wolf knew he was better if a predator was near. Logan took a breath and continued to prowl the perimeter of the cabin. Something was out here but what—he couldn't quite tell. It wasn't Hansen or his men. They weren't clever enough to stay hidden, plus they smelled bad. Logan would have honed in on them like a beacon. No, this was a presence, one to be aware of but not a threat. At least not yet. Whatever it was, it was gone now. Logan circled the cabin once more, then went back inside.

He slipped through the door to find Kate was standing in the living area, worry pinching furrows in her brow.

"Is everything okay?" she asked.

"Fine," he smiled to reassure her. She didn't look assured, and he felt his chest tighten at the thought of her being afraid, lonely, or hurt. He didn't want any of those things for her.

"I'd really like to look at those wounds if I could. Just to be sure."

Against his natural instincts, Logan relented. He knew he was healing, but if it made her feel better, he would tolerate it. Wolf perked up as Kate came near.

He stepped into the living room and removed his shirt. Kate was glad his back was to her so he couldn't see her expression as she drank in the sight of him. Wide shoulders tapering to a narrow waist, the muscles across his back begged to be touched. His hair curled slightly at the nape of his neck and she had to force herself to not let her fingers sink into those rich dark curls.

She reached toward the small incision where she had removed the micro-chip. Two stitches but the wound looked as though the stitches were ready to come out instead of having been put in less than twenty-four hours before. She lightly ran her finger alongside the cut. She swore she felt electrical current as her finger grazed the smooth skin. Her mind drifted as she thought about what it would be like for her hands to have free range over the plains of his body.

"Is this normal?" she asked. "It looks like it's nearly healed."

"It is," he replied. "I told you, we heal faster than humans."

She let her finger stay in contact with his skin as she trailed it down his shoulder to where she had removed the bullet. The Telfa pad was still taped over the wound. She removed it carefully. This time, she let out a surprised gasp. The skin was knitting itself back together and a rough scab replaced the hole she had stitched up. It would probably leave a scar, but the degree of healing was far beyond what it would have been for a human.

"Incredible," she murmured.

Logan was trying not to concentrate on the feel of her hand trailing across his back. He shrugged at her comment. "Told ya."

"So the leg?" she questioned.

He turned to face her. She took a step back and nearly tripped. Without thinking, he reached out and pulled her in close against his chest.

"Broken bones heal a little slower. It's sore, but in a few days I won't have that," he breathed, as he felt her in his arms and his wolf stirred with a hunger that had nothing to do with food.

He lowered his head and took her lips into his, tender only for a moment as the wolf stirred. When she didn't protest and instead gave a small moan as her arms snaked around his neck, Logan gave the wolf more rein and kissed her harder.

Kate gave herself up to the kiss. *Oh my god I'm losing my mind and I don't care.* He was all heat, flame, hard muscle and smooth flesh. He was firm lips claiming her mouth while his tongue found its way between her lips to dance with hers. Kate twined her fingers in the curls at his neck as his hands sought out her hair. She arched her back as he slid his hands down her back to cup her buttocks and pull her hips closer to his throbbing erection. Kate couldn't help herself, she pushed even tighter against him, pressing her breasts into his chest, feeling the length of his erection through her jeans.

He growled low in his throat and pulled back from her. He looked at her with uncertain eyes. "I can stop if you want me to, but it will have to be now."

Kate made up her mind then. "Don't stop."

He lowered her gently to the floor in front of the fire. Kate was touched when he reached to the sofa to get a blanket and laid it down for them. Before she even saw him move he had arranged the blanket and his mouth was back over her hers, exploring, seeking, tempting. Kate reveled in the feel of him.

Logan's hands were on fire as they pushed her

shirt up, his hands roaming her belly, her ribs and up to cup her breast firmly. She moaned and tried to press herself deeper into his hand. He trailed kisses down her neck, behind her ear, across her collar bone. His fingers worked her bra aside to tease the nipple. He rolled it gently, then harder as the bud rose to him. When he lowered his mouth to the nipple Kate gasped. He teased it with his teeth, with his tongue. She only wanted more.

Kate moaned and reached for his jeans. She unbuttoned and unzipped them, freeing his erection and giving herself a mental high-five that she hadn't provided him with underwear. She smiled as her hand reached down to stroke his erection while he peeled the remainder of her clothes from her body. He was hot and hard, his erection throbbing, straining against her hand.

He cupped her breasts in his hands, bringing them together so he could suckle both of her nipples at the same time. Kate gasped with pleasure. His hands slid down her side ribs to her hips, his mouth trailing hot fiery kisses down her stomach. Her hands reached down to twine in his hair and he looked up at her in the soft firelight, poised over her belly. The look on his face was feral, and it was obvious the wolf was close to the surface. It gazed at her with a passion that made her body flood itself in anticipation. He lowered his head to take her into his mouth and she arched to meet him.

God, she didn't know it could be like this.

She writhed and moaned, her movements, her sounds driving him to madness with wanting her. Her scent was here, at her center, her core, and he knew she wanted him every bit as much as he wanted her. It surrounded him, filled him with her essence. His wolf howled triumphantly, at long last his mate was found, and she was his.

Logan paused as the realization hit him full

force, Kate looked at him, her eyes wide and trusting. It took only a moment for him to make his decision. He would deal with that later. Right now he wanted her, wanted this moment. He shoved the realization to the back of his mind and lowered his mouth to claim what was his.

He lifted his hips and poised himself at her center. She ran her hands up his arms, encouraging, welcoming him to her body. Her fingers traced delicate patterns across his chest and shoulders as she lifted her hips to him, demanding he take what she was offering.

Her eyes were glazed with passion, her lips swollen from his kisses. Logan lowered his hips and sank into her, slowly at first. He gasped at her tightness, the slick feel of her against him. With a deep moan, he withdrew and plunged into her to his full length. She arched, wrapping her legs about his waist, urging him forward again. The feel of her legs around him, the feel of her taking him in, urging him to go faster, harder only made his body respond to her that much more. Logan stroked her in the most intimate of ways, long and slow, picking up tempo as he couldn't stand it any longer. He buried his face in her neck and her hair as he brought them both to a climax.

As Logan came with her, his wolf let out a victorious howl. He could hear it in his head, the wolf was pleased. Logan had been with other women, kissed them, made love to them and his wolf had never responded this way. Logan knew what just happened, he just wasn't sure how to explain it to Kate, or if this was even the right time.

The exertion took its toll on his body and he tried not to collapse on top of her. He lowered himself down beside of her. Burying his face in the hollow of shoulder, he inhaled deeply, letting the silk of her hair surround him. He stayed there, breathing heavily, his eyes closed.

He felt her reach up to stroke his head.

"Am I too heavy?" he started to move but she stopped him.

"No, stay, please."

He lifted his head to look at her. His eyes were smoky with passion and Kate was more than a little aware of his naked body next to hers. Firelight flickered along his skin, bathing him in soft light. *God he was beautiful.*

He tilted her chin to look at him. "Are you sorry?"

She was surprised by his question. "No. Absolutely not. It's just, is it, I mean?"

"What?" he asked.

She took in a breath and let the words ride out on the exhale before she could be too embarrassed to say them. "Is it always like that? Because I have never…it's never…oh crap, it's never been this good!"

He rolled onto his back and laughed. He was even more incredible when he smiled, especially when he was naked.

"I don't know, to be honest with you. You're the first human I've ever done it, well, not done it but, I mean shared...uh…ah hell, now you've got me doing it," he laughed.

Kate propped herself up on an elbow. "You've never done it with a girl?" she teased.

He looked exasperated. "Of course I've done it with girls. I've just never done it with a *human* girl. Only other weres. We tend to keep to ourselves for obvious reasons." He leered menacingly at her.

Kate laughed. "Oh, great, so now here comes my crash course in werewolf mating habits." She mimicked a documentary narrator. "Once copulation is complete, Rover will proceed to eat the human female..."

"Rover! You did not just call me Rover!" he exploded into mock anger, as he moved, eerily fast, to pin her arms and pull her to him once again, "I'll show you eat." He raised his eyebrows suggestively.

Kate laughed and collapsed back to the floor. She didn't know why she felt so comfortable with this man and she certainly never laughed in bed with one. With Logan it all seemed so natural, so right.

Long after Kate drifted off to sleep, Logan continued to hold her, listening to her breathe. He had never felt an attraction so strong and he certainly never lost control like this before. Kate filled a place in him he never knew he had, much less was empty. Logan hated the thought of dragging Kate into all of this. At the same time, he didn't think he could let her go either. She would still have to choose of course, and as the female, whatever choice she made was law. Kate would have to accept Logan as her mate, despite the fact he was an alpha. He wished he had more time to court her properly.

Even more worrisome was the matter of Sig Hansen, Pro-Gen, and Eden's Children. It was a terrible time to bring a human mate into pack society and politics. She deserved safety and stability, not a life of living on the edge, of being hunted. He drifted off to sleep, knowing he could never be safe or stable.

Chapter Eight

Kate awoke the next morning with Logan sleeping peacefully beside her. Morning sunshine filtered across his sleeping features. He looked so peaceful. She lay there, drinking him in. When he shifted and tossed an arm over her hip, his face softened in a brief smile as his hand squeezed her once. She smiled. He was beautiful.

Michelangelo's David had nothing on this man. He was perfection personified, even in sleep. Clinical Kate noticed his color seemed brighter, healthier this morning and she suppressed a giggle as she wondered if that was what was meant by the afterglow. Kate stirred and Logan's eyes came immediately open, his arm snaking around her protectively.

"Shhhh, it's okay," she said, touching his face lightly. "I'm just going to get up, maybe make some breakfast, look over some notes, okay? Just sleep."

His eyes cleared and focused on her. He smiled briefly, gave her a wink, kissed her nose, and fell immediately back to sleep. As Kate stood and glanced out the window, she could have sworn she saw branches move across the meadow. Fear flooded her but she pushed it away. This area was full of wild life and the cabin had been deserted for a year. It was probably just a deer.

She went upstairs to brush her teeth and shower, then made her way quietly back downstairs to begin going over her father's notes. She had no idea where to start so she began by looking at the most recent entries.

Kate was thankful it only took an hour to familiarize herself with Dad's material. He was obsessed with the genetic makeup of weres and the fact some weres could be born while others were made. Of the made weres, he was fascinated with why some humans survived the transformation and some didn't. His most recent theories centered on the idea that a specific protein chain in the DNA sequence determined whether humans survived the change or not.

As Kate reviewed her father's notes and emails, she came across an interesting email from a name she recognized, or at least a last name she recognized. Lawton Turner emailed her father two months before he died. The note told her dad that three more citizens—which Kate read to be weres—passed away recently from an untreatable condition. The email stated each citizen was from out of town and had not visited any relatives recently. Kate felt certain the email was a code telling her father the people who died were made weres and none of them had been away from the pack recently. She made a mental note to ask Logan to confirm and went to the kitchen to make breakfast.

Kate did her best to be quiet and allow Logan time to sleep, but making food in silence was impossible, especially for her. She was at the stove, pushing eggs with a spatula when she felt warm arms encircle her waist and a long, hard body press against her backside.

Kate sank against him as though it were the most natural thing in the world to do. "Good morning." She smiled.

"Mmm hmm," he said, nuzzling her neck.

His hand began to work its way toward her breast, and though Kate knew it was stupid after last night, she turned.

"Uh-uh buster. Not now. You have time for a

shower before you to eat. Then we'll decide what we're going to do later," she said with a wicked gleam in her eye.

Logan grinned and wordlessly prowled to the bathroom. When he returned, Kate noticed he had found a razor and shaved. She gaped. He was glorious with precise high cheekbones, square jaw, and strong chin. He was shirtless and his hair was still damp from the shower. Kate nearly turned the stove off and attacked him. She congratulated herself for having enough forethought to think of turning off the stove.

As they ate, Kate shared with him what she found in her father's work and email. Logan tipped the chair back with his hands behind his head. She could see the worry on his face. He was concerned, not just for himself, but for his people. People he knew personally and was close to.

"So my dad emailed Dr. Barrister information. Is there anything that tells you why some of us are dying and others aren't?"

"Dad thought it had something to do with genetics. He understood there are considerable genetic differences between a were that is born and one that is made. From what I can get, he thinks a specific protein sequence that links together the DNA molecules is responsible for a successful transformation. What Pro-Gen is doing might be trying to reverse the wolf aspect or it could be intended to kill. Dad was frustrated because there was no data to help him out. Apparently the packs are hesitant to give up information like this. He had no way to determine the method of exposure. He questioned if there was some type of geographic link, or if there was a common source they were being exposed to. I think that's why your dad noted that the victims had not been out of the area."

Logan looked thoughtful. "It all sounds

plausible, what you've gotten so far. Anything that might be telling you how to reverse it, or how to cure it?"

Kate shook her head. "The big question is what exactly is the proper sequence? If Pro-Gen is exposing weres to something that is trying to reverse the DNA structure back to human, it stands to reason that there is also something to restore the original programming, so to speak. The other problems are method of exposure, method of administration, and most importantly, what kind of timeframe do we have to work within? That's why data from the other affected packs would have been helpful. If we could establish how the others are being infected, we could possibly counteract it."

Logan looked at her skeptically. "You're not exactly filling me with hope here, doc."

Kate looked apologetic. "I'm sorry, but those are the clinical facts. Normally something like this takes years of research."

Logan's chair slammed down onto the floor. "We don't have years! My people are dying! All because some crackpots think we don't have a right to exist! Do you have any idea what these people are up to? I just spent four weeks locked in a cage while they plied me with God-only-knows-what!"

"What do you mean, Logan?" she asked quietly.

He took a breath. "The night you found me on the road, I just escaped from a Pro-Gen lab. I was taken Kate. They took me because they knew who and what I am, and they tried to kill me."

Kate considered what he was saying. She managed to keep her voice steady. "Are you infected?"

"I don't know."

She wanted to touch him, to comfort him, but she knew if she reached for him right now, he would pull away. Instead she asked, "What do you know about Pro-Gen?"

"I know that it's a front for the Eden's Children Group.

"Do they really have that kind of influence? And power? And money?"

"Lots of money in religion, cupcake. Especially when there's a cause."

Kate considered Logan's words. He was right. There wasn't a lot of compassion for weres.

"For a civilized society we certainly carry our share of torches and pitchforks, don't we?" she asked.

Logan answered her honestly. "You have no idea."

"So how does the guy who showed up at my door fit into all of this? This Hansen guy? What do you know about him?"

"Hansen runs the lab I escaped from."

"So that's why he wanted you. You escaped. How quickly are the other wolves dying once they've been infected?"

Logan looked at her questioningly. "As far as we know within a few days, why?"

"Because," Kate answered. "Depending on what they gave you, you could be the first one that lived."

Logan shook his head. "So how do we find out?"

Kate dropped her head to her hands as the enormity of the situation descended on her. "Well, all I need is a blood sample from you and a research grade lab complete with genetic processing equipment. You know, no big deal, just like they have at major colleges and pharmaceutical companies."

Logan smiled. "I may be able to help you with that, cupcake."

Chapter Nine

Thunder rumbled as rain continued to fall. Kate and Logan spent the day pouring over her father's research material. Their plan was to head for Logan's pack territory in northern Montana first thing in the morning. Logan explained how when werewolves began dying, his father built a small lab in the basement of their home. It wasn't university quality, but it held enough equipment Kate could get started.

For now, she was snuggled into the safety of Logan's embrace, enjoying the moment. She turned her cheek to his chest and listened to the beat of his heart. She inhaled his scent, earth and musk and male. She thought she could live a thousand years and never get enough of breathing him in. She didn't know why she felt so safe, so secure with him. She was secretly looking forward to going to his family home. If nothing else it was more time to be near him.

A crash sounded from the direction of the porch and Logan's body stiffened, his hand tightening protectively around her waist. She watched as his nostrils flared and his eyes changed, the wolf coming to the surface, on the alert.

She tried to reassure him. "It's okay. It was probably just a branch or something."

Logan turned his gaze on her. "Someone's out there." He stood and put himself between her and the door.

A voice called from the other side, over the falling rain. "Logan. It's Lucas. Open the door."

Logan stepped forward and opened the door. The man outside was soaked to the bone. His hair was plastered to his head and water ran down his face. He stood in the doorway, shivering slightly. His dark eyes were rimmed by large circles and he was pale. Though his shoulders were wide and he was nearly as tall as Logan, it was the slight, defeated stoop that made him appear older and smaller. There was intensity about him as he averted his eyes from Logan and assumed a submissive posture. He stood shivering as water pooled around his feet.

The two men stood on the threshold, grim faced. Logan didn't invite the other man in; rather he stepped to the side, putting himself between the newcomer and Kate. The air around them was strained and it was clear Logan's wolf was at the surface, growling. Lucas smiled softly and raised his hands.

"I'm not trying to get between you and your girl, man, so just put him away." He stepped back so he was against the door and as far from Kate as possible. Logan was clenching his teeth so hard his jaw muscle twitched.

"What are you doing here?"

Pain passed over Lucas' face as he replied, "I'm here to help you, Logan."

Logan roared, "You've done enough! Get out!"

Kate stepped forward, putting her hand on Logan's arm. "Logan, who is this? What's going on?"

A look of mild surprise crossed the newcomer's face as he looked at Kate's hand on Logan's arm.

When Logan didn't reply, Kate tried again. "Logan? Please tell me what's going on." She looked back and forth between the two men. Their physical similarities were not lost on her.

A moment passed. Then two. Logan's hand tightened on hers. "He's my brother. And, he's a traitor."

Chapter Ten

Fifteen hundred miles away, Dr. Sig Hansen was in a rage. His face was purple, his tufted hair stood on end, and spittle flew from his lips as he cursed the heavens. The bodyguards watched the tantrum with expressionless faces. It wasn't the first time the mad doctor had flown into a rage. It wouldn't be the last.

Hansen discovered the small town veterinarian had led him on a goose chase. He screamed and railed, shaking his fists and waving his arms like a child in the throes of a tantrum.

The partially decomposed carcass of the dog had been retrieved. Hansen rushed it to his lab to confirm the small town vet had dimwittedly euthanized his enemy for him. His sadistic glee turned to incomprehensible rage when he realized the truth. After an hour the torrent subsided, and the doctor made a phone call.

"She has deceived us. The GPS was planted in a dead canine, and then buried in the city dump. I will find them. No sir, I don't know at this time. Yes, of course, I will search them all. Sir, I can find them, I assure you. They could not have gone far. No, no sign of the other one yet. Yes, that was also a dead end. I don't know why they are still alive, I am working on it. Sir, if you will allow me to take the men and…yes sir. Yes, I understand. Yes, of course."

Hansen turned to the guards, his eyes wild. "We stand down. For now."

Hansen turned and stalked to the holding room where the test subjects were held. After a while, a pained, anguished howl echoed throughout the compound.

****

Kate stared at the two men for a moment. The tension was palpable. She stepped away tentatively though stayed behind Logan.

"I'm going to go get some dry towels." She quietly left the room.

Without warning Logan lunged, knocking his brother to the floor. Rather than return the fight, Lucas lay unmoving, chest, belly and neck exposed. He wouldn't make eye contact with Logan.

Logan roared with frustrated rage. "Fight back, damn you. Fight me!" He pummeled the man on the floor.

Kate rushed into the room to find Logan's brother on the floor, head turned away, as Logan raged.

"Logan. Stop it." Her voice was sharp and full of authority and for a moment Logan paused. Both men looked at her. Lucas with a look of incredulity, Logan as though she had struck him.

"Logan, come to me," she said softly and held out her hand.

Logan rose off his brother. As he strode toward her, she tossed the dry towels to Lucas. Without a word, she turned and went to the sofa where she sat and regarded the two men. Logan took a place near her and crossed his arms.

She watched as Lucas removed the soaking jacket and hung it by the door. As he turned, he flashed a grin at Kate. It lit up his entire face and made him look almost angelic. Kate could imagine all the women he won over with that grin.

"Not much of a talker is he? He never was. Thanks for the towel, by the way." He removed his boots and left them by the mat. When he reached the chair he dropped into it. He put the towel over his head, roughed it up, and removed it. His hair stood up wildly but the change to his green eyes was astonishing. Instead of looking like a transient, he looked like a mischievous schoolboy.

Anger poured from Logan in waves. "Stop it, Lucas. It won't work with me."

As quickly as it came, the smile vanished, and Lucas was once again the beaten transient who stood at her door a few moments ago.

"I had to try." He winked at Kate.

The barest hint of a smile betrayed her as she dropped her gaze to her lap.

Lucas looked speculatively at Logan and rubbed his hand over his head. "Logan, I didn't betray you, or our family. I came here to help."

Logan stiffened but didn't move.

"We had to know what was going on in there. Somebody had to go. People are dying, Logan. Our people. I would never turn on them, or you. You have to believe me."

"You're lying," Logan growled through clenched teeth.

"No, I'm not, but if we don't get a handle on Hansen and Pro-Gen he's going to destroy us all. You were the first one they haven't killed. When you escaped, Hansen nearly had a stroke. He doesn't know why you made it this long and he's desperate to find out why." Lucas nodded at Kate, "How much does she know?"

Kate narrowed her eyes at Lucas and crossed her arms. "How much do *you* know?"

Both Logan and Lucas remained silent, staring at one another. Finally, Logan spoke. "She knows. She's Doc Barrister's daughter."

Lucas looked at Kate sidelong. "I figured as much. I knew you were hit so I managed to track you to the road. I started checking the local vets. Thank God there weren't too many. I found Dr. Barrister's and when I went in, the lady was, uh, really helpful."

Kate burst off the couch. "You didn't hurt Margaret?!"

Lucas looked shocked. "No. I didn't do anything to her. I can just be, charming when I want to be, and people tell me things." He looked questioningly at Logan.

For the first time in years, Lucas heard his brother's voice in his head. *Well, okay, maybe she doesn't know everything.*

Lucas grinned at his brother and Logan looked away, impassive.

Kate looked at the two, she knew *something* was passing between them, she just didn't know what.

Lucas turned to Kate. "So, you know about the research then? That Pro-Gen is infecting lycanthropes with a toxin that changes their genetic structure?"

Kate looked at him for a moment. "My father's notes tell me he suspected something of the sort. Most of Dad's work centers on the genetic makeup of weres. His focus was primarily on why some lycanthropes were dying and others weren't. "

"And what have you decided?" Lucas looked once more like a boy with a secret he was dying to tell.

Kate couldn't help it, she smiled. "Here's what I suspect. The toxin is attacking specific protein chains in the were system. These protein chains are uniquely based on the specific genetic makeup of the infected party, in other words, some lycanthropes are more wolf than others. This toxin attaches to the protein chains, breaking them down and killing the subject."

Lucas smiled at Kate. "You're pretty good, Doc. Do you know what specific protein chain you need?"

"Knock it off, Lucas, if you've got something to say, come out and say it." Logan growled.

Lucas turned back to Kate, unfazed by his brother's grousing.

"Fine. I left the lab in a hurry after Logan broke out. By the way big brother," he looked pointedly at Logan. "I had a plan to get you out but you couldn't wait one more day." He turned his attention to Kate. "I was able to get into the server room and download the research data. Pro-Gen knew what I was, and they were taking no chances. When Logan escaped, I knew they would come after me. I would have been here last night but you guys seemed kind of busy." He grinned wickedly.

Logan stared at his brother. "So that was you."

Kate looked at Logan but pressed Lucas, "What kind of information did you get?" she asked, suddenly hopeful.

Lucas looked nonchalant, "Oh, just the protein sequencing information for the toxin, that's all."

Kate's eyes sparkled with joy as she turned to put her hand on Logan's arm. This was the information she needed that could help her to help Logan and his family. "This is great. This means we can pinpoint the opposing sequence that should counteract the effects of the Pro-Gen toxin. We can reverse the effects of the virus as long as we get there in time. Lucas, this is great! I can't wait to get started."

Suddenly, the smile Lucas had been wearing was gone. "I hope you can use it, and soon. I'm going to be your first test case."

Chapter Eleven

Kate found Logan on the deck later that night. He was leaning on the rail, looking over the water. The air was cool and moist, smelling of rotting leaves and water. Night birds called occasionally over the steady hum of crickets. She could tell from his posture he was pensive, worried about his brother. His expression did little to belie the depth of emotions that lurked beneath the surface. She closed the door and walked over to stand beside him.

They stood there for the longest time, not saying a word. Kate couldn't tell if her presence gave him comfort or irritation, but since he didn't attempt to push her way, she chose to go with the former.

Logan continued to stare over the lake. Kate was a strange woman. She came and stood beside him, not saying a word. Just her presence was enough to calm his wolf, who, had he been out, would have been pacing with anxiety. Logan was glad the wolf was in and the full moon was nowhere near.

Logan was worried about so many things. Lucas. Kate. The fact he couldn't stop watching her. He couldn't stop thinking about her.

He wasn't sure he could take care of her, wasn't sure he couldn't be overly possessive, wasn't sure he was the kind of man she would choose. What Logan did know was the wolf had already chosen his mate, and he would not rest until all parties involved came to the same realization. The wolf controlled the more basic of life urges, like eating, establishing territory and breeding. He knew Kate was the one. Logan hoped he could convince her of that.

Kate broke the silence when she quietly said, "I don't know how much time we have…for Lucas."

Logan nodded. "I know. I know you will do what you can. We should be able to make it to my father's in about twenty-eight hours, give or take. Even if we aren't in time for Lucas, there are others we will be able to help.

Kate fell silent again. Shyly, she put her hand over his. Logan suddenly grabbed her into his arms and held her tight.

"I appreciate everything you've done for us, for me," he whispered.

Kate leaned back and looked at him closely. He loosened his grip on her enough that she could reach up and run her fingers through his hair. "Why would you think I wouldn't help you?"

"Kate, I don't make it a habit of sleeping with women, especially ones I don't know."

Kate's hand stopped its travels. Her eyes narrowed.

Logan felt her stiffen, and his wolf uncurled. He knew he was saying something that bothered her, his wolf knew she was upset. What did he do?

He tried again. "I'm just trying to tell you that I don't get around that much, that I don't expect anything, like a relationship, or commitment."

Where was he going so wrong with this? His wolf was howling with rage. The man was confused because he didn't want to force her into something she didn't want and he was trying to tell her so. Why was she so upset?

Kate pulled back from Logan's embrace and straightened her shoulders.

"I certainly would never expect a relationship just because you slept with me. If you think that's what I'm after you're wrong. Don't worry, once I help your people create the protein sequence, I'll be on my way, and won't bother you again." She was nearly crying.

She truly didn't expect a relationship, so why the hell did he have to bring it up? Sure it would have been nice, waking up with him every morning, going to bed with him every night. But damn, she barely knew him, save for a chaste kiss many years ago and the best sex of her life the night before, where did that constitute a relationship? Kate's anger began to get the best of her.

"And another thing, buster. If you think I make it a habit of going around sleeping with strangers, you're wrong. It just happened, okay? End of story. I'm not looking for a relationship, I'm not looking for commitment, and I'm not looking for anything from you, Rover, so get past yourself!" She whirled to run into the house but Logan stopped her.

"I wasn't trying to imply that you sleep around, I was trying to give you some room and not run you off! This is new to me too, Kate. I don't know what's happening. Well, I do, but, look—I didn't want to tell you this way, like this. My wolf has chosen you as my mate and I don't know how to handle that. And—don't—call—me—Rover!"

Kate stopped and looked up at him through tear-filled eyes. Now she was really confused. He was trying to run her off, right? This was the big break-up scene, but did he say something about his wolf choosing her as his mate? She shook her head, trying to fling the thoughts and emotions aside.

"What are you saying? And what do you mean your wolf has chosen me as a mate? Aren't you trying to get rid of me?"

Logan looked at her incredulously. "No, I'm not trying to get rid of you. I'm trying not to make you feel forced into something you may not want to be a part of."

Kate took a step closer to him, "And the part

about your wolf choosing me?"

Logan took a deep breath. "Look, we're different. For someone like me, the wolf nature has more control over certain areas. The wolf chooses the mate. My wolf has chosen you. Look, I didn't want to tell you, at least not this way. I don't want to scare you."

Kate's tears stopped as realization flooded her. "Does that mean your wolf likes me?" she asked with a wicked gleam in her eye.

Logan was stunned now. "Yes."

"So if your wolf likes me, does that mean that you like me too?"

Logan swallowed. "Yes."

"I think I like your wolf," she said as she slid her arms around his neck and pressed her body against his. Logan couldn't believe it. He wrapped his arms around Kate and it was all he could do not to take her right there, on the deck, under the night shadows with the trees framing a night sky filled with stars. She moved against him, slowly, seductively.

The door opened and Lucas stood there, holding a shirt. "Sorry," he said, but the grin on his face said he wasn't, not one bit.

Logan left his arms around Kate as he growled at his brother. "What?"

Shaking with laughter, Lucas handed Logan a shirt. "Found it in my pillowcase. Thought the doc might want it back, to slip back in your pillow." Howling with laughter, Lucas turned and went back into the house.

Logan held the shirt in his hand while he looked questioningly at Kate.

"I hoped you wouldn't attack me if you recognized my scent. I put it in your pillow so that you might know me when you woke up. It worked for pups when I was growing up." She finished softly.

Logan continued to stare at her, then at the shirt. Finally he shook his head and tossed the shirt over the deck rail. “I don’t need to be scent marked, cupcake. I know what you smell like already.” He nuzzled her shoulder and pressed her hips to his so she could feel his awakening erection.

Kate tilted her head back so he had full access to her neck and chest. “Whatever you say, Rover,” she said breathlessly. “Whatever you say.”

Chapter Twelve

The three of them headed for Montana the next morning. Lucas estimated he'd been infected three days ago, and insisted he still was not displaying signs of infection. However, as the day wore on, the shadows under his eyes darkened and his face became more drawn and pale. The miles seemed to stretch endlessly before them. Logan's hands tightened on the wheel and his mouth set in a grim line. Kate attempted not to notice that he too, had shadows darkening his eyes and the faintest traces of dampness across his forehead.

Kate turned constantly to check Lucas. His brow became damp with sweat and he was prone to bouts of chills. In between, he would tell Kate what he observed at Pro-Gen and what to expect from him. He estimated they had enough time to get him to Price Falls and once there he would need to be isolated. He explained to Kate that all packs had facilities where wolves could be contained. Lucas didn't explain for whose safety and Kate didn't ask. He told her once the toxin started to affect his system, he would be prone to fits of rage as he changed from wolf to human and back and if the anti-toxin didn't work, he would die after a couple of days. He shared this with a growing clinical detachment Kate found troubling.

They passed through the town and Logan headed out on a two-lane state road. After a few miles, he turned off the road and followed a tree-lined track that seemed to wind and twist back on itself. He crossed a narrow stream and continued, deeper into the forest. Kate was glad she had the model with all-wheel drive. They emerged from the trees and Kate could see across the valley, nestled into the far tree line, a normal looking home with several outbuildings. The drive wound behind the house to allow access to the other structures.

As Logan pulled to a stop Lucas was taken over by a seizure. His back arched, veins bulged on his neck and his hands bent in close to his body. Kate looked on, speechless. The skin under Lucas's hands began to roll, as though the musculature was enlarging beneath the skin. His nails began to darken and extend from his fingertips. Logan leapt out of the car and wrenched open the SUV's back door. He gently gathered his brother into his arms as Lucas mumbled, "Hurry, Logan, I can't hold it in much longer." Lucas' eyes began to change, turning golden and Kate noticed his canines elongating.

"Here now, what's this, what's going on…Logan?" a man burst onto the porch. There was no mistaking the family resemblance. Kate assumed this must be another brother. She was shocked when Logan shouted, "Dad, hurry. We have to get to the cage!"

Without a word the man ran back into the house with Logan behind him. Kate followed in silence. Lucas was shifting in Logan's arms, writhing.

They passed through a normal-looking middle-class home then descended a staircase that Kate assumed led to the basement—dungeon? She noted the makeshift lab in one corner of the basement complete with microscopes and autoclave. Down a short passageway, through another door, Logan and his father disappeared.

Kate was pulled up short by arms like steel bands wrapping around her, not tight, but secure.

"No, no sweetie. Let the men folk handle that. It's no place for a girl."

Kate twisted to see she was being held securely by a woman her age. She had long brown hair, green eyes, and beautiful skin. She smiled at Kate.

"It's okay honey, they'll be back in a minute. Since you're with Logan I'm going to go out on a limb and say you must be little Katie Barrister, right?" She guided Kate over to a table with four chairs, her tone cheerful and even as though they were meeting for a craft circle.

"Now, tell me how you met my boys."

Kate gasped and before she could help it she blurted, "You're Logan's mother?"

The young woman tilted her head back and laughed. "It's one of the advantages. We age pretty good," she said, nodding her head as though it was something she once knew but had forgotten.

"Just between me and you, I'm sixty-two, which is still really young." It was apparent where the mischievous look Lucas got came from—his mother had the same sparkle.

Kate walked over to the lab and began poking through the drawers and cupboards. "I'm Kate Barrister, Dr. Barrister's daughter. My father and mother died in a car accident less than a month ago. I picked your son Logan up off the road three nights ago. Lucas found us early yesterday morning. He's been infected, but he brought me the data Pro-Gen had and I think I can make an anti-toxin, but I need some naphthalate blue. Do you have any of that?"

Logan's mother's paused.

Kate realized how she must seem. "I'm sorry to be so forceful, but if I'm going to have any possibility at all of saving Lucas, I have to work fast."

The other woman smiled. "I think we're going to get along just fine, Katy. The naphthalate is in the second cabinet on the right."

With that, the two women went to work. Logan's mother oriented Kate to the lab as they went.

Chapter Thirteen

Logan carried Lucas into the stronghold that served as their holding facility. Lucas was shifting, transforming, but something wasn't right. His face twisted in pain and his body seemed confused. There was an order to a transformation, normally beginning at the head and working back. Lucas writhed as various parts of his body attempted to transform before they were ready. It was a gruesome sight.

Logan placed Lucas gently on the pallet on the floor then carefully shut the door behind him. His brother twisted and moaned. It wouldn't be long before they wouldn't be able to contain his screams.

Laramore came over to stand beside his eldest son. He didn't speak but there was pain and compassion in his eyes for his son. Logan touched his dad on the shoulder, then slipped into the holding cell across the aisle and quietly shut the door between himself and his father.

Lawton grasped the bars with desperation. "Logan, son. No, not you too."

"It's okay Dad," he said quietly. "Just do me one favor, please?"

Lawton Turner looked his son in the eye, the pain on his face clear to see.

"Don't let her see me this way."

His father swallowed and nodded. He turned and left his sons.

Lawton entered the lab to find Kate and Logan's mother, Brie, chatting amicably as Kate worked. She looked up smiling when Lawton entered the room, expecting to see Logan behind him. When she looked past Lawton's shoulder and saw no sign of Logan, her shoulders dropped.

Lawton approached Kate and the only sign of his emotion was the trembling hand he laid on her shoulder.

"Kate," he said his voice full of raw emotion, "Thank you, thank you for getting my boys home." He glanced at Brie. "Can you help them?"

Kate attempted to run for the room she had seen Logan disappear into. Lawton held her.

"No, girl. He doesn't want you to see him like this. Can you make whatever it is we need to fix them?"

Kate didn't respond as tears of grief poured from her eyes. She fought Lawton. "Let me go, I want to go to him!"

Lawton held her as she cried. She cried for her folks, cried for Lucas, cried for Logan, and she cried for herself.

Lawton gave her only moments before he turned her face so he could stare directly into her eyes. "Kate." He commanded. His voice was deep, like the voice of God. It filled her, not with fear, but with warmth. "Kate? Are you listening to me?"

She nodded.

"I need you to do what you can. You are the only one who understands and there is no time to lose. Can you do that?"

A door closed on Kate's emotions. She felt nothing. No pain. No sadness. No regret. Only emptiness. Determination filled her, fueled her with an energy she didn't know existed. She straightened and without a word, returned to the lab.

Kate worked through the night. Her first test results failed and she nearly cried. Logan was depending on her. She couldn't let him down. She wouldn't let him down.

She began another sequencing agent. Lawton had drawn blood from both of his sons, as well as himself. Kate was able to test the protein sequences Lucas had given her on the blood samples to monitor the changes to the DNA structure.

Her third sequence was her breakthrough. She called to Lawton and Brie who were sleeping fitfully on the couch. She had barely explained her results before Lawton pulled out what appeared to be a gun.

"You aren't going to shoot him?" she asked incredulously.

Logan's father looked grim. "This is a tranquilizer gun. I only use them as a last resort. Considering the condition Lucas is in, he's too dangerous for any of us to approach. This is the only way to get it into him. Logan isn't so bad. I can administer his directly." He looked at Kate with grim amusement, "Unless of course you have a better idea?"

Kate narrowed her eyes at Lawton. "I want to see him."

"No. I promised my son. He loves you too much, and doesn't want you to see this. You can be mad at me later, but right now, I want you to make another round of this stuff in case we need it. I don't intend to lose my sons to those bastards." Lawton left Kate standing as he disappeared through the door where his sons were confined.

Kate returned to her lab to make more antidote. Hours later Kate was exhausted. Subsequent samples taken from Lucas after the first few injections showed the antidote was working. His cells were returning to their original genetic structure. Logan however was a different story. His condition was slower to react and steadily declining. Kate was frustrated. Why didn't his body respond? Kate asked Brie for the hundredth time if she was certain about Logan's parentage.

Brie replied with only mild irritation, "I'm fairly certain, Kate. I was there for the whole thing, from conception to delivery."

Kate dropped her head into her hands. "I'm sorry. I'm frustrated. There has to be something I'm not getting. Something I'm missing. I'm just not getting it!"

Brie looked helplessly at Kate. "I wish I could help you. I just don't know anything about this sort of thing. All I know about DNA is it's what makes everybody different."

Kate looked up. "That's it!"

Brie stared.

Kate stood up and went back to the vials that held Logan's blood. "I'm such a bonehead. Of course. Everybody's different. That's why it's working on Lucas at a different rate than Logan." Kate continued to work until she realized Brie was still standing there, staring at her.

Kate explained. "Pro-Gen has to have a sample of an individual's blood in order to develop a toxin. It's like a designer disease. Each one is unique because it's specific to the person it is intended for. My antidote isn't working for Logan because it's for Lucas. Logan and Lucas are brothers; they share similar DNA, but not the *same* DNA. Their bodies are reacting differently because their genetic makeup is different. I've been giving Logan the same anti-toxin I gave Lucas. It's slowed the reaction down in Logan but hasn't reversed it because it isn't affecting him in quite the same way. I have to tailor the antidote specifically to Logan's DNA."

Two hours later Kate triumphantly handed her antidote to Lawton. He disappeared once again into what Kate had dubbed *the secret room*. He came out a few minutes later to tell Kate that Lucas was continuing to improve.

"Why don't you get some sleep? It's up to Logan

now; all we can do is wait." He put his hand to the small of Kate's back and guided her over to Brie. Kate felt she was abandoning Logan but she was nearly asleep where she stood. She allowed the woman to take her upstairs to a comfortable bedroom. Kate barely removed her shoes before she fell onto the bed, still dressed and fell fast asleep.

She awoke sometime later to the feel of a warm, lean body lying close to hers. She sat up, frightened but a strong arm snaked around her waist and pulled her close. Kate turned to see Logan smiling at her through sleep-filled eyes.

"S'ok, cupcake. Go back to sleep," he mumbled.

Kate grabbed him by the shoulders. "Logan!" She was frantic.

His eyes flew wide open as he sat up. "What is it?"

"What is it?" she spluttered. "It's, it's you. Are you okay? What happened?" She was crying with joy.

Logan smiled at her as he lay back down on the bed. "Don't I look okay?"

Kate looked him over from head to toe. "Well, you look fine. But…"

Logan pulled her into his embrace. "No buts, cupcake. Sleep now. Talk later."

Kate relaxed and allowed herself to sink into his arms. He was okay. Even better, he was here, with her. Kate wrapped her arms around him and held him tight, breathing him in. She was so grateful to have him here.

"Logan?"

"Mmmm-hmmm?"

She smiled. "My wolf likes your wolf."

About the author...

Autumn Shelley currently lives in Central Texas with her helicopter pilot husband and 3 dogs. When she isn't scuba diving, riding her sport bike or reading she can be found at her computer working on her next book.

Raven's Shelter

by

Dariel Raye

Dedication

Special thanks to
Tauris, Jackson, and Isis
for keeping me young at heart

Chapter One

Karen swiped at her face, wiping at unwanted tears. *In the arms of the angel, far away from here...*Sarah MacLachlan crooned on the wall-mounted waiting room television. “Shit! If they’re gonna play that song all day Animal Planet is definitely going on mute. How am I supposed to get any work done listening to that and thinking about all the poor animals I can’t do anything for? Huh? What do you think?”

The brown and white Brittany spaniel watched Karen with warm brown eyes as she continued to lather his back and talk to him. Karen took on a playful tone as she changed the subject. “Ooh, you’re gonna smell so good! Your mommy’s gonna be so happy with you!”

The dog wagged its tail and began swishing around in the large tub.

Fia, one of her assistants, stuck her head in the door. “Karen, Betty is on the phone. How much longer before you think you can call her back? It’s nearly five and she says she needs to leave at five.”

“Ah, give me another twenty minutes. I need to dry this beautiful baby off first. Tell her I’m really serious about expanding the no kill shelter, though. Twenty minutes.” She raised her voice to call after Fia. “Oh, and Fia, tell her please don’t do anything until I call! Get Auriel or Carl to check in our two boarders.”

Karen finished bathing and drying the spaniel, carefully preparing him for his owners to pick him up. Then, she washed her hands and grabbed her ham and cheese croissant, her first meal of the day. She glanced at the clock. It was after five.

Karen picked up the phone and called Betty, wondering what she had for her this time.

"Hey, Karen, I've got one for you to look at."

Karen took another bite of her croissant. "Male or female?"

"Definitely male. He's huge, and now that he's awake, he won't let any of us near him. He just came in yesterday, but he's not eating."

Swallowing quickly, and reaching for a 32-ounce Gatorade, Karen frowned. "Has Ron checked him out?"

"Yeah, he says he's healthy, but somebody must have tried to poison him. Ron found traces of something in his blood he couldn't identify. He wanted to take him, but I told him no."

"I'm on my way. Don't tranq him until I get there. I wanna get a feel for him. Okay?" Karen picked up her keys and headed for her SUV, headset already in place. Animal Services was only a few miles from her clinic, so she continued asking questions until she got to the kennel.

Betty was locking the office and heading toward Karen when she arrived. Karen turned off her headset and followed Betty down the walkway that led to the animal.

"I put him back here because I didn't want anybody to try to adopt him. I've named him Mr. Vicious."

"Oh, my God! That's a wolf mix! Where'd they get him?" Karen knew immediately this was no ordinary house dog. He actually looked pure wolf. He stood nearly four feet tall with shiny black fur, and glared at them with baby blue eyes. His expression was one of suspicion and unadulterated fury.

Karen stooped down in front of the crate to see if he showed any further signs of aggression. The animal remained completely still. "Betty, you said he growled at the other attendants?"

Betty stood a distance behind Karen. "Mr. Vicious not only growled, he snapped at them. He meant business, and you know what that means. They want to put him down tomorrow. That's why I called you. He might be a mean SOB, but he's just too beautiful to be killed."

Karen watched as the animal's gaze moved to Betty. "I think he knows what beautiful means." She laughed and stood to join Betty. "Did you bring the stuff?"

"Yeah." Betty reached into a large duffel bag and removed a collar and muzzle attached to a long stick. "I could watch you do this a thousand times and still be amazed. Still…be careful." She handed the stick to Karen and took a few more steps back.

Karen spoke to the wolf with reverence. "Hello, beautiful. I'm not about to let anything happen to you." She offered him a closed mouth smile as he stared intently into her eyes. "Nobody's gonna hurt you. I won't let anybody hurt you ever again."

****

"What do you mean he got away? You had five men at your command! How could he have gotten away from all of you?"

The blonde haired man shuffled his feet, unable to look his superior in the eye. "We had him, Mr. Moore, but then he got hold of Luke and we had to unlock the cage so Luke could get out. We'd already given him the shot and thought he was fading, but the bastard nearly killed Luke. As soon as we opened the cage, he got past us. That's why Luke ain't here. We still could have got him except some damned bleeding heart activist saw us chasing him and started making threats.

"You gave him the shot and it didn't put him under?"

"Yeah, that's what caught us by surprise. Like I said, he should have been fading when we opened the cage."

Mr. Moore scratched his round, hairless chin. "You searched the area and visited the kennels around here?"

"Yes sir, but there was no sign of him. He's gotta turn up, though, right? I mean, he can't shift with that stuff in his system."

"You have one more day, at most, to find him. After that, the formula will be of no assistance if it is not reinforced. The fact he was able to walk after the injection tells me he is very strong. The other one was unconscious for days. It's possible we only have hours before his system reverts to normal. Unless he is forced, he will avoid ingesting solid matter. The formula requires solid matter to remain active in his system. As it stands, the effects of the formula are temporary at best. If he manages to shift, he can only be identified by his body temperature. Even in human form, his temperature will be that of a wolf."

Mr. Moore held a vial between his thumb and index finger. "Do you realize the significance of finding one of them here? Here with this damnable heat? No, I don't suppose you would." His gaze never left the vial.

These idiots had no idea who he really was. An award-winning neurologist, yet he had been unable to save his daughter. Following his daughter's death, he closed his practice and disappeared into the Georgia hills where he encountered his first shifter. He would not allow himself to be called doctor until he found the answers he sought. *No more. With the blood of these ungodly creatures, not another human life will be lost.*

"Can't you..."

Mr. Moore interrupted him. "No. I know what you are about to ask. Can't I just utilize what I already have? No. I need a continuous supply, and the one we have is even more valuable to us in her present condition. I will take no chances with her. It was not by chance I learned of beings like Mr. Raven. His presence here alone is proof that I've been given another opportunity. I will not fail again. *You* will not fail me again."

****

Raven followed Karen into the small cottage-style house. The collar chafed, and he didn't even want to think about the muzzle. He was immediately inundated with the scents of other animals. He attempted to pull back toward fresh air. Karen was having none of it.

"I know, I know. It's a new environment and you've gotta get used to our scents. Nobody here will hurt you."

She nudged him forward, stopping to introduce him to her apparent infestation of four-legged pets. He realized suddenly, Karen thought he was one of them. She actually thought he could be a pet. There were two hissing cats, a small mixed-breed female dog, and one male dog that appeared to be a Doberman mix. The Doberman mix growled and stepped into his path. As soon as Raven squinted his eyes and gave him an dark look, the dog backed up.

All the while, Karen issued orders in an attempt to keep peace. He looked at her and sat down. If she wanted to keep leading him along, she was going to have to drag his 230-plus pound ass. Although she looked quite healthy, a little extra softness in all the right places, dragging him would still be a feat worth watching. He had much more important things to do than sit around acting like a pet.

Raven sat, the equivalent of a large man planted in position with arms crossed over his chest. Karen tugged at the collar a couple of times and then stopped to give him a thoughtful look. *Well, at least she took the hint.*

"Okay, well you're here now, so I guess you can move around on your own and get comfortable. I have two rules." Karen bent to remove the collar and muzzle.

Raven could hear her heart beating in quick time, and she seemed to have stopped breathing. Once the collar and muzzle were removed, he heard her let out a deep breath.

He watched her as she spoke, admired her bravery. He was listening for the rules. Raven needed to follow them, at least until he could figure a way out of here.

She must have understood his silent acquiescence because she continued. "No bathroom privileges in the house. If you need to use the bathroom, you ask to go outside." Karen walked back to the door and opened it, illustrating what she apparently expected him to do.

"That's rule number one. Rule number two, no fighting. We are a family, and we do not fight one another."

Water. He needed water. Raven moved toward the kitchen, assuming that was where Karen kept water for her pets.

There they were, a row of water and food bowls along a kitchen wall. Raven stepped up to the largest bowl and was met with the growling Doberman mix again.

Raven made eye contact with the dog. *Don't mess with me dog, I'm not in the mood.*

Once again, the Doberman mix moved away. *Smart dog.*

Just as Raven was about to drink, a hand swooped down and slid the bowl from under him, replacing it with another bowl full of water. He growled at the sudden movement.

She completely ignored his warning, placing the

bowl of water in front of him. "This one's yours. What would you like me to call you?"

Raven started to drink. *Oh, here we go. Another stupid-ass name. Buddy, Blacky, hell what's it going to be this time?*

He glanced up and noticed Karen's pensive expression. She was serious about this name thing. When he took a moment from berating himself for the mess he'd gotten himself into, he could see she was actually kind of cute. Definitely not an appropriate mate—the human thing and all—but yeah, definitely worth a bit of his time. She had warm brown eyes, short black hair, and skin the color of baked pecans. Raven loved baked, salted pecans with a sprinkle of sugar.

He started to drink again. He had no idea how long he'd be locked in his wolf form, but he had to focus on finding Syreena. Although Karen saved him from the gallows, she had nothing to do with his original mission.

He dimly heard her soothing if incessant voice as she prattled on. "What about Brutus? You like that name?" She looked as if she really expected an answer.

Raven allowed his tongue to hang from his mouth, signaling approval. The name made him sound like a bouncer, but he had certainly been called worse, and it might shut her up long enough for him to think.

"Are you hungry, Brutus? Kip and Tammy eat all day, and Nate and Peggy ate before I came to get you. They stay at the clinic with me during the day. I have all kinds of..."

Raven was no longer listening. What was with this woman and the constant yakking? There was something he was supposed to remember about eating. He wouldn't have dared eat anything at the kennel. Karen seemed nice, and she smelled good.

Most of all, he was hungry. He watched her as she continued to talk and pour the contents of a bag into another bowl she placed on the floor.

"I'll bet you lived with a family. You're too domesticated to have been on your own for long, even if you *are* a wolf. We might have to figure out a way to disguise you. Your kind isn't supposed to be in the city limits. Did you know that?" She laughed. "Stop looking at me like that. It's as if you understand everything I'm saying. Come here and eat your food. I hope it doesn't upset your stomach."

Raven could smell the food from where he was. It didn't smell like anything he wanted to eat. He was hungry, but not that hungry. He stretched his forepaws out and collapsed on the floor. The tiles felt good against his stomach. Cool. To his surprise, Karen sat on the floor next to him, slowly moving her hand closer to his fur.

She touched him, going straight for the fur between his ears and massaging gently. The area was the equivalent of the nape of his neck in human form. He had never been able to resist a woman's touch there, not to mention she was actually silent for a minute. Just as Raven started to relax, leaning into her hand, his eyes closed, the phone rang.

Karen slowly stood. Raven could tell that she didn't want to startle him. "Be right back, Brutus."

He heard her conversation. "Hey."

The voice on the other end was male. His hackles rose instantly. The voice was familiar though something blocked his memory. "Hey sweet thing. How about some company tonight?"

"No, it's probably better you don't come over right now. I've got a bit of a project going."

"Come on, sweetheart. I haven't seen you in days. What is it? What are you working on so hard you can't even let me come over?"

Raven listened attentively. Whoever this jerk

was, he wanted to come over and screw Karen. Raven might be stuck in wolf form, but he wasn't about to let that happen.

****

Raven sat up and nudged Karen. She had been stroking his back since she returned from the telephone, and he started to doze. Now he could smell the jerk from the telephone. He hadn't even gotten out of his car yet, but Raven knew it was him. Karen told him not to come over, yet here he was.

"What is it, Brutus?" Her human ears couldn't hear anything yet. She glanced up as Nate, the Doberman mix, passed the kitchen door.

Raven stood and moved toward the front door to join Nate. Karen followed. Just as they arrived at the door, there was a knock. Nate barked and Raven growled, a deep bass rumbling that startled Karen.

She opened the door. "Ron, didn't I say *not tonight* when you called?" She stood in the doorway with her arms folded across her chest.

Raven recognized Ron from the kennel. He had examined him while he was drugged. So, this Ron was a vet. That meant he couldn't kill him. Maybe he could just maim him in all the right places, instead.

Raven stepped in front of Karen, growling ominously at Ron, who glanced down, a peculiar glint in his eyes, as if just realizing they were not alone.

Ron backed away from the door, pointed at Raven and watched him warily. "Isn't that the wolf-mix from the kennel? Sweetheart, he's vicious. He was scheduled to be put down tomorrow."

He shook his head as if another realization just dawned. "Oh, now I get it. That's why you didn't want me over tonight. You know you can't keep an animal like that, sweet thing. You're a vet, too, for crying out loud. You know better."

Karen did not move from her position. "Ron, go home. He's mine now, and there is no way I'm gonna allow you or anyone else to take him. Put-down, my ass. Look at him."

She glanced down at Raven. "Come on, Brutus. The rude man is leaving."

Ron tried to push through the door.

Using his preternatural speed, Raven had him on the ground, his canines at Ron's throat before Karen could stop him. He wanted to bite a plug out of him just for being such a shithead. That would put Karen in a difficult position and she'd been nothing but kind to him. Growling, he backed away from Ron and stood in the doorway beside Karen again. Raven kept his eyes on Ron as he moved to allow Karen room to close the door. He listened until he heard Ron leave, then turned to Karen.

Raven couldn't quite make out the expression on her face. She stroked his fur again, so she probably wasn't angry with him. Was she upset about Ron coming over against her wishes? Yes. There was more. She kept stroking his fur, her brow puckered. She was worried for him. Raven never had anyone besides his sister worry for him before, let alone try to protect him. Not that he needed protection. Still, it felt kind of nice. So, Karen was a vet. That certainly explained a lot.

****

Karen opened the closet and removed the largest pallet she owned. She looked at her new friend. "I hope this is gonna be big enough for you. Kip, Tammy, and Peggy sleep with me. You and Nate are big boys, so the pallets will have to do."

She stood there long enough to see Brutus glance over at the bed, then paw at the pallet before lying down. There was no question about his intelligence. Those baby blue eyes followed her every move, and he seemed to listen intently to everything she said. Too bad she couldn't find a man to do the same. *With my luck, he'd probably need a leash and a muzzle, too.*

Nate intercepted her trek to the shower, nodding his head toward the door. "You need to go out, boy?" She turned to Peggy, curled up on the bed between the two cats. "Come on, girl. You go out with Nate." Karen turned to Brutus. "Come on, let's go outside and take care of business."

As she let them out, she was surprised Nate hadn't put up more of a fight. She had kept other male dogs temporarily, and Nate had done his best to make their lives hell. This time, however, it was almost as if Brutus had been there all along. Nate acknowledged him and then stayed out of his path.

Her large backyard was fenced and well-lit, so she wasn't concerned when Brutus trotted to a spot outside her vision. She realized he was one of those shy ones who didn't want anyone to see him take care of business.

Inside, Karen made sure her pets had water for the night, gathered her things to shower and get ready for bed, and stepped into the shower.

The warm water felt good against her skin. She wished she could wash away her concerns as easily as she washed away the grime of the day. She decided to take Brutus to the clinic with her in the morning. She didn't trust Ron. He meant well—maybe. Out of some misguided imperative, he might try to hurt Brutus. As long as they had dated, he still did not understand her. She would never be able to forgive him for hurting one of her animals.

Although she had more than enough evidence Brutus could be vicious, somehow she knew he would not turn against her. He made it clear biting Ron's head off would not bother him in the least though he had been gentle with her even when he had to have been frightened and traumatized. He was such a beautiful animal. She wondered where he came from. It was obvious someone had cared for him, but his unwillingness to eat disturbed her.

According to Betty, Ron said Brutus had been poisoned. Perhaps his stomach was still sensitive. She would try giving him some sensitive stomach food tomorrow at the clinic, and maybe do some blood work herself to make sure he was okay.

She grabbed her towel from an overhead rail and slid the shower door open. Usually, Nate stood in the doorway while she took a shower. To her surprise, Brutus stood there. Something about his facial expression made her aware of her nakedness in a way she never did when Nate watched her. Heat rose to her cheeks.

She wrapped the towel around her and frowned. "Brutus, go to bed."

****

Raven trotted back to the pallet and glanced at the bed again. Being locked in wolf form was becoming more problematic by the minute.

He pawed the pallet and fell on it, groaning. He closed his eyes as he tried to figure out what he'd gotten himself into. After a telepathic message from his sister, Syreena, he left their home in Washington State and traveled to her last known location in Georgia.

Most shifters were only able to communicate telepathically over short distances. Raven and Syreena were sibling alphas partially because they had extraordinary abilities. Always on the outskirts of pack territory, they were accepted only because they protected the packs.

Orphaned as cubs, and ostracized from area packs, they came to rely on one another. As they matured, they learned they were mutations with heightened senses. As they grew to adulthood, they developed into sentinels. No one was certain why the change occurred, but the siblings made legends reality just as their parents before them. They were faster, stronger, and larger than pack wolves. They were also the only ones able to shift at will. Others were limited to the phases of the moon, only able to shift during the new or full moon. Because of their differences, Raven and Syreena were not allowed to mate with shifters in the local packs.

Syreena traveled south seeking a possible mate. According to the legends, a hidden wolf pack still resided in the hills of Georgia, and some of them had been born with the same abilities as Raven and Syreena.

Raven followed Syreena's scent to a large warehouse where he was ambushed. They used some kind of electrical charges. The only identifying marks on the building were the capital letters SH. There were no windows.

The last thing he remembered was shifting into wolf-form in an attempt to escape. In wolf-form, all of his senses were astronomically heightened. Somehow, whoever was behind this managed to inject him with poison. It weakened him, disabling his ability to shift back to human form.

His parents died protecting wolf packs that never truly accepted them. Valuable to the packs only because of what they could do, it infuriated Raven that he and Syreena were expendable. Expected to sacrifice themselves for the pack just as their parents had. Without his sister, he was on his own.

His next memories seemed surrounded by fog, his movements in slow motion. He had no idea how Animal Control captured him and retained only hazy memories of Ron's examination.

****

Karen woke to a coughing sound. Peggy nudged her hip while Nate rested his chin on the side of her bed. Kip and Tammy were also staring at her, their round faces reminding Karen of uppity little people. She heard the sound again. It was coming from her bathroom.

She glanced at Brutus's bed—empty. Reaching quietly into her bedside table, she pulled her .38 and slid out of bed as carefully as she could. The sound stopped. Karen moved toward her bathroom anyway, Nate and Peggy flanking her.

Karen stepped into the bathroom and flipped the light switch on, pistol ready to fire. The room was empty. The tiny curtains at the bathroom window fluttered toward her. She exhaled and sagged against the light switch. Now, she knew what happened. Brutus became ill during the night and found a way outside through her bathroom window.

Karen closed the window, dashed to her bed and threw her silk robe around her shoulders. She slipped her arms through the sleeves as she moved to the front door. She had to find him. He wouldn't be safe roaming the streets, especially if he was sick. Although her parents had been wealthy, Karen knew what it was like to be alone. She shuddered, thinking about what could happen to him in the wrong hands. He was simply too beautiful an animal to roam free.

She stepped onto her front porch and called to him, her voice echoing through the quiet neighborhood. "Brutus. Brutus, come here baby and let me help you." When she still didn't see or hear him, she instructed Nate and Peggy to watch the house, grabbed her keys, and headed for her truck. The best way she knew to entice a canine was with a ride.

Completely oblivious to her appearance, Karen slowly rode through the dark streets, stopping at intervals to call for Brutus. After riding for over an hour, she returned home. She absently swiped at her tears. How she could have been so careless as to leave that window open? Incidents of horrible animal slayings had been on the rise since the New Year. Every day or two, Karen received reports of mutilated animals, some pets and some livestock. She treated at least three dogs that had been electrocuted, and a cat whose body had been nearly drained of blood. The thought of her beautiful Brutus becoming the victim of such a senseless act made her heart race.

Nate whined as he nudged her thigh. "Oh, Mama's okay, sweet boy. I'm just a cry-baby." She ran her hand along his sleek back, still swiping at her tears with the other hand. Karen returned to the bathroom and opened the window, unwilling to take the chance Brutus would return and find himself unable to come in the way he had gone out.

Karen sat on the side of the bed staring at the empty blue wall. Since childhood, she had shed tears over the senseless pain of innocent animals. One reason she loved them so was because they kept her from being completely alone. Karen supposed she would always be more comfortable with them.

She rested her forehead in one hand and reached over to cuddle Tammy to her chest with the other. She knew she shouldn't feel so attached to Brutus, yet she already felt responsible for him. She glanced at the clock and whispered, "Damn it! Another sleepless night."

Chapter Two

Raven lay in a fetal position behind Karen's home. Moments after shifting to his human form, the remainder of the poison was forced from his system. His head felt as if someone worked on a welding project inside his skull. He was weak and vulnerable. His yowling stomach reminded him he had not eaten anything in nearly three days. Normally, he would have shifted back to wolf form. In his current state of fatigue, forcing too many shifts over a short period of time could damage his system.

Donning the boxer shorts and T-shirt he'd taken from Karen's closet, he was at least able to cover himself. The boxer shorts were so tight they would chafe with movement, and the T-shirt rode well above his navel, baring his sculpted midsection. The uncomfortable clothes would at least allow him to manage for a few more hours without more clothes. After that, he'd have to figure out something.

He listened as Karen returned to the house and walked back to her bedroom, her quick steps light and precise. Running his index finger along the tiny silver cell phone, he felt bad about taking it from her bedside table. He wondered how long it would take for her to miss it in the morning.

Raven could hear her heartbeat as well as the slight puff of air when Karen pulled the sheet over herself. He immediately started imagining how silky her pecan-brown skin would feel against him, her legs wrapped around his waist and clasped at the ankles, her soft feet pressing….

Raven shook his head, clearing the unexpected image of Karen from his thoughts. First of all, he was wearing some other man's underpants, and second, he was not here to fantasize about Karen. Like everyone else in his life, the moment she found out he was different, all of her caring and concern would vanish as if he'd never existed.

He was reminded he hadn't heard anything from his sister for some time now. His link to her was completely silent, but he felt sure he would know if she was dead. His internal clock told him sunrise was in approximately three hours. He needed the darkness to shield him as he procured suitable clothes and shoes. This was his least favorite part of shifting away from home—the damnable things he ended up wearing because humans had such a problem with skin.

Raven stood. Karen had once again turned off all the lights inside the house. The throbbing in his head became exponentially more severe and the tight boxer shorts became more uncomfortable as he moved toward the tall privacy fence. He leapt over it in one agile bound, his six-feet-five frame landing like a rabbit leaping through a field.

Running along the dark streets, much like a jogger from a different time zone, Raven moved toward his hotel room. He was grateful he'd had the forethought to get a room before he went to the warehouse, the last location his sister had contacted him from.

He began to formulate a new plan. Previous communication with Syreena led him to the warehouse. Her scent there was faint, meaning she had not been at that location for at least a day before he arrived. Raven and his sister never lost contact before. The absence of her voice in his head was disorienting. Although he felt certain she was still alive, he could not imagine what force could be strong enough to break the telepathic bond they shared since before birth, and certainly not for this length of time.

He used Karen's cell phone to dial home. "Hey Letha, this is the first chance I've had to..."

Letha hit Raven with a barrage of questions. Whenever a pack member was away, mandatory check-in was scheduled at twenty-four hour intervals. As the pack's chief information officer, communication was Letha's specialty. She knew which questions to ask and what information to relay to the pack.

"Raven, where the hell have you been? I've been worried sick. The whole pack's in an uproar because our field protection is gone." She seemed to catch herself. Her tone became softer and less accusatory. "Are you okay? I really was worried about you."

Raven scoffed, happy to hear a familiar voice, but reminded instantly of the superficiality of the pack's concern. How badly he wanted someone besides his sister to care for him without conditions. "I'm okay, Letha. I think. There's definitely something going on down here, though."

After Raven filled Letha in on the events over the last three days, she gave him an update from her end. Unfortunately, no one in the pack had heard anything from Syreena.

****

Raven bypassed the hotel clerk, a middle-aged, balding white male with sagging blue eyes, by taking the fire escape to the fifth floor and climbing to the window of his hotel room. In moments, he was freshly showered and dressed in his usual denim and cotton. He called down to the front desk and asked the clerk for the location of a twenty-four-hour restaurant. His stomach would not wait until dawn to be satisfied.

With keys and room card in his pocket, he left

his room again. This time through the door. He took the elevator down to the garage to his truck. As his mind cleared, he realized he'd been locked in wolf form for more than two days. He had no desire to shift anytime soon.

Raven reviewed his mental rolodex while eating his pre-dawn breakfast. He quickly made a list of the images of places Syreena went before their telepathic bond was severed…before the warehouse. Perhaps he'd find clues to her disappearance in one of those places.

His sister's face, a softened replica of his own, smiled at him as he heard her bell-like voice in his head. *"This place is huge, Rave, and I smell Alpha wolf! Wish me luck!"* Moments later, he no longer heard her thoughts. Syreena's transmission from just outside the warehouse had been his last contact with her.

He had to find a way to get more information about the warehouse and its owner before returning there. One ambush was more than enough.

While mapping out his schedule for the day, his thoughts unexpectedly returned to Karen. Would she continue to look for him? He smiled, remembering the look on her face as she stepped out of the shower to find him watching her. He chuckled, thinking in that moment she had to have sensed something different about him.

Karen was an unusual woman. Raven wished for more time to explore her, to see what she was like when she wasn't nervously prattling on about nonsense. Time he couldn't have, for it raised the chances she would find out what he was.

****

Karen's alarm sounded at six sharp, waking her from a terrible nightmare. She couldn't remember the details, only that her animals were involved, mutilated again. She glanced at Brutus's bed in the hope somehow he had returned through the bathroom window left open for him during the night.

She leaned back on her elbows and sighed. His bed was still empty. “Where are you, my pretty boy?” she whispered. Where could he have gone?

Karen slowly stretched as she stood and tip-toed to the shower. Peggy, Tammy, and Kip still slept soundly in her bed, and Nate was already at the bathroom door waiting for her. She rubbed his head and massaged his back before she stepped into the shower.

As part of her usual routine, Karen returned to her bedroom to place her cell phone in her bag. It wasn’t there. She walked through every room of the house looking for it. Her next move was to dial her cell phone number using her home phone. The house remained silent. She must have left the phone at work. Frowning, she locked the door and headed for the clinic. As she drove along the quiet streets, she watched for signs of Brutus.

Fia came in just moments after Karen arrived at the clinic. “Hey, boss, how ya doin?”

“I might be losing my mind, but other than that, I’m fine. You didn’t see my cell phone yesterday, did you?”

“Uh, no. Don’t tell me you’ve lost the silver chalice. I thought you couldn’t do without that thing.”

Karen sighed. “I was thinking maybe it fell out of my pocket while I was in one of the dog crates except I distinctly remember taking it with me yesterday because I was talking to Betty on it when I got to the shelter.”

“Oh yeah, what did she have over there this time?”

Karen choked up as she answered. “I am such a cry-baby. Fia, she gave me a wolf and I let him get away.”

"What happened?"

She looked up and noticed Carl, another of her veterinary assistants who now leaned against the open door. She gave him a small nod before continuing.

"I left the bathroom window open. I think his stomach was upset because someone tried to poison him. I heard him coughing, but when I got up he was gone and the bathroom window was open. Actually, at first I thought it was a person coughing. Then I realized it had to be Brutus."

"How'd he get out of the bathroom window? Isn't it too high?" Carl asked.

"He must have really needed to get out. He probably jumped." Karen looked at both of her employees.

"Come on, boss. He'll turn up. They always do." He stepped closer and wrapped his meaty arms around Karen.

"I just don't want anything to happen to him. With the horrible things people have been doing around here to animals, shooting them, electrocuting them, beating them to death, even draining their blood, it's just a bad time for me to have been so careless with him."

She stepped out of Carl's embrace. "Fia, Carl, you should see him. He is the most beautiful thing." She snatched a tissue from the box on the counter in front of her. "Oh, this is so stupid. Come on." She started for the kennels. "Let's check on everybody. Hopefully, they had a better night than their doctor did." She turned to Carl. "Man the front for me until opening time. Some of the others should be here by then."

Fia smiled indulgently, falling in behind her and patting her on the back as they stopped to check on each animal, Karen still blowing her nose in the tissue.

****

Raven read the name on the glass door. *Karen S. Marshall, D.V.M.* It couldn't be. This just couldn't be the same Karen who'd saved him from the gallows. It was her, though. Although his instincts led him to this location, he caught her clean scent before he even got to the parking lot. He also caught his sister's scent in this place, days old, but still discernible. Why then, had he not caught even the slightest hint of his sister's scent on Karen? Had Syreena been here when Karen was away?

It was as if fate insisted he cross paths with this woman in human form. Syreena would love this. She was always going on about fate. He opened the door and stepped inside, ignoring the stares of every cat, dog, and woman in the waiting room.

"May I help you, sir?" The tall, German chocolate-colored woman smiled at him from across the pass-through.

Another animal lover. He considered how honest he could be with her and decided to go for it. "Hi Auriel." He had seen her name on her gold name tag. "My name is Raven Adler. I'm visiting the area for a few days and I'd like to speak to Dr. Marshall about a project I'm working on."

"Certainly. She'll be available for conference in about thirty minutes. She's performing a neuter right now. Would you like to wait or shall I have her call you?"

Raven kept his face neutral though he winced on the inside. There was just something disturbing about a woman who routinely hacked-off balls. "I can wait. Would it be a problem for me to look around your facility while I wait for the doctor?" Raven removed his wallet from his jeans and showed Auriel the miniature of his veterinary license.

Her visage seemed to tighten instantly and she glanced at the slightly shorter woman next to her.

"Doctor, I am not authorized to allow a tour without my boss's permission. I'm sure you understand."

"I understand. Thank you." Raven wondered what Dr. Marshall might be hiding. He didn't miss Auriel's physical reaction to his question. The formerly friendly young woman was suddenly wary and suspicious. She was obviously very loyal to her boss.

Raven stepped away from the counter and sat near the waiting room door. A thin blonde woman made eye contact and smiled. Her smile was beyond friendly. He smiled in response then glanced at his watch. He considered showing her his canines, but wasn't in the mood for games. Inwardly, he smiled again considering how quickly her meatless bones would break if he even started to unleash his sexual demands on her.

****

Karen rubbed her patient's head and removed her surgical gloves. Surgery went well and the freshly neutered dog was doing fine. Fia approached her as soon as she stepped into the hallway.

"Boss, there's this gorgeous guy here to see you. He says he's a vet, too and was asking Auriel if he could look around the clinic."

"Look around? Damn it, Ron must have sent him." She stepped into another room, removed her scrubs, and washed her hands. "Where is he? Waiting room?"

"Yep. I must say all the female clients are enjoying the view."

Karen frowned, genuinely puzzled. "What are you talking about?"

"The view! You know—good looking man—enjoying the view? Even the pets stopped whatever they were doing and looked at this guy when he walked in."

Karen shook her head. "Well, view or no view,

he'd better not be one of Ron's minions coming in here to piss me off or he's gonna get cussed out today."

"And that would make today different how?"

Karen gave Fia a *no you didn't* look. "I don't cuss every day."

Fia laughed. "*Ahem.* Okay. You're the boss, but I've never met another woman who can cry real tears over a dog or cat getting hurt or lost, and turn around a minute later to cuss every human around her like a sailor. I'm just saying..."

Karen rolled her eyes and started walking to the waiting area. "Where's my guest?"

"Dr. Adler?" Fia called Raven to the front counter to meet Karen.

Karen stared as a tall man with wide shoulders and wavy black hair approached the counter. She knew her lips were parted, but couldn't seem to force her jaw closed. He moved with the grace of a predator, slow, sensual movements as if his muscles rolled when he walked.

"Hi Doctor."

A few moments passed before Karen realized Dr. Adler still held his hand out for her to shake. All suspicions about him working for Ron flew from her mind as her lower abdomen lit up like a furnace and her lower limbs melted from the heat.

"Oh, hi Doctor. You are from?" She tried to cover, something she seldom had to do. She was not a woman who spent much time thinking about men, let alone falling all over one. She was not accustomed to having to control her reactions.

"I'm from Washington State. I do apologize for keeping you from your patients, but I only…"

Karen found herself staring again, his words dropping to a low hum. His eyes were like water, liquid pools of baby blue in an olive-colored complexion framed by the blackest hair she had ever seen on a white man. He had high cheekbones, full lips, a straight nose, and as he spoke, she could see just a hint of pearl white, pointed incisors. The imperfection made his features perfect.

"Doctor Marshall? Are you all right?"

Karen noticed as the baby blue pools narrowed, his entire expression becoming one of concern. She blinked slowly, realizing he was awaiting a reply from her. She covered again. "Oh, I'm sorry. I didn't get much sleep last night. You were saying?"

"If I could bother you for just a few minutes longer in private." He smiled.

Bother? His smile gave her an even better view of his imperfect yet perfect white teeth, and it was as if a light switch turned on causing the fire inside her to flare. "Oh, no bother." She looked around the waiting room. "Five minutes?"

That smile again. "Five minutes."

Karen led him back to her office. She managed to compose herself during the time it took to walk down the corridor even though she could feel his baby blues on her behind as if he touched her. She stepped inside the room and reached around him to close the door.

She turned to face him. "How may I help you, Dr. Adler?" *What is it that feels so familiar about him?* She motioned for him to sit adjacent to her.

"Dr. Marshall, I understand you are the local no-kill expert. I would like to help with your shelter."

"My shelter?" Karen recently opened a small no-kill facility outside the city limits so homeless animals had an alternative to the city's shelter. No one knew she was the owner with the exception of her employees and Betty. Many of the animals who lived there were not *legal* pets. On record, she was just one of many veterinarians who donated free services to the shelter. Ron had tried everything to keep her from opening it.

"I understand if you prefer others not know about your dual role at the shelter. I assure you I only want to help."

"Who told you?" She watched as his gaze moved from her breasts to her face. She crossed her legs to control the pleasant thrill his subtle action triggered between her legs. It was just too much to hope this gorgeous man liked big girls. Despite her extra pounds, she usually didn't have too much trouble attracting a man's attention, but other men who expressed interest in her never looked like this one. He could have easily stepped from the pages of *Esquire* magazine.

"No one told me. I simply put the pieces together and came to you."

He was staring into her eyes as if he was trying to determine whether she was being truthful. She stood abruptly.

"Dr. Adler, what would be the nature of your..." she narrowed her eyes, "help?"

"Since I don't live in the area, it would have to be purely financial."

"Oh." This man was unnervingly calm.

She definitely needed the financial help. The shelter was full, and most of its residents were not adoptable, yet Karen saw more homeless animals walking the streets every day. First, though, she wanted to know more about this Dr. Adler. "Do you have a no-kill shelter in your area?"

"Yes. In fact, I am the owner and supervising veterinarian." His smile widened, offering her an unobstructed view of his canines again. "Like yours, our shelter is home to many animals who were sentenced to death."

A knock on the door drew Karen's attention. "Come in."

Auriel stepped into the doorway. "Boss, Mrs. Lee is in the waiting room with Arnold. She asked how long you'd be." Auriel's deep set brown eyes darted between Karen and Dr. Adler, a tiny pucker at her brow.

"Thanks, Auriel. Tell her I'll be right there."

Karen turned to her guest. "Dr. Ad-.."

He interrupted her. "Please call me Raven."

Karen felt warmth rushing throughout her face. "Raven." *How fitting.* "I'm Karen."

"Karen." Raven stood. She liked the way her name sounded falling from those full lips. His voice was deep and a bit raspy in a bad boy way, yet there was something particularly polite about his manner. "I know you're busy right now. I'll be here for a few more days. Why don't we discuss this further over dinner tonight?"

Karen took a quick breath and felt as if she were having an out of body experience when she answered him. *The audacity!* "Okay." She reached on her desk and picked up one of her cards. She turned the card over to write her cell phone number on the back, and then remembered she'd lost her phone.

She glanced up at him, wanting to kick herself for being so nervous while he looked so placid. "Um, my cell phone…I haven't been able to find it today." She glanced at him again, eager to gauge his reaction. There was none. "I'll tell you what. Just call me on my land line."

She wrote the land line number on the back and handed the card to him.

"How's seven? I'll call you and get directions to your home."

"Okay." *Is that all you can say?*

Raven opened the door and accompanied her to the front of the clinic. "Thank you, Karen."

She watched him leave, fighting the strangest urge to run to the door and watch him as long as she could.

Fia popped her lightly on the shoulder. "Ah, he's

gone now. You can close your mouth."

Karen closed her mouth, rolled her eyes, and walked quickly to see her next patient. It occurred to her she had given a virtual stranger her phone number, and he'd be calling in a few hours to get her address as well. Somehow, though, it felt right.

She looked up and Ron was standing in front of her. She hadn't even noticed him as he came in. She'd been too busy staring after Raven.

Chapter Three

Raven sat outside the no-kill shelter. The place appeared to be guarded as if precious jewels were located inside. A brick wall surrounded the facility, but he could still tell Syreena had been here. Somehow, she had been to Karen's clinic and her shelter without actually coming into contact with Karen. He considered jumping over the wall. Decided it might be wiser to wait until he knew more about what he was dealing with.

He needed Karen's help to figure out how her clinic and her shelter were related to the warehouse. He didn't know how much Karen was aware of, but there was a connection. He bumped into Ron as he left the clinic, and the man stared at him, a strange look on his face. Something about Ron wasn't right, but Raven still did not want to believe he was wrong about Karen.

The only two places Syreena had gone before the warehouse were Karen's clinic and Karen's no-kill shelter.

Seven hours before he could call her—a long time. Images of Karen's full, round bottom swaying from side to side made his jeans suddenly too confining. In wolf form, he had underestimated his attraction to her. He always liked lots of hair, but even Karen's short hairdo was sexy on her. He sighed and headed back to his hotel room.

The moment he entered the hotel lobby, he sensed it. A low growl rumbled in his chest, threatening to break free as he scanned the area. An unknown shifter had been in the lobby.

"Dr. Adler, you have a message." The hotel clerk held her hand up, beckoning for him to come to the front counter.

Satisfied the shifter was no longer in the immediate vicinity, Raven approached the counter.

"Someone left this for you, sir." She smiled and leaned toward him as she handed him a sealed white envelope.

"Thank you, Cile." He always paid close attention to name tags. "Did you see the messenger?"

"No, sir. Unfortunately, I wasn't here when the envelope came. It was in your message box, so when I saw you I just thought I'd hand it to you personally." Her heart sounded as if it would leap from her chest, but it was steady. She was being truthful.

Raven glanced at the note, blinked slowly, and then offered her a warm smile, slightly baring his teeth. "Thank you very much, Cile. I won't forget your…consideration."

He shared a laugh with Cile as she fanned her face with her hand. She leaned closer to him, almost touching, and whispered. "If you're interested, I get off at midnight. I've lived here my whole life. I could show you some of the sights around here, just between us, of course, if you're interested."

Raven studied the envelope, held between his thumb and forefinger. It occurred to him Cile might be useful. After a moment, he looked into Cile's hopeful eyes again. "I might take you up on that."

She nearly fell over the counter when he backed away and sauntered up the stairs.

As soon as he stepped into his room, Raven ripped the envelope open. Inside, he found a simple, handwritten two-line note: *I have what you're looking for. Stay away from the doctor and I'll come to you.* The script was not familiar to him, and the scent of another shifter was strong. Whoever wrote the note was male.

Raven reread the note, making sure he hadn't missed anything. He glanced at Karen's cell phone, still in the center of his bed where he'd thrown it this morning. He wondered why someone would try to keep him away from Karen when his instincts told him otherwise. Never one to follow directions particularly well, he decided to continue on his present course. Carefully.

****

"Dr. Marshall's got a date." Fia made her sing-song statement for the fifth time.

"I do not have a date, damn it! I told you we're just discussing business over dinner. Nothing more." Karen flicked her fingers at Fia. "Why do I bother trying to explain to you? You know how much I need…"

"I know how much you need somebody better than Ron. I can't stand that ass."

"Fia!"

"Don't try to act like you don't know he's an asshole. Any man who wants to screw every time you turn around yet won't lift a finger to…"

Karen held her hands in front of her in assent. "Okay, okay. You're right. He's an asshole, but it's not like there's been anyone else beating down my door. He's not all bad. He doesn't want me to lose my license."

"Uh huh. Whatever." She turned back to the computer. "Personally, I like blue eyes."

Karen rolled her eyes. "When is Mr. Stobbins coming in with Lexie?" She flipped through the chart in her hands. She knew Fia was right. Ron was a jerk, but he'd always been there waiting on the rare occasions when she got lonely.

"His appointment's not until two-thirty." She grinned, turning around to face Karen again. "So where are you taking blue eyes for dinner? Why don't you take him to that new place on the lake?"

Karen let out an exasperated sigh and walked away with the chart. She heard Fia's laughter as she continued down the hall.

Karen sat down at her office desk and called Betty at the animal shelter. "Hey, Betty, I'm still kicking myself over this, but my new guest jumped through my window and got away last night. I need you to keep your eyes open for him and call me if you see anything."

"Sure, sure." Betty lowered her voice. "Ron's been here today. He must have figured you got Mr. Vicious from me."

Karen sighed. "Yeah, he came by the house last night after I'd told him not to. That's how he saw him."

"You took him home with you? I thought you were taking him to your shelter."

"When I looked into those eyes of his, I wanted to keep him. Surprisingly, he even got along with Nate!"

Betty laughed. "And I guess Nate's approval of him was proof enough for you, huh? I'll keep my eyes open for him and give you a call if he turns up."

"Thanks, Betty. See ya later."

Karen made her usual call to the no-kill shelter to check on the animals there, then made another round to check on the boarding pets at the clinic. Restless energy crackled along her spine when she thought about her date with Raven. She was actually looking forward to learning more about the mystery doctor. She smiled at the fact she really was anticipating a date. Fia would never let her forget it if she knew what she was thinking.

Karen was fairly sure she sensed interest on Raven's part. She didn't want to get ahead of herself because she also sensed he was hiding something.

Even more reason to find out as much as she could about him tonight.

She mouthed his name. Odd name, but it felt good, and it fit his appearance—everything except the blue eyes. Those eyes were so striking, she hadn't been able to stop staring into them. She wondered if he noticed, decided he had probably been too busy staring at her breasts and her ass to care.

****

Karen changed clothes for the third time and turned to face Peggy, Tammy, and Kip. "What do you think? Do I look okay?"

Kip yawned, hopped down from the bed and left the room. Peggy and Tammy simply stared at her.

Karen wasn't bothered by their apparent lack of interest. "I want to look nice, but not too nice. You know. I don't want to look presumptuous." She turned to peer into the mirror again. "Ugh! I don't have anything that's exactly right." She tugged at the waistband of her pants and ran her palms along her outer thighs.

She stepped over to her closet and pulled out two more outfits. Choosing a sapphire blue sleeveless sheath, she quickly changed out of her pants and into the dress.

Just as she was about to change again, deciding that the sheath was too dressy, the phone rang. The Radisson Hotel showed on her caller I.D., and she picked up. "Hello?"

"Karen, this is Raven. I'm about to head your way. What's the address?"

She prattled off the address to him and asked if he needed directions.

"No. I'll find you."

Karen turned back to the mirror and opened her mouth in horror. She still had to do her face, and the Radisson was only ten minutes away. She seldom wore make-up, limiting the practice to special occasions, so she knew she needed the entire ten minutes or more. Her stomach fluttered as she grabbed her make-up bag and got busy.

She jumped when the doorbell rang. Normally, Nate forewarned her before anyone got near the bell. When she stepped into the foyer, he was just sitting there quietly, watching the door. She touched his head, looking into his face as she spoke to him. "You okay, boy?"

Nate wagged the nub of his docked tail, the only cosmetic surgery she had allowed for the Doberman mix. She refused to allow his ears to be clipped, and they stood out on the sides of his head like two black felt caps as he tilted his head to the side and continued to watch the door.

Karen checked the peep-hole and opened the door when she saw it was Raven. The butterflies in her stomach seemed to have company now. He stood outside in faded jeans and a gray T-shirt. This man was too gorgeous to walk the streets. Her palm moved automatically to glide down her hip. "Um, Hi. Come in."

Raven stepped inside. Nate walked over to Raven and pressed his forehead to his leg in greeting. Peggy ran out of the bedroom doorway and leapt up before Karen could stop her. Raven opened his arms to catch the tiny dog as if he had known she would leap into them.

Karen looked at him and laughed. "My goodness. You're definitely a vet, aren't you? Nate doesn't like *anybody*, but look at him. You'd think he was saying hello to an old friend."

Raven offered her a smile that didn't quite reach his light blue eyes. "They always know dog lovers."

"That's for sure." Karen ran her palms along her dress again as she looked up at him. She felt overdressed and exposed, and more than a little turned on despite the fact he hadn't really done anything.

He stood there holding Peggy, Nate sitting next to his leg as he watched her with a slight smile still tilting his lips. Otherwise, he was expressionless. Karen caught a glimmer of something in his eyes. She couldn't identify it, and it was gone as quickly as it appeared. She smiled again, clasping her hands together. "Well, I guess I'll just grab my purse. You want me to drive since I know where the place is?"

"No. I like to drive. You just tell me where."

Something about that statement set the butterflies in action again. "Okay."

Karen turned and walked back into her bedroom to get her purse. Once again, she was sure she felt his eyes on her backside as she walked away from him. *Definitely an ass man.* Something about knowing he was watching made her want to swivel her hips more, but she fought to control it.

When she returned, Raven reached out and touched her shoulders, turning her quickly so that her back was to him. She didn't have time to react before she felt a tug and heard a zipping sound.

Karen turned to face him again, pressing her palm to the base of her throat. A short, nervous laugh escaped before she could stop it. "Thank you. I forgot this dress even had a zipper."

His smile was genuine now as his gaze moved slowly from her lips to her eyes. "You're welcome. I wouldn't want anyone else to take that as an invitation."

She laughed, unsure what she should say to that statement.

As they left, she gave him directions to the restaurant. He double checked her door to make sure it was securely locked, then walked beside her with his palm at the small of her back. He held her door as she climbed into his truck. Karen had forgotten how good it felt to have a gentleman at her side. Her work took precedence over everything, and with the exception of an occasional night of mediocre sex with Ron, her love life was pitifully empty.

She glanced at Raven. He was a big man. Wide shoulders, narrow waist, solid ass, long legs. It had been a long time since she'd been with a man who turned her on like this. She imagined how his solid weight would feel on top of her. She knew she was probably old fashioned, but her favorite position was still on her back.

He slowly turned his gaze from the road ahead and smiled at her, a knowing look on his face. Too knowing, as far as Karen was concerned. She turned away from him, realizing too late that her mouth was slightly open again. She was grateful she wasn't a drooler.

"So, tell me about yourself, Karen. What is it about animals you love so much you just had to become a vet?"

Grateful for a diversion from her thoughts, she answered. "Everything. I think the main thing though, is their honesty. They either like you or they don't. There's no pretense." She turned toward him again. "What about you? Why did you just have to be a vet?"

"I believe I was born to be one. People can be so cruel. I just wanted to offer a safe haven."

"Yeah! Exactly! That's the very reason I started the no-kill shelter. Every time I see a homeless animal walking the street, it hurts. I know I can't help them all, but being able to offer, as you say, a safe haven, at least that's something." She suddenly thought about Brutus and turned her head to stare out of the window.

"Karen? You okay?" It was strange the way his raspy, bad boy voice still had a soothing effect.

"I'm fine. I was just thinking about my

woo...dog." She caught herself before admitting to keeping a wolf inside the city limits. Although she felt unusually comfortable with Raven, she didn't want to take any chances. "I just got a new dog from the shelter yesterday evening, and he got out of my window and ran off. I rode around and looked for him most of the night, but couldn't find him. We've had a lot of horrific things happen to animals around here lately, and I'm just really worried about him."

She wiped at her tears as quickly as she could, glancing at him in hopes he wouldn't see her crying and come to the conclusion she was insane. Tears might be pressure valves, but sometimes she hated being such a cry-baby.

He leaned back in the seat and turned to face her after he parked, frowning as he stared at her tear-stained face. "You really liked this dog, huh?"

She looked at him, shaking her head. "Yes, I liked him a lot, and no, I'm not crazy, in case that's what you're thinking. I just cry easily about my animals. They're the only thing I cry about, though."

"That's not what I'm thinking at all." He touched her forearm with his hand, signaling her to wait. He opened his door and came around to open hers, offering his arm to help her out of his truck.

Looking around at other couples as they walked into the restaurant, Karen noticed everyone was attired similarly to the way she was dressed. Raven, in jeans and a T-shirt, would draw even more attention. He appeared to be completely unconcerned. She wasn't sure what she thought about that, but her body warmed to him even more. She decided she'd have to figure that one out later.

Karen looked around as the host led them to their table. Every female in the restaurant turned to gawk at Raven as if they'd never seen a man before. Karen had the urge to sink her nails into him and declare *"Mine! I saw him first!"* She sat across from him and smiled sweetly.

"I don't drink, but please get whatever you want," he told her.

Something else they had in common. "I don't drink, either. I've heard their oyster dip appetizer is..." She pressed her fingertips to her lips and released them as if blowing him a kiss. "Mmm scrumptious."

Raven raised one of his brows as he smiled at her. "Well, we simply must have some of that, then."

The longer they were together, the more relaxed she felt. She beamed, lifting her fork to reach his plate when he offered her some of his entrée before he touched it. *Okay, so he's perfect. When are the horns coming out? A tail, maybe?*

According to Raven, all he wanted was a tour of the no-kill shelter, and he would send her a check each month to help with expenses. She had to ask one more question. "Not to look a gift horse in the mouth, but where do you get the funds from? Seems to me, you'd need every penny to help with your own shelter."

"I have some fairly wealthy sponsors."

"Oh." Karen reached across the table and wiped the sauce from the corner of Raven's mouth. His gaze followed her index finger as she transferred the sauce from the corner of his mouth to her tongue.

Okay, maybe one more question. "Are you married?" The question hadn't seemed so out of place while it was still running around in her head. Now, she felt as if she had to minimize the damage. She lifted her hand, palm toward him. "I'm sorry. Don't answer that. I don't..."

"No. I'm not married."

"Oh." Karen wanted to crawl under the table long enough to stop her body from making her say stupid things.

"Raven, I'll be right back." She had to get away

from him for a minute. Desire was overwhelming her, and she didn't want to ruin what could just be a very healthy business relationship. *Yeah, right.*

She noticed the ladies' room as they came in because it was located near the entrance to the restaurant. She stood and walked quickly to the restroom, finally exhaling after she closed the swinging door.

Karen dashed cold water on her face and patted it dry with a paper towel so the water wouldn't tamper with her make-up, then stared at herself in the mirror until her breathing was steady again.

As she stepped out of the ladies room, someone pulled her to an abrupt halt and her torso rubbed against a hard chest. She looked up into those gorgeous blue eyes, the prettiest blue eyes she had ever seen. It didn't matter to her at that moment other customers and restaurant employees were all around them. Her body wanted this, and it didn't care who was watching. She lifted her arms, clasping her hands behind his neck, and flicked her tongue between his slightly parted lips. He was hot in more ways than one. His body seemed to sear an imprint into hers as she pressed against him.

Raven opened his mouth and Karen did her best to swallow his tongue. It was as if she hadn't just eaten a healthy meal. He tasted like everything she'd been missing, and she didn't want to let him go. She felt his arms wrapped low around her waist like iron clasps, and with her thin sheath and underwear the only layers between her body and his jeans, she felt a huge bulge pressing against his denims and into her abdomen. She ran her teeth along his bottom lip and bit him, drawing blood before she could stop herself. *So much for a business relationship.*

Surprised by her own actions, she slowly pulled back from him and ran the tip of her tongue along the outline of her lips. The slightly metallic taste made her want him even more.

Karen held onto him, her hand clutching his T-shirt, as he reached up and wiped the blood from his lip. His gaze never left hers, and she knew exactly what he was thinking.

His voice was even raspier than before. "I've already taken care of our ticket. Are you ready to go?"

It was not a question, as Raven was already pulling her to the truck by her wrist. Karen stumbled after him, caught in a cloud of desire and fascination.

Again, he held her door for her and helped her into the truck before he went around to the driver's side. As soon as he got in, he pulled her to him in one quick motion, wrapped his arm around her shoulders, and those perfect lips covered hers as his tongue entered her mouth like he lived there. Karen slid her hand from the seat and allowed it to glide along the inside of his thigh, just grazing the rock hard bulge in his soft jeans.

Raven made a hissing sound and unzipped her sheath, sliding the dress and her bra strap from her shoulder as he ran his tongue from her collarbone to the sensitive area behind her ear. He touched the top of her breast reverently with his finger and she dropped her head back against the seat, offering them up to him.

Suddenly, as abruptly as he had pulled her to him, he pushed her away and started the truck. "Sorry. Not here."

Karen could barely understand what he said at first. She wanted to wail. Then it dawned on her if he hadn't stopped, she was about to get laid in the restaurant parking lot.

The silence was deafening as they rode to her house.

Karen wasn't sure what she would say when they got there.

Embarrassment started to set in by the time they pulled into her yard.

Chapter Four

Raven sat staring at the steering wheel for a moment before he turned to Karen. His politeness returned, though now she had an idea what was barely contained under the surface. "May I walk you inside?"

Karen smiled as she nodded. Raven's sudden apprehension was precious to her, and her embarrassment melted away as she sat waiting for him to open her door.

"How long have you lived here?" He reached for her hand as they walked toward the front door of her house.

"About six years. I bought this place when I moved here with my veterinary license." She simply couldn't pass up the opportunity. "So do you live alone?"

Raven frowned. "No."

"Oh." Something inside her seemed to drop as she considered his answer. When she was able to speak again, she asked, "Who lives with you?"

He seemed to think about that for a long while. "I guess you'd call it an extended family. My sister and I live on the estate our ancestors left us."

"Uh huh." With the exception of her pets, she had always been on her own. A home-schooled only child, her wealthy parents bought her pets to keep her occupied and away from them. The idea of an extended family was so foreign to her she didn't even try to process it. She was happy he hadn't mentioned another woman.

Raven stood behind her as she opened the door.

She knew he was extremely close because she felt the heat coming from his body.

Karen stepped inside and greeted Peggy and Nate, who repeated their previous behavior with Raven. Nate butted his forehead against Raven's leg, and Peggy jumped into his arms. After a few moments, Nate trotted off to the kitchen, and Raven put Peggy down so she could do the same.

Karen's smile faltered when she noticed Raven's eyes smoldering. His gaze traveled from her toes to her head and back again, a totally different kind of smile tilting his lips. He reached for her. "May I help you with your dress?"

Once again, it wasn't a question. He grabbed her wrist, pulling her forward until their bodies met, then he turned her around so her back was to him. Raven lifted her dress and pressed against her back. She felt that same bulge against her backside as he slid her dress over her shoulders and bent to drop it at her ankles. He stooped lower, sliding his palm along her calf and lifting one foot, then the other to remove her sling-backs.

Karen wanted to turn and face him, but he kept one hand splayed against her back, keeping her in place as he removed her stockings. She was glad she'd worn her lace panties.

He stood, sliding his palms from her waist to her hips, massaging every contour of her plump, round behind through her panties as he moved. Those pointed incisors grazed her neck at the juncture of her shoulder.

She relaxed as he nibbled along her neck and shoulders, her body stabilized by his legs behind her and the wall in front of her.

Raven slid one hand under the elastic of Karen's panties, making contact with the soft skin of her backside as he slid his hand lower, lower, until his fingers touched her ultra-sensitive folds. She whimpered and he turned her to face him, dragging his fingers slowly over his nose and mouth, then flicking his tongue out to taste her juices. “Mmm. You taste as good as you smell.”

Karen wanted him so desperately, her legs went limp. She tugged at his T-shirt, trying to remove it. He placed his hand on hers and shook his head. “Later.”

Raven unclasped her bra and slid the straps along her arms. Karen had the fleeting thought he’d obviously done this a lot. She found the thought disturbing until he touched her right breast, continuing the treatment he’d started outside the restaurant. He made tiny circles along the soft, smooth tissue, lowering his head as he approached her espresso-colored nipple. All she could see was his long dark lashes as he examined her. Sensation flooded her body creating a waterfall from the point of his contact to her throbbing core. Still holding her in place, he licked and sucked her hardening buds, giving both of her breasts equal attention while he explored her yearning center with his gifted fingers.

Raven lifted Karen, and she wrapped her legs around his waist as he carried her to her bedroom. Karen was too lost in what she was feeling to notice he already knew where her bedroom was.

He dropped her in the center of the bed and lifted her legs to remove her panties. Completely naked, she reached for him. His exploration of her core had left her wanting something much bigger and harder to fill the yawning space. Using his hands to spread her legs farther apart, he bent down and lapped at her clit, causing her entire body to shudder with pleasure. She buried her hands in his wavy black hair, moving her hips to maintain contact between her clit and his lips.

He nipped her lightly, those canines at work again. Karen knew there was a reason she liked those teeth so much. He clutched the globes of her ass, keeping her immobile while he slid his tongue along her labia, flicking the tip intermittently into the entrance of her cavern. When he pressed his undulating tongue against her clit and slid two fingers inside her, pressing against her G-spot, she exploded. Her body convulsed involuntarily as she arched off of the bed as if she were being healed.

Karen's body finally relaxed and she reached for Raven, running her hands through his hair to the nape of his neck. She massaged the area with one hand and tugged at his T-shirt with the other as he moved to lean over her on his knees. He quickly pulled the T-shirt over his head and Karen gave his sculpted chest all of her attention. She ran her index finger through the silky black hair between his breasts, leaning up to flick her tongue over his copper-colored nipples. She smiled, leaning back to view her handy-work when they hardened and his chest muscles flexed in anticipation.

Raven pulled her to him, leaning over to kiss her, his movements urgent as she slid her hands along the waistband of his jeans, loosening the brass button and sliding the zipper down. The dark trail of silky curls continued from his navel to the base of his impressive erection. She wasn't surprised to find that he didn't wear underwear.

Karen gripped him in both hands, touching her index finger to the pearl of pre-come at the head, and sliding her hands along the hard, velvety smooth skin. She glanced at his face when he shuddered, the planes of his handsome face tight with forced control that did not extend to his eyes, sparks of silver roiling within the beguiling pools of blue. He hissed a warning just before he grabbed her hands, lifting her arms above her head and pressing her flat on the bed. He slid the thin condom over his pulsating organ, grunted, and slid the palm of his other hand along her hip, directing her to wrap her legs around his waist again.

As soon as she locked her ankles at his perfectly muscled ass, he surged forward, stretching the walls of her vagina with the biggest, hottest rod she'd ever encountered. When her body adjusted to his heated assault, he pulled back a fraction and plunged inside her again, this time filling crevices she didn't know she had. The movement brought an anguished cry from her like a dam overflowing, and she punctuated each thrust with an uncontrollable combination of his name and unintelligible cries.

"No! Please!" She fumbled, trying to grab hold of him when he pulled away from her and flipped her onto her stomach, tipping her ass up to continue his invasion. She tried to turn and face him again, but he growled, sliding pillows beneath her to keep her tilted up for his intentions. *Did he just growl at me?*

Before she could scream again, he slid into her slick channel, this time slowly as he rocked back and forth on his knees, nearly pulling all the way out each time, and plunging forward again, in, out, in, out. His pelvic bone bumping against the soft globes of her ass was more amazing than she could have imagined, and her body grabbed at him greedily, milking him. He responded with a feral growl, increasing the rhythm of his deep, hard thrusts to a frenzied crescendo.

She teetered along the edge of consciousness when her body opened, pulling him impossibly further, and a volcano erupted from her center, sending sparks throughout her entire system. She was convulsing again, and vaguely aware of his heartbeat as he shuddered behind her, finally releasing an extended breath as he rested against her back, the weight and heat of his body an unexpected aphrodisiac.

Raven rolled away from her and removed the

pillows so she could face him as he rested on his side. His face was expressionless now as his gaze moved slowly along the contours of her face. She touched his brow to move one of his sweat slick curls. He turned her hand over, bringing it to his lips, and kissed the inside of her wrist, his gaze never leaving her face.

Karen smiled, stifling her urge to ask him what he was thinking. "Raven, that was unbelievable."

He returned her smile, but kept silent, choosing instead to tilt her jaw and cover her lips with his in an almost crushing kiss, his tongue tangling with hers. He whispered the words into her mouth. "You're addictive. I want more."

Karen's body instantly became pliant as he covered his miraculously engorged shaft with a new condom, moved closer, fitting their bodies together again, and slid inside her without preamble. She moaned, pleasure overcoming her surprise that both of them could be ready again so quickly. After another slow burn, Raven finally drifted off to sleep.

Karen awoke refreshed and exuberant. She tip-toed quietly to the kitchen, bypassing the shower because she wanted to smell like Raven as long as she could. It dawned on her when she saw Nate, Peggy, and the cats sleeping in the kitchen, their behavior was odd. Neither she nor Raven even thought to close the bedroom door, yet they had not been interrupted.

"Good morning, sweethearts."

Karen opened the refrigerator. She had a strange maternal desire to cook breakfast for Raven. They made love for hours, and he actually apologized for not being able to go longer because he hadn't slept in three days. She laughed softly, then grew serious. Amazing.

Her stomach lurched. She could very easily fall in love with this man. In fact, she felt as if she'd already started falling, and she'd known him all of one day. He felt so familiar, though, as if she had known him longer.

Damn it! No eggs, no sausage, and no bacon. Karen closed the refrigerator. She turned to Nate and Peggy. "Wanna ride with me to the store?" They both hopped up, ready to go, their mouths open in anticipation.

Karen tip-toed back to her bedroom to check on Raven. His light snore told her he was dead to the world. *What are you doing? Why not just lie down and let someone else dance on your heart?*

She stood, watching him. He was too good to be true. Could he care for her, or was she just something to do like she'd been for her parents? Her parents always treated her like a science project, sparing no expense, yet making it clear that she was an inconvenience. Suppose he was just passing the time? Something inside her screamed, shutting out the rational pessimist. *But I want him!*

She grabbed the dogs' leashes and headed to the store. By the time Raven woke up, she'd have a hearty breakfast before him. Fears of rejection be damned! Talk was cheap. She wanted to show this man what a good time she'd had last night and how much she wanted him to become a partner in more than business.

****

Raven sensed danger, but couldn't seem to open his eyes. Three days without sleep had weakened him. A familiar male voice said, "Get up, you fucking freak! I got something for you."

Raven finally managed to open his eyes. Ron stood in the bedroom doorway. Although Ron was a distance from the bed where he lay, Raven could smell the man's fear and rage, his heart beating dangerously fast. Ron held a tranquilizer gun, and it was aimed at Raven.

Where was Karen? Because it was her home, her scent was everywhere, but he couldn't hear her heartbeat. Good. Maybe. Did this bastard do something to her? Raven tried to keep his body as still as possible, assessing the situation. Ron was too unstable to reason with.

"I knew what you were when you bumped into me at Karen's clinic. If it had been up to me, I would have blown you away right then." Ron glanced at the rumpled sheets and spat on the floor. "It makes me sick to think of you touching her—a fucking dog!"

Without provocation, Ron fired. Raven anticipated the first shot and managed to avoid the tranquilizer. He shifted to wolf form as he leapt from the bed lightning fast. Ron began to fire in rapid succession. There was no escape.

At least two of the tranquilizers ripped through his flesh. His strength and consciousness waned as the tranquilizers took effect almost instantly. Trapped in wolf form, his limbs no longer responded as he watched Ron coming closer to him.

"They told me you got away the last time, so each of those shots contained a double dose. It won't kill you, but you're going to wish you were dead."

By the time Ron stood over him, Raven's eyes could barely focus. His last thought was of Karen and then everything went black.

****

Karen returned with everything to prepare breakfast. Since she wasn't sure what he liked, she picked up breakfast meats, cereals, fruit, eggs, jam, syrup, waffles, and pancakes.

Nate growled as soon as they entered the house, and Peggy started to bark. Both dogs ran straight to the bedroom and appeared to be searching for something. Karen followed them, her arms full of bags.

"Oh, my God!"

She glanced around the room. Raven wasn't there. The bed was even more rumpled than before she left. Her bedside table was displaced and there was blood on the rug. When she saw Raven's clothes on the chair where he left them the night before, her mind raced in panic.

Karen picked up the phone and called the police. Satisfied that they were sending officers to investigate, she sat on the side of the bed to wait. "Ow!" Something pierced her hip and she sprung off the bed as if bitten. Closer inspection revealed a small black dart. She felt around on the bed and located two more. Unsure what to do, but needing to do something, she started pacing from one end of the room to the other.

Within minutes, two officers arrived. They collected the darts, found four more on the floor of the bedroom, and took a sample of the blood. After questioning Karen, they left, stating that she would be informed of their findings.

She was surprised when tears started to flow. She never cried over people, only animals. She was so worried about Raven, she wanted to wail.

An idea suddenly occurred to her. She searched Raven's clothes until she found his room key, then grabbed her purse. She took the dogs and cats to the clinic to keep them safe. Once they were in place, she left for the Radisson. Maybe she would find some clue there.

A tall, attractive man with straight brown hair and hazel eyes smiled at Karen as she approached the Radisson's elevator. "Hello."

Karen smiled and watched the numbers as the elevator came down. She turned around as she got on the elevator. The man was gone.

The hallway was quiet as she exited the elevator. Karen still felt uneasy, as if she was being followed. She located Raven's room and slid the keycard through the slot. As soon as she touched the handle to push the door open, someone grabbed her from behind and placed a large hand over her nose and mouth.

"Please don't make any noise. I don't want to hurt you," a man hissed in her ear.

Karen had always been told to never enter a secluded room or car with an assailant. So, she lifted her foot and slammed her heel into his insole.

He jerked, but held her even tighter as he pushed her into the room. "Shit! Woman, Goddamn it, didn't I say I didn't want to hurt you? That shit hurts!"

He closed the door behind them, locked it and took several deep breaths before letting her go. She turned to face him and backed toward the patio doors leading to the balcony. "Who are you?"

"What are you backing away for? I'm the one who's hurting. Let's just say I'm a friend of Raven's." He mumbled something Karen couldn't make out.

"Do you know where he is? Is he okay? What happened? What's going on?"

The man stared at her, an incredulous frown marring his attractive features. He was tall and muscular like Raven, but the physical similarities stopped there. Finally, he took another deep breath and motioned for her to sit. "I need you to listen to everything I'm about to tell you without asking any questions until I finish. Can you do that?"

Karen swallowed, nodding quickly. She wanted him to cut to the chase so she could see Raven.

"My name is Cord Ramirez, and I'm married to Raven's sister, Syreena. We don't have time to go into a lot of details, but the same people who took Raven, took my mate, Syreena." He looked at her for a moment, then continued. "They operate out of a warehouse here in town, and they're the same ones who've committed a lot of the animal mutilations lately. I'd been watching them for a while, and Syreena got involved. I tried to tell her not to, but she wouldn't let it go."

He looked as if he was in pain. Karen was surprised that she actually understood how he felt. Although she'd only known Raven a very short time, her stomach lurched painfully when she thought of him hurt.

Karen stared at the man, her mind a blank slate. She had so many questions, she didn't know where to start, and the questions seemed to have cancelled one another out at the moment. She was unable to separate one question from another long enough to ask anything.

Something about Cord felt right to her though, and she had always been an excellent judge of character. She realized she had forgotten to breathe, but when she took a breath, the questions rushed back into her mind at once and tears ran down her cheeks, uncensored.

Cord frowned, staring at her now with his mouth open. "Um, I, uh..." He sat beside her on the bed, his voice soothing. "So I take it you really like Raven. I was counting on that." He leaned across her and pulled a tissue from the box on the bedside table. Handing it to her, he stood again and waited.

Her voice was muffled through her tears. "The police. I called the police. They could go to the warehouse."

"No!" Cord spoke quickly and emphatically, moving to sit beside her again. "If the police go in, these people will run and take your Raven and my Syreena with them. I have some people who can get inside and get them out, but we need your help."

Karen sniffled. "I'm listening."

Cord was still frowning. "You sure you're okay?"

"I'm fine. I usually just do this over animals. Right now, I can't seem to stop. I'm okay, though. Go ahead."

He gave her a dubious look before he continued. "Your friend, Ron is involved." He waited for her reaction.

"Ron? He's an asshole, but kidnapping? Why would he do something like this?"

"I'm not sure. I think it's about money. It doesn't matter."

Karen rested her forehead in her hands before she spoke. Her next words would have been inaudible to human ears. "So that's where he's been getting the money." She looked up again and slid her hands along her thighs. "Ron told me he inherited some money from a rich uncle. I remember because I resented the fact he never offered to help me with the shelter. In fact, I remember thinking he never mentioned an uncle before."

Cord nodded. "Makes sense. Must be a shitload of money. He carries a key card and code to the warehouse in his wallet. I need you to help me get it from him."

Karen's mouth opened in horror as she considering what she might have to do to get those from Ron. "Ugh! I could kill the sonofabitch!"

Cord smiled. "I like your style, lady, but leave that part to me. All you have to do is set a date with him and leave his back door open. They keep a tail on him, so someone is always watching." He looked down, a sheepish expression coming to life.

"What is it?" she asked.

"I thought the best way to protect Raven was by keeping him away from you. I sent him a note warning him. I watched you enough to know you weren't really involved. It was just that Ron was always hanging around you, and with them watching him, you know. It put Raven at risk, and I was counting on him to help me figure out how to get Syreena back."

"You told him to stay away from me?"

He stared at his feet. "Yeah, but..."

She held up her hand, stopping him. "No. You've already explained. I was just wondering why he didn't listen."

Cord scratched his jaw. "Well, I don't mean to be out of place, but I guess he thought being with you was worth the risk."

Karen looked at Cord, but spoke as if she was talking to herself. "I have to help him. If he hadn't been with me..."

"I didn't tell you that to make you feel guilty. I've got a corner on that myself. If Syreena hadn't gotten involved with me, she wouldn't have been at the warehouse in the first place. All we can do now is get them out of there. They won't think anything about seeing you with Ron. If they catch me approaching him, they'll kill Syreena. I didn't have to worry about that at first because they needed her too much. Now, though, since they have Raven, she's expendable." His fists were tight balls as he spoke.

"Why do these people want them? Who are they?"

Cord's hazel eyes shifted uneasily. "They're using their blood for experiments. 'SH' stands for Super Human. Apparently, they think they can raise human performance."

"Using their...why would they...?"

Cord sliced through the air with his hand. "There's no time for that. The more time we talk, the more time those bastards have to hurt them."

Karen's stomach did a flip as she thought about Raven's smile, his blue eyes, and the fact she felt more comfortable with him than she ever felt with another person. "Tell me what to do. Ron calls me every day. I don't always talk to him, but he never misses a call."

Cord gave Karen the details she would need to

help save Raven, then stopped abruptly. He reached behind her to pick something up.

Karen stared at what he held. "My phone! What's my phone doing here?"

Cord frowned again. "I was hoping it was Raven's. I wanted to find out who else he's called since he's been here." He handed her the phone and shrugged.

After noticing two calls had been made from her phone, Karen looked up at Cord again. "Raven?"

Cord looked sheepish. "Imagine so. I guess he thought he needed it."

She shook her head and stuck the phone in her purse. "I'm ready."

He sighed. "Good." The next few minutes were spent gathering details and ironing out their plan to free Raven and Syreena.

Chapter Five

Raven awoke with a blaring headache. The wounds from the darts had healed, but he was weak, hungry, and his mouth was dry. He lifted his lids slowly. He was in a crate in the warehouse again. More iron crates, some empty, and others holding various kinds of animals surrounded him. More than anything, he needed to know Karen was safe.

"He's awake again, and he's shifted back! I gave him enough to make him forget how to be anything *but* a wolf!"

He recognized the voice from his first visit to the warehouse. The man was large, blonde, and smelled evil. His limbs tingling, Raven tried unsuccessfully to move.

The blonde man started toward Raven. Ron stopped him. "What are you doing? You've already given him three double injections! He wasn't supposed to have more than one. Don't give him more. He's had too much and has been shifting back and forth all day. We don't know what effect this stuff will have on him."

Raven was surprised Ron of all people wanted to keep him alive. Then again, if he'd wanted him dead, he certainly could have finished the job at Karen's. He seemed satisfied just making Raven *wish* he was dead. With Syreena captured, he found himself in a position he'd become accustomed to throughout his life—on his own and fending for himself.

Blondie pushed Ron. "Get out of my way! Moore put me in charge, and he said he wanted results."

Before Ron could stop Blondie, another dart

pierced Raven's side. It lodged between his ribs. Involuntarily, his body shifted back to wolf form and he lost consciousness again.

****

"Hello?" Karen fought to keep anger out of her greeting at the sound of Ron's voice.

"Hey, beautiful. How about dinner?"

Karen sighed, not wanting to sound too eager. "I've been thinking. Why don't I fix dinner at your place? You're always taking me out. It's my turn."

He hesitated. "Sure! Tonight?"

"I guess I can whip something up tonight. Might as well. Around six-thirty?"

"Yeah! This is an unexpected surprise. I'll come pick you up."

Karen smiled, wishing she could poison him. *Idiot.* Every time she thought about the fact she'd actually slept with him, she was tempted to take another shower. "That's why they're called surprises. I'll drive. I have to go by the store and pick up some things."

"Oh, okay."

"See you tonight." Karen hung up, her nerves a tight coil around her throat. What if she did something wrong? Would they kill Raven? His sister? What if Ron figured out what she was up to? *What if? What if?* She paced until she was nearly too tired to stand. Just two days ago, she hadn't known Raven existed. Now, she couldn't cope with the possibility of never seeing him again.

****

Raven awoke to a loud noise. He wasn't sure if it originated outside or inside the warehouse. Still in wolf form, Raven watched Ron open the crates and draw blood from the captive animals. Every part of his body was in pain, the excessive forced shifts taking a toll on his system. He shook with the effort to stand. His limbs simply would not respond.

He heard Syreena speaking to one of the guards, but hadn't been able to make out what she was saying. The anger in her tone sounded like a cover for fear.

He would never forgive himself for letting his guard down. The note left at the hotel warned him to stay away from Karen. Still he couldn't believe she was involved with anything causing harm to animals. Although Ron had gotten into her house, Raven knew from experience it was not hard to do. Besides, he felt Karen's instinctive distaste for Ron.

The loud boom sounded again. This time, Raven was certain it came from outside. Seconds later, he heard feet hitting the concrete floors, running. He couldn't turn to see what was happening. He tried to move again, adrenaline pooling in his stomach when a body landed on top of the crate he was in. Suddenly, he smelled another shifter, the same shifter who left his scent at the hotel, accompanied by several humans. Next, he heard several soft popping sounds followed by heavy objects hitting the floor. Silencers. They were using silencers.

Someone jiggled his crate. A flurry of activity ensued and Raven realized the animals were being rescued. "Help him." It was Syreena's voice. She must have been talking to the other shifter, because he came closer and lifted Raven from the crate floor. He felt Syreena's hand in his fur, and an additional heart beat a quick rhythm inside her body. Not only had she found her mate, she was expecting. This explained the absence of her voice in his head.

Syreena's mate started to run, each step jarring Raven's aching body. The smell of sulfur reached Raven's nose just before he was placed in the bed of a truck. Syreena jumped in to cushion his throbbing head in her lap.

The truck lurched forward and Syreena spoke softly. "Rave, we got Doctor Ron and Evan, the blonde guy. Karen helped us. Unfortunately, the one they all called Mr. Moore got away. He'll turn up again, though."

Raven closed his eyes, too tired and sick to be elated over Karen's safety or his freedom. Syreena grew silent, resting her cheek against his head. He wanted to ask how much Karen knew. He wondered if she would have helped if she had known they weren't human. Even packs refused to accept them until they found out how useful they could be. He winced, but not from physical pain. Would Karen feel like she'd slept with an animal?

****

Karen jumped up from the sofa, covering her mouth with her forearm. On the ten o'clock news was a vivid image of the warehouse up in flames. She hadn't been able to eat much, but other than that, her dinner at Ron's went off without a hitch. Cord was in and out so quickly and silently, she could hardly believe he'd gotten the key and code before he left. She'd given Ron a string of plausible excuses as to why there would be no sex. That had been nearly three hours ago, and she hadn't heard anything from Cord or Raven.

She ran to the restroom, her stomach ridding itself of what little she managed to eat. The thought of Raven trapped in that building was more than she could stand. In that moment her thoughts about developing feelings for him were old news. She was undeniably, unbelievably in love with Raven. She put her head in her hands. *Oh dear God, help me.*

Karen had just rinsed her mouth out and splashed cold water on her face when she heard the doorbell. She flew to the door, her feet barely touching the floor.

She opened the door to find Cord standing there with a large, limp wolf in his arms. "I didn't know where else to take him."

A gorgeous woman stood at his side. She had the same impossibly black hair and blue eyes as Raven. “Syreena?”

Syreena nodded, leaning in to hug Karen. “Thank you for everything you’ve done.” Karen watched as Syreena kissed the top of the wolf's head. She thought it odd, but perhaps their entire family loved animals as she did.

“Brutus?” She stroked his silky black fur. “He was in the warehouse, too?” The animal’s breathing was shallow. It was obvious he had been abused.

Cord nodded, stepping through the doorway and depositing the wolf on Karen’s sofa. “Is this okay?”

She nodded, watching the door for Raven. Tears rose in her throat before she could ask. “Where’s Raven?” When Cord didn’t answer immediately, Karen went to the kitchen and poured water for Brutus, bringing it back into the room. She dipped her fingers in the water and rubbed droplets along his mouth, stroking his fur with her free hand. Still crying, she began to murmur to him as she covered his large, furry body with a cashmere blanket.

When Karen glanced at Cord, he looked uneasy again, his eyes shifting from her to Brutus. Finally, he sighed. “Uh, he’ll be here soon. He’s pretty weak, but…” His gaze fell on Brutus again.

“But what, Cord? Where is Raven, damn it? Answer me!”

Syreena frowned, matching Cord’s expression. She turned to Cord, her voice barely above a whisper. “I told you we shouldn’t have brought him here.” She pressed her hand to her lower abdomen.

Karen glanced at the couple’s faces, a question in her gaze. “Are you all right?”

Syreena answered. “Yes. If not for this baby, there’s no telling what more they would have done to me. They thought I was worth more because I’m pregnant.”

Karen frowned. "I still don't understand what they..."

She felt a wave of electricity and turned to look at Brutus. When she turned back, Syreena was glaring at Cord, her lips pursed in frustration.

Cord rolled his eyes and sighed. "Ree, she needs to know. She loves him."

Karen frowned. "I *am* still in the room. What am I supposed to know?"

Brutus began to shudder, his large frame threatening to leave the sofa. Karen started to run for her medical bag.

"No. You need to see." Cord's voice was calm as he appeared to block her path so quickly she didn't see him move. He turned her around so she had a view of Brutus, who continued to shake violently until his limbs began to lengthen, the thick hair disappearing.

Karen's legs became watery, abandoning her as she landed in Cord's arms.

****

Mr. Moore limped into the opulent foyer. "James! Come at once and pack my bags."

A short, stocky man with thin gray and blonde hairs slicked over his large balding pate approached as quickly as his legs would carry him. He reached toward his employer, a lilting Irish accent adding urgency to his words. "Oh, Mr. Moore! What happened to you, sir?"

Mr. Moore waved him away. "Don't waste time asking questions, man! Do as you are told! I will be leaving for my island estate. Please provide enough for a lengthy stay."

James nodded and moved away as quickly as he had approached.

Mr. Moore stopped in his living area, his injured leg nearly giving out. "Damn those blasted creatures! Abominations, all of them! Time. All I need is more time to develop a stronger serum. I underestimated their intelligence. It will not happen again."

****

Karen woke the next morning in her bed. She sat up and memories from the previous night flooded her at once. "Raven." She whispered his name, hoping she wasn't alone in the house.

Syreena stepped into the room wearing a tentative smile. "I heard you moving, so I thought I'd come in and say good morning."

Karen returned her smile. "Good morning. How's Raven?"

Syreena came closer and sat on the side of the bed. "He's still a little weak, but getting better. We heal very quickly."

Karen worried her bottom lip with her teeth. After a moment of awkward silence, she laughed nervously. "I don't know where to start, what to ask. So, what are you, exactly?"

"We call ourselves shifters. There are lots of other names for us, but I think you should be talking to my brother." She hesitated.

"Is he here? And Cord?" She laughed. *Hysteria.* "Seems so backward, me asking you when it's my house." Karen looked down and started pulling loose threads from the bedspread. "I feel so bad about fainting like that…this is just beyond anything I've ever imagined. Well, maybe I've imagined it. I just never expected any of it to be real. I guess I just got overwhelmed."

Syreena smiled again. "I think I understand. Rave is in your guest room, and Cord went home to take care of some things. He wanted to make sure everyone knew to keep a watch for the man who is apparently behind the whole warehouse thing. Then there's the business with the police." She stood. Karen wanted to ask her so many questions, but she knew Syreena was right. She should be talking to Raven.

Confident Syreena was taking good care of Raven, Karen showered and dressed before she left her bedroom. She went straight to her guestroom, where Syreena sat quietly, watching him sleep. When Syreena saw her, she stood to leave. She touched Karen's arm. "He's worried about your pets. Says he still wants to help you with your no-kill shelter."

Karen stammered. "Th-they're f-fine. I took all four of them to my clinic."

Doubt and hope flitted across Syreena's beautiful face, so much like her brother's. "I guess I should leave you two alone." She did.

Karen sat beside him. The hard planes of his face were perfect, his black waves framing his face now that it wasn't tied back. She reached to move the same stray curl that always seemed to find its way into his face, and his eyes fluttered open. They were unfocused at first, but when he smiled, the entire room seemed to brighten, the light striking his canines at just the right angle.

Karen shook her head as she whispered. "I must be insane."

She saw the concern in his blue eyes before he spoke. "Syreena told me that you..."

Karen placed her index finger against his lips. "Before you say anything else, tell me you don't have any more secrets."

"No more secrets."

"There was something innately different about you. I felt it. I've never been able to let myself go with anyone else before. Call it human instinct, I guess. I was overwhelmed at first, and I should be angry with you for not telling me before we slept together. Maybe it's because I sensed something from the beginning, but none of it changes the way I feel."

He looked away. "And how is that?"

He still didn't look at her, as if somehow not looking could cushion the blow if she didn't care for him enough to accept what he was.

She touched his cheek with her palm. "I left you sleeping yesterday morning so I could make breakfast for you." She stopped, turning him to face her. "I have *never* done anything like that before. I think I started falling in love with you the moment I met you, and when I almost lost you, well...that hasn't changed."

"I think I fell in love with you when you stepped out of the shower."

She laughed and hugged him, pulling back when he gasped in pain. "Sorry. I'm just so glad you're okay. When did you? Oh, you *dog!*"

He shook his head, the corners of his lips curving into a smile. "Animal lovers."

Karen laughed, moving in to kiss him. "Make that singular. Animal lover, and proud of it."

She had planned to give him a nice closed-mouth kiss and pull away, but he wrapped his arms around her, pulling her closer. When she pressed against him, she drew back. "Um, wait a minute."

Raven nodded, a confused look on his handsome face.

Karen closed the bedroom door. When she came back, she frowned slightly, nibbling her bottom lip with her teeth. "Is Cord like you and Syreena?"

"You mean is he a shifter?"

She ran her palm lightly down his chest, watching the silky black hairs spring back in place as her hand glided over them. "Mm-hm."

"Yes. Why do you ask?" His extreme politeness returned, and his voice sounded strained.

"We can talk about this later when you feel better." She turned to leave. He caught her arm fast, before she had barely taken a step away. He pulled her back to the bed.

"Tell me what's on your mind, Karen." His voice was even raspier than usual.

"I was just thinking because Syreena's pregnant."

Raven frowned, waiting for her to continue.

She sighed. "Okay, obviously our bodies are compatible enough to have sex, but can we...will we be able to have children? I mean, would I be able to carry your child?"

"Technically, that's two questions, and honestly, I don't know the answer to either of them. I can tell you we're born in our human form, though." Every fear of rejection and disappointment was evident as he gazed into her eyes. "Do you think you'd want my children?"

She smiled, desire pooling at her core. "Well, not right this minute. I was just thinking about it. I think we need lots and lots of practice first." She leaned in and kissed him again, allowing more of her weight to rest on his chest. She broke the kiss almost as soon as their lips met, reminding herself he was still in pain. "I'm sorry. I know you're really not up to this. I don't want to hurt you.

He smiled, running his tongue along the tips of his incisors. "Hurt me. I heal really fast."

Karen didn't need another invitation. She straddled him and commenced with practice sessions one, two, and three.

About the author...

Dariel's love for books, as well as her fascination with animals and all things paranormal, prompted the beginning of her writing journey at the tender age of 8. A classically trained pianist and vocalist with a degree in piano and vocal performance and a master's in counseling psychology, she is presently studying for a Ph.D. in Instructional Design.

She lives on the Gulf Coast with her 3 large house dogs, where she is working on her next paranormal romance.

Visit her at:
http:// www.pendarielraye.blogspot.com

Marek's New World

by

Renee Wildes

Dedication

To Vee, critter extraordinaire—and my friend

Chapter One

Wrongness. The fine hairs rose on the back of Cheyenne Rafferty's neck. She crouched beside the ice-laced pond and surveyed the too-still Montana forest. She sniffed the air, catching only the normal scents of an early mountain spring: spicy Ponderosa pines, new quaking aspen leaves and the mineral tang of mud-tinged snow. She strained to listen. Silence. Dead silence. No animals, no birds. She wanted to melt down into true-self and let Sister take over. The white wolf's senses were more acute, but she needed to record and report for the Forestry Service. Hard to do with paws and a growl.

Biting her lip with a frown, Cheyenne pulled her handheld radio from her belt. "Eagle Two to Nest."

"What's up, Chey?" her cousin Amber asked.

"You got anything from USGS on recent seismic readings?"

"No alerts for Kootenai. Why?"

Cheyenne closed her eyes and reached for the inner stillness that allowed her soul to touch the earth. *Wrongness.* A single ripple on the water's mirror surface. "Too quiet. Sister's twitchy."

"I'll double-check." Silence on the line, then "Hang on, Chey. Tremor appeared out of nowhere."

The earth shivered, a sigh building to a low groan. With a mighty heave, the ground arched like the back of a newly saddled mustang. Cheyenne lost her balance and tumbled to the ground. The pond crested into a single giant wave that crashed over her. Boulders cart wheeled down the mountainside toward her truck. With the speed of thought, Sister emerged. The nimbleness and claws of the white wolf gave her better purchase on the shifting ground than her human self. She danced amidst the rock slide, Cheyenne's thoughts buried beneath Sister's instinct to stay up, keep moving. It seemed forever, but was over within minutes.

Sister shook herself free of debris. Now that it was safe, Sister retreated. Muscles stretched, joints popping as bones lengthened. Skin burst through fur. There was a moment of dizziness, of disorientation as Cheyenne straightened upright and rose in her wet filthy uniform. She grimaced at the cold, clammy material clinging to her skin. She wished she could shift into clean dry clothes, but that wasn't how it worked. What you left was what you re-entered, exactly as you left it. A little extra fur made back into clothing. She wrung out her dripping ponytail and tossed the scraggly ash blonde rope of hair back over her shoulder. Her boots squelched in the mud as she picked up her squawking radio. "I'm fine. What, no warning?"

"It was gone just as quick. If it wasn't for the 'graph, it'd be like it wasn't there. Six-point-two, very localized. I think it barely brushed the towns, but Evan's checking. Phone and power lines are down. What's the damage there?"

Cheyenne looked around. Rocks had carved jagged paths through the underbrush. Evergreen trees lay toppled in every direction, the pond a shallow mud puddle. "Looks like an amateur logging event. I need to check my truck." She returned the radio to her belt and half-staggered, half-slid down a newly created trail to the gravel road where she'd parked.

A moan sounded from nowhere, from everywhere, like a dying moose magnified a hundredfold, building to a roar. A sense of glee, of malice and rage, hammered into her.

Cheyenne drew her service revolver, looking around for the source of the sound. Sister cowered deep within. Cheyenne frowned. Sister didn't cower from anything, not even a mother grizzly with new cubs. Whatever it was, her inner wolf wanted no part of it.

She quickened her pace. Her other weapons were in the truck. This early in the season, bears weren't out unless they were critically short on body fat. For taking soil samples and measuring water depths, she didn't need weapons. Just a pen, notepad and test tubes.

Was it just her imagination, the feeling of eyes boring into the back of her head? Twice she spun around to see nothing. She cursed her overactive imagination. The truck was just around the next bend…

"Holy Hannah!" Cheyenne plowed to a halt and stared at what was left of the rust-laced, once-slightly battered Dodge Ram. A huge boulder had crashed into the driver's side door, crumpling it like a beer can at a frat party. Another still rested in the bed, but had flattened one side. Something had grazed the front end, hard enough to tear off the bumper and the grille. The fluorescent green puddle beneath the remains of the radiator proved she wouldn't drive out of here. The missing truck parts were probably halfway down the mountainside.

Ram tough. Except for earthquakes. Holstering her sidearm, she blinked back tears, growled her frustration and grabbed her radio. "Truck's gonna need a tow. I'll hoof it down to Brady's cabin and get a lift from there."

"Stick to the road."

Cheyenne shook her head and then rolled her burning eyes. Like Amber could see her. "Cross-country's more direct."

"Stay on the horn, Chey."

"Yes, Mama." Cheyenne stomped over to the truck and kicked the tire. Not helpful, but she felt better. She considered letting Sister make the ten-mile hike, except she needed to haul her gear and wasn't comfortable leaving loaded weapons in an unattended damaged vehicle. Yanking open the passenger's side door, she stuffed her GPS, samples and notebook into her backpack before slipping it on, and slung her shotgun and canteens over her shoulder.

"Now I know why llamas always look so crabby." Bending over to grab a sturdy branch, she stripped it down to a walking staff and headed east down the mountain.

****

Marek awoke to the earth shaking. The seal of his tomb cracked open, shattered by tremors. The earth fell away, revealing the overwhelming brightness of an early afternoon sky. He shielded his watering eyes as best he could from the forgotten brilliance of the sun and stumbled out on shaky legs, stiff from disuse, into an unfamiliar wilderness. No priests, no temple singers or pyramid of stairs. Where was he? *When* was he? If the priests had not summoned him, why was he awake? A mere earthquake should not have sufficed. Surely the land had withstood many during his long sleep?

Long indeed for a pyramid to vanish into forest.

As the ground settled beneath his feet it hit him, like the war club of his sparring partner, Veynar. If he hadn't been summoned, then only one thing would have awakened the Guardians of the Reynak. The accursed Reynak had somehow escaped back into the world of men.

He fingered his *ahnkeisha* crystal amulet. It should have glowed a brilliant lavender as it focused all the belief and will of the people. Instead it was a dull purple-gray, darkened and lifeless. The focus of his strength, powerless. He glanced around. He was to awaken with his brethren at the call of the priests, to lead modern warriors against the Reynak. Except no warriors awaited instruction. Were people aware of the danger?

Marek re-entered the tomb to grab his weapons, the spear and the scythe like *druia*, also tipped with *ahnkeisha* crystals, molded to a razor's edge. First, find Veynar and Levan. Then plan. He took a deep breath, trying to overlap what his mind remembered of the tombs' layout with the current landscape. Veynar slumbered to the east, Levan, north.

A moan grew to a roar. Primordial fear gripped him. His gut burned. He steeled himself, squaring his shoulders as he strode northward, toward Levan. This was why they had stayed behind, to convey firsthand knowledge of the ancient demon. Knowledge was power, even if—he glanced down at the dark amulet—power was not. Leaving the people of this world to be slaughtered by the demon was not an option. Not while he still drew breath.

Marek cursed his stiff limbs. His muscles tingled as the blood flowed faster through his veins. The farther north he traveled, the more twisted the landscape. Foulness tainted the very air. No living souls lingered in the Reynak's wake. He quickened his pace. He stretched his arms overhead, swinging the deadly curved *druia*. Rather than a harvester of grain, it was a harvester of flesh, of lives. Stars willing, of demon.

It hunted, the Reynak. It knew its greatest threat was the three warriors that followed it. The first thing it would do would be to destroy its weakened adversaries, before they could band together as *The Three* and challenge it.

Marek had to get to Levan first.

A pulse of darkness flashed ahead; triumph roared over a man's despairing scream. With a warrior's battle cry, Marek broke into a run. Was he already too late? He knew how fast the Reynak struck. How many times had he witnessed the aftermath of the demon's kills?

The crystal amulet sparked, a faint tingle against his skin. Marek burst into a clearing. The Reynak reared up onto its hind legs and shook its horned head. Levan's lifeless body flopped like a child's doll in the demon's jaws. The Reynak eyed the darkened amulet with a knowing glint in its flame-red eye. Snorting, it tossed its victim at Marek and leapt away.

East.

Levan's body crashed into Marek and bore him to the ground. The *druia* landed several feet away. Horror warred with rage. He'd forgotten the savagery of the Reynak's kills. Levan's blood coated Marek's body—his skin slick with it.

No time to grieve. Veynar was next.

"I shall return for thee, my brother." Marek placed Levan's amulet around his own neck, gathered both their weapons and ran after the Reynak, using the foul taste of demon to track it eastward. Too slow. He recognized futility but continued on. His legs burned, the muscles protesting overuse. Cold air seared his lungs even as sweat trickled down his bare back. Still he ran, leaping over logs and boulders.

Again the Reynak bellowed, followed by a human scream of defiance. True to their code, Veynar fought. Fully charged, the *druia* was a formidable weapon. Even when just a blade, it could still do considerable damage in fast enough hands. Veynar was almost as fast as Marek.

Almost.

The Reynak's roar carried a note of pain. Veynar must have gotten in a solid blow, but the warrior's cry was suddenly silenced. By the time Marek got there, the Reynak was gone. What remained of Veynar's body sprawled in a pool of blood-melted snow. Demon blood coated Veynar's *druia*, a yellow-green ichor.

Marek dropped to his knees, sliding his arm beneath Veynar's shoulders. The Three were broken. He had failed. Failed the gallant old men, who had used every last bit of power they possessed to send the three warriors forward with the Reynak. Failed to protect his friends. Failed to capture the demon.

He was alone.

Or was he? A twig snapped behind him, a footstep. A woman's imperious voice spoke an unintelligible order. He didn't recognize any discernible words, but the tone of command, that of a warrior, was unmistakable. Dropping his weapons to the ground, he held his arms out from his sides. Slowly he stood and turned.

Chapter Two

"Don't move!" Cheyenne pointed her shotgun at the blood-smeared stranger as he stood and turned away from the prone body. Sister growled at the stench of the yellow-green goo that splattered the ground and the men. Cheyenne feared she'd come upon a murderer, but the raw agony in the living man's eyes belied that. "What's your name? What happened here?"

He frowned. Puzzlement clouded his gaze. She repeated her questions in every Native language she knew. Frustrated, her repertoire exhausted, she fell silent and studied him.

Clad only in moccasins and intricately tooled leather breeches that buttered his muscular thighs, he stood tall and straight before her, covered in human blood and bits of that weird sulfur-smelling goo. Long raven hair tied back with a leather thong revealed a proud, almost raptorial visage, with piercing black eyes and a strong jaw. Native cast, but with an aristocratic edge that set him apart.

Used to fit men from the *braw* males of her own Pack, she still couldn't repress a feminine shiver. This was without a doubt the most ripped man she'd ever seen. She wondered if he was some kind of soldier, doubtful with that hair.

Leave it to her to find a romance-cover-model-turned-ax-murderer in the middle of nowhere.

Sister insisted the man was blameless. Involved in the tragedy, but not responsible. Even though the self-recrimination in the man's eyes stated he thought otherwise. No Pack member had ever been murdered in cold blood. They could read a person's intentions and steer clear. Accidents, illness and old age, yes—but never murder.

Cheyenne decided to trust her instincts. "Who are you?" When he didn't respond, she tapped her chest. "Chey-enne."

Comprehension lit his gaze, and he pointed to himself. "Mar-ek." He then indicated the body of the man on the ground. "Vey-nar." His voice choked as he pulled off the dead man's amulet and placed it around his own neck.

"Marek." Relieved he spoke, Cheyenne lowered her gun until the barrel pointed toward the ground. Her eyes widened; his skin reddened where the goo clung. Some kind of acid? That had to hurt, although he appeared not to notice. There was a stream where he could wash, but how to convey to someone who spoke a different language?

She held out a hand, palm up. "Come." She pantomimed as she backed away, motioning him to follow. He nodded once. She forced herself not to react when he picked up his strange weapons and took a step toward her, cradling the lethal-looking crystal blades like an armload of firewood.

Understanding dawned in Marek's eyes when the sound of rushing water reached their ears. He glanced at her; with a forward sweeping motion, she indicated he should go ahead of her. He waded into the icy stream and began to wash away the filth from himself and the blades.

Cheyenne flinched. Those burns looked nasty. She took off her backpack, opened it, pulled out her first-aid kit and a survival blanket. She grabbed a tube of ointment that relieved pain and prevented infection.

Marek watched her approach with wariness in his eyes. She applied some of the ointment on her fingertips and rubbed it into her inner wrist, holding it out so he could see it wasn't harming her. Eye-level with the worst of the burns, she put more on her fingers and reached for his chest. He caught her wrist, stopping her, and frowned.

Dormant femininity uncurled. Cheyenne quivered as his long, calloused fingers caressed her skin. She hoped he wouldn't notice. "Shh, it's okay. Trust me, this will help."

He didn't release his grip, but allowed her touch. He watched her apply the medicine, and she knew the moment his pain eased by the way he jerked and then relaxed. He released her hand and let her tend to the other wounds.

His three pendants drew her gaze. They looked like huge diamonds. Sister growled, bristling at their latent power. Cheyenne didn't recognize the symbols etched into the settings, but she steered clear of the silver metal.

That cliché was all too real for Pack.

He had to be freezing. She held the survival blanket out to Marek. He wrapped it around his shoulders and led the way back to Veynar's body. Cheyenne studied the wounds, spacing the claw marks with her hand. Careful to avoid the mysterious acid compound, she frowned and reached for her radio. "Amber, switch to the alternate frequency." She made the change to ensure privacy. "Let Brady know we've got a mauling death here."

"Will do. How far are you from his cabin?"

"Casting Creek. Maybe a half-hour." Cheyenne turned off the radio. "We have to take him to Brady's." She motioned putting down the weapons and scooping up Veynar's body. To her shock, Marek clenched his jaw and shook his head. His knuckles whitened around the shaft of his oversized scythe. She recalled the mysterious roars from earlier. What manner of creature was out there, that Marek was more concerned with guarding the living than honoring the dead? What would make him so reluctant to release his weapons, even for a moment?

"Come on." Cheyenne headed for Brady's. Brady would help them retrieve Veynar's body. Marek strode beside her, tension in every line. Both of them scanned the surrounding forest. Even when she smelled wood smoke and Brady's cabin came into view, neither relaxed.

Brady awaited them on the porch, dressed in his brown Lincoln County sheriff's deputy uniform. He eyed her dirty, crumpled khakis. "You look like hell. Are you all right? Amber mentioned a body."

"We're fine." Cheyenne handed him her shotgun and slipped off the backpack. "Rockslide got the truck. Found Marek here with his friend Veynar dead. Looked like an animal attack."

Marek motioned for them to go inside.

Brady stared at him with open suspicion.

"Quit being such a cop." Cheyenne frowned at them both. "Brady, he's innocent. It was some kind of animal—something Sister wants no part of. We have to retrieve Veynar's body." She led the way into the cabin; Marek followed.

Brady brought up the rear, watching Marek remove his moccasins before he crossed the threshold and laid his unusual weapons just inside the door. "Those look like acid burns. From what?"

"I don't know. Some kind of gelatinous substance littered the area. Washes right off. Water doesn't make it worse."

"Marek, where are you from?" Brady demanded. Marek looked up from folding the survival blanket but shook his head. Brady then attempted every other language he knew.

Cheyenne rolled her eyes. "Don't you think I tried that, Einstein?" Frustration lit Marek's gaze. Cheyenne placed a hand on his arm, waited until he looked down into her eyes. "It's okay. You're safe now. We'll go back for your friend, and we'll find the creature that did this." Hopefully her tone would reassure him if her words couldn't.

Brady growled, showing a flash of teeth.

Cheyenne whirled on him. "Pipe down, Fido. Try putting yourself in his skin for a second—he's the only one who knows what happened and he can't tell us a thing. Show some empathy."

"Empathy? He's wearing silver."

"Yet more proof that he's not from around here. He doesn't know its effect."

Brady strapped on his revolver, opened the gun case to retrieve a rifle. "Leave the pack. Radio, weapon, stretcher."

"Got it." Cheyenne pulled the stretcher off the wall, disassembling it for transport while Marek watched with wide eyes. "Let him bring one weapon. No one should go unarmed."

Brady's gray eyes ignited in open threat. "One wrong move, he joins his friend." He pointed to Marek's cache of weapons and then held up one index finger.

Marek's jaw tightened. He nodded, selecting one of the scythes. Brady tossed him a Missoula Ospreys sweatshirt, but kept his rifle trained on him. Cheyenne knew that was all the concession her alpha older brother was going to give Marek.

"Ladies first?" she quipped.

"Hell, no." Brady handed her the shotgun. "He leads the way. You stay behind me."

Marek set out at a fast walk that had Brady stretching and Cheyenne almost jogging to keep up. Brady opened his mouth to speak, but something in Marek's urgency registered because her brother opted for silence all the way to Casting Creek.

Marek threw up a hand with a clenched fist and plowed to a halt. Cheyenne held her breath. There was that creepy sensation of eyes on her again, the faintest trace of sulfur. She watched Brady turn in a slow circle, frowning as he scanned the surrounding woods. An unnatural silence hung over the landscape, as if every living creature cowered in terror. A shiver ran up Cheyenne's spine and she gripped her shotgun until her knuckles turned white and her fingers ached. Sister tried to emerge. From Brady's rigid stance, he fought the same impulse to shift.

Marek broke into a run, toward where they'd left Veynar's body. With an anguished cry he dropped to his knees.

Veynar was gone.

Brady scanned the blood-soaked ground. "Where's the body?"

Cheyenne stared around. "We left him right here."

Marek leaped to his feet. He pointed to himself and held up one finger. Then he pointed to the ground where Veynar had lain and held up two fingers. Last he pointed toward the northwest, held up three fingers and motioned them to follow him before he took off running.

Brady frowned at his sister. "There's another one?"

"First I've heard of it." Cheyenne dashed after Marek, Brady bringing up rear guard. She ran until she staggered, until her lungs threatened to burst, but Marek showed no signs of slowing. He cleared logs and dodged boulders with ease.

Foulness thickened the air. Sister gagged. A sense of menace pressed against them when they stopped before a crevice in the rocks. Blood and bits of flesh littered the ground, but again there was no body. Cheyenne fought nausea as she bent over, hands on her knees, and struggled to draw breath through the knifing pain in her side.

Marek collapsed in on himself. He dropped to

the ground like a retracting spyglass, posture screaming defeat, despair.

Black laughter rolled over them and then was gone.

Brady glared at his sister. “What the hell is going on?”

Chapter Three

Cheyenne took a deep breath to stop her trembling. It didn't help. "Animals don't laugh."

"There's no such thing as the boogeyman," Brady declared.

"Then you explain it!"

"I can't! All I have are two bloody crime scenes with no victims and a witness who can't tell me what happened."

Marek staggered to his feet. Motioning around him at the clearing, he shook his head and pointed back toward Brady's.

"I don't think we should stay out here in the open," Cheyenne said. "Can you give us a lift back to my trailer?"

Brady frowned at Marek. "He's not staying with you."

"Well he can't stay alone in your cabin while you're at work. You can't leave him out here with whatever-it-is running around killing people and stealing their bodies." She couldn't bring herself to voice the thought, *or eating them*. It was enough to see Brady's jaw tighten. The same thought had already occurred to him.

"Brady, Sister's adamant he's harmless."

Brady eyed the crystal-tipped scythe with a snort.

"I've got two bedrooms, a hot shower and food. You think I can't take care of myself?"

He didn't rise to the bait. She was trained in self-defense, she was armed and she was Pack. "He's no stray."

"No, he's a man without money, friends or gear. He can't even speak the language. He's filthy, exhausted and in shock. He needs food and rest. I have a radio."

"I'll check on the tow truck," he grumbled.

She stood on tiptoe to kiss his cheek. "Thank you."

"Let's get your stuff. I'll drop you off on the way into town—if your trailer's still in one piece. Otherwise, you're going to Gran's." Brady's tone brooked no argument.

"Deal." Cheyenne set off toward the cabin. Marek didn't relax until they entered the building. Cheyenne found his reaction interesting. "Maybe it can't enter homes."

"What, like a vampire it has to be invited in? You watch too many movies." Brady grabbed Cheyenne's backpack and pointed to Marek's weapons. "He can put those in the back."

They piled into his Expedition. Marek closed his eyes, his knuckles white around the armrest, but never made a sound. He acted like he'd never ridden in a moving vehicle before.

Who was this man?

Cheyenne half-expected him to kiss the ground when they got out, but Marek just glared at the SUV, then turned to her trailer.

Brady circled her home and started the generator. "I don't smell any leaks and it looks solid enough."

"I've got food and fuel for a month. Now get to work."

With a last frown at Marek, Brady drove off.

Cheyenne smiled at Marek and unlocked her door. "Come on in." Motioning him to follow her inside, she dropped her backpack just inside the door and unlaced her boots. She grimaced at the pile of clean laundry on the recliner she'd folded, but neglected to put away. Geological survey charts lay scattered across the kitchen table and dirty breakfast dishes littered the sink. Her cheeks warmed. "Sorry for the mess."

She locked the door behind them and returned her shotgun to the gun case. The trailer had always seemed big enough for one. Until Marek trailed behind her. He crowded the too-narrow hallway with his heated male presence. Every Pack hormone went on high alert. She indicated the second bedroom and pointed to him.

He ducked into the tiny room, lit by a single west-facing window, eyeing the twin bed, nightstand and chest of drawers. She pulled back a curtain to reveal the closet and pointed at his weapons. Marek put them in the cubby and closed the curtain. He looked around him and nodded, then turned to her.

She sucked in a breath when his gaze met hers. Unexpected desire made her blood shimmer with heat. Her hand groped for the handle on the top drawer. Blindly she pulled out a pair of men's socks and boxer-briefs, fumbling to withdraw a pair of black sweatpants. Marek was taller and leaner than Brady, but the clothes would do in a pinch. At least they were clean. "I'll show you the bathroom…where you can clean up…"

Awareness and amusement shone in his eyes. She shut her mouth and backed away. Cheyenne grabbed towels from the linen closet and led the way into the bathroom. Her cheeks flamed as she mock-demonstrated the use of the toilet and showed Marek how to turn on and adjust the water for the shower. She put out another tube of ointment on the counter by the sink. She grabbed her shampoo, tugged on her hair, poured some in her hand, and did the same for her shower gel. Lucky for him she went in for herbal scents rather than something girlie.

"I'll leave you to it." She closed the door.

****

Marek wanted to laugh as he watched her retreat. What a wondrous place this future was—heat without fire, warm rain for bathing, and a way to remove body waste without going outside where the Reynak waited. So long as they stayed within manmade structures, the Reynak could not touch them.

It hated men for that reason, amongst others.

Marek stripped and entered the shower cubicle, washing away the grime of untold centuries. He frowned. Who would have thought languages could shift so much as to be unintelligible? It gave him the sinking feeling that the barrier the elders had erected to contain the Reynak had lasted much longer than anyone had thought possible. How long had he been imprisoned?

He shuddered, recalling the last memory he had of *before*—the feeling of panic as he tried to draw one last breath and failed, as his heart stuttered in his chest and then stilled. Momentary panic that he had made a terrible mistake, before everything went black and he knew nothing at all.

Until today. He was not supposed to do this alone, but he was all there was. There had to be a way to communicate. He turned off the water and grabbed the thick, fluffy drying cloth. The dye was amazing. What plant or shell did the blue come from? The same blue as her eyes. He applied more of the cream that stopped the pain from the Reynak's venom, and dressed. The clothes Chey-enne had given him, with the shirt from Bra-dy, were soft and warm, but of an unknown fiber.

Chey-enne. She was a marvel. A true daughter of the earth, with a split soul. His body stirred at how her eyes went dark and hazy with need, how the warm scent of her body called to his. Such a passionate, forthright soul. At least her kind had survived the ages.

He stiffened. If her people were still around, perhaps old legends of *before* still survived. The children of the earth had once been the foremost story weavers in the land. Surely something, some hint of his people and their struggle, their sacrifice, survived even now. The thought that no one remembered them, that they had been swept away by the passing of time, was too horrific to contemplate.

An idea tickled the edges of his mind. In addition to being one of the ablest warriors, he had been chosen for the strength of his mind. He was one of the few that could communicate without words. A talent the children of the earth had also possessed. Chey-enne's shields were strong, but shields tended to weaken during sleep, especially in the young and unwary. If he could touch her dreams, he could change them. Share his memories so she would understand the danger. In doing so, he could also acquire hers. And the language he needed.

He shied from that thought. One did not just help himself to another's mind without invitation. That was anathema, akin to rape, a crime punishable by death. But how was he to ask permission when she understood not a word he said?

The needs of the many outweighed the needs of the few...or the one. But a lesser degree of wrong was still wrong.

Haunting flute music drifted down the hall. Running a hand through his wet hair, Marek strode out into the main room of her unusual lodge—and stopped. There were no musicians. Chey-enne set the last dish on a small drying rack. The meaty smell of fowl wafted from a big box standing against the wall. His stomach gurgled to life. The table was cleared. The folded clothes, gone.

She still needed to bathe and change. Chey-enne turned at his approach, and her eyes widened. He paused at the flash of interest in her gaze, veiled by her lashes. The air thickened around them. So, he had not imagined her earlier reaction to him.

He had not anticipated this complication. Pain lanced his heart. There had been no one since Ama. His dove. The Reynak had slain them, her and a half-dozen other women, while they worked in the fields outside the village. Innocent women. Their screams haunted him even now. He still saw the accusation in Ama's sightless eyes. Her blood stained his soul.

If he traded dreams with Chey-enne this night, all would be revealed to her. There could be no secrets in such a bond. Could he let another share a path he himself feared to tread?

Chey-enne glanced down at her appearance, and her cheeks flushed. She mumbled something and retreated down the hall.

As soon as she left, taking the scent of need with her, he could breathe again. Marek wandered into the main room. The music emanated from a small white box atop a table. He sat in the chair, listening to the flutes.

The smell of food distracted him. Restless, he got up to pace. Stopping where Chey-enne had washed dishes, he pulled a cup from the branch of a small, carved tree. Remembering how Chey-enne had turned the handle to make water come, he half-filled the cup with tepid water and took a cautious sip, not knowing how his stomach would react. The elders had cautioned him to take it slow when he reawakened.

Thus far, his day had been anything but slow.

The water hit his stomach, and it clenched in shock. A wave of nausea rolled over him, but he breathed through it and the feeling subsided. He took another sip and carried the cup over to the clear-covered hole in the wall to watch the sun setting behind the trees. He tried to block the sound of running water from down the tunnel. The mental image of warm water streaming over Chey-enne's naked curves was…unsettling.

To distract himself he wandered about the room. Potted plants hung from hooks in the ceiling, vines trailing down the sides. A fragrant dish of dried leaves, petals, bark and herbs sat in the middle of a long low table in the center of the room. There were turtles everywhere. Pottery painted with their images, little engraved statues, pictures on the walls.

Odd, but charming. Marek frowned. The room overflowed with her presence. A blanket draped over the back of the long chair on the other side of the room. He picked it up. Her scent—warm, wild, woman—clung to the fuzzy folds. He dropped it.

Shadows lengthened in the darkening room as the sun dipped behind the trees. The sound of bare feet padded behind him, and with a "click", the room flooded with light. Startled, he turned to see light blazing from an odd-shaped statue on the small table beside the chair, banishing the shadows.

All he could do was stare. The pale skin of Chey-enne's bare arms and shoulders shimmered above the clingy material of her top, held in place by the thinnest of straps. Strands of wet hair ended just above her breasts. The faint outline of her nipples showed beneath tiny yellow flowers on a blue background.

An all-but-forgotten heat sparked. His body clenched in a way that had nothing to do with the water. Marek took a deep breath to steady himself, realizing his mistake when her scent curled around him, through him. Cursing his unexpected weakness, he turned away.

Chapter Four

Cheyenne stared at the rigid set of Marek's back and shoulders. Odd how his rejection stung. She'd not set out to tempt him. What was so seductive about plain old faded flannel sleepwear anyway? It was comfortable, naught else. But she hadn't imagined the too-brief flare of heat in his chocolate eyes.

The timer dinged. She left him to his thoughts over Sister's protests. Setting the table for two, she pulled buttered acorn squash and chicken potpies from the oven, then grabbed spinach salad and raspberry vinaigrette from the fridge.

"Marek," she called, filling salad bowls.

He entered the kitchen with an air of resignation, as if he'd reached some sort of decision he wasn't altogether happy with. He sat down in the chair across from her and avoided her gaze throughout the uncomfortable meal. Cheyenne watched him pick his way through a small piece of squash, plain salad and one potpie. She'd have bet money on a larger appetite, a man his size, and lost. He seemed distant, melancholy.

Sister was agitated. She wanted to go out and run under the moon and stars—a nightly ritual. A bad idea, until they figured out what was out there. If only Marek could say what was wrong.

The sound of the radio broke the awkward silence. Brady's voice, strident as always. "Chey, pick up."

Cheyenne moved to the desk in the living room, where the radio and her computer sat. "I'm here.

How's my truck?"

"Everything okay?"

"Fine—we just finished supper. What about my truck?"

"Joe towed it to his place. He can have parts from the dealership in the morning. It should be back in your hands by tomorrow night. Evan said he'll give you a ride in the morning, and drop those samples you collected off at the lab."

Cheyenne sighed, relieved. "Sounds good."

"You sure you're okay?"

"Why do you keep asking me that?"

"Because Gran's pitching a fit. Amber says she keeps muttering about a 'blood moon.' Hell, Gran called me three times at the station. Dispatcher's gonna have my hide. She wants to see you and your new friend ASAP."

"Tell her we'll drive over tomorrow night after I get my truck back," Cheyenne said. "I've got work to do tomorrow."

"So do I," Brady groused, "and it's not playing go-between for you and Gran." He paused. "Why is it the older we Pack get, the freakier we get?"

Cheyenne had to laugh. Her pragmatic older brother was the most literal person she knew. Their grandmother, a practicing witch and midwife for the past century, drove him to distraction with her hunches and dream interpretations. "Longevity gives us too much time to think," she replied.

"You're telling me. Well, gotta go—break's done. Want me to stop by when my shift ends?"

"No, I'll be asleep by then. I'll call you tomorrow."

"Okay. 'Night, brat."

"'Night, bro'." Cheyenne glanced at Marek. How was she ever going to coax him into another vehicle? She put away the leftovers and did the dishes, then turned off the kitchen light and rejoined Marek. He stared at the oversized, Montana geographical map on the wall, tracing the paths of the rivers and lakes that watered Kootenai National Forest.

She moved to his side and pointed to a spot on the map. "We're right here." She pointed to herself, and him, then down at the floor and tapped the map.

Marek nodded and returned to studying. How much did he understand? She left him to it. She had the latest land management report to wade through—guaranteed to induce a good night's sleep in the worst insomniac. She couldn't wait to see the latest insanity the committee-from-hell proposed.

The third time she reread the same paragraph she gave up and put the folder down. She'd just rest her eyes for a minute... A hand shook her shoulder and her eyes snapped open to focus on Marek's face. She glanced at the clock on the wall. Eight o' clock. Holy Hannah, she was turning into an old lady.

She stifled a yawn. "Guess it's time to turn in." She let him help her to her feet and went over to turn off the light. Sister's eyes immediately adjusted to the moonlight, but Cheyenne waited a minute in case Marek still had trouble. Then she turned and made her way down the hallway to her room. He followed her with no apparent difficulty.

She turned at the door and smiled at him. "'Night. See you in the morning." She slipped into her room, shut the door and collapsed into her unmade bed. "Sleep. Must have sleep..."

****

Marek lay down atop his bed. She had to smile at him, open and trusting. Would she understand the necessity of what he was about to do, or would she view it as a betrayal? He racked his brain for another way. Nothing came. This was it.

Taking slow deep breaths, he cleared his mind of the day's events, of his emotions. More difficult than he recalled. He was out of practice. He drifted, seeing himself lying on the bed, the shadows of the furniture in the indirect moonlight. He shut off the visual, feeling the hard surfaces of the wall, the furniture. Then he shut off the feeling, the observing, becoming a blank cloud of non-being, expanding through the wall into the next bedroom.

Chey-enne tossed and turned on her mattress. Seeing her soft skin bathed in moonlight, glowing as she sprawled across tangled bedding, made Marek's heart beat faster. As blood pumped through his veins, need thickened hot and heavy in his groin. Awareness of his own body tumbled him back into burning flesh. He cursed the fire licking along his skin. He had to reenter the calm, or it would never work.

One breath…two. Clear mind. Stillness. Cool nothingness. Again he misted free of his body, through the wall. Marek hovered above her, a passive vapor of nothingness. Jumbled images flowed into him, unknown people and events. He let those slide through him, catching nothing, allowing them to fade away. He waited…waited for today's events to surface, the questions.

The world shook; the ground lunged up to meet her as she fell. Chey-enne's dreams were extremely vivid, full of color, sensation and emotion. No wonder dream-swimming was so regulated—it could become addictive. Marek saw himself kneeling beside Veynar's body, heard Chey-enne's order to rise. He felt her human fear, felt her wolf's reassurance.

"What's your name? What happened here?"

The words. He understood her words. The perfect opening. He slid into his dream-self, felt anew the horror and rage at the violent deaths of his friends, and knew she felt it too. He flashed back to a sparring match with Levan and Veynar.

Ama walked by, catching his eye at a critical moment. Veynar's club tapped him on the back of his head, dropping him to his knees. Levan howled with laughter as Marek rubbed the back of his aching head. Ama smiled at him. Shy interest flickered in her doe-soft brown eyes.

Chief Kua's daughter, interested in him? Who would have thought...?

Marek slid away from that thought. He was not there to share his personal loss with Chey-enne. The Reynak...he needed to focus on the Reynak.

A baby cried, too far from his mother as the Reynak stalked him. The woman screamed and ran toward her child. Unarmed, not caring. The closest warrior was Ama's brother, Kiel. He snatched up his druia, *ran to stand between the Reynak and the baby. Alone.*

Ama cried out in denial and lunged for Kiel. Marek grabbed her arm, restraining her out of harm's way as Veynar and Levan ran to join Kiel. She fought him, wolverine-fierce. He held on, grim, desperate, despite the names she called him. He had to protect her from the Reynak, from herself.

The baby's mother grabbed her son up, dashed for the safety of their lodge. Kiel gave her time to get away, distracting the demon with his deadly blade. He was fast. The Reynak was faster.

Ama had hated Marek that day. Chief Kua was grateful he had not lost two children to the demon. That thought twisted Marek's gut. Eventually Kua *had* lost both his children to the Reynak...

They buried Ama in her wedding dress, her and their unborn daughter. Marek barely remembered that day, so clouded was his mind with disbelief, with loss, with hate. The calming drugs the priests had given him barely made a dent in his rage. Veynar and Levan hovered close, lending him their support with wary, worried eyes...

Then came revelation, when the elders emerged from the sweat lodge after days of fasting and prayer. An answer from the gods. A way to remove the Reynak from the here-and-now, banishment behind a wall of earth, *ahnkeisha* and human will. But the hope of success came with a stern reminder from the gods that nothing manmade was eternal; the banishing was doomed to fail. One day…

"Then someone should be there to warn them," Marek said.

Chief Kua shook his head. "The Reynak is immortal. We are not."

"We shall leave records of what we have done," Tith, the head priest, stated.

"And if they understand our cords as well as we understand the Ancestors' wall-paintings?" Marek challenged. "Records are lost or misinterpreted, languages shift, change. The earth itself changes. Would you doom those-that-follow because of ignorance? Would you leave them with the possibility of failure, or a chance for success?"

"What we do could be done again," Veynar said.

Chief Kua shook his head again. "Whom would you condemn? Whom would you ask us to remove from this world, to the coldness of death, only to have them awaken in some unknown time, far away from all they know and love—with the Reynak the only thing familiar? What future is there in that?"

"Whose daughter would you condemn without us?" Marek argued. "I would not ask another to go. I offer to go myself. I have no ties here, none I leave behind. All have gone before me. Because of the Reynak. It has taken everything from me. Maybe someday, someone can find a way to defeat it once and for all. I would be there to see it done."

Their faces said it all. They thought he was a madman. Death-hungry. Marek knew it was a decision made in haste. He also knew he was right.

"You have much to live for, young one," Chief Kua said. "Do not throw away your life so rashly."

"All men die," Marek said. "The Reynak and I are bound by the blood of my kin. My heart is empty, Father. It holds only hate now. I am not a fit companion for anyone, and if I am to die alone, I would have it be for something greater than myself."

"You do not go alone." Veynar spoke up. "We are sworn to brotherhood, and I shall not let you go on such a great adventure without me. Who knows what amazing things we shall see in the not-yet-happened?"

"You need three," Levan added. "Sun, moon and stars. Earth, air and water. Body, mind and heart."

Tith nodded. "So decided, it shall be done."

The preparations took days. Days for the trap to be built. Stone held together with clay-mortar, laced with human blood. The blood of a willing sacrifice, the one-for-many. Marek's, Veynar's and Levan's, ensorcelled with spells of binding and thrice blessed. Days of fasting and prayer. Marek's faith wavered under a wave of hate, a burning need for vengeance, for retribution. The gods must have taken pity on him, for it was that very fire in his heart, which hardened the walls and sealed the Reynak within its prison.

The last thing Marek saw as his eyes closed was the glowing ahnkeisha *crystals around the necks of the priests, of Chief Kua, of every surviving member of the tribe. The power of belief, to send him on his journey into the Great Unknown.*

"Fare thee well, Guardian," Tith said.

And now, here he was, far into the future, alone and friendless, with dark crystals and *The Three* broken. The gods help them all.

Chapter Five

Cheyenne awoke with a start, gasping for air. Her heart pounded like the drums from her dream. Tears soaked her pillow. Her throat ached. She sat up in bed, in the still-dark room; it was not yet dawn. What a horrible dream…

Sister growled. Cheyenne froze. A dream, yet…not a dream. More. A memory. Marek's memories. And there was only one way for *his* thoughts to be in *her* head.

He'd put them there.

With a shriek, she jumped out of bed and stomped to the next room. Not bothering to knock, she burst in. Marek awaited her. The amulets lay atop the chest of drawers; with no warding silver around his neck, she had a straight shot to his throat. Their eyes met; as if he read her intent, he raised his head.

"Give me one good reason why I shouldn't," she snarled.

"I can't," he replied. "What I did broke every rule."

She blinked at his even-handed admission of guilt. "Why?"

His eyes flashed in the dark. "Your people were supposed to be ready! Instead, I find you oblivious."

Cheyenne curled her hand around his throat. This close, his heat, his scent caressed her with every breath she took. A new fury took hold as her treacherous body stirred to life. "I'm not your damned playground!"

"I needed your language." A muscle ticked in his

jaw. "What's killing people is no wild animal. Brady's wrong—the boogeyman does exist."

"So I've seen." Her fingers tightened ever so slightly. "You're telling me the Balrog is real."

Marek frowned. "I do not know that word."

"A fire demon in a legend recorded by a man named Tolkien."

"Legends often have a grain of truth. How was he defeated?"

"Slain by a wizard with an elven sword."

His eyes lit up. "A wizard is like a shaman? That might do. Where can I find one?"

Sister growled. "It's just a story, Marek!" Cheyenne burst out. "It's not real. There are no wizards or magic swords."

"Then we are in real trouble, because your Balrog—my Reynak—*does* exist, and it shall kill your people as easily as it did mine, without pause for thought or regret. That's what it does, what it has always done. Women and children, not just men."

"Why?" Cheyenne pressed. "There has to be a reason."

Marek stared at her in disbelief. "It's a demon. It kills people. That's what it does. *That's* your reason."

"No. Not good enough. Even the devil had his reasons." Cheyenne released him, knelt before him beside the bed. She slid her hand to his cheek and searched his face. "Why are you here? Why did you come? For your own revenge? Or for us?"

Marek closed his eyes and swallowed hard.

"Don't close your eyes. Don't shut me out." Cheyenne's voice was a mere whisper. "You've dragged me into the deepest part of this, Marek. There's no going back for either of us, now. So, which is it?"

The raw pain in his eyes broke her heart.

"Both."

"Fair enough." She backed away. "It's almost dawn. I'll start breakfast."

She considered those dream-memories as she heated butter in a skillet, added frozen spinach and whisked eggs with milk. She heard the shower. *Good luck washing those memories away*, she thought. Having his wife and child ripped from his life, to go home every night to an empty lodge, filled with ghosts and memories…that would play havoc with anyone's mind. Marek wasn't thinking clearly. He was reacting, lashing out at the thing that caused him pain—and perhaps everyone that got in the way.

She needed to talk to Gran. Brady could mock all he wanted. Gran had a unique way of looking at the big picture, without the personal getting in the way of clarity. As the second-oldest Pack member, she held a lot of what-came-before.

Only as a last resort would she consult Old Josiah. The only living person who could personally recall shoeing Paul Revere's horse, he was just plain scary. Half in the past and half in the present, she never knew whom he addressed when he spoke. Like Brady said, freaky.

Three hundred years could do that to a person.

How old was Marek, time-sleeping-wise? Cheyenne poured the eggs over the butter-softened spinach and popped slices of whole wheat bread in the toaster. She mulled over the puzzle that was Marek while she set the table, stirred eggs and buttered toast.

He appeared just as she poured orange juice. "It isn't safe to be outdoors," he told her.

That's all she needed—another bossy big brother telling her what she could and couldn't do. "I'm not cowering behind walls. I have a job to do. Besides, I'll be armed. You can come with me, but you'll have to leave your weapons behind. It would be very hard to explain to my boss why I'm traveling with the grim reaper."

Of course, he didn't get the reference. Cheyenne sighed. It was hard to crack jokes when all she got was a blank stare.

A knock sounded at the door. Marek flinched. Cheyenne laid a hand on his shoulder. "Do you really think the Reynak would knock on the door and politely ask to come in?" she asked.

Evan stuck his head in. "Got any coffee?"

"You're early. Come on in and shut the door," Cheyenne said. "I'll get a pot started."

Evan eyed Marek with curiosity and raised an eyebrow at Cheyenne. "Morning, I'm Evan Lee." He held a hand out to Marek. Marek held his own hand out, and Evan shook it. Marek stared at his hand when Evan released it.

"It's our custom when meeting new people for the first time, and introductions are made," Cheyenne explained. "This is Marek," she told Evan. "He'll be observing me today."

"How exciting for him. He'll be observing you doing paperwork."

Cheyenne turned from filling the coffeepot with water. "No way."

"Way. I'm spending the day at the lab. Your truck's in the shop. Dan and Chris are on field rotation. It's your turn to man the desk—you've got two weeks' worth of catch-up to do."

"I'm not a desk jockey and you know it."

"Woman, your desk looks like a Cathy cartoon and the boss needs you to assist him with that committee report rebuttal. You *did* read it, didn't you?"

"The first part," she confessed. "It put me to sleep."

"Damn." Evan threw her an exasperated look.

"*I'll* make the coffee—*you* park your butt in a chair and start reading."

Marek's lips twitched as Cheyenne stomped into the living room to snatch the folder off the coffee table. She glared at him. "Don't start. You'll be sorry—Evan's coffee is lethal. You'll wish I'd made it." *Paperwork. Crap.*

He innocently ate his eggs. Evan started the coffee and grabbed a plate, helping himself. Cheyenne opened the report, nibbling on toast and scribbling in the margins as she read.

"So, who are you?" Evan asked Marek.

Marek glanced at Cheyenne.

"Foreign exchange student," Cheyenne replied.

Evan eyed Marek with skepticism. "Uh-huh."

"Graduate school," she added.

"I seek a way to improve conditions for my people," Marek clarified. "A way to balance nature and human use."

Evan poured three cups of coffee. "Did I miss the memo?"

"Must have," Cheyenne evaded.

"Did the *boss* miss the memo?"

Cheyenne didn't even bother to answer as she added cream and sugar to her cup. *Lots* of cream and sugar. "Here." She shoved both toward Marek. "Trust me, you'll need these."

"So the boss doesn't know. Oh, this ought to be good." Evan plopped down into his chair.

Marek took a cautious sip of his coffee, and his eyes widened. "*Kany'l?*" His tone was reverent.

"Coff-ee," Cheyenne clarified. "You've had it before?"

Marek threw a cautious glance at Evan. "Only twice, for very special rituals."

"Well, here it's a common stimulant drink," she told him.

His eyes flashed. "Do you people take *everything*

for granted? Is *nothing* sacred to you?"

Cheyenne's temper flared. "Now wait just a minute, Conan. I said I'd help you, and I will, but you can't just show up here and start passing judgment on people."

"So much for UN diplomacy," Evan commented. "Chey, do your homework. Marek, you want some more eggs?"

"Yes." Marek took another sip of coffee.

Breakfast finished in silence. Evan did the dishes while Cheyenne made her notes and Marek contemplated his...*kany'l.* The ride to the station was silent, except for the country music on the radio. Marek sat tensely between Cheyenne and the door, and kept his eyes shut. She almost took his hand, then remembered she was still mad at him. Evan observed them both with quiet amusement. Cheyenne decided she was mad at him, too.

"Rafferty? My office—*now.*" Kane Shields was waiting, arms across his chest, when she strode into the room. "Lee, don't you have an appointment with the lab?"

Evan escaped with a look of relief. Over their boss's shoulder, Amber shot Cheyenne a sympathetic glance.

"Would you like some coffee, sir?" Cheyenne asked.

He glared at Marek. "Who the hell is this?"

"This is Marek, the foreign exchange graduate student I emailed you about," she replied, hanging her coat over her chair. "He's observing today. You didn't forget, did you?"

"Email? What? Oh, hell—was that today?" He scratched his head, looking befuddled. "Well, whatever. Park his butt in a chair with a manual or something and grab a notebook. The governor's head piranha already called twice to remind me about our meeting at eleven, and the sheriff's office called.

Seems some campers had a run-in with a bear last night. Two dead. Chris is investigating."

Marek tensed.

Cheyenne shuddered. Not another attack. *Please, God, let it be just a bear.*

"Local paper's on line one," Amber called.

"Tell them we're investigating and I have no further comment at this time. Let them hound the sheriff for a while," Kane snapped. "Lord, what a day—and it's not even eight yet. Yes, I need some coffee. Bring the whole damned pot."

The door opened, and in strode Collette Rafferty.

"And now my day is complete," Kane groused.

Cheyenne blinked. "Gran, what are you doing here?"

Chapter Six

Marek stared at the Old One, standing proud as royalty, a wooden staff in her hand. Ancient. Ageless. She stared back at him, and he shivered. She Saw. She *Knew*, without him saying a word. He inclined his head. Her eyes smiled at him, and she nodded back, then turned to her granddaughter.

"Brady said you were coming to see me."

"*Tonight*, Gran. I'm working now."

"Could've fooled me," Kane muttered.

"So I thought I'd save you a trip and come and see you."

"Gran, I can't visit with you now." Cheyenne shot Kane a nervous glance. "I'm *working*."

Collette's gaze also traveled to the head ranger, and her eyes narrowed. "So, did you catch your bear, big man? Foul doings...foul doings under a blood moon."

"Oh, for the love of..." Kane rolled his eyes and stomped over to the coffee machine. "Five minutes, Rafferty." He poured a cup and slammed into his office.

"Gran, I have work to do." Cheyenne's expression was equal parts affection and exasperation.

"Aye, you do, girlie." Collette's voice was distant. "You do."

Marek shivered as her gaze sharpened and pinned him. "As do you, traveler. Last of *The Three*."

"What do you know of my people?" he demanded. "What do you know of what-came-before?"

"What came before comes again," Collette

replied, in that same mystical voice that told him she was not entirely in the here-and-now. "It walks among us, its mission unchanged. Would you stop it, river man's son?"

"That's why I'm here," he snapped.

"Is it?" Her eyes sparked with the humor of one catching a child in a lie, knowing. "Is it now? Come with me, then. We have much to discuss." She turned to Cheyenne. "Join us when you finish here."

"Have you seen her desk?" Amber called. "That'll be next month. Hello, Auntie Collette."

"Greetings, child." Collette turned to Cheyenne. "Tonight."

Cheyenne nodded, grabbed a notepad off her desk and retreated into Kane's office.

"She forgot her *kany'l*." Marek caught himself. "Her coffee."

"I'll take it to her as soon as the shouting starts," Amber promised.

"Come." Collette took his arm with surprising strength. "Escort an old woman home. It's not safe to walk alone these days."

Marek caught the undercurrent. "But I am alone, grandmother."

She whacked him across the backs of his thighs with her staff; it stung. "Are you a martyr now? Ready to lie down and die? Or will you fight, warrior? As you promised?"

Marek glared at her. "I have not forgotten my oath, but things have changed."

They strode out onto the bright sunlit porch. A black-cap cocked its tiny feathered head at him from its perch on the railing. Collette smiled. "Yes, some things have changed. Others stay the same. Those who survive are they who change. Too stiff, too resistant, and they crack under pressure like brittle wood fit only for the fire."

"You speak as a shaman, in riddles."

"I am not of The People." Collette shook her head, and for a moment, Marek felt fur brush his hand. "But I have vision, and I am not without power of my own."

"So what do we do first?"

"First?" Her blue eyes twinkled up at him. "First we drive to a clothing store and go shopping. Brady's clothes do nothing for you."

Drive. Marek stared at the tiny green chariot-from-hell. His stomach lurched as Collette opened the door.

"Relax. I'm a much better driver than my grandson."

The morning passed in a dizzying array of traders, with an overwhelming selection of...everything. Marek tried not to think, letting Collette choose a variety of materials and colors. He rebelled at modern footwear, however, allowing only a pair of simple leather boots. By the time Collette determined they had enough, the sun was high in the sky and Marek's head ached from sensory overload.

He collapsed into a chair in her cabin and closed his eyes.

"Here." She handed him a cup of tea. "Willow bark."

He took a sip, recognizing the bitterness, grateful for the painkiller. Finally, something familiar.

"I'll start lunch." She pulled a covered bucket from the cold-box and dumped the contents into a pan. "Hope you like venison stew." She set out dishes and sliced bread. "Come eat."

They spoke of her healing arts through the meal. Afterward, Collette gave him a tour of her workroom. Many of the dried plants hanging from the ceiling were known to him. His heart clenched at the familiar scents, at the yearning ache they invoked. *Home. Family.*

Gone. Alone.

Collette patted his hand, bringing him back from the chasm. "What do you call this one?" She fingered a spidery fern.

"*Tinsa,* for fever." Marek told her all their names and uses from his recollection. Collette scribbled furiously in a notebook, and shared with him the uses for the ones he didn't recognize.

"Cheyenne has a bowl on a table that is full of…"

"It's called potpourri," Collette explained. "It's used to make your home smell nice, to help a person relax. Were you a healer as well as warrior, Marek?"

He shook his head. "Not for the whole tribe. But we knew what to gather on our travels, and how to heal ourselves while we were away."

"Whom did you fight?" she asked. "Other tribes?"

"Why should the people fight amongst themselves? That benefits no one. We trained to fight in case we were attacked. We trained to fight the Reynak."

"The creature set loose last night? Was it born in your time?"

"Not my generation. I was born to the attacks. My whole life in the demon's presence. I know no other way."

She frowned. "Demon, you call it?"

Marek stiffened. "For demon it is."

"Where did it come from? What brought it forth?"

"You sound like Cheyenne."

"Do I, now?" Collette looked pleased. "So she is starting to question. Good." She said no more on the subject, simply handed him a "mortar and pestle" and set him to work grinding various roots for her potions.

They worked through the afternoon, and the simple task cleared his mind and body of tension. Every time he started to ask a question, she shushed him with, "Later. We will speak of it later, when Cheyenne arrives. Until then, breathe. Be."

She really did sound like Tith. Marek shut his mouth and ground the roots until the sun dipped behind the trees.

Collette finally called a halt and they went out into the "living room." Marek thought that a curious term, since one "lived" in the entire dwelling. Collette had just started a fire in the hearth when Cheyenne slammed into the cabin.

Her cheeks were flushed, her eyes glittered. Her pale beauty struck him a solid blow. Air left his chest; for a moment he forgot to breathe.

"Brady's in a rare mood," she announced. "I'd steer clear of him for a while."

Marek took in her crumpled khakis, noticed her hair in disarray. "What happened?"

"Rattlesnake got into the office and made its home under my desk. It's April! They're supposed to still be hibernating. You ever fish a venomous snake out of a nice dark hidey-hole when it doesn't want to go? Loads of fun, lemme tell ya."

Marek's face paled. He recalled all too well the blackened, bloated limbs of snakebite victims, the slow lingering deaths that sometimes took days. He wrestled down the urge to strip her naked and see for himself that she was unharmed.

"Where was Kane?" Collette demanded.

"He's probably still in the snarl-fest with the council and the sheriff. Brady dropped by on his way to work to report that he'd spotted Gremlin crossing the road in front of his truck, near where those campers were killed. Gremlin's an ornery old sourpuss of a grizzly bear," she added for Marek's benefit. "Anyway, I'd just gotten a good hold of

Little-Miss-Hiss-and-Scales when he came in to find Amber atop her desk and me beneath mine."

Marek could just imagine what her older brother had to say on the subject. Much of Brady's attitude was explained…and explainable.

"Have some wine, dear, you'll feel better."

"Why are they waking up this early?" Cheyenne mused, taking a glass of dark red liquid from her grandmother. "There's no food for them yet. It's all in disarray."

Collette offered a glass to Marek. Wrinkling his nose at the sour, fermented odor, he shook his head. She shrugged and took a sip herself.

Cheyenne rubbed her free hand up and down her other arm. Marek had an insane urge to wrap his arms around her, to comfort her.

"If they're emerging and there's no food, they'll come down out of the mountains and start grabbing livestock and garbage," Cheyenne stated. "Mothers with babies to feed will be especially desperate—and bold. Last thing we need are for folks to start shooting." She pinned Marek with her gaze. "Did the earthquake do this? Is the Reynak doing this?"

"I don't know." Marek ran a hand through his hair in frustration. "In my time the Reynak was a constant, well-established presence."

"What tales were spun of how it appeared?" Collette asked. "Come tell us while I make supper. Chey, start a salad."

Marek paced the floor of the tiny kitchen, too agitated to sit down at the table. "It was a dry, hot summer. No rain for weeks. There was a fire, a huge forest fire that consumed half the mountain in a matter of hours. People and animals fled to the river, taking refuge together from the heat of the flames. Smoke and ash choked the very air they breathed. The river stopped the flames, too wide for the fire to jump. When it died, the survivors left the water, grateful to have been spared.

"That was the night the Reynak first appeared. All went quiet and still, as if all the birds and animals cowered. Hunters went to investigate. They were found slain the next day, torn asunder by some wild, clawed beast. And so it began. A quiet, a feeling of hate and malice, and then the attack. We hide within walls and it cannot reach us. We fight, but cannot kill it. A stalemate, for generations."

"How did the fire start?" Collette asked.

"A campfire poorly tended," Marek admitted.

"So men start a fire that destroys half a mountain, and the Reynak appears to start killing men," Cheyenne mused.

"What are you implying?" Marek demanded.

"Marek, how do you like your steak?" Collette asked.

Distracted, he turned to the old woman. "Just past pink."

"I'll put yours on first, then."

"I'm not implying anything." Cheyenne took a sip of the revolting beverage. "I just find it an interesting coincidence."

"Coincidence?" Collette shook her head. "I'll pour iced tea for you, Marek."

Dinner was steak and steamed vegetables, with salad. Marek noticed the women's steaks were much redder than his own. "Did you finish what you needed to?"

"For now." Cheyenne cut into her meat with unnecessary force. "I'd rather do things than write about them afterward."

"Knowledge shared with others is never wasted," Collette reproved.

Cheyenne growled at her. For just a moment, her eyes glowed silver.

Marek was riveted by that fierce light. She was so unlike any woman he had ever known. The women of his village had been quiet, self-contained. Ama had been shy, even in their sleeping furs. Cheyenne had a temper; she didn't have a shy bone in her body. Chasing after demons, taking in strangers that walked in her dreams, wrestling with poisonous serpents...she tackled all life threw at her with headlong, perhaps heedless courage.

Amazing Brady's hair wasn't gray.

Cheyenne's gaze met his across the table. The challenge in her blue eyes shifted. "What are you staring at?"

She'd never circle where a straight line would do. Marek wondered if she was as bold a lover as she was in every other aspect of her life...and stopped. Where did *that* have its birth? "You."

Her eyes darkened to a look that heated his blood and clouded his mind. "Never seen a crabby werewolf before?"

None he wanted to pin naked to the nearest wall.

"Cheyenne, stop teasing the poor man," Collette ordered.

Just like that, the burning desire subsided. Marek froze, and stared at Cheyenne with growing anger. "What did you do?"

Chapter Seven

Cheyenne flushed and refused to meet his gaze. "Nothing."

She lied. Marek knew it. But he held his peace in Collette's presence. They would speak on it later. A newly awakened part of him reveled in the thought of that upcoming confrontation. That he was familiar with—head on—challenge. He felt more alive than he had in…well, years.

"Come, both of you. Marek, I have something of yours," Collette stated. "We have much to discuss."

Marek frowned. "Something of mine? What do you mean?"

She reached out to take his hand. "There's something that has passed from hand to hand, generation to generation. All we were told is to save it for the one who would come. It *feels* like you. I know it—you're the one we've awaited."

"What do you mean, it *feels* like me?" His heart pounded. "Are you saying something of my people survives even now?"

She nodded. "Let me show you. Cheyenne, take him into the living room. I'll be right out."

Marek sat cross-legged on the floor in front of the hearth and clenched his fists to keep his hands from shaking. What could it be? Weapons? Tools? Ceremonial mask? When the Old One returned to hand him a box of sanded cedar, Cheyenne curled up on the rug beside him. She laid a hand on his thigh for a brief squeeze, then pulled back. He was grateful for the comforting gesture.

He stared at the box, oddly afraid to open it.

Hope. Fear. Death and demons he faced unflinching, but hand him a small wooden box and he broke out in a cold sweat. Cheyenne slid behind him to rub his shoulders with small capable hands, close enough for Marek to feel the soft press of breasts against his back. Her solid presence was soothing, an anchor of familiarity.

"Do you want me to stop?" Her voice was a whisper of breath in his ear. "Would you rather do this alone?"

Marek shook his head, unable to form words. Slowly he slid off the cover and reached inside. His fingers tangled in corded thread and knots. He froze. Impossible. "Do you know what this is?"

"We have never opened the box," Collette told him. "It was not our place. We were its keepers, nothing more."

He took a deep shuddering breath and drew the *quipa* from its nest of darkness into the light. It was huge, the tale of centuries, and its colors were bright still. They shimmered out of focus through a haze of tears. "This belonged to Tith in my time." He could barely form the words around the lump in his throat; his voice was hoarse. "It is the record of my people, kept by the high priest of each generation."

He searched through the knots. "Here is where we moved north. Here is where we built the pyramid." His fingers stilled on a black knot. "Here is where the Reynak came." He shuddered. "Here is where our tomb was built." Blood thundered in Marek's ears as he counted the strands after he left. "So many." He did a quick calculation.

"A thousand years?"

Cheyenne draped her arms around his shoulders. Collette shook her head. "No, Marek." When he looked up, her eyes were sad, her face compassionate. "We have held onto this for that long, passing from caretaker to caretaker, one in each generation."

It took a moment for her words to sink in. "*Two* thousand?" He could barely comprehend such a vast stretch of living. "What happened?"

"It was found in the ancient ruin of a stone pyramid, with catacombs inside," Collette reported. "Our best guess is a tremendous earthquake that leveled the mountain."

"Are they gone? All?"

She nodded, and placed her work-roughened hand atop his. "Since long before our time."

Gone. All gone. Lost. Forgotten but for this. He was alone. Knowledge of the Reynak, too, had been lost to the passage of time. None lived who remembered the great struggle—or the demon. Despair crushed the breath from him. Hidden beneath his shirt, the amulets sparked against his chest. Shoving the *quipa* and box aside, he dropped his head and wept.

"You aren't alone, Marek." Cheyenne rested her head over his shoulder. "What can we do to help?"

He shook with dark laughter. Entire war bands had been lost in the fight. What was he to do with two women who could not even touch the power amulets? Belief powered the amulets—the belief of a dead religion, long gone. "Nothing. There is nothing you can do."

Cheyenne slid around to face him, until she was practically in his lap. "Oh, yes there is." She placed a hand on either side of his face, forced him to meet her burning gaze. "We are children of the earth, guardians of the earth. We have existed since before your time, and there are hundreds of us if we summon all Packs together. Surely we can come up with a way."

Incredibly, the amulets stirred, a faint spark of life against his skin. A glowing warmth in his heart. Marek stared at Cheyenne, shocked. Could it be that any belief would do? Then there *was* hope.

Collette nodded, her eyes thoughtful. "Good idea. I'll contact Tomas to get the elders together. We'll meet tomorrow night at Josiah's." She looked at Cheyenne. "You should go home and try to get some rest."

****

Cheyenne rose and reached down to help Marek to his feet. He looked exhausted, wrung out. Sad, tired, stunned. His hand trembled in hers. He had lost everyone and everything, an island of before in an unfamiliar sea of now. What did he have left? Leather clothing, crystal weapons, silver amulets and a knotted *quipa.*

"Come on," she said. "Let's go home."

Marek shuddered at the words, but followed her to the door. They went out and climbed into the truck. Cheyenne watched him take a deep breath as he put the seatbelt on, saw him pale and close his eyes. He really hated this, the driving from place to place. She remembered his earlier explosion over coffee. Maybe he hated everything about his new world. He needed to be reminded of what was still similar, familiar. That the people today weren't any different inside than those he'd left behind. That respect and caring still existed.

It was a silent ride back to her trailer. Cheyenne wanted to wait until they were home to have their discussion. All looked normal around her dwelling. She rolled the window down and listened intently for the familiar sounds of the night. She led the way inside, not daring to tempt fate—the Balrog, the Reynak—by lingering. She started a fire in the woodstove, grabbed a pitcher of lemonade from the fridge and some fired-clay mugs, and turned out the living room lights. Her eyes rapidly adjusted to moonlight and the glow of flames through the cracks in the stove door.

Marek sat down beside her on the floor, watching her. Puzzled. Wary.

"I think you've had all the 'modern' you can take for one day," Cheyenne told him. "Am I wrong?"

"No." He leaned back against the couch and closed his eyes, making a visible effort to relax.

Cheyenne turned on the flute music and took Marek's hand, leaning against his shoulder. She, too, closed her eyes. *Breathe. Be.*

Big mistake. His warm masculine scent curled around her, through her, with every breath. Part green, spice, and part musk. *All* male. Every nerve danced to attention in the light of the moon. She couldn't deny her attraction to him, not to herself. She might have been able to bury it, had she not seen the same spark of interest in his gaze. Here and there, quickly doused.

"'*Listen to your body*,'" Collette had oft advised her. "'*Listen with your heart.*'" Sister trusted Marek with every fiber of her being, had since the beginning. Cheyenne did, too. It was Marek who had to trust and believe in himself, here in the now where he'd landed.

Once he'd known want, need. He'd been married, almost a father. Sister growled; Cheyenne mentally rolled her eyes at the absurdity of being jealous of a woman two thousand years' dead. But Marek was still alive. He regretted it. The scope of his mission seemed too vast for one man to handle. He needed something smaller, more immediate. More personal. A bridge from then-to-now.

"What were they like?" she asked. "My people in your time?"

Marek was silent for a long time. "Shy. Distant," he finally answered. "Packs of wolves lived all around us, but every once in a while we would cross one and it would look at us with piercing blue or gray eyes, with human intelligence, and you just *knew* it was no mere wolf." He shivered with the memory.

Marek didn't strike her as an observer. "Did you never speak to one of us?" Cheyenne pressed.

"Actually, I did. There was an *agrilu*, a singer-storyteller, who spent many a night at our fires. He could make up a song about anything, at the time of happening. Berry picking, planting, hunting, harvesting. He shared weddings, births and deaths. Once I fell into the river while fishing and it was the topic of that night's unfolding." His lips quirked at the memory, then he sobered and opened his eyes to look at her. "The wonder of your kind. To be both wolf and human."

"We're born this way, a separate people. The wolf shares our soul, but the human half rules. Contrary to popular myth, we don't need the full moon to shift. The wolf is always with us. It gives us a tie to the earth, to nature. You've known our kind. Did you never meet someone like me?"

The sudden spark in his gaze made her shiver. "I have never met anyone like you."

The heat in the room shot up ten degrees in a moment. Sister sighed, yearning to move closer, and Cheyenne's breath caught in her throat at the honest, open desire on his face. His cheeks flushed. She felt his body calling to hers, and she trembled with the need to answer him.

"What—a crabby, snake-catching werewolf?" she quipped.

Marek ran his hand through her hair. "A beautiful woman ruled by her heart. Fearless. Who throws herself into whatever life brings. You took in a stranger after very suspect circumstances. I could have been the worst sort of criminal."

Cheyenne fought the urge to close her eyes and lean into his hand. She shook her head. "No. One of our strengths is we can read another's heart. You were blameless. You needed my help. Made perfect sense to me. It still does. You need me." *I need you.*

"What do you know of what I need?" he demanded.

She gave up trying to tamp down the wanting. Desire coursed through her, sang its heated song in her blood. Her skin tingled, too sensitive. Her clothing chafed; she needed it off. All she wanted was his skin against hers, his body on hers. In hers. Now.

His grip tightened just shy of discomfort. Cheyenne thrilled at his strength, his control. God, she wanted to see him lose that control. He *needed* to lose that control. He glowered at her, flickers of sexual heat igniting his gaze. Her nipples tightened with anticipation.

"You are doing it again."

She blinked at Marek's accusatory tone. "What?"

"Making me want you. Cease."

Cheyenne wanted to laugh. She wanted to cry. She had to make him understand. "I can't *make* you do anything, Marek. I want you. Your hands, your mouth. I need you, burn for you. But I can't *make* you feel the same against your will. If you want me, you want me. I want you. You want me. What could be simpler?"

"You must not speak so." His voice was strangled. His breathing, heavy.

"Why? Because it isn't proper?" Cheyenne unbuttoned her shirt, pulled it loose from her slacks. His gaze lowered, and froze on her breasts, glued to the nipples she felt pressing against the pink satin of her bra. "Or because it's making you hot? Hard?"

He shuddered, clenched his jaw.

Her body wept with need. Cheyenne saw his nostrils flare as the scent of her desire curled around him. She reached out to take his hands, lacing her fingers with his, and placed them over her breasts.

The heat of his hands was incredible. "There's no one here but us. You…and me. Alone in the night…wanting…needing. Don't say no. Please."

She held her breath. What would he do?

Chapter Eight

Marek stared at her, shocked, speechless. Never had a woman spoken so…bluntly…to him. But her honest words, her intoxicating scent, aroused him in a way he had never felt before. A fierce burning need so intense he would ignite if he did not take her. "Are all women so…forward?"

She smiled, her eyes glowing. "Most of my kind is raised to say what's on our mind, yes. Less chance of misunderstandings that way."

There was no misunderstanding this. Not with her holding his hands to her breasts. Marek slid his thumbs over her nipples, which pebbled at his touch. He rubbed slow circles over the soft material that covered her as Cheyenne closed her eyes and threw her head back with a shivery moan. His body jerked at that sound, and his mouth watered to taste her skin.

He nuzzled between her breasts, kissed his way up the column of her neck to her ear. Her skin burned beneath his lips, and he found a particular spot that made her gasp. He teased her there, with his tongue, with the lightest scrape of his teeth, until her gasp turned to a raw moan and she started to shake.

Cheyenne let go of his hands, reached out to slide hers under his shirt.

"Wait." He pulled the silver amulets off and laid them on the cushion above them, not wanting to hurt her.

She swallowed, and nodded. Desire replaced the chagrin in her eyes, and she touched him again. Now it was his turn to groan. The sensation of her small feminine fingers sliding over his burning flesh… Her touch was pure heaven. She pulled his shirt up, and he helped her get it over his head.

Skin against skin. Her gaze met his for a moment, and her honest, open passion warmed the chill, filled the emptiness. She was there, with him, breath for breath, heartbeat for heartbeat. Not alone… She stroked up his chest, pinched his flat nipples lightly before curling her arms around his neck. She pulled him to her, brushed his lips with hers.

Marek poured himself into the kiss, unashamed of the depth of his need. Somehow, she understood. He slid his hands down to grasp her hips, dragging her closer. Cheyenne moved to straddle him, angling her core to cover his aching, turgid shaft. He stopped thinking, only able to feel. Heat. Need. Barely able to breathe, drunk on her scent. He caressed her back, slid his hands along her sides.

She broke off the kiss with a flinch and a giggle. "That tickles."

"Sorry." He slid the shirt from her shoulders and frowned, huffing out a single frustrated breath. The breast harness stymied him. "How does this come off?"

She reached behind her, gave an agonizing wriggle against him that made him momentarily blind with lust, and the scrap of cloth fell away.

His vision cleared, riveted on delicate pink tips and tightly puckered nipples. Her breasts were small but firm, soft and glowing in the moonlight. So pale, so perfect. They quivered with her every breath. Marek closed his mouth over one, teasing her with his tongue, suckling hard.

"Marek!" Her nails dug into his shoulders.

His heart soared at that breathy cry, at her fierce reaction to his touch. To him. The blood pooled in his groin, straining the seam of his jeans. His body tightened to the point of pain. He switched to her other breast, needy, starving. She wrapped her legs around his waist; her hips rocked against him, bathing him in fire.

He rose to his knees and fell forward, laying her back onto the rug, covering her body with his. Cheyenne writhed under him, her searching hands everywhere on his skin. Everywhere she touched left a burning trail in her wake. Marek dipped his fingers under the top of her pants, growling as he fumbled with the unfamiliar button. The zipper proved easier, and he pulled back long enough to tug them down. Cheyenne helped, arching her back and raising her hips so he could slide them down her legs and toss them behind him.

The merest scrap of lace covered the drenched curls between her legs. Proof of her desire. He stroked under the barrier, sliding his fingers over her wet, swollen folds. He clenched his jaw at the rush of fire, the ache to bury himself within her body. All that wet heat, calling to him. Cheyenne parted her thighs for him, granting him permission, access to the most intimate part of her. He breathed in her heady scent.

"Please," she whispered, arching into his hand.

Marek tugged on the lace until it tore free. Then she was bared to his gaze, his touch. He leaned down, felt her shiver as his hair brushed her inner thighs, heard her take a deep shaky breath—and hold it. Anticipation crackled along his nerves. The tension in her thighs said she felt it, too. Such a miracle, Cheyenne. So accepting, so honest.

"Please."

He ran his tongue along her, soaking her scent, her taste, into his very bones. Wild. Salt. Musk. Cheyenne. He drank her in, needing her in his very soul, where she could stay with him forever. Licking, sipping, holding her hips still while she bucked against his mouth with raw, broken sobs. Her thighs gripped him tightly, the muscles rigid as she strained toward completion. He wanted to see her break, explode with a satisfaction that he gave her. His lips sought, and found, the small sensitive bud that was the focus of a woman's passion. He gently traced in with the tip of his tongue, using but the slightest pull as he suckled.

"Marek!" She broke against him with a wild cry, shaking.

He shuddered at the sound of his name on her lips, at the liquid passion flowing from her quivering flesh. His shaft ached to bury itself in that wet heat, feel her intimate muscles pull him into an explosion of his own. He nearly burst at the thought.

Cheyenne raised her head to stare down at him. Sweaty, panting, eyes dazed. He moved up to capture her lips in an open-mouthed kiss, tangling his tongue with hers, swallowing her every whimper. He ground his hips into the cradle of hers, his body straining against hers. She stroked her hands down his back, into his pants to grip his rear, kneading like a kitten. She clutched at the material, sliding it down over his hips.

"Take them off," she whispered. "I don't want anything between us."

He had them off before she could blink, and choked when she curled her fingers around his shaft. Squeezing, pulling. Marek jerked in her hand, almost exploded then and there. She circled the tip, spreading the creamy drop that escaped his control over the sensitized flesh.

He could wait no longer. Pulling free of her hands, he nudged his aching shaft between her thighs. She moaned as he teased her slick folds, still quivering with aftershocks, and he shuddered as she bathed him in wet heat. He eased into her, groaning as her hungry body sucked at his, drawing him in further. Clenching his jaw against the excruciating pleasure, he backed out. Pumping his hips in a torture of short, teasing thrusts, heightening the tension, the anticipation until Cheyenne growled. She wrapped her legs around him, arched her back and pulled him all the way home.

Hot. Tight. Voracious. Her body throbbed around his. His world exploded in a haze of carnal need. Pulling back, thrusting home, with a force that might have hurt her had she been less primed, less ready for him. She rocked against him with hungry little mewling cries. Her hands burned his flesh as she clutched him closer, as she tilted her hips to take him deeper. She squeezed around him, and his control snapped. Need consumed him, and he thrust. Harder, faster, deeper, until his blood boiled. With a rush, the world exploded, and he shuddered as he flooded her with his seed.

Incredibly, she pulsed around him with her own completion, having matched him stroke for stroke. The pleasure went on and on, shaking him to his soul. He collapsed onto her, utterly spent. She wrapped her arms around him, keeping him close, her body still milking his softening shaft.

He never wanted her to let him go. His body remembered night pleasures, the physical satisfaction of release into a woman's wet, willing body. But never had he burned so fiercely, needed a joining heart and soul. Until now. Until her, Cheyenne. Unlike Ama, who had accepted but never offered, Cheyenne held nothing back, met him touch for touch, need for need, and heat for heat. He had never known a woman's fire could burn so hot, so bright.

He wanted to make her burn again.

****

Cheyenne shivered at the sense of loss as he

slipped free of her body and rolled onto his back to pull her close. His heart hammered against her ear. The scent of sweat and sex hung in the air and she snuggled closer, into his warmth. Contentment stole over her, and she closed her eyes, letting her breathing gradually slow to normal. The shimmering in her blood subsided. Her body cooled. She sighed as his hands soothed where before they'd aroused. He trembled as her breath tickled his skin.

Please, no regrets, she prayed.

Marek rolled to his side, so he could see her without craning his neck. He couldn't seem to stop touching her, stroking slow and firm over her skin, rubbing circles over her still-quivering belly. His touch felt so right, like she'd been waiting all along for him to come into her life.

She reached out to brush the hair back over his shoulder, running her fingers through the long silken strands. She shivered, recalling the sensation of his hair sliding over her inner thighs, right before his mouth... God, she was a goner. She wanted him still. Again.

Heat flickered in his dark-chocolate eyes. "You are a dangerous woman, Cheyenne," he stated. "You make me feel things I swore not to, not ever again."

Definitely not a man from her time. No man she knew was so open about his feelings, not to a near stranger. No, not strangers, she amended. Through their extraordinary connection, they knew each other on the deepest level. Now, as lovers, that final barrier down, what would they become?

"You can't shut your feelings out, Marek."

"Pleasure only brings remembered pain." He grimaced. "Never have the memories threatened to consume me as they have tonight. Once I loved a woman, and the Reynak ripped her from my life. You make me want to care again. Were the Reynak to harm you, I do not know what I would do."

Well, there was a compliment. "Pain buried only festers," she reminded him. "It must be freed and dealt with. Only then will it lessen. Only then can your heart heal."

"As long as the Reynak breathes, it shall never heal."

He really was a tangled mess. As long as he believed that, it would be so. His own nasty little self-fulfilling prophecy. She gripped his hair in her fingers, cupping her hand along his jaw. "Then we make it go away. If there's one thing I heard loud and clear from your story, it's that it can be defeated when everyone bands together. Together, we're invincible."

He frowned. "You truly believe that?"

"With all my heart." She pulled him in for a kiss. Slow. Tender. Soul-deep. "I believe in you, Marek. You came here with strength of purpose. It's not in you to concede." She wanted to fill him so full of the light and heat of *now* that the shadows of the past would find no purchase in his heart. Once, he had loved, had laughed.

You will do so again, she vowed, sliding her leg over his hip and scooching closer until they touched. Skin to skin, pressed together from thigh to neck. She trembled with reawakened yearning as his hand gripped her backside to haul her closer still, as if he'd have pulled her into him if he could.

She wanted that, to be so close he'd never get her out. In his blood, in his bones. She breathed in his scent, traced her tongue up the column of his neck to his ear. She felt his pulse pounding against her lips, tasted the salt and the heat. Desire. Need. Hunger.

Cheyenne pushed against him, using the leg hooked around him to flip Marek onto his back. He tensed and stared up at her, questions in his eyes. She ran her hands over his chest, down his sides, his thighs. She smiled as his skin flushed and he shuddered, his gaze igniting with renewed wanting. His cock stiffened under her gaze. She couldn't help herself.

She licked her lips.

Marek closed his eyes and groaned.

Cheyenne circled his navel with her tongue, fondling his heavy sac. She took his growing erection in her hands, squeezing, pulling. He thrust in her grip, and she circled just the tip with her tongue, and then took him in her mouth. Hot. Hard. Huge. So male, so sensitive. Wet heat tingled between her legs as she teased his cock, careful not to use her teeth. God, he tasted good. Salt and spice. She sucked him all the way in, working him with her tongue.

He pumped his hips with a strangled shout. "Woman, cease."

She growled. *Give it to me.* She almost released him, then sucked him back down. Again…and again. His hands knotted in her hair, and every muscle in his body tightened as he came in a rush. She swallowed every rich, creamy drop, slowly releasing him with a final lick.

Marek stared at her with stunned disbelief.

"Haven't you ever -"

He shook his head, gasping for breath like an unconditioned Thoroughbred.

Cheyenne blinked. Wow. She was his first. The thought blew her mind. She shivered at the crackle of energy that arced between them. "Welcome to the new world. I've been waiting for you."

Chapter Nine

Marek frowned, confused. "Waiting for me?"

"Don't you feel it?" Cheyenne sat up and motioned her hand between them. "It's like I was waiting to come alive until you showed up. Believe me, I don't normally tumble into lust with the first guy I see."

He did feel it, the energy. Hence the confusion. It was almost as if... He raised himself up on his elbows and glanced up at where he'd tossed the amulets. To his utter shock, they glowed softly in the dark, a gentle—but definite—lilac. He glanced at her, seeing their glow reflected in the silver tinge in her blue eyes. Belief. Power. One person was not enough, but that it responded at all gave him a shiver of hope.

Cheyenne, too, stared at the amulets. "Whoa. Look at that. Why are they doing that?"

He grinned at her wide-eyed wonder, almost that of a child. In some ways, Cheyenne still spoke with the forthrightness of a child, before they learned control. Now he sat up and motioned between them. "They respond to positive energy of the heart, the mind, and harness it into a force the wearer can control. It also trickles into the crystals in the weapons if I hold them while wearing the amulets."

She frowned, looking thoughtful. "Harnessing the power of man's mind against the power of...what? What *is* the Reynak? Where did it come from?"

"I told you -"

She held up a hand and shook her head. "No. You told me when it came, what happened before. What we assume was the cause. Man's destruction of nature. The Reynak's retribution."

"The fire?" Marek knew he sounded skeptical, even to himself.

"Did it ever kill my kind, in your time?" Cheyenne asked. "Did it ever kill animals?"

His temper flared. "You're suggesting it's out to kill man because of *fire*? Lightning starts fires, too."

Cheyenne gripped his arm as he glared at her. "The amulets respond to man's power of the mind. Man starts fires far more often than lightning. Has the Reynak killed animals?"

Marek reeled in his temper to actually consider the question. "No."

"Then it doesn't harm the natural." Her eyes narrowed. "Which means it's probably an earth spirit made flesh."

He didn't like that look in her eyes. "What are you talking about?"

"What does man do differently, out of all the creatures on this planet?" she demanded.

He tried to think.

The soul of patience she wasn't. She answered her own question. "We change things. Nature left to itself coexists within itself. Change, in nature, comes slowly, over ages of time. And it never harms itself."

"Fire?"

"Fire. Logging. Clear-cutting. Mining. Tilling the soil. *Change*," she clarified. "And it's way worse now. We have pollution, global warming, reduction of the ozone layer, unprecedented extinctions." He must have looked lost—what did those words mean?—because she stopped. "We change nature, push it out of balance. Only an earth spirit would care. Only a god would have the power to send something like the Reynak."

"Are you saying the gods themselves conspire against us?" he demanded.

"I'm saying it's not a demon. It has reason, motivation. It has a mission and it's selective in its prey."

"You don't know that. You're guessing."

Cheyenne stood up. "There's only one way to find out."

Before he could blink, Cheyenne was gone. She just...melted down, into a beautiful white wolf with Cheyenne's blue eyes. She trotted over to the door, pawed at it, looked back at him and whined.

His heart stopped. No. Absolutely not. No way was he opening that door. She would go to her death. The Reynak killed everyone he ever cared for. If she perished, too, Marek knew his heart would die forever.

The wolf shimmered, grew, and Cheyenne returned to take his hands in hers. "Your amulets work on belief. I believe in you, in your story. But I am more than human. I am also nature, animal, which you say the Reynak has never harmed. Now you have to trust me. Believe in me. Let me be a bridge between nature and man, the Reynak and you." Her eyes burned with conviction. "I know I'm right. It won't harm me. You have to trust me."

She asked too much. He couldn't do it. He held her very human curves to him, took her woman's mouth with desperation. "Don't do this," he whispered against her lips.

"Trust me," she replied.

"I'm coming with you."

"No." She shook her head. "You're entirely human. We know it will kill you without a second thought. I have to do this alone. I'll be fine."

She truly believed that. What she said made perfect sense—*if* she was right. He watched her shift back into the white wolf, and this time found himself walking over to the door. He hesitated when his hand grasped the handle. Her gaze was steady, unafraid. Heart in his throat, he opened the door and stepped aside.

****

Well, this was a brilliant idea, Cheyenne thought. Sister, however, yipped with excitement at being free to run. Through fields and forest, under the moon and stars. One with the forest, with the night. What she was born to do. She trotted toward the tree line, stretching her muscles into an easy lope.

Where are you? Come to me.

It couldn't be far. The Reynak and Marek were bound together. If she was going to break that bond, she had to examine the other end of it. See if the Reynak truly was demon, which Marek believed, or overzealous guardian, which is what it seemed. A demon would be random. This Reynak was very precise. Too precise. Plus, there was the fact that it couldn't touch anything manmade.

The night breathed around her, creatures stirring all about. She startled up a rabbit, still in winter white. Sister itched to give chase, but Cheyenne let it go. *Where are you? Come to me.*

The night stilled. Fearful. Sister plowed to a halt. A tremor shook her fur as the distinct smell of sulfur burned her sensitive nose. Cheyenne held the wolf steady. *We need to stay. We need to know.*

The Reynak stood between two hemlock trees, waiting. She stared up at it—way up. It would tower over her even in human form. From Sister's vantage, it appeared big enough to block out the stars. But the stars were still there, overhead. Whether blocked by clouds or Reynak, she reminded herself, the night went on. Sister wanted to cower before it. Cheyenne forced herself to sit. Wait. Calm. Mostly. *I know I'm right.*

She'd never seen anything like it. Not in a book. Not in a nightmare. It was huge, and walked upright, with cloven hooves on its hind legs and razor claws on its front. Ram's horns curled around its ears, and its eyes glowed red. She'd expected fur. Instead, it sported an armored hide like a crocodile, which crackled with dark earth energy.

It cocked its head, seeming puzzled by her behavior. When it snorted, its nostrils flared as red as its eyes. Heat radiated from it—she felt it from where she sat. Fire within a shell, almost like a volcano. Definitely earth. If she could sense that about the Reynak, could it sense that about her?

She'd bet her life on it.

Greetings, guardian, she opened.

A feeling of surprise. No words. It understood her, but was limited to feelings. Maybe images?

What are you?

She got an exact mental image of what she looked at with her eyes. Oh-kay. Not exactly a rocket scientist. Got that.

Why are you here?

Images flooded her mind. Fires, cutting down trees, planting. Exactly as she suspected. The Reynak killed the tree cutters—the trees grew back. The Reynak killed the planters—the meadow grew back. Its message was clear. Kill the humans—keep the status quo.

Cheyenne felt an unexpected twinge of sympathy. It was way worse than the Reynak knew. It could not single-handedly stop "progress" no matter how many individual humans it killed. Two thousand years ago, maybe. Now…never.

She could empathize with its mission. The same need drove her. To protect the land. But it couldn't go around killing people.

How did you get here?

A rift in a fire-mountain. The Reynak just

walked through, from its fire realm into a world of air and water.

Who sent you? That was the key. Find the sender; convince him or her to send the Reynak back.

And they'll listen to you why? Sister challenged.

Because the old ways no longer work. If the sender who wished to protect the earth was an immortal deity, then it knew full well what was going on in the here-and-now. The Reynak was doomed to fail, and if the sender truly wished to protect the planet then it would be open to hearing about Plan B.

Who sent you?

It cocked its head as if it didn't understand the question. A creature just intelligent enough to obey a simple command—"Stop man"—but not intelligent enough to question, or learn, adapt or alter its path. Basically, a golem, a deadly, single-minded automaton.

It was but the bullet. Who held the gun? There in the darkness, under moon and stars, Cheyenne waited. *Who sent you?*

Small.

Now it was Sister who cocked her head, Cheyenne who frowned in confusion. Small? What did *"small"* mean?

The Reynak snorted. *Big.* A rush of planets, moons and stars. Suns, galaxies, the entire universe. It made Cheyenne's head spin. *Small.* Down to one planet, Earth. Cheyenne actually felt herself plummet, and her stomach churned in protest.

Aha. So, there *was* a deity in charge of the earth.

Bad. A sense of disappointment, anger, outrage.

Not bad, Cheyenne insisted. *Just…misguided.*

Bad. The Reynak grew before her very eyes.

Oh-kay, no gray in the Reynak's world. Black

and white left little wiggle room. Humans were bad. Kill the humans. She definitely had to find the gun for this bullet.

Sister rose and loped off. Cheyenne had the information she wanted. The white wolf saw no reason to linger. The Reynak let her go, back to the trailer.

Marek awaited her in the doorway. It was a testament to his trust in her, and his self-control, that he simply waited in the doorway. Unarmed. She brushed by him and shifted as he closed the door, only to find herself in a bone-creaking hug.

"You're unharmed." There was wonder in his voice. "How?"

"I was right," she told him. "Now I know what to say at the council meeting tomorrow."

He silenced her with an open-mouthed kiss that left her breathless, shaking when he broke it off. "What?"

What was the question? What was the answer? Cheyenne shook her head to clear it. "The Children of the Earth have the same mission as the Reynak. To protect the earth. We convince the sender to take the Reynak back, to let us stand in its place."

"I'm not one of you," he reminded her. "It won't listen to me. I'm one of the hated humans, personally responsible for wounding it countless times. For imprisoning it. I followed it here. I'm not one of you."

Lightning struck. "But you could be."

Chapter Ten

Marek stared at Cheyenne. Suspicion, skepticism narrowed his eyes. "What do you mean? How?"

"The Reynak recognizes our blood. We could make you blood brother to us." Cheyenne gripped his arm. He had to listen. He had to believe. "With moon serum running through your veins, you would no longer be considered a threat by the Reynak."

He shook his head. "I was sent to fight the Reynak. To not do so would be to dishonor my people, everything they sacrificed and died for."

Cheyenne wanted to scream. "To fight the Reynak single handedly is suicide. Where's the honor in that?"

"There *is* honor in death." His eyes blazed at her.

"Yours was a temporary banishment. You were sent to *defeat* the Reynak. To teach others to defeat it. If we can defeat it, without anyone else dying, then let's do it."

"How?"

Cheyenne straightened. "I told you it was sent. We convince the sender to take it back. We offer to take its place."

"As what?"

"Guardians of the earth. Protectors of the land. To teach respect and responsibility to others, so the land stays balanced and endures forever. *That's* what the Reynak wants. *That's* what it fights for."

"By killing people?"

"I never said it was a good *method*, only good

intentions."

Marek's expression said he clearly thought her mad. "So where do I fit in?"

Cheyenne choked at the image that came to mind. Curling her arms around his neck, she stepped close, skin-to-skin, and shivered as the heat flared anew in his eyes. "We're born what we are. We can't change that. Shifters are born. Contrary to popular myth, they can't be made. However, humans can be altered. Healers have done it to heal a near-mortal wound."

His hands cupped her backside. "I don't want a tail."

She grinned, then pulled him down into a pulse-pounding kiss. "You won't," she whispered. "No fur, no paws, no tail. Heightened senses, faster healing, threefold longevity."

Lovers had also done it, when they discovered a human life-mate, to extend the human's years and make interbreeding possible. Heightened senses and a new awareness of the moon also increased libido, but she wasn't ready to share that little fact with him.

"But you would feel like a child of the earth and moon to the spirits, to the Reynak." She searched his eyes, his expression. He looked like he was thinking it over. She ran a hand through his hair, letting the cool strands slide over her fingers like a silken waterfall. "You would be part of our community, no longer alone."

Pain flashed in Marek's eyes. A human's fear of being alone. One also shared by Pack. His arms tightened around her, and he tilted his head to nibble down the curve of her neck. "Later," he growled. "I'll think about it later."

Passion rose, hot and swift. Cheyenne trembled with need. Later. Later was good.

Marek stared at the circle of Pack council members. He recognized Cheyenne, Collette, Brady, and surprisingly Kane. Kane wasn't Pack, but an honorary human member. Unchanged. Brady glowered at Marek, at the arm Cheyenne kept around Marek's waist. Marek tore his gaze from Brady's to scan the others. Warriors like Brady, Shamans like Collette—all older, wiser. His gaze was captured by the oldest. What had Cheyenne called him? Josiah, that was it—Old Josiah. He Saw. He walked in both the *then* and the *now*.

"This meeting is convened." Josiah rapped on the floor with his staff. "As the host, and the eldest, mine is the speaking staff. Let he—or she—who holds my staff be the sole speaker."

Everyone inclined their head in agreement.

Brady motioned for the staff. When Josiah handed it to him, he growled at Marek. "What is this human doing here? He isn't one of us." He indicated the silver amulets. "It's an affront to wear those here."

Collette took the staff. "He is the reason for this meeting. I called it on his behalf. The deaths of the humans are no accident." She glared at Kane. "Nor is it by a bear. There is a creature set loose by the quake, a creature locked up some two thousand years ago—by Marek's people. Now it is free and only Marek possesses the knowledge of it."

Marek glanced at Cheyenne, who nodded encouragement. This they had previously agreed on—that he would explain what she'd found out. He fingered the *quipa*. Two thousand years…he still reeled to think about it. The *ahnkeisha* crystals glowed softly against his skin, from the belief and support of Cheyenne and Collette.

Belief. He took a deep breath and motioned for the staff. "The Reynak, we call it. An earth spirit, summoned by a god long dead to prevent change. A killer of humans, who change their world to suit themselves. It does not suit the Reynak, nor the gods. For years we fought this creature, in a war we could not win, a war it could not win. A...stalemate."

"We have better weapons now!" Brady retorted.

Half a dozen growls greeted this breech of etiquette, his lack of control. He met those burning eyes for but a second before he lowered his gaze to the floor. Marek read the tension in Brady, but the alpha backed down to the Pack council. For the moment.

"Fighting it gets us nowhere. Killing us does not stop human 'progress'," Marek continued. "The Reynak cannot win, does it soak the earth with the blood of every human in this land. Killing is not the solution."

Kane took the staff. "Then what is?"

Cheyenne squeezed Marek's arm as she motioned for a turn. "It does not harm the natural. I spoke with it, just last night. It is sentient, self-aware, after a fashion. It greeted the wolf in me. It was sent, a warrior for the earth." Her gaze met Kane's. "As we are. All over the world, people fight the Reynak's battle. We convince the gods to take the Reynak back, to let us take its place."

Collette took the staff from her granddaughter. "We do a summoning."

Marek caught the puzzled looks that flew around the room. Cheyenne had told him no one had performed the ancient ritual since nearly his time. The old gods were forgotten, dead. Collette had assured him that Josiah held the necessary knowledge, but he seemed a bit...unreliable to Marek. He knew what Brady and Kane's reactions would be. They were men of the here-and-now, with no time or patience for the mystical.

They were in for a rude awakening.

His gaze strayed to Cheyenne. She stood

straight and proud beside him, her constant physical contact a warm reassurance. So beautiful. So *sure*. She looked like Collette, felt like Collette. The mystical ran deep in her veins, and she had just started to acknowledge its presence. If she began her serious studies, she would be a force to be reckoned with in another century or so, just like her grandmother. Destined to be on the council herself one day.

A century or three of living. Now there was something to consider, what Cheyenne proposed. He knew that would be the second part of the meeting. They would need the council's blessings. He already knew Brady would say no. But he needed to stop reacting like an older brother and start thinking like a Pack leader.

Could he do it? Marek wondered. Could he allow Cheyenne to change him so fundamentally? Somehow, he knew, she would be the one to do it if he chose that path. He had a feeling there was more to it than she let on. Joining of body and spirit, like the dream-sharing, but more permanent. What would be the long-term repercussions of such an act?

The word "amulet" snapped him back to the here-and-now. Collette was speaking. "The *quipa* is his," she remarked. "The amulets are made of a resonating crystal. Marek?"

He took the staff. "The crystals are *ahnkeisha*, as are the blades on my weapons, which Cheyenne and Brady have seen. They focus human will, turning purple, and can injure the Reynak and drive it off. At one time, all the warriors wore one. Here, there were just three. Veynar and Levan were killed when the Reynak emerged." That thought still caused his gut to clench. "Now there is just me from *before*, but the crystals work the same. Collette and Cheyenne proved they respond to Pack thoughts as easily as to my people's. Together, focused, we can do this."

Brady motioned for the speaking staff, just as Josiah started to rise. Josiah sat back down and granted Brady permission to go first. Marek handed Brady the staff, and Cheyenne's hand tightened on his arm. She glanced at Marek nervously. Marek shook his head. Whatever Brady had to say, he would answer.

"I saw the ground where Veynar and Levan fell," Brady stated. "We never found the bodies. I saw the burns on Marek, caused by the Reynak's venom. I heard a cry that turns a man's blood to ice, and makes my wolf want to cower in fear." He glared at Marek. "You have never defeated it with the weapons in your time or of your time. We have better weapons in the here-and-now, and I trust in them more than in a bunch of psychic mumbo-jumbo. I say we use them."

Josiah stood with a snort, and motioned for the staff. "So certain are you, young one? The flesh cannot defeat the spirit. Besides," he looked to Kane, "I cannot see you allowing tanks and bombs to rip up the wilderness."

Kane shook his head, and motioned for the staff. "I usually hold silent at these meetings, as I am not a council member, and am but a guest here." He stared at Cheyenne and Marek hard, until Cheyenne squirmed beneath his gaze. "Foreign exchange student? That was the best you could come up with, rather than the truth?" He held up a hand. "No, I know why you did it. I would have responded with disbelief. I am usually in Brady's camp, and I should know better, after so many years of living with the Pack, with having Cheyenne and Amber working for me. I have seen creatures emerging from winter hibernation early, before Mother Nature is prepared to feed them. They're hungry and cranky.

"But it was no grizzly that killed those campers.

I now have a name to this menace, and I would see it gone." Kane glared at Brady. "I would not have my wilderness torn apart by manmade weapons. It seems to me that would be counterproductive and the very thing that reinforces the Reynak's mission. It doesn't sound like anything manmade will work, regardless of the power or generation. Manmade is manmade. We need to try something else."

Marek watched Cheyenne blink, and he caught a sense of surprise from her. It seemed out of character for the irascible, pragmatic ranger. But, it appeared there was more to Kane than he'd first thought.

The conversation continued, until Josiah called for a break and then a vote. Collette brought Marek and Cheyenne water. "They'll discuss it privately, in small groups. I think we have a chance. They know we have no time."

Cheyenne's blue eyes searched Marek's. "Have you thought about the other?"

Collette moved off to give them privacy.

How to answer? "Thought, yes. Decided, no," he confessed. "There is no going back from that. I would hear what your council would say, first."

"Fair enough." She bit her lip, and Marek found his gaze drawn to that unconsciously provocative action. Even in a room full of people, Cheyenne drew him to her without even trying.

"What?" he asked.

"I can't stand the thought of the Reynak hurting you," she told him.

"Well, that makes two of us." Her frown indicated she found his grim humor less than amusing. "I find much of interest in the here-and-now." Cheyenne foremost among them. Marek reached out to cradle his hand against her cheek, tracing her lower lip with his thumb. He watched her eyes darken in reaction to his touch. Would it always be like this between them?

"I knew you were going to be trouble," Brady growled over Marek's shoulder.

"I'm a big girl," Cheyenne retorted. "My personal life is no concern of yours."

"Everything about you concerns me, little sister," he told her. "Especially a demon-toting stranger we know nothing about."

Marek felt her shimmer against his palm, watched a glint of silver light her eyes as she glared at Brady. She bared growing fangs in a parody of a smile; her growl more felt than heard. He turned to meet Brady's less-than-amused expression. "I would un-tote the demon in question, and I would never deliberately hurt your sister."

"And what do you have to offer her, stranger?" Brady challenged.

That was the question, wasn't it?

"Holy Hannah, Brady, let's deal with today before we worry about tomorrow," Cheyenne snapped.

"It's a guardian's duty to worry about tomorrow," Brady argued.

"True," Collette commented, striding up to defuse the tension. "But tomorrow starts today. They're ready."

Chapter Eleven

Cheyenne swallowed hard. Josiah stared at them. She shivered as Marek's hand rested against her lower back, a comforting heat. What would they say about her offer to Marek? Would they understand her rationale?

"You make an interesting suggestion, young one," Josiah stated. "But it must be Pack only. Any humans would be vulnerable."

Cheyenne straightened. It was now or never. "Marek needs to be there. This is his battle, his honor. He can be there, if he becomes kin to the Pack."

Brady's eyes just about popped out of his skull, and he growled, but did not respond to her audacity. His expression clearly stated he thought the council would take care of it for him.

"You suggest changing him." Josiah's own eyes glowed at her. "Who would sponsor him?"

Gran stepped forward. "I would. He has knowledge from before that would be invaluable to scholars, the only expert of his people. He could make his way as a teacher."

Heart in her throat, Cheyenne nodded. "I would share my life with him, until such a time as he chose elsewhere."

"He would be your responsibility," Josiah stated severely.

She turned to Marek. "Are you willing to stay in the here-and-now, to learn our ways and to share your own?"

His gaze burned into hers. "I would do anything

to see the Reynak gone and people safe and free," he replied. "I believe there is much I can learn from you and you from me, and I would be willing to teach any who seek the knowledge."

Josiah frowned. "Would you stay with Cheyenne, under the guidance of Collette, and lead us in the petition of the old gods?"

"I would."

Cheyenne's heart pounded. Was the council granting their approval? Was her impulsive notion about to become reality for all time?

"All those in favor, say aye," Josiah stated.

Most of the council ayed—save Kane and Brady. Kane turned to Marek. "I was made the same offer—twice. I turned it down—twice. Have you had time to consider the ramifications of what this means? You would no longer be human. Neither would you be Pack. You would be cursed with seeing all you come to know and love die and be gone, while you lived on. You would feel the moon but never change entirely. You would have a foot in each world, but your soul would be neither."

Cheyenne winced. Kane didn't pull his punches. When put like that…

Marek stared back at the ranger, unflinching. "I have already outlived all I've known and loved—that pain I know intimately. I freely came here, and I must make of it what I would. Cheyenne has been my anchor, and we have a connection." He turned to her. "For all the short time period, this feels right. We know each other on a different scale than most, a bond of heart and mind."

Brady didn't bother to tamp down his growl. "You slept with him." His tone was accusatory as he glared at Cheyenne.

Sister's hackles rose. Cheyenne burned. "We dream-walked together, shared memories and language," she retorted. "And who I chose to sleep with has been none of your concern since I turned eighteen."

"If Marek is certain," Kane broke in before brother and sister could start fighting in earnest, "then I vote aye."

"We have a majority, but for those crystals of Marek's to work it must be unanimous," Gran stated. She frowned at Brady. "Stop thinking so small. If you would ever be a true leader for your people, then you must see past the obvious and embrace who you really are."

"And who am I?" Brady challenged. "I'm a Pack guardian, sworn to keep people safe. You're talking about summoning an ancient god who may or may not exist, to banish a demon that may or may not exist. Does that sound safe, or even sane?"

"We've seen it," Cheyenne retorted. "It exists. Therefore, whatever sent it has to exist."

"Then it's not safe," Brady argued. "I can't in good conscience condone a face-to-face with something we can't defeat. That's just crazy talk."

"Would you like me to introduce you?" Cheyenne asked with saccharine sweetness. "I'm sure we could arrange something."

"As a matter of fact, I would." Brady's eyes burned. "No offense, Gran, but I believe in the physical, not the spiritual—what I can see, touch, hear. I haven't seen anything that would suggest this is anything other than an attack by a predator."

Cheyenne's heart stopped. Sure, the Reynak hadn't killed Pack—up until now. But Brady was likely to piss it off just enough to become the first.

"That is not a good idea," Marek stated.

"Ya think?" Cheyenne drawled. "Okay, big brother. Let's just shift and go for a walk under the stars." She turned to Marek. He was not a happy man. His jaw tightened, and his eyes were haunted. "I'll be fine. Remember?" She laid a hand against his cheek.

Heedless of his audience, he pulled her into a hard embrace. His kiss tasted of desperation and stole her breath. "Stay safe," he whispered against her lips. "Should anything happen to you, I would be lost."

Now there was a telling statement. Cheyenne shivered. Bit by bit, Marek wound his way into her heart. She didn't want to step out of his arms. She glanced over to see a thoughtful look on Josiah's face. What was he pondering?

"I think all Pack counselors should go," Josiah stated. "Kane and Marek stay here, but we should see what we're up against—and let it see us, as well. Cheyenne can lead the way."

Gran and Josiah exchanged a *Look*—as if they were privy to something the rest of them could only guess at. Before she could distract herself, people started melting into wolves. Kane and Marek stared in wonder.

"That never gets old," Kane stated. He nodded to Cheyenne. "Go on. Marek and I will just get to know each other a bit while you're gone."

Cheyenne frowned. Trepidation made her heart skip a beat. What would they talk about? Her? *Now you're being paranoid*, she scolded herself. So what if they did? Sister pushed, distracting her from her thoughts. She yearned to dance under the stars. With a sigh, Cheyenne turned inward…and down, dropping onto all fours in a shimmer of white fur. She snapped at the big gray wolf beside her, barely missing Brady's ear.

Josiah, a rangy, rather moth-eaten gray wolf, growled at her, and Sister subsided, dropping into a submissive crouch. Marek knelt before her. "Hurry back to me."

Both woman and wolf thrilled to those words. Kane opened the door, and with one last look at

Marek, Cheyenne lead the way outside. Flanked by Brady and Gran, she loped into the trees, the older council fanning out behind them. Sister yipped and stretched her legs, launching herself over a fallen log. They startled up a young buck and gave chase, not trying to catch it but simply running for the sheer joy of it all—reveling in the pouring moonlight, the crisp air, the twinkle of stars against the black velvet of the night sky and the fellowship of being Pack.

Sister's tongue hung out the side of her muzzle as she panted. Her muscles burned. Cheyenne eventually swung back toward Josiah's home and dropped from a lope to a jog.

Wrongness. Sister plowed to a halt. Brady crashed into her, nearly bowling her over. The entire Pack halted, noses twitching as they scented sulfur on the breeze, as the crackling darkness descended and the forest stilled. Cheyenne shook it off, like water from her fur. Gran cocked her head at the huge shadow sliding through the trees. The Reynak's front claws clacked together like a testy lobster as it approached. Cheyenne flattened her ears at the irritating sound.

Brady stared up at the flaring red eyes of the earth-spirit. Cheyenne caught a sense of puzzlement from it. They weren't attacking, or running, which were the only two things it was prepared to deal with.

Small, Cheyenne sent her thoughts its way. *Show us "small."*

Again the dizzying rush of stars from the universe to the earth. Gran whimpered and gagged. Tomas flattened his ears. A pair of female eyes glared down at them from the clouds. Gold. Pupils like a cat's. A hand reached down to caress the head of the Reynak. *Sina,* a voice purred in Cheyenne's head. Then *She* was gone—if *She'd* ever really been there. Was it just a memory of the Reynak's?

The Reynak snorted at them. Again the sense of puzzlement.

Go back, Cheyenne thought. *Go home.*

It shook its head and snorted again. Its nostrils flared red as it backed away through the trees until it was gone. Cheyenne felt its retreat, but knew it was still just beyond Sister's senses. She streaked toward Josiah's house, where Marek awaited her return.

A shiver sparked along her nerves at the thought of going home to Marek. Her heart turned over.

The porch light was on. Almost as if he sensed her approach, Marek stood in the open doorway. Cheyenne shoved Sister aside and reached for him, encircling his waist with her human arms. He held her tight. Cheyenne took a moment to soak in his warmth, then turned to Brady.

"Well?"

His face was gray, a stunned look in his eyes. She fought the urge to say, "I told you so", and reached for his hand. It was ice cold. He focused on her face. "You were right," he said. He turned to Gran. "If you were right about this, what else are you right about?"

"Oh, everything," she replied loftily. She turned to Marek. "Does the name *Sina* mean anything to you?"

"You heard that?" Cheyenne asked.

Gran threw her another one of those Looks.

Marek paled. "The goddess of misfortune?"

"Well, if that's what you thought of Her, no wonder She's got it in for you," Cheyenne huffed. "You've got a lot to learn about women—even goddesses."

Josiah strode up. "She's the sender. She's your gun." He turned to Brady. "Seen enough, guardian?

What's your answer now?"

Brady swallowed hard. "Aye." He turned to Marek. "I owe you an apology. Whatever I can do to help, you can count on me."

Cheyenne stared at Marek's brightening amulets. "Look."

Marek shuddered. "I don't have to look. I can feel it. Belief. Conviction."

"What does it feel like?" she asked. Curiosity was her besetting sin, Gran had oft told her.

"Lightning." His gaze burned into hers. "Together, we can do this. I accept your offer. Let's finish this."

A surge of heat greeted those words. Cheyenne could only nod. Brady sighed, but inclined his head. He was a changed man, eyes wide open. Gran patted her shoulder. "Go home, both of you. We'll work out some of the details tonight. Marek can fill in the rest tomorrow."

Cheyenne found herself alone with Marek on the porch as everyone else went inside. She stared up at his strong, handsome face. Familiar. Beloved. Hers. Did he know what he was agreeing to?

"Do you know what you're doing?" he asked.

No, but Sister did. "The marked is always tied to the marker," she warned him. "It makes you forever mine, and me yours."

He frowned. "Are we getting married?"

She smiled through the unexpected pang. "No. It's just a bond, almost familial. The serum in you is noticeably mine. We'll be able to link to each other like in the dreams, but even when waking."

"You're going to bite me?"

Need made her tremble. Sister burned to possess him, to bind him to them forever. "Yeah." Her brow wrinkled at the hoarseness in her voice. "But it won't hurt a bit."

Chapter Twelve

Marek frowned as his body tightened in response to that voice. Anticipation. Damned if the thought of being tied to her didn't make him hard as *ahnkeisha*. Her eyes were dark in the lamplight, her cheeks flushed. He'd be willing to bet that heat went a lot farther down her body, too. He lowered his gaze, to see her nipples pebbling against her shirt. Was she already softening, swelling? He took a deep breath, scenting her need. It called to him, pulled at him, and he felt himself twitch and lengthen in response. He pulled her against him, letting her feel his own growing arousal, and shuddered when she gasped.

He bent down, until his lips were but a breath from hers. "Let's go home," he murmured. Desire licked along his skin as she whimpered. Whimpered…moaned…writhed under him, around him. He shook himself back to his senses.

Cheyenne stumbled down the steps and climbed into her truck. Marek barely noticed the vehicle. So long as it got him there faster, it could fly for all he cared. She missed the hole with her key the first two times she tried, her hands shook so badly. But she got it started on the third attempt, and the truck roared to life. The ride home was tense silence. Anticipation was an excruciating crackle down his spine; even his fingertips tingled.

He had no idea how they made it home. He all but dragged her into the trailer. She'd just locked the door when he knotted his hand in her hair and took her mouth like a starving man at a banquet. He moaned at her wild taste, the slide of her tongue against his own. Her arms came around his waist, her fingers curling her nails into his back—he felt their bite through his shirt, and he burned to feel them on his bare skin. He shook with need, the blood roaring in his ears, rushing down into a pulsing erection. He swore he felt every stroke of her tongue there. The memory of her sucking him down her throat almost dropped him to his knees.

She arched into him, cradling him between her thighs. He slid his hand under her shirt, tugging her breast harness up until her breasts sprang free. Her nipple bored into his palm. He circled it with his thumb, pinched it lightly between his fingers. Cheyenne gasped into his mouth. The sound was a shock of fire. This loving was different—a fierce, primal craving.

He pulled off the amulets, dropping them to the floor. She reached around to the front of him, grasped his shirt to tug it free from his jeans and yanked it open, scattering buttons in every direction. He laughed and shrugged out of the ruined garment, pulling back to tug her own shirt over her head. Her eyes glittered up at him, her pale skin flushed rosy with desire. Her nipples beckoned. He maneuvered her over to the long chair that she called a couch, and she shoved him down to climb atop him.

The sight of her breasts hanging over him inflamed him. He pulled her down to take one in his mouth, teasing the nipple with his tongue, drawing hard enough to make her cry out. She reached down to rub him through his jeans, and his hips surged upward, pressing his aching erection against her hand. His heart hammered in his chest. He gripped the lush curve of her backside, settling her over him. She slid her hands up over his chest, and he drew her down, rocking his hips to rub against that exquisite heat.

"Marek!"

His heart tripped at that breathless cry. He undid her pants, tugged them down over her hips. She staggered up long enough to slide them and her undergarments to the floor. Her eyes narrowed on him. "Off," she ordered.

"Whatever you want," he agreed, kicking free of his own clothing before dragging her to him. "Come here," he growled.

She leaned down to take his mouth with hers, plundering the depths with her tongue, in a carnal dance with his. Her hands trailed over his chest, down his sides and abdomen. Marek's muscles clenched at her touch, in anticipation of her curling her fingers around him. He grasped himself, and her hand joined his, fingers entwining as they tightened around him, stroking up and down his shaft.

She nibbled along his jaw to his ear. Hot panting little breaths licked along his skin. "God, you make me burn!" she whispered. He groaned as her tongue swirled around his ear, and he buried his fingers in the fiery cream between her legs. Her swollen core sucked at his fingers, and the need to bury himself within her made him shake.

"You're killing me," he groaned aloud.

"Not yet," she whispered. She suckled on the skin of his neck, nipping lightly over the pulse pounding in his throat. She positioned herself over him, dragging his sensitized flesh over hers until he was near begging. With shocking suddenness, she plunged her hips down, sucking him into her voracious body, and clamped down onto the curve of his shoulder with teeth that were suddenly razor-sharp.

Marek's world exploded in a rush of pain and white-hot lust. Molten need surged through him, the need to take, to conquer. *Mine*, echoed in his mind as she fed on him and he pounded into her. His blood boiled until he thought he would combust. She flowed around him, and he into her, until they were a single swirl of hunger and need. It was too much, and with a roar, he came, shuddering into her as she growled and pulsed around him.

He shook. He burned. The world shifted back into focus. She licked at his wound, already healing. Incredible. Her eyes gleamed down at him. Glowing silver in the moonlight. She threw her head back with a howl as she broke in pulsing waves around him. He felt the pleasure crashing though her, through him. Wild. So beautiful it almost stopped his heart.

Mine.

Her sentiment or his? Marek drew her down into his arms, and she snuggled close. He waited to speak until their racing hearts slowed, until their ragged pants returned to normal. He wrestled with a heavy mixture of satisfaction and guilt. Never had he taken a woman so roughly. He'd all but attacked her. Not that Cheyenne was complaining, but still.

"Is it always like that?" he asked.

She stared into his eyes, and he felt the shock of it deep in his soul. Already the connection was there. "I've only ever heard the word 'intense.' I think I'll have to tell them that is a gross understatement. But it's making you over, giving you a connection to the earth and the moon, which is why human sensibilities are stripped away to the most basic core needs. The human becomes the beast, even if just for a moment. It's the way it has to be. Don't feel guilty. You didn't hurt me." She grinned, then sobered. "Did I hurt you?"

He shook his head, still dazed.

"Now what?" she wondered aloud.

Incredibly, his body stirred anew at the husky note in her voice, when he'd have sworn he'd never be able to move again. "Let's go to bed, where I can love you properly." She quivered, her eyes darkened. His heart warmed at the wild woman the gods had granted him. "Your bed or mine?"

"Mine's bigger," she whispered.

Somehow, her inviting him into her bed felt like more. He felt the pull of it through his heart, through his very soul. No longer alone, in truth now. The emptiness was gone. He pulled her down for a long, gentle kiss. "Yours."

She melted against him. "Mine," she agreed.

****

Had it only been three days? Cheyenne asked herself as she stood beside her mate and faced the council. Sister recognized that little fact immediately—only mates knew that explosion of passion in the Bonding. He was truly soul-mate of the Pack now. Even Brady had backed down, after two seconds in Marek's presence. Now it was time, time for the summoning. Time for the Reynak to return to its own place, so they could live free. Free of fear and guilt.

Gran nodded to her, to Marek. Like the rest of the council, she stood naked in the moonlit clearing, bearing nothing of the manmade. Marek alone wore the amulets, but bore no weapons. "Are you ready, child?"

Cheyenne took a deep shuddering breath. The council, in a moment of apparent pure insanity, had decreed that she be the one to do the calling, since she was bound to Marek—as was the Reynak. Marek's warm touch was reassuring. Whatever happened, they'd face it together. The amulets glowed bright lilac now—a people united despite their aversion to the silver. It had to be a good omen.

The moonlight poured over them as she raised her arms. *Come to me.*

The Reynak stepped forward. Seeing Marek and the crystals, it let out a tremendous roar, a blast of heat and darkness. This time, Cheyenne refused to cower. It couldn't harm them. It wouldn't harm them. She protected Marek. She did.

The Reynak charged. Marek stiffened, but did not retreat.

Cheyenne stepped between them. Surprised, the Reynak plowed to a halt. Sniffing. It cocked its head, shook it. Puzzled. It stared, at the amulets, at the moon. She knew what it saw—one of the hated warriors. She knew what it felt—earth kind. The contradiction confounded it.

The time had come. "Sina!" she called.

Golden cat's eyes in the clouds, a feeling of supreme irritation. The very air crackled around them. *Who dares call My name?*

Cheyenne's hair blew wildly in a nearly nonexistent breeze. She dropped to her knees; the entire council followed suit. Marek, too, knelt, and took her hand. Their submissive gesture mollified the deity—irritation turned to curiosity. *Who are you?*

"Your children, who guard your lands in the here-and-now," Cheyenne replied. She curled down into herself, and Sister emerged for a moment, then retreated again. Cheyenne shook her head, disoriented by the suddenness.

Sina stared at Marek. *He is not mine.*

"He is mine," Cheyenne replied. "There are humans sworn to our cause, who believe as we do that we do not inherit the land from our ancestors, we but borrow it from our children."

The goddess' eyes narrowed on the amulets. *He bears the symbols that stood against me and mine.*

"They focus belief and will," Marek replied. "The belief in the need to protect the earth, and the will to see it done."

What would you have of Me?

"Return the Reynak to its former home and

leave us to ours," Cheyenne pleaded. "It would be ineffective, and killing people just brings undue attention. If You don't, there would be war and destruction on an unprecedented level. Allow us to take its place, working to protect Your realm, our home."

You called My name. In doing so, you resurrected a religion long forgotten. I would not be lost again. Since you say you would replace My pet, then I would demand a price from you.

Marek tensed.

"What would you ask of me, Lady?" Cheyenne trembled.

Become My priestess. Defend My world openly, publicly, on a grander scale than you do now.

"If I do this, You'll remove the Reynak from this world?"

Yes.

Cheyenne nodded. "Done." A rush of heat and light flooded her, a burning anger at the waste, the desecration. A burning need to set things right.

Done, Sina replied. *But you shall hear from Me again.* She and the Reynak vanished.

The sounds of the night gradually returned. One by one, they clambered to their feet and looked around. Cheyenne threw herself into Marek's arms. "It worked!"

"And you are now bound to the past and the future," Gran commented. "A priestess to the past, sworn to protect the future. Looks like you both have your paths set."

"And we take those first steps together," Marek stated. He captured her lips with a burning kiss.

Her heart soared. Cheyenne distantly felt the Pack loping off into the woods as Marek eased her to the grass. "Together," she whispered.

About the author...

Renee Wildes is a former RWA contest diva and now an award-winning, multi-published author of both fantasy romance and contemporary paranormal romance.

A former vet tech, she has an AAS degree from MATC Madison in Laboratory Animal Science but now works in health insurance. She lives in central WI in a small town two hours north of Madison, east of Wausau in a region she calls "paper mill central." She's married with two kids, a calico cat and two gray half-Arabian mares.

She enjoys horseback riding, reading and scrapbooking. She's a huge PBR fan, especially of Wiley Peterson from ID. She's also the only Washington Redskins fan in die-hard Green Bay Packer territory.

She has a website: http://www.reneewildes.com
She also has a blog:
http://www.reneewildes1.wordpress.som

Werewolves in London

by

Karilyn Bentley

Dedication

To my wonderful, supportive hubby, I love you.
And to the Spanksters,
I couldn't have done it without you!

Chapter One

"Your dog doesn't respect you." Vonda reached down to scratch behind Sam's ear. "I can help you with that problem, but I can't help train him to herd. Do we have a deal?"

Tom took off his hat, scratched his head and slammed it back on as if to hold in steam. Judging from the color of his face, he should have let his hair wave free in the breeze. It might cool things off. One long finger pointed at Sam. One nicely shaped, work hardened finger. The list of things that finger could do to her body rushed through Vonda's brain on fast forward. It didn't help that the man whose finger provoked such lascivious thoughts was the best-looking thing in this little podunk town.

Why was she thinking such thoughts? *Concentrate, Vonda, concentrate!* Last time she thought this way about a man she was in heat. Oh shit. *Not again.* No wonder Sam stuck to her like proverbial glue.

Wait. Tom's mouth was moving. "...me?"

"Huh? I'm sorry, what did you say?" *Good job Vonda, way to look stupid on your first visit with a client.*

"I said, how can that dog not respect me?"

"Well, dogs see things differently than humans. If you don't act like the alpha, then they assume they are the alpha. That's what creates problems. That's where I can help."

"Yes, yes. I know. But I have other herding dogs. None of them give me problems. What's up with that?" His frustrated green stare bored into her.

Men frustrated so easily. Humans in general. Ever see a canine with hypertension?

Sam licked her hand. She took in a shallow breath when his tongue rasped against her skin and it was then that she smelled it. The scent of a man. Not just any man. A man she wanted to mate with. A man about six four, with sandy blond, almost brown hair and green eyes. A man who stood less than three feet from her.

Damn hormones.

If she didn't get out of here soon she'd lose any chance of ever being a dog trainer.

She looked at her wrist. *Two hairs past a freckle.* "Well, all dogs are different and therefore react differently. Look, I really have to run. Do you want me to come back and help you with Sam or not?"

Say yes, say yes, say yes. He opened his mouth, closed it, looked at Sam, then her, then Sam. He sighed. Oh yeah, she had the job.

"Okay. When do you want to start?"

She looked at the evening sky, the oranges and pinks blushing across the horizon. Tonight was one day from the full moon and she felt the pull of its magic creep under her skin, touching the beast inside her, coaxing it out of hiding. She would be hard-pressed not to change for the next three days. Well, Tom had waited this long for help. What would be three more days?

"Thursday. Will that work for you?"

He stuck out his hand. "Sounds good. What time did you want to come out?"

She gripped his hand, holding tight despite the tingles shooting straight into her core from where their palms met. Desire ripped through her hormone sensitive veins and she fought the urge to pull him against her. *Damn heat.* He pulled away, shaking his hand.

"Did you feel that?"

"I'm sorry. Sometimes I build up electricity. Would nine in the morning be okay?"

"Umm, sure."

"Great. Gotta run. It's been real nice meeting you." One last pat to Sam's head and she zipped back to her car.

Thank God she had irregular heat cycles. The last time the heat ran through her veins seemed mild compared to the desire Tom evoked in her, and yet she hadn't resisted the urge to mate. Look how that ended, with her husband screaming to the divorce judge that she was a furry dog.

What had she been thinking? Her ex couldn't even tell the difference between a dog and a wolf.

But he had taught her an important lesson and that was to stay away from men. Electronic devices worked quite well, thank you very much. And until she met Tom McGowan her philosophy had worked. A bit lonely at times—*okay, who was she fooling, all the time*—but a little sacrifice never hurt anyone. Her core tingled as she remembered the electrical spark from his touch, the desire she fought while in his presence. Tom had the potential to shatter her philosophy and her heart. Fear colored her thoughts and made tonight's impending change seem easy in comparison.

****

Tom took a deep breath and held it, trying to get his bodily functions under control. Anger and arousal; what a combination. At least he'd learned one thing from the shapely brunette, and it wasn't a lack of respect from his newest dog. His hand reached for his crotch, feeling the hard ridge of his arousal. Nice to know the thing still worked.

He'd all but given up on his ability to function as a man since Anita's passing four years ago. And not only did his dick suddenly come on line, but what was up with that electric tingle Vonda gave him when she grasped his hand? Last time he'd felt anything remotely like that was from his mother, and Mom sure hadn't provoked what was going on in his pants.

Maybe he should ask Vonda out. Provided he remembered what to do with a woman on a date. Okay, some parts he remembered quite clearly, which is why he hadn't dated since Anita. How would he explain to the poor woman his lack of arousal? *Really, honey, it's not you, it's me.* Yeah, right. Thinking about how that conversation would go scared him away from the dating scene. Now that things seemed to be working again, he might just give it a try.

Thinking about Vonda drove away the anger he felt over her assessment of Sam and the dog's lack of respect for him. Everyone knew that dogs thought of Tom as their natural leader. Sam was just crazy. Who cared what her assessment of the situation was? Tom would take the eye candy any way he could get it.

Dark brown hair, shot with silver highlights, hung to her shoulders and framed an elfin face with amber eyes. She barely reached his shoulder and yet her body moved with the grace of an athlete. He'd love to strip off her clothes and see the play of muscles under her skin as her legs gripped his waist while he....

Tom shook his head, clearing away most of the fantasy. Later tonight he'd marvel he actually managed a fantasy, but for now his ranch deserved his attention, not the woman.

"Come, Sam." Tom patted his leg.

Tongue lolling from the side of his mouth, Sam's ears perked up as he stared intently at Tom's leg. The tongue slipped behind teeth as he stood and shook himself, trotting over to where Vonda's car had been parked.

No respect. Man that burned.

Tom sighed. As impossible as it seemed, Vonda had a point. "Come on, Layla. Let's go make a round."

Layla rose from where she lay, her arthritic legs shaking as she stood. Her tail wagged like a pendulum as she limped to him. He slowed his pace so she walked beside him. At least she respected him.

Sam sat in the driveway staring forlornly after the trail of dust from Vonda's car. He felt the instant the dog's attention turned to him as he and Layla walked toward his truck. Not one to be left behind, Sam yelped as he ran after them, pole-vaulting over Layla so he could lead what he considered his pack to the truck.

His pack, his left ass cheek. Sam had a dominance issue, and he had too soft of a heart where canines were concerned. Dogs loved him, recognizing a friendly leader when they saw one. Until Sam came into his life, he'd had great success training dogs.

Sam was a breed unto himself and he had no idea what to do with him.

If Tom told him to sit, he walked off, come happened only occasionally and down was more elusive than a willing steer at branding time. No wonder his friend Steve had a friend of a friend more than willing to get rid of Sam.

He should get rid of him too, but every time he thought it, the damn dog would lick his hand, staring out of those eyes mismatched blue and brown, and he couldn't do it. Sam stayed.

Funny thing was, the dog seemed to like Vonda and Sam didn't give his attentions easily. As far as he could see, Sam only liked him and his daughter Elizabeth. Until the sexy dog trainer stepped out of her red SUV, revealing jean-clad legs.

He shook his head at the image that thought formed and picked up Layla to put her in the bed of his truck. Sam jumped in without being asked. Tom slammed the tailgate shut and started for the door.

He didn't have much time left before the remaining rays of sunlight slid behind the horizon. Gunning the engine, he started across his property, heading to the last hole the vandals had torn in his fence. They were getting braver; this spot was close to the house, almost within visual distance.

So far the only evidence of the vandals' activities was cut fences. His herd hadn't been touched. The damage wasn't even that extensive? Nothing was stolen, so why were they bothering?

The whole thing gave him a bad feeling. As if someone hunted him. Once he arrived at the damaged fence, he hopped out, leaving the dogs in the bed. Correction; Layla stayed in the back of the truck like a good girl. Sam saw the need to jump out and chase a rabbit.

It was useless to call him back. He grabbed his tools and used the remaining sunlight to repair the hole in the barbed wire. He heard Sam barking in the distance, Layla whimpering in reply. The wire felt warm under his palm, through the leather glove. Perhaps his skills honed as a lad and unused since that time still worked. He closed his eyes, focusing on the heat, imagining who held the wire before him.

It took a minute before the picture came to him, flashing in fast-forward like a racecar, the colors a blur. Concentrating, he brought the whirling pictures into focus, slowing them down until he could make sense of them.

Scents came first; the acid smell of fear, terror, and the sharp tang of blood. The wire dropped from his hand as he stumbled backward, his chest constricting, a tight belt suffocating him. He looked to the house, not seeing the structure, but seeing the light from it glowing on the horizon. A cold finger of darkness swept down his back as he saw in his mind's eye Elizabeth running through the house, playing as ten-year-old girls were wont to do. Alone.

Oh, God, no. Not Elizabeth.

Chapter Two

Vonda slammed the car door and scurried up the steps to her house. Not much time left before the sun slid below the horizon and she needed to be in place when darkness hit. The moon wouldn't rise until complete dark, but the change would happen promptly at sundown. All those rumors about werewolves changing when the full moon rose were a little off. Or at least they were off for her, she knew no other werewolves.

Orphaned when she was two and raised by a foster family in Dallas, Vonda never knew about the wolf within her until puberty came and the change hit. The terror she felt that first time still haunted her. When most girls her age got cramps with their periods, she changed into a beast. Like she could discuss that one with her foster mom. Luckily that first time she didn't share a bedroom and no one saw her. For three days around the full moon she changed into a wolf at sundown and back at sunrise.

After that first time, she learned how to sneak out of the house and stay in the shadows. Winter was the worst, when the nights were long and darkness hit around five-thirty. Lying became second nature, fear always present. When she turned eighteen and rented her own place things became easier. She learned how to hunt, how to temper her amazing physical strength and what the auras around people meant.

Just when she thought she had it all figured out, that being a werewolf was no different than having some strange disease, she went into heat.

Intense sexual urges she couldn't resist accompanied the heat cycle. Any man in her vicinity risked being used like a stud. Not like most men minded. Her ex sure didn't. She, on the other hand, hated how she acted, hated having to get laid like an addict needed to shoot up. While her ex loved her carefree sexual attitude, her conservative upbringing caused her to hate it. But with the heat coursing through her veins, forcing her mind on only one thing, she had no choice; she needed a man like an addict needed a fix. After a whirlwind romance consisting of a bunch of now-embarrassing sex, her ex had proposed, clearly confusing lust with love. Try as she might, she couldn't blame him for using her, not when she returned the favor ten times over.

It lasted all of two months, until her husband saw her change. No amount of great sex could hurdle that barrier. He ran out of their apartment faster than she could howl, screaming Vonda was a dog. How insulting.

And now she was in heat again.

All she could think of was Tom; his scent and the electric zing that shot through her body when his hand touched hers. If she remembered correctly, the heat only lasted the time of the full moon. All she had to do was avoid all men, including Tom, and she shouldn't have a problem.

Vonda dropped her purse on the table by the door, striding down the hall to her bedroom. The house was silent except for the ticking of the mantle clock. Tick, tock, each click of the minute hand tugging her one step closer to the change. Kicking off her shoes, she pulled her T-shirt over her head, laying it on the bed. The bra came next, and she tugged off her jeans, folding them in a neat pile on top of the rest of her clothes. The lace thong made a nice bow on the pile.

She felt the magic now, humming in her veins,

flowing along her skin. Not much time remained.

Vonda walked down the hall, into the kitchen and out the back door. Under her feet the grass felt warm, soothing. She stood facing west, watching the sun slip beneath the horizon, drawing its rays across the ground like a web. Magic seeped under her skin, rippling muscles, quickening her heart rate. The power built, until her jaw clenched against the pain. Bones snapped, elongating, shortening, changing. Fur streamed over her skin as her hands turned into paws.

Dropping to the ground on all fours, the wolf let loose a howl, shaking the pain free. The grass sprang under her feet as she padded toward the edge of her property.

The hunt was on.

As a wolf, she followed her instincts. As a human, she followed reason. Despite her upbringing, or lack thereof, she learned how to merge her wolf's mind with her human one; how to use her heightened senses no matter what physical state she was in. She listened to her instincts now. They were never wrong when it came to food and that meant food ran ten miles to the east.

A good night's exercise.

Howls sounded from the direction she headed. Her heart leapt at the sound. Cousins. Not a hundred percent like her, but close enough. Wolves accepted her into their packs, although they remained wary of her, uncertain if she was an alpha or omega. Vonda never fought for status in a pack, why should she—even though they were cousins, she didn't belong with them.

She didn't fit in anywhere. As a human she was stronger, faster and had a big hairy secret. As a wolf her scent smelled like a human, puzzling her cousins, causing them to remain wary of her. She walked among both worlds, but belonged to neither.

But at least here in London, Montana she could become a wolf without worrying if humans saw her furry half. There were no wild wolves in Dallas or anywhere in Texas that she knew of. Moving to Montana had been self-preservation and so far, it had been a good move.

No one questioned one extra wolf roaming here and she didn't have to hide for three days like she used to. Why she waited so long to move here was beyond her. She should have moved sooner.

Maybe then she could have avoided the ex. She could have had Tom instead.

Stop it, Vonda! Tom needed to be avoided. At least until the heat went away. Thank God her next appointment with him was after the full moon. Hopefully the heat would be gone then too.

Howls sounded to her right and she veered toward them. She saw images in her mind, images sent by her cousins, their way of communicating. A herd of deer standing in a copse of trees, their ears pricking forward, listening. Feelings of quietness, the hush of paws on grass, the excitement of the impending kill crept through her veins.

Telepathy rocked.

Vonda found her cousins watching the deer, biding their time. She trotted to the back of the hunting party and lowered her tail and ears. The wolves nearest to her sniffed her in a proper how-do-you-do. She felt their uncertainty, but they didn't chase her off and more images of wolves killing deer slashed through her mind.

And then they were running, the deer sprinting away, wolves pounding after them.

Vonda stayed in the back, helping chase, but not taking down a deer. She wouldn't eat first either, that treat belonged to the alpha pair.

Trees flashed by her as she sprinted after the deer, low foliage slapping her face. The smells of the forest excited her, the word "home" a constant thought. Her breath sawed in and out of her lungs, she really needed to hit the track in human form.

Three feet from the deer, she smelled *them* on the evening breeze. A scent that left her salivating. *Cattle.* Directly to her left.

She veered. To hell with the deer. Why have venison when she could dine on steak tartar?

Even as a human she liked her meat raw. And what better to eat than steak, straight off the steer?

Vonda thought the image of cattle and sent it to the nearest wolf, who stumbled in his flight after his dinner. Emotions crashed over her; fear, fright, followed by thoughts of humans. Bad, scary, she should stay where it's safe, where humans with explosive sticks couldn't hurt her.

She almost stopped, but why should she be scared of the humans? She was half-human after all. And there was steak. Did she mention that? Raw, fresh. Much better tasting than deer.

Adios cousins. She was on a new chase.

Her legs picked up speed, churning dirt and leaves as she raced across the ground. A barbed wire fence stopped her progress. The cattle lowed on the other side.

Close. So close. She could dine on steak tartar tonight. Her stomach growled.

Vonda eyed the fence. Two rows of barbed wire were strung between wooden posts. It didn't look like an electrical fence. The fence was meant to keep animals in, not out. And as a werewolf she had her own way of getting through the fence that her canine brethren found impossible to do.

She ducked her head between the two wires, following with her left front leg, then left rear leg. The right side followed and she was through. The cattle looked her way. She snarled and leapt.

Cattle scattered as she attacked. Not as fast as

deer, they still ran for their lives. She picked out one at the back of the pack and jumped at its throat, taking it down. The cow screamed, the sound ending in a gurgle as its throat tore open, blood streaming. She shook her head, spraying blood across the grass.

She waited until the blood slowed to a trickle, the spirit of the cow flying free. Once it was dead, she sank her teeth into its hide. Dinner, ah.

Steak tartar was her monthly treat since she had arrived in town three months ago. Last thing needed was for wolves to be blamed on monthly cattle killing, which is why she tried to hit a different ranch each month. Problem was she hadn't learned the boundary lines of each rancher, or who all the ranchers were. Tom was the only one she'd met and he managed to turn her on even when she was in wolf form.

From the darkness came barking, riding the wind as it blew across the ground. She raised her blood-soaked muzzle and inhaled the wind. A dog was closing in, running full force toward her. Shouldn't be a problem, dogs lacked the strength of wolves.

You can't be seriously considering killing a dog, Vonda. Get real! Her human mind overrode the wolf's instincts, she turned and faced the oncoming dog.

Vonda snarled at it, baring teeth, letting it know the cow belonged to her. A brown and white dog pulled up short, its tail initially dropping, then curling as it snarled back.

Tom wasn't kidding around when he said Sam presented a problem. The damn dog was willing to go up against a wolf, and a werewolf at that. Not the smartest animal around, but Vonda had to give him points for bravery. Or maybe it was pure stupidity.

What was he doing over here? Shouldn't he be on Tom's property? She sent the dog an image of her talking to Tom, petting Sam, telling him to sit.

Sam cocked his head as his growls stopped. Vonda pushed the images harder, her petting his head as he sat. Sitting was good, he wanted to sit, he didn't want to attack. Attacking bad, sitting good.

Sam sat.

She pictured the house and sent it to Sam. Unfortunately, the house reminded her of Tom, and her blood ran hot, her sex swelling. Sam whined.

Eww, yuck. He wouldn't dare. She ventured a glance under the dog's hindquarters. Whew. Neutered.

She snarled again, trying the house pictures once more. Sam sat, the tip of his tail wagging. Vonda saw Tom sitting at a table with a girl of around ten, the scent of fear rolling off him. Vonda closed her eyes, shaking her head. A dog sent her pictures?

She'd never had that happen before. But why shouldn't it? Dogs were distant cousins and all canines had the ability for telepathy. Which was why dog training came so naturally to her. She pictured what the dog should do until the animal understood which sound went with the picture. However, no dog had sent any image other than chasing critters back to her.

Maybe she could only communicate with them while in wolf form. If being a werewolf only came with a how-to manual, things would be a lot easier.

Tom's fear, as seen through Sam's eyes, strode through her brain, triggering a like response in her. Sam's ward was in trouble. She had to help. Wait a minute; Tom didn't belong to Sam, which was the whole root of the trouble in that relationship.

Vonda shook her head. It didn't matter at the moment who was in charge, Tom or Sam. All that mattered was that Tom was in trouble. Something was wrong. Vonda probed into Sam's memories, seeing nothing to cause fear in Tom. His daughter was smiling, but something was wrong.

What? Sam had ducked out the dog door, smelling her scent even across the distance. He hadn't wanted her kill, he'd wanted her.

And now she had to help him.

Sam barked once, signaling he understood her decision to help him and took off across the darkened pasture, heading toward the house. She followed.

****

"Hey Dad, look what I did in art class." Elizabeth held up a canvas with a picture of the mountains.

"You painted that?"

She nodded. "Yep. Whatcha think?"

"Wow, girl. You're quite the little artist." He smiled, impressed with her picture. Who knew his daughter drew like that?

"Daaadddyyy." She slapped a hand down on the kitchen table. "I'm NOT a little girl. I'm almost grown."

Problem was, she spoke the truth. Amazing how time flew. He'd swear that yesterday he first held her in his arms, her tiny fists balled, her face red and grimacing. She sat at the table, her features identical to his, her hair, though, the dark brown of Anita's. A girl on the cusp of adolescence. What would he do with a teenage girl? Weren't there things only a woman could tell her?

He really needed to start dating. If not for himself then for his daughter. She needed a mom. A mom like Vonda.

Visions of tanned legs wrapped around his waist while he drove into her, again and again, harder, faster, rushed through his brain. What was it about that woman that got him hard while he cooked dinner? There was nothing sexy about raw meat.

He flipped the burger on his indoor grill and

continued his conversation with Elizabeth.

"Yep, you're growing up. Pretty soon you'll be able to cook for me while I sit and watch you."

"Don't be ridiculous, Daddy. I can't cook."

He laughed. Elizabeth always said that. She looked so peaceful sitting at the table, doing her homework. Nothing at all like his vision, where a huge man held her, her face dripping blood from a cut on her head, her eyes wide, as she struggled in the man's grip.

Just thinking of what he saw gave him chills.

"Daddy, it's burning!"

So it was. He flipped it, shooting Elizabeth an apologetic smile. "A little charcoal never hurt anyone, honey."

"Whatever." She waved a hand, returning to her books.

Would he be able to keep her safe? Where was he in that vision? That man he saw was huge, like a steroid-crazed wrestler, and he was no lightweight.

Why...how? His visions always came true. Or at least they had when he was a child. He hadn't tried to see anything since he saw his mother's death a day before she died. Now he needed to learn how to stop that man from getting Elizabeth.

The man had been in the house, he realized with a start as he flipped the burger onto a plate. He put a raw meat patty on the grill. How did that man get into his house?

The scariest thing was, what had happened to him? Was he dead? Why wasn't he helping Elizabeth? Once caught, that man would be dead, that much he knew for sure. Murdering the son of a bitch sounded like a good idea.

"Hey, Daddy," Elizabeth's voice dropped him into the here and now. "It's a full moon. You think another steer is going to die?"

"I don't know, hon."

Unknowingly, she managed to derail his morbid thoughts onto another little problem his ranch had. As if vandals breaking fences to get to his daughter wasn't enough bad luck, for the past three months something, probably a wolf, had been gnawing on his herd. Each full moon brought another dead steer. If he didn't know any better, he'd think it was a werewolf, but those only existed in folklore. They couldn't really exist.

If he stuck like barbed wire to the herd for the next three nights, he might catch the wolf, but what was the loss of another steer when compared to his daughter? Nope, he'd stay home where he could watch her. Maybe next month he'd catch the wolf, if the thing gnawed its way through another cow tonight.

"Daddy, where'd Sam go?" Elizabeth looked at him, her amber eyes reflecting the light. His mother's eyes. Although the color was oddly like Vonda's.

Damn. He had to think of her again. The fantasy started playing, an endless loop in his mind. Double damn. Elizabeth had asked him a question. He should be thinking with the head on his shoulders. What the fuck was wrong with him tonight?

"I'm not sure, honey. Why don't you clear off the table and set it? I'm almost done over here."

Dinner. Think of dinner not Vonda. Dinner. What about strawberries used to paint chocolate down her firm flesh, leading to...

He flipped the overcooked burger onto the plate, turned off the grill and slammed the spatula onto the cabinet. Elizabeth squeaked.

"Sorry, honey. It slipped." Slipped in and out of hot, wet, warm flesh. In and out, over and over...

"You okay, Daddy?"

"Um, yeah. I have to go pee. I'll be right back."

Hoping Elizabeth didn't see the bulge in his

pants, he walked to the bathroom and slumped against the door. Taking himself in hand, he grasped the length of his dick and stroked. Once, twice and he came over his hand, teeth gritting against the pleasure. Well, whatcha know? The damn thing still worked.

Grabbing a tissue, he cleaned up the mess. He really needed to get control of himself. He couldn't just run to the bathroom every five minutes like a horny teenager. Elizabeth would know something was wrong and this was one conversation he didn't feel like having.

Yeah, honey, Daddy has the hots for the dog trainer, which causes him to have to jack off every so often, but it's good to know the ole dick still works. Uh-huh. Right.

He finished washing his hands and was reaching for the towel when the lights went out. What the hell? No storm or high winds were in the area. Maybe the fuse had shorted for the bathroom. He'd have to go check.

Layla growled. Tom's heart rate jacked up a notch. He'd owned the dog fourteen years and never once had she growled. Barked, yes; growled, never. Until now.

The doorknob slipped in his wet grasp. He used a corner of his shirt to twist the knob, managing to barely turn it, when he heard Elizabeth scream. The scream died as flesh met flesh and a crash sounded. Oh, God, no. His nightmare had just begun.

He yanked the door open, rushing into the scene from his vision. The room was dark, dappled in moonlight filtering through the blinds, unlike his vision where the room seemed lighter.

He blinked, rage consuming him. When he opened his eyes, the room seemed brighter; he smelled blood and the sharp tang of terror. A chair lay on the floor, papers scattered everywhere. A huge man with a shaved head and more tats than a prisoner held Elizabeth, one hand clamped over her mouth, one muscle-bulging arm wrapped around her waist. Her feet pummeled his shins, but the blows meant nothing to the man.

He felt his lips peel over his teeth as a red film settled across his eyes. That son of a bitch hurt his daughter. He heard an inhuman howl echo through the kitchen and the skinhead's eyebrows skimmed skyward. For a minute He wondered how Layla could make a noise like that, and then he realized it didn't come from the dog. It came from him.

Odd, but then no one had ever tried to kidnap his little girl before.

His limbs tingled as if he'd stuck his finger in an electrical outlet, energy pulsing through them. His muscles felt like they were growing, lengthening, becoming stronger. His teeth, especially the incisors, ached. His throat quivered as that inhuman howl broke out again. Elizabeth's eyes widened.

He focused on her, noting how her eyes glanced behind him as she struggled to speak, her words muffled incoherently. A rush of air to his right caused him to turn, but he was too late. A heavy weight struck his head and he crumpled.

He heard Elizabeth's muffled yells as he struggled against the darkness in his head. The front door banged shut and he knew he'd failed her. Darkness consumed him.

Chapter Three

Vonda saw the house from a distance. Uh-oh. It looked as if she'd been eating cattle from her newest client. That couldn't be a good thing. Maybe Tom hadn't noticed. It could happen.

Sam trotted along beside her, glancing at her occasionally from the corner of his eye. She hadn't gathered anything else from his canine brain in their journey to the house. Just like a male to be the silent type.

In the distance she saw the house, shining like a lighthouse to a weary traveler. Her steps slowed. She was in wolf form and would be until morning. What would Tom do when he saw her? Shoot her? What was she thinking to trail after Sam like this?

Sam looked at her and she felt his mind touch hers.

Hurry. Fear. Help.

Sam had a point. Even from this distance something seemed off. A discord in the harmony of nature. What the hell. If Tom needed her help she was there. Maybe afterward he'd repay her with sex. Yeah. That sounded like a great idea. He might be a bit freaked out when she changed, but he'd know she helped him and he'd throw her on the bed, thrusting inside her, and...

The lights shut off at the house, effectively throwing her out of her fantasy. She stopped, startled by the sudden loss of light. Sam's ears cocked forward as he sniffed the air. She dragged a deep sniff in too, smelling the scents of evening along with a new scent.

Her nostrils flared. What was that? The smell triggered a response in her brain that resonated in her body. Despite the fact she had never smelled that scent before, she knew what it was. It smelled like her. A mixture of magic and evergreen.

Werewolves.

What were werewolves doing here? Who cared about that, would they want to meet her? Where were they?

She scanned the perimeter of the house, looking for wolves, but all she saw were two men, one of them carrying what looked like a bundle of blankets in his arm. The bundle jerked and even from where she sat Vonda could see the man's muscles bulge as he tightened his grip on his load. Sam growled.

Elizabeth.

Vonda looked at Sam and back at the men as they walked toward a car parked along the main road. She breathed in, thankful the wind carried the men's scents to her and not hers to them. Sure enough, there were three different scents, two werewolves and one scared girl. She should have picked up on that earlier.

Sam darted through the grass, heading toward the men, she followed. This was worse than she thought. She hadn't imagined this when Sam came to her, telling of Tom's fear.

These men were like her, she knew it; she smelled them. So why were they in human form? How could a werewolf stay in human form when the moon shone full and bright?

She'd have to ask, after she knocked their asses down for stealing a little girl. What kind of perverts were they, taking a kid like that? Where was Tom?

She didn't care to think where he might be, or the condition he was in. She'd find Tom after she stopped these bastards.

Legs churning, she overtook Sam, passing him

as if he were a turtle on a sunny day. If she didn't get a move on, those perverts would have that girl in their car. Good thing she ran faster than the average wolf, although that steer in her stomach slowed her down.

The giant man carrying Tom's daughter laid her, blankets and all, in the backseat, and wrapped the seatbelt around her, while the other one got behind the wheel. Trying not to puke—not even a wolf should exercise after eating—she sprinted toward the giant.

The car's engine turned over, headlights splashing over the ground, blinding her. She veered out of the bright path, noting that the giant stood watching her, one hand on the car door.

She leapt, aiming for his throat. He took a step toward her, catching her around the neck and throwing her to the side. She landed with a thud, the air knocked out of her. The vibration of his steps ran across her skin as he walked toward her, but it was a little hard to move when she couldn't breathe.

As quickly as it had left, the air rushed into her lungs and she rolled, standing up even though her legs felt like they would collapse. Ears back, she snarled at Giant Pervert as his voice resonated in her ears.

"Where the fuck did you come from?"

"What is it, Big G?" The man from the car hopped out, staring at them.

She saw Sam leap at the man, slamming him into the car frame. The man let out a screech as he hit. The noise turning into a growl, followed by a yip.

Sam, danger! Get Tom!

A beefy hand clamped on the ruff of her neck, lifting her into the air. She put all four feet against GP's chest and pushed as she snapped at his wrist.

Blood gushed from his arm and he dropped her with a curse. She darted out of his reach, eyeing him for any sudden movement.

Who the hell are you and why aren't you a wolf? In case you didn't notice, the bloody moon's full.

"Someone needs to teach you a lesson, bitch. Who's your pack leader?"

Don't have one. Why are you taking Elizabeth?

"Why don't you have a pack leader?"

Because you're the only werewolf I've met. Now give me back the girl and no one will get hurt.

His teeth flashed. "Funny one, aren't you? In case you didn't notice, you're a bit outnumbered. And you didn't answer my question. Who's your leader?"

Maybe you're just deaf. I said I'm my own leader, I answer to no one. Let me have Elizabeth, you perv.

His brows carved a row in his forehead as he ignored her request. "Seriously? You be telling the truth about no leader?"

She stared at him.

"Well, well. Isn't this interesting. Hey, Jace, the bitch here has no leader."

She ventured a glance at Jace, and immediately wished she hadn't when she saw Sam lying in the grass. She growled. Jace put up his hands.

"Hey, now, he attacked me. He's not dead; don't get your fur all ruffled."

"What should we do with her? She shouldn't be left alone." GP looked worried.

I'm fine. Just give me back the girl. You perverted or something? What do you want with a little girl?

"I'm not no perv. That's sick. You don't understand our ways."

Then explain them. That should be interesting to hear. After all, she'd been waiting most of her life to hear some explanation of what she was and maybe the ensuing conversation would give Elizabeth enough time to unroll the blankets, and jump out of the car.

Unfortunately, Jace had more brains than his skinhead friend and figured that little bit of info out on his own. Dammit.

"Big G, leave the bitch. We'll find her later. Get in the car before things go to hell."

In Vonda's opinion, things were already there. How much worse could they get?

Jace gestured at Big G and slipped behind the wheel.

Big G scratched his bald head. "I hate leaving you here. Wolves should run together. Don't worry. We'll come back for you." He walked to the car and waggled his fingers at her.

She followed, trotting to the driver's side. She might be able to open the door and pull Elizabeth out. But again, her plan was foiled by Jace, who gunned the engine before Big G had time to shut his door.

She started running, chasing after the car for all she was worth, mortified she had just let a child be kidnapped by a couple of werewolves. At least she had their scents imprinted on her brain. She'd be able to track them.

****

Tom woke with a headache, a constant pounding in his ears. Why was he on the floor? And then it rushed back with a sickening thud, a crushing weight on his ribs. He'd failed Elizabeth. They took his daughter and he couldn't stop them. Tears stung his eyes as his breath caught in his throat. Her life from infancy until now flashed in his mind, each picture generating another invisible sucker punch to the chest.

The cops. He had to call the cops.

Slamming his palms against the floor, he pushed himself to all fours, the room spinning as if he were drunk. As he levered himself to his feet, the room stopped its merry-go-round dance. Why was the room so bright?

Light poured in from between the blinds, flooding the room. Had he really been unconscious for the remainder of the night? He heard a motor rev and ran toward the window, peering between the slats of the blinds, his eyes blinking in the car's headlights.

Elizabeth must be in that car. Screw the police. If the kidnappers were sitting outside, he would take care of them himself. It wasn't too late to kill the bastards that took her.

He ran to the door, and saw the gun case with his rifle standing against the wall. Yeah, capping the bastards in their asses sounded like a great idea. Problem was, the case was locked and damn it if he couldn't remember where the keys were. Like he had time to find the fuckers.

Wrapping his hand in his shirttail, he slammed his fist through the glass, imagining it was the kidnappers' faces. Shards sprinkled around his feet. He grabbed some ammo and with shaking hands slammed it into the rifle and pulled the bolt.

Locked and loaded.

The door took longer to open than it should have, but then it fell open with a squeak and a thud, and he bolted through it. His head pounding, bile choking his throat, he jumped off the porch and took off at a dead sprint after the car.

Was that a wolf chasing the car? He blinked, shaking his head. What the hell? He must have taken a harder hit than he thought.

Legs pumping, he ran faster than he thought himself capable of. He had to catch them, had to get Elizabeth back. And what was that weight in his hands?

Oh, yeah. The rifle. Shit for brains, he could fire on the motherfuckers. Except if he did that, the car could flip and Elizabeth could die. But he had to stop them and chasing after the car on foot wasn't working. How to stop them?

He had a truck. Yeah, the truck. Four wheels chased faster than two feet.

His lungs burned with the exertion, but he couldn't rest, couldn't rest until Elizabeth was back in his arms.

He took off, sprinting back to the truck. Halfway there, he heard footsteps behind him. His heart picked up the pace, triple-timing it as he realized the wolf was following him.

Shit, he didn't have time to be eaten by a wolf. He needed to save his daughter.

If he got to the truck, he could leave before the wolf caught him.

Keys, he needed his keys. Neither of his pockets contained them. He remembered his rifle, but left his keys who knows where? How could he chase after Elizabeth without his truck? Fly? Stupid idiot. And the wolf was still behind him keeping pace, stalking him.

He darted behind the truck, aimed his rifle at the wolf and tried to get his breathing under control.

****

Circling around, Vonda followed Tom back as he sprinted toward the house. She saw Sam push himself to his feet, his body undulating, his collar jingling with the motion.

Thank God he didn't seem hurt. She reached out with her mind, rummaged around in his thoughts, learning he was sore, but not badly injured.

Since Sam was okay, her attention turned back to Tom, only to see him on the other side of his truck, his rifle pointed at her. Oh, shit.

Tom, it's me Vonda. Put the rifle down!

Like her thoughts would help. Most humans couldn't understand her telepathically. But she had to try. Being shot was not high on her to-do list.

****

Tom felt a buzz like insects in his head and heard words. *Tom, it's me, Vonda. Put the rifle down!*

Oh, yeah. He definitely got hit harder than he thought.

But what if that really was Vonda? Okay, he didn't get hit that hard, like a woman could turn into a wolf. He tightened the grip on the rifle, his chest pumping like a bellows.

Tom, please! You don't believe it, but it's true. It's Vonda, please don't kill me. Please. Shit, he doesn't hear me.

What if it was Vonda? The blood that wasn't pounding in his head rushed to his dick at the thought of her. Great, just great. Kidnappers just drove off with his daughter; he sees a wolf, hears voices in his head, and gets a hard-on. What kind of a fucking freak was he?

Why not humor the voices? How much worse could it get?

"Fine. If you're really Vonda take two steps to the right, sit, and wait right there."

The wolf walked two steps to the right, eyes on him, and sat. Damn.

He had no time for this shit. Each minute he spent aiming the rifle at the wolf, his brain obviously tripping on a hemorrhage, was one more minute those fuckers had his daughter.

To hell with that. The wolf was either Vonda or it wasn't. Some things you just had to trust to fate no matter how unbelievable.

"Get your ass in the truck while I get the keys."

Not waiting to see what the wolf would do, he lowered the rifle and darted up the steps into the house. Layla poked her head out from behind the couch. Ignoring her, he grabbed his cell phone and keys off the table by the door. Spinning around, he almost tripped over Sam as the dog came into the house.

Cursing, he side-stepped Sam and yanked the door shut. The wolf sat by the passenger door of the truck, looking over her shoulder at him.

"Are you really Vonda?" he whispered.

In the flesh.

He paused, trying to stop breathing like a race horse. If that wasn't Vonda, his ass was pretty much screwed. One foot after another, his breath caught in his throat, he walked toward the wolf. Dear God, let her be Vonda. One thing finally went well on this hellacious evening—the wolf didn't bite him and jumped straight into the truck when he opened the door.

Okay, that went well. The only thing left for him was to get in the truck and drive hell-bent after the fuckers who had his daughter. Provided the wolf in his truck didn't eat him first.

What the hell had he been thinking?

He slammed a fist on the hood of the truck as he walked around to the driver's side. Yanking open the door, he was greeted by a lolling tongue and a lot of overgrown pearly whites. Was that blood on her muzzle? His heart skipped a beat.

Oh, get in already. We went through this earlier.

He took a deep breath and placed the rifle on the gun rack before sliding behind the wheel. He fumbled with the keys. Two tries later he had the key in the ignition and the engine turned. Adrenaline raced through his veins. The bastards that took his daughter would pay for it. He'd make sure of that.

Shifting into reverse, he backed out of the driveway, gunning the engine when he dropped it into drive.

"Which way?" he growled, then blinked at the sound.

What was up with those strange noises coming out of his mouth? He sounded almost animalistic. Well, hell, he felt animalistic and would go medieval on their asses once he found the kidnappers. What did they want with Elizabeth? He shuddered, thinking about what his daughter must be going through as he white-knuckled the steering wheel.

He'd always protected her; what would she think of him now? How would she be able to look up to him when he let her be taken?

You didn't let her be taken. They took her. There's a difference.

He whipped his head to the right, staring at Vonda.

"How the hell did you know what I was thinking?"

You weren't thinking it, you said it. I heard you.

"Nope. It was in my head." Was he actually arguing with a wolf? Even if said wolf was the sexiest woman he'd seen. His groin throbbed thinking about Vonda's hair, her beautiful amber eyes, her hot body. How the hell could he be thinking of sex at a time like this?

You think I'm sexy?

"You need to work on that telepathy thing."

Sorry. I usually talk to wolves, not humans. You're the only human I've been able to talk to like this. They can't understand me. I'm surprised you can.

"Yeah, I can understand you just fine. The problem is that you're reading my mind."

Well, I wouldn't be reading it if you weren't broadcasting it all over the place. Seems to me like you're talking. Hey, stop! I need to get out and smell for tracks at the corner.

He slammed the brakes, thankful he had just turned the corner and wasn't going fast. Vonda waited, staring at Tom. He stared back. If she needed to scent the tracks, she'd better get out.

Do you see any hands over here? One paw dangled in the air.

He reached across the seat and pushed the door open. Vonda leapt out and put her nose on the ground. She sniffed all four corners of the road, then stuck her nose in the air and walked around the corners. Her nostrils quivered as she breathed.

As he watched Vonda make her rounds, he wished she'd hurry. This whole sniff-out-the-bad-guys routine took too long. He tapped his fingers against the steering wheel, feeling his blood pressure rise the longer Vonda sniffed the ground. Enough already. He could have driven to the Canadian border and back in the time it took her to sniff around the road.

After what the dashboard clock claimed was only two minutes—he obviously needed to take it in for service since it wasn't working right—she trotted back to the truck. The seat dipped as Vonda landed next to him, a wolfish grin on her face. She glanced at the door, then him, one paw waving back and forth.

He grunted, reached around her and shut the door, holding in the chills that inched their way to his low back as his arm brushed her muzzle.

Head to the right, their scent is the strongest in that direction. Stop if you come to cross streets.

He shifted into drive and stomped on the gas. On this stretch of road, heading in this direction there were no cross streets for miles, which made it easier to track he supposed. Thinking about tracking Elizabeth gave him fresh chills as to what those men, particularly the giant one, wanted with his daughter.

"Why would they take Elizabeth? Why would they come into the house and take her? It's not like she was on a street alone or something. What kind of freaks break into a house and take a little girl? I don't even know them!" He slammed his hand on the steering wheel.

They're werewolves. Like me.

Tom's lip curled, exposing his teeth. "You know them?"

What? You think I hang with kidnappers?

"Until tonight I didn't even realize werewolves existed."

It was a surprise for me too.

"What do you mean?"

****

Vonda sighed. She might as well tell him. He was stuck with her until they caught up to Elizabeth. And judging by the whine of the engine, that shouldn't be too much longer.

I grew up in a foster home and didn't know werewolves existed until I turned into one when I was thirteen.

Tom faced her, mouth agape. "That must've been hard."

You have no idea. My foster parents thought I was doing drugs or something, since I snuck out of the house every full moon. Figured it was easier for them to think I was snorting coke than to have them see me turn into a wolf.

"Yeah, I can imagine. That would be weird. Can you change at will?"

She shook her head. *Nope. Only on the day of the full moon, the day before and the day after. I turn when the sun sets on those days.*

She licked her lips. What would Tom do if she ran her tongue over his ear? Maybe he'd reciprocate in kind. Yeah, she could deal with that. After the ear, he'd move on down...

Tom turned to her, eyes raking her. She smelled the scent of arousal swimming through the truck's cab, thick and heady. Hot damn, he actually found the wolf attractive. Not like she cared at the moment, with the mating heat coursing through her body. She'd take him any way she could, but maybe this relationship wouldn't end like the other one.

Tom faced forward, hands tightening on the wheel.

"Look up there. Are those taillights?" One finger pointed straight ahead.

She looked down the road, squinting. Yep, definitely taillights. Her lips peeled back from her teeth.

I think we've caught the bastards.

Chapter Four

Tom flipped the lights off as he rolled to a stop. He jumped out and tried the gate the kidnappers had driven through.

Locked.

The red of the taillights disappeared in the woods, swallowed in the shadows, leaving him alone with his failure.

He kicked the gate a couple of times before yanking on it.

Keep that up and the whole world will know we're here.

Vonda trotted to where he stood fighting the gate.

"Well, what do you suggest? I can't just Superman over the damn thing." The gate stood at least seven feet tall, a wrought iron monstrosity, attached to an equally impressive fence. No footholds to be seen. Whoever lived here didn't raise cattle.

And Elizabeth was behind those formidable walls.

We can go under it. See, it doesn't go too far into the ground. Look at that rabbit tunnel underneath.

He looked to where Vonda gestured with her nose. The light seemed brighter than normal, and he saw the small hole a rabbit had dug under the fence.

"Well, what are you waiting for? Dig!"

Vonda shook her head and trotted over to the rabbit tunnel. Dirt flew as the hole deepened. What a woman, um, wolf. He ran back to the truck and grabbed his rifle. By the time he returned, Vonda was under the fence.

Hope you fit through. I tried to dig it large enough for you.

Tom poked the rifle through the space between the bars before lowering himself into the hole. His head poked out the other side of the fence easily, but the rest of him didn't want to pass through.

A scream died in his throat, the only sound an escaped grunt.

Back up and I'll dig some from this side.

He pulled back and let Vonda work. This time he was able to pull himself through. Picking up the rifle, he followed Vonda as she led him through the woods.

The road wound between trees for what seemed like miles. Time crept forward, slower than Layla in the winter. Probably because they took the scenic route through the woods instead of the dirt-packed road. Less chance of being seen. Hopefully.

At least it gave Tom plenty of time to think, to plan new ways of killing the bastards that took his daughter. Shooting was too clean. So was snapping their necks. He should have brought the axe.

They're in the clearing.

"Huh?"

Shh! Just think it. Do you really want them to hear you?

He glared at her. She stared back, amber eyes unblinking. Brave women were sexy.

Canines gleamed in the darkness as Vonda stood a little straighter.

Damn. He'd projected thoughts he hadn't meant to. Again. Well, he was new at this telepathy thing. He planned on getting better at it once he had Elizabeth back. Then he could concentrate on Vonda. Until then visions of long legs wrapped around his waist and amber eyes glowing in the moonlight were relegated to the back of his mind.

Dropping to the ground, Tom crawled toward the clearing, Vonda following.

Wonder if they can smell me.

Why...he started, remembered why and shut his mental trap. *Can't you mask your scent?*

Her head tilted to the side as she stared at him. *See any dead animals around?*

What does that have to do with it?

Vonda shook her head. *In order for me to mask my scent, I need to roll on something dead.*

Before he could think a reply to that little pleasantry, they arrived at the clearing. Numerous men, women, and wolves—which he assumed to be of the *were* variety—stood huddled in a circle, staring in the middle of ring. Too many for him to take out, even if Vonda managed to take a couple down.

Where was Elizabeth? He looked around the clearing, surprised by how light it seemed. The moon was full, but it should be shadowed in the woods, clearing or not. He looked to the tops of the trees, searched for lights and saw none. Maybe there was something he couldn't see that reflected the light, making the shadows disappear.

Or maybe his eyes had adjusted so well to the dark that the dark now seemed light.

A person moved, allowing him a glimpse into the circle, a glimpse into what they were hiding, a glimpse at his daughter.

Elizabeth huddled on the ground, knees to her chest, face buried in her knees.

And then the person moved again and his glimpse was gone.

He felt an almost overwhelming need to kill them all. His heart pounded in his chest, beat in his head, pulsed in his teeth, down his throat.

An unearthly sound echoed in his ears, turning every head in the clearing to him.

Like he cared.

They had his daughter, his only child, and they would die.

He sprang forward.

Chapter Five

Vonda turned to Tom as he howled. *Howled.* Since when did men howl?

Okay, maybe in the heat of passion, but nothing like what he let out. Her bones felt like ants crawling through them, small tingles burning deep.

She took a deep breath and gasped. What the....

Tom sprang from where he lay, muscles bulging. She tried to reach for him, remembering at the last second she had no hands to pull him back.

Tom, no! Wait!

Of course he didn't. Since when did men listen to a woman? And he'd left his rifle behind. Brilliant. Fight a bunch of werewolves barehanded.

If what she smelled on him was accurate, and her nose didn't lie, he might have a better chance than she thought.

By now the startled werewolves were flocking around Tom, while Elizabeth screamed, "Daddy!"

She should help Tom fight, she really should, but fighting was so not her thing. Sneaking, now that she was good at. She could sneak right around the clearing while Tom distracted them all and try to free Elizabeth. Two women stood by the girl, obviously guarding her.

She slunk through the shadows, blending into the night, until she stood about thirty feet from Elizabeth. The girl still screamed for her father, but from the looks of things, Tom had lost. She didn't have much time left to do what she planned. Thankfully she had learned while running with the wolves how to speak telepathically to one wolf and not the whole pack.

Elizabeth, I'm behind you in the woods. She projected the thought into the girl's mind, praying Elizabeth could hear her.

The girl's head whipped around, eyes frantically searching.

Score one for the wolf. Now to convince her.

I'm a friend of your dad's and here to help. Start crawling to me. I'll distract them.

But Dad—

Let's get you out first.

She picked up a stick with her mouth and pitched it. She heard it hit, but the two guards didn't. Shit. Quick, Plan B. She howled.

That got their attention.

Hey, Bitch. To your right. You wanna piece of this? She turned and stuck her tail into the clearing, waggling it.

One of the guards gestured for the other one to check it out. The woman trotted right, the other one watching her.

Elizabeth, change of plans. Run left, quick, go!

Elizabeth, bless her heart, jumped up and hauled ass. Tom really needed to put the girl in track.

"Hey, she's getting away!"

Elizabeth was to the edge of the clearing before the wolves started moving. She circled around, shocked that she could feel the wolves' surprise and indecision over whether to stay with Tom or chase Elizabeth. Half stayed, half chased.

Damn.

Before she made it to Elizabeth, the same giant who had stolen the girl came from behind a tree and grabbed her again. She leapt, slamming into Big G and Elizabeth, taking them both down. Elizabeth scrambled out, and she went for Big G's throat.

She never made it.

A hand grabbed the scruff of her neck, shaking. She knew she should submit because the hand was attached to what smelled like a dominant leader, but submitting meant letting them have Elizabeth and Tom and she couldn't do it. She snarled, turning her head to bite.

A wave of power washed over her, power she had never before felt, a power that froze the bite on her lips. She looked up, right into the face of one of the women that had guarded Elizabeth in the clearing.

Pack leader. Alpha. Submit.

She snarled. Another wave of power crashed over her and she felt her body start changing. What the hell? The moon was still out. She fought against the power that coursed over her, through her, trying to force the human half of her back into hiding.

For the first time in her life, she fought to stay in the wolf's body. With everything she had, she concentrated on maintaining the wolf, until her vision narrowed to the tall, athletic, brown-haired woman holding her scruff. Just the two of them, locked in a battle of wills.

The woman's eyes widened, then narrowed as she felt more power slam into her. She imagined a wall between herself and the pack leader, a wall that blocked all power, a wall that let her remain a wolf.

The hand slipped from her neck, allowing her a toe-hold in the struggle.

Submit, dammit! The words reverberated in her head, willing her to lie on her side, the urge almost overpowering.

Like hell. She was too far into this fight to back down now.

I don't think so. I want...Elizabeth...and...Tom.

You don't understand what you ask for.

Then...why...don't...you...explain.

The woman screamed, throwing her hand

toward Big G, who cowered on the ground. The power beating against Vonda's body suddenly lifted as Big G shrieked, his body exploding into a wolf.

Holy shit.

Elizabeth screamed. The wolves and humans dropped to the ground, rolling on their sides. Vonda fought to remain standing, the clash of power and her own struggle against the leader leaving her drained, her legs shaky.

The last note of Elizabeth's scream dripped from the trees, coating them with silence. The pack leader's chest heaved, her frustration evident in her scent.

"Who the hell are you?" Hands fisted on her waist, she glared at Vonda.

Who the hell do you think you are, kidnapping a little girl?

"You didn't answer my question."

You're not answering mine.

The hands dropped to her sides as she took a breath. "Are you challenging me?"

Words like ice lanced through her veins and the just-returning forest noises went silent. Some deeper meaning to the pack leader's words existed, but for the life of her, she didn't know what it was. Time to bluff.

All I want is Elizabeth and Tom back. If you call that challenging, then I guess so.

"Does your pack do things so much differently?"

What do you mean?

"Does your pack not raise pups from interspecies unions?"

Interspecies unions? Could she sound any more stupid? What did the woman mean by that one?

"Surely you can smell it on her. Elizabeth belongs to us, she's one of us. Tom never changed, he can't raise her. How would he explain what she's going through when she changes? It's in Elizabeth's best interests to live with the pack."

Whoa, Nelly. Elizabeth was a werewolf? She glanced to where the girl stood, mesmerized by the alpha. At least she stood, instead of groveling around on the ground like the rest of the pack. That was a good thing, right?

Tom's a werewolf?

"You really didn't know, did you?" The woman bent closer, sniffing Vonda's neck. "Who are you? You don't belong to us."

She side-stepped, but the alpha grabbed the scruff of her neck again. Geez, if the pack leader didn't cease and desist with that scruff-grabbing routine Vonda would have to bite her.

"She told us she had no leader."

She darted her eyes in the direction of the voice. Jace crawled into her line of vision. Uh-oh. Not good. She had the distinct impression that not having a leader was a bad thing.

"Really?" Ms. Pack Leader gave her a curious look. "How did that happen?"

The fight left her. She'd always wanted to meet another werewolf, but didn't know how. Chat rooms didn't cater to the real thing and she didn't know where else to look. Couldn't ask anyone either, without running the risk of men in little white suits heading her way. She smelled frustration and curiosity from Ms. PL, not hatred. Maybe these wolves knew why she was what she was. But first she had to ensure Tom and Elizabeth's safety.

What did you do with Tom?

"You like to avoid questions. Fine, I'll answer some of yours but you owe me in return, got it?"

She nodded.

"Tom will be fine. I'm not sure why he's so upset over the matter. He should know that we mean only the best for Elizabeth."

But you kidnapped her and knocked him out!

How could that be the best for her?

"Kidnapped? Tom's mother should have explained all this," she waggled her fingers back and forth, "to him before she died. He knew we'd be coming for Elizabeth."

Um, hate to be the one to tell you, but I think someone dropped the ball on that one.

The PL dropped her and turned on Jace and Big G. "What did you tell Tom when you fetched the girl?"

Jace dropped on his side. "We was supposed to tell him something?"

Vonda watched PL practice deep breathing exercises. Maybe she counted to ten. In four different languages. She would've just smacked the werewolf, but obviously this woman ran things another way.

"Thanks to my enforcers, it seems we owe Tom an apology."

She marched over to the clearing, Vonda hot on her heels, Elizabeth staying put like a good submissive. Tom lay on the ground, two wolves lying beside him. Vonda ran over to him, licking his face.

His eyes opened. The pain in their depths made something twist deep inside Vonda. He hurt and she wanted to kill the cause of it.

"Daddy!" Elizabeth came running as Tom struggled to sit. Apparently the girl wasn't as submissive as she'd seemed.

Throwing her arms around his shoulders, she buried her face in his neck as Tom's arms surrounded her with the grip of a desperate man.

Not intending to barge in on their reunion, but in case PL decided to take Elizabeth back, Vonda edged her way closer to Tom, close enough for her fur to brush against his arm. Probably not the best position to take, seeing how even that littlest of touches sparked another bout of the mating heat.

The alpha knelt in front of Tom. "Seems we owe

you an apology. We assumed you knew we would come for Elizabeth. But it looks like your mother never told you about herself or about you. Elizabeth belongs with us, the pack. You didn't change, but she will."

****

Tom looked at the woman, willing breath into his lungs. Change? What the hell did she mean, change? But one glance around the clearing told him what she meant. Even if he didn't want to believe it, he knew deep down he was different. It didn't take a genius to realize the sixth sense type of thing he experienced his entire life didn't happen to everyone. Being a werewolf, and a genetically defective one at that, never crossed his mind.

Breathe, Tom. In through the nose, out through the mouth.

Now that air managed to flood his lungs, he wanted nothing more than to laugh. Wild, hysterical laughter that meant craziness knocked at his door.

Well, hell, laughter was the best medicine, right?

The writer of that cliché obviously didn't have his problem.

"Huh?" squeaked out. Embarrassing. So much for sounding coherent.

The woman sighed. "Werewolves, Tom. You should have changed, but didn't. Sometimes it happens. Usually one that does not change doesn't have a child that does, but Elizabeth will change."

"How do you know that?" Goody for him, his voice didn't sound like a pubescent boy.

"We can smell it on her. You have a similar scent. Rather surprising since you don't change." She shrugged. "But the point is that Elizabeth needs to be raised by us. How else will she know how to be a wolf?"

Tom's arms tightened around Elizabeth. They'd

pretty much proved he'd lose the fight, but that wouldn't stop him from trying again.

Um, excuse me. Vonda interjected. *But why can't she just live with Tom and you can check in on her? Wouldn't that be better for her? To, like, live with her father?*

He and the alpha stared. Why hadn't he thought of that? His first reaction had been to fight, not talk it out. God, he loved that wolf, um, woman.

The alpha blinked a couple of times, clearly mulling over Vonda's suggestion. She looked at Elizabeth held in Tom's white-knuckled grasp.

The damn bitch best go for the idea. Tom held his breath as it wasn't doing much good going in and out of his mouth.

He watched as her head tilted to the side. Emotions played across her face as her eyes drifted to various pack members.

Tom heard what sounded like thousands of bees buzzing in his skull. He shook his head, but the sound didn't go away. Vonda's head turned as she looked around the pack with the alpha.

No way. But after everything else that happened tonight, why not? He focused on the noise in his head, turning the cacophony into a single strand of conversation. Check him out, eavesdropping on a private conversation.

He should have remained ignorant, because who wants to know what the gossip is saying about you?

Seems like there was some debate on who the lucky wolf that got to visit Elizabeth was. More debate on if Vonda's idea should even happen, which took longer than he'd like. Back to the wolf that got to visit Elizabeth—of course it was the brown-haired woman. And, whoa Nelly, were they now deciding who he slept with?

Like hell if they thought they could decide that. The only one he wanted was Vonda.

The buzzing stopped as most of the pack, including Vonda, turned to stare at him.

Oh shit. Looked like telepathy wasn't his thing. They all heard who he'd like to sleep with.

The pack leader smiled. "That can be arranged."

Excuse me?

"Huh?" Wasn't he full of intelligent remarks tonight?

The pack leader tucked a strand of hair behind her ear. "You," she pointed at Tom, "can mate with her," the finger turned to Vonda, "and we can let you keep Elizabeth. Of course, that's dependent on the bitch there," the finger returned to Vonda, "joining our pack. You have five minutes to decide."

With that declaration, she marched to the other side of the clearing, the pack following. Tom felt the wolves' eyes on him, staring, watching, daring him to make a run for it. If he hadn't seen one of the creatures change before his eyes, he'd think it was all a nightmare from the blow to the head.

But small things in his life, little things he had stuck in the back of his mind over the years, whispered to him, made him know that what the alpha said was true. Werewolves existed and he carried their genetics.

Made him wonder what other secrets Mom had neglected to mention.

"Daddy, if I'm a wolf and they wanted me to join them, why didn't they just ask?" Elizabeth's amber eyes turned toward him, her head resting on his arm.

"Um..."

Because their momma never taught them any manners. I swear, thinking there's nothing wrong with kidnapping little girls. These folks are nuts.

****

But she'd still like to get to know them. And

with the mating heat upon her, sleeping with Tom sounded like a wonderful idea. Best idea she'd heard all night.

Of course, she'd have to wait until morning, when her human body returned, to engage in any fun.

Permanent, slid across her mind. Yeah, it would be a permanent type of thing. Would she be able to do that? To move in with Tom? Staying with him when the mating heat vanished?

At least he wouldn't call her a dog.

And he was way ahead of her ex on the attractive scale, the nice scale, and the family man scale. All in all she wouldn't mind a bit of horizontal time.

"I'm sorry to drag you into this."

She gave Tom a wolfish shrug, wishing she had her human features so he could read on her face how much she wanted him. Not all of the desire came from the mating heat. Sure, her core pulsed and she wanted nothing more than his cock thrusting into her, filling her, but a part of the desire throbbing in her veins was for Tom. Just Tom.

Something within him spoke to her on a base level.

And she wanted that in a permanent way.

You didn't exactly drag me, you know. I saw them taking her first.

Tom nodded and swallowed, his hand stroking Elizabeth's back, his eyes refusing to meet Vonda's.

A shaky hand shoved through his hair. "Are you willing?"

He spoke the words to the trees, but turned to face her before the sound died.

She didn't hesitate. If he was willing to have her, knowing she turned furry once a month, she would take him. And she got a hot body in the bargain.

Yep. If you don't mind me looking like this monthly.

He shook his head, opening his mouth to speak, but the alpha chose that moment to return.

"So, what's the decision?"

"She'll move in with me. And you won't be taking my daughter," Tom growled the last words.

Damn, if that wasn't the sexiest thing she had heard.

The alpha nodded. "That is acceptable. We will check on you monthly to see how Elizabeth is." Her eyes moved to Vonda. "And to see if you have questions about us. You need a pack."

Thank you. I would like that.

"Now, since you've decided to mate, we will need to make sure you consummate the relationship."

"And just how do you suggest you do that?" Tom's lips pulled back, exposing his teeth.

"I'll follow you back to your house and ensure the mating is consummated. I'll return later to talk more to Vonda about the pack. Are you ready to go?"

She exchanged a glance with Tom. PL was going to watch them? Eww. She didn't get into starring on sex tapes. Talk about performance anxiety.

Elizabeth lifted her head from Tom's shoulder. "Hey, Dad, what's consummated mean?"

Chapter Six

Vonda touched the silver picture frame containing a photo of a black-haired woman in a white, strapless wedding dress and a younger looking Tom. Husband and wife. Until death do us part.

They'd looked so happy, so in love. How could she hope to achieve that with Tom?

First things first. They needed to consummate this agreement, something Tom looked rather hesitant to do. He paced the room, running fingers through his short hair until it stood like captured soldiers, nervous and trembling.

"Elizabeth will be okay. She'll sleep for awhile. Margie put her under and promised she'd stay asleep." The alpha, Margie, had claimed she had the ability to make Elizabeth catch eight hours of ZZZs, and set about proving it with a wave of her hand.

Tom stopped his pacing and stared at her. "I should be up there with her, not down here with you." He ran his hand through his hair again, making matters up top worse. "Dammit, that didn't come out right."

"I know what you mean." And she did. Tom should be with his daughter, not trying to have sex with her.

Although the sex sounded great at the moment. And how screwed up was that? Mating heat was a bitch.

"Did it hurt?" Tom gestured at her.

Vonda looked down her body, from Tom's tee shirt around her torso, to his sweat pants on her legs and wondered what the hell he was talking about.

"Um, did what hurt?" Having his shirt rub against her sensitive nipples or his pants rest against her already wet core? Somehow she didn't think that was what he wanted to know.

"The change back."

Oh, yeah. That. "Well, it wasn't the best feeling I've ever had." The only thing she could imagine worse would be having your tonsils ripped out through your nose. "But it doesn't seem to have any lingering effects. I didn't realize changing back to a human while the moon was still out was even possible."

Margie was one powerful bitch. Holding her hand toward Vonda, she had forced her wolf back to its hiding place, bringing out the human half to writhe in agony on the cold linoleum floor of Tom's kitchen. For the first time since she hit puberty, Vonda saw the moon out of her human eyes.

It was worth every bit of pain.

"Maybe she'll show me how to do that. She's going to teach me what it means to be a pack member." Vonda couldn't wait. After all these years alone, she would learn what it meant to be a werewolf. There had to be more to it than getting furry once a month.

"That's good. That's real good." More with the hand through the hair routine. "I need to go check on Elizabeth."

Tom headed for the door, but Vonda beat him there.

"You can't go anywhere until we, um, until we mate."

Her hand on his arm sparked heat, a tangible arc that crossed the air to Tom, stilling him. He took a deep breath, turning to face her. His green eyes smoked with desire, firing the blood in her veins, whipping it into a frenzy being with her ex had never produced.

It was callous of her to want sex after all that had happened tonight, knowing that a ten-year-old frightened girl lay upstairs. But with the mating heat firing her blood, she couldn't help it. All she wanted was Tom. His arms around her, his body pressed to her, his thick cock inside her.

Her imagination kicked into overdrive as she pictured him pumping into her, in and out, his big body slamming into her over and over again. She felt wetness between her legs as her core wept, wanting him in her, needing him to complete her.

His nostrils flared. "You smell good," he said, his voice a low growl that distorted the words.

She didn't think she could get wetter, but that growling thing sent her core into overdrive.

Holding his gaze, she started working the buttons on his shirt. His breath sawed in and out of his lungs as her hands crept down his torso. Once the shirt was unbuttoned, she pushed the sleeves down his arms, dropping it onto the floor. She ran her hands up his arms, feeling the muscles tense at her touch. Gaw, but the man was strong. She loved the feel of his pecs under her palms, the way the springy hair dusted his chest.

She needed her skin against his. Now.

Working quickly, she yanked her shirt over her head and reached behind her to unhook her bra. Tom stared transfixed as she pulled off her shirt, but snapped out of the trance as she unhooked her bra, pushing the straps off her shoulders.

His hands shoved her pants over her hips and Vonda kicked them off. A wave of embarrassment passed through her. What if he didn't like the way she looked? Her sexual experiences were limited to a man who called her a dog.

If that growl meant anything, she shouldn't have worried. Tom brushed a hand over her collarbone, across her breasts, down her stomach to her core, the feather-light touch scorching like fire.

"You're beautiful."

Vonda felt her muscles relax at his words.

"You're pretty good looking yourself."

He bent his head, his lips pressing against hers. The tip of his tongue traced the crease between her lips and she opened for him, letting the strokes of his tongue against hers carry her into that place where nothing mattered but the two of them.

Tom held her head with one hand, while his other flicked her nipple into a hard point. Vonda stopped thinking, her body pure instinct, wanting him, needing him in her. She fumbled with the button on his Levis, while his fingers flicked against her nipple. A moan escaped her and she finally freed the darned button, which allowed her to yank the zipper down. She shoved the jeans over his hips, then pulled the waistband of his tighty-whities out and over his cock, freeing him for her feeling pleasure.

Vonda ran her hand up the length of him, loving the velvety skin, the thick head, the swollen sac. Damn, but he was huge. She'd be sore tomorrow.

She could hardly wait.

Tom moaned in her mouth as she stroked up the thick length. His thumb rubbed against her swollen nipple as his other hand stroked from her waist to her hip, each pass drawing closer to the place between her legs that ached for him.

He kissed her until her surroundings dimmed, until the only thing that mattered was his lips on hers, his skin against hers, the feel of his cock in her hand as she drew it through her grasp. She circled the broad head, once, twice, feeling wetness seep out of the slit. Rubbing the moisture into his skin, she continued her lazy strokes, up and down, up and circled around, while Tom's hand moved closer to her mound.

He touched her core, his fingers sliding in the wetness he found there. She felt his cock kick in her hand, spurts of cum coating her stomach.

"Shit!" Tom exploded, as his hips bucked against her hand, while she milked him dry.

Well, that didn't take long. What about her?

He dropped his head to her shoulder, breathing deeply. "I'm so sorry. It's been awhile since I've...yeah." He tried to take a step and tripped over his jeans, falling into her. "God, I'm sorry. I'm so sorry. This just isn't going to work. Not now anyway. I just..." He ran his hand through his hair.

Vonda blinked. "But what about Margie?"

"Fuck. I don't know."

Vonda looked down and saw the cum running down her stomach. She wiped it off, smearing it onto her core and the insides of her legs.

"Hey, Margie! It's finished!"

Hopefully the alpha would smell him on her and leave before this night got any worse.

Vonda heard Margie on the other side of the door, breathing deeply.

"Ah, good. The mating is complete. Is Tom...okay?"

"Yeah, I'm good." His hand did another run through the hair.

"Oh. Well, then. That's great. Great." Why did she sound so disappointed? "I'll let myself out and leave you two lovebirds alone. I'll be back tomorrow afternoon to talk to Vonda."

Vonda and Tom listened as Margie's steps echoed down the hall, the sound of the front door shutting propelling Tom into action.

"God, I'm sorry." He reached for his underwear and jeans, drawing them up in one motion while he talked. "We can...yeah...maybe later, right? I'm going upstairs with Elizabeth. You can have the bed in here."

He yanked his shirt off the floor and closed the door behind him, never once looking her in the eye.

What was it with her and men? She slid one finger inside her while circling her clit with another. Two strokes later and her hips bucked, the orgasm rippling through her. Her body relieved, she wished she could say the same about her heart.

She walked into the bathroom and started cleaning herself with a wet washcloth. How would she face Tom tomorrow? She understood his need to be with his daughter and it was just plain weird to even try to have sex under the circumstances, but still. He could have stuck around long enough get her off too.

Although that wasn't fair, was it? Yes, yes it was. Even if he was embarrassed. Everyone knows men can't always control those things. She pitched the washcloth onto the rim of the bathtub. Still. The mating heat hadn't abated. She could do with a dose of Tom right about now.

But she knew getting him back into the bedroom would be a challenge.

Good thing she loved challenges. She had what was left of the night and all day tomorrow to come up with a plan. Vonda smiled. Yep, Tom would soon discover werewolves didn't give up so easily.

Chapter Seven

Tom walked in the back door, leaned against the wall, and pulled his muddy boots off. He heard the female voices like a squabble of geese, pecking around the kitchen. Vonda's laughter rang out and then the squabble dropped to a manageable volume.

Shit. He'd managed to avoid Vonda all day. What did you say to a woman when you came all over her and then left the room? Thanks? And what an ass he was, didn't even bother to see to her pleasure.

The only good thing that came of it was he knew his dick still worked in front of a woman.

Now he had to face Vonda and how embarrassing was that? Maybe he could sneak up the back stairs...

"Daddy!" Elizabeth ran around the corner, smack into him, her skinny arms surrounding his waist with a squeeze.

Or maybe he couldn't sneak anywhere.

"Is that you, Tom?" Vonda called.

Yep, not sneaking anywhere. Time to face her. He was a big boy, really. Yep, yep.

"Come on, Daddy. Margie's been telling us about the pack." Elizabeth tugged his hand, drawing him into the kitchen.

Within a few hours, Margie had gone from Elizabeth's worst enemy to her best friend, and wasn't that a good thing. Made things easier on him too.

Margie and Vonda sat at the kitchen table, tea cups in front of them. An extra cup sat in front of an empty chair. Elizabeth slid into the empty and took a sip out of her cup.

"Want some tea, Dad?"

"No, sweetie, I'm good. Just going to change out of these clothes, then I'll come back and fix dinner, okay?" He rubbed his hand over her head, chuckling as she ducked and squeaked, "Daddy!"

He walked out of the room, feeling Vonda's eyes on him. *Way to continue to avoid her, Tom.*

He had to face her eventually, no getting around that. She would be living here now. Taking Anita's place. He grabbed onto the dresser, steadying himself. Not only did he have to deal with his little failure in the bedroom last night, but now he realized he had to come to grips with Vonda, for all intents and purposes, being his wife.

Anita looked out at him from the photo taken the day of their wedding, her eyes glistening with love. Some of the last coherent words she'd spoken to him, asked him to find someone else, someone to keep him warm at night. She was gone, had been gone for four years, her death releasing him from his wedding vows, so why did he feel like being with Vonda was cheating?

It wasn't. Definitely wasn't cheating.

Layla walked into the room, her nails tapping a rhythm on the wood floor as she made her way to the rug under the bed. She huffed as she plopped down on the rug, her expression one of extreme exasperation.

He took a breath and shut the door. "What's the matter, old girl? You think I need to move on?"

As usual she remained silent. Like a dog can talk. Wolves on the other hand....

He ran his hand through his hair. In the last twenty-four hours he'd had his daughter kidnapped and returned, been given a mate who turned furry once a month and discovered he was half werewolf.

If he had anymore revelations, he'd need to change his name to John the Baptist.

Tonight he needed to talk to Vonda. He would, once Elizabeth went to bed, which gave him even more time to avoid the unavoidable. Yee-haw.

He dropped his shirt and pants into the clothes hamper and shrugged on a tee-shirt and jeans. Layla remained curled on the rug by the bed, waiting for him to dress. He looked from his dog to the bed, the bed where he spent many a fine night with Anita, the bed where he would spend many more nights with Vonda.

All day he'd thought about Vonda, what he would say, and more importantly, what he would do to her body. He felt his cock grow at the thought of Vonda, her brown wavy hair, her amber eyes, her small hand as it grasped his cock, drawing out his pleasure.

Damn. He couldn't go out to the kitchen looking like he'd stuffed a potato down his pants. Think, think. Yeah, fixing fences, nothing sexy about that one. Or he could look at the picture of his wife on their wedding day. Yep, that one did the trick.

Tom ran his hand through his hair.

"I hope you don't mind," he whispered to the picture. "I mean, you asked me to find someone and I did. More like she found me, but whatever, I'm going to take her tonight. Elizabeth will have the mother she needs and I, well, I like her too. I hope that doesn't bother you."

Was it his imagination or did the picture shake its head? He definitely needed some water; he must have been out in the sun too long.

"I love you, Anita, I'll always love you. But Vonda's here with me now and I need her. I hope you understand and that you aren't mad. What the hell am I saying? You're not even here. I'm talking to ghosts again."

The picture frame felt cold in his hand. With a last look at the picture, he placed it in the dresser drawer. She was dead. Four years now. Time he got on with his life.

The woman he wanted now sat at his kitchen table and there was no room for ghosts.

****

Vonda watched as Tom walked back into the kitchen and started to pull things out of the freezer. Pots and pans flopped on the stove in a rush of movement. Nothing more sexy than a man that can cook. Especially a man that rocks a pair of faded Levi's.

She took a sip of the now-cool tea and openly ogled Tom's butt. Damn, but the man was hot. She needed to stop ogling, especially since Elizabeth sat next to her. Needed to set a good example, especially since she was going to be the girl's step-mom.

The tea went down the wrong way. Margie slapped her on the back as she wheezed and hacked.

"You okay?" Tom stopped chopping vegetables and looked at Vonda.

She nodded, whacking herself on the chest. Apparently drinking while thinking of impending motherhood, even if it was motherhood by step instead of birth, should be avoided. At least Elizabeth seemed to like her and the feeling was returned. Of course she doubted Elizabeth realized that she was the new mother figure in her life.

"Well, I should run. Things to do on the full moon. Will you be running with us tonight, Vonda?" Margie stood and hung her purse over her shoulder.

She coughed one more time. "I'll probably just stick around here, but will look for y'all."

"Well, if we don't see you this time, there's always next month."

"True. Hope you have a good run."

"Same to you. Bye, Elizabeth. Bye, Tom."

"Bye." Tom raised a hand and went back to seasoning meat.

Margie showed herself to the door, while she picked up the used tea cups and placed them in the dishwasher.

"What did you do today, Elizabeth?" Tom asked.

Elizabeth leaned on the counter, watching Tom work.

"Vonda took me to her place to grab some clothes because she said she's crashing here for awhile. Then we went to eat at the deli. Margie was here when we got back and she talked to us for the rest of the afternoon. What did you do?"

She listened to them talk as she set the table. It was not her imagination that Tom was ignoring her. On another day that would bother her, but today she didn't mind. Margie had explained some things, some very interesting things, when Elizabeth offered to play the piano for them. Once she heard what Margie had to say about the matter, she could hardly wait to see if the alpha was correct.

And to do that, she had to convince Tom to sleep with her before the sun went down.

Time was running out and she still hadn't figured out how to get Elizabeth out of the way. All she knew was that before the moon rose she would have Tom between her legs.

Chapter Eight

"Elizabeth, why don't you go practice the piano? Vonda and I have some things to discuss and we don't need an interruption, okay?" Tom looked at Elizabeth as they cleaned up the kitchen after dinner.

"But I practiced this afternoon for Margie."

"Is there something you could do in your room?"

"So like, you're kicking me out of the first floor?"

"Pretty much."

Elizabeth shook her head. "Adults. You guys are just weird. Fine, I'll go read a book, okay?"

Tom patted her back. "Thanks honey."

"And I'm going now. You can finish up the kitchen."

"Hey...."

"You asked for that one," Vonda said, as Elizabeth huffed up the stairs. "Not like I'm complaining. You just solved my big dilemma of the day."

She leaned against the counter, hand outstretched for a plate to put in the dishwasher.

"Glad to be of service." He handed her a plate to put in the rack. "Now if I could just solve one of mine. Something's been eating my herd each month. Only one or two head, but...."

She looked at the ceiling. That corner might need a broom. Looked like cobwebs hung there. She glanced back at Tom. That white-knuckled grip he had on the dishrag was bound to hurt.

"You? You've been eating my herd?"

Busted.

She shrugged. "They were there."

"So are deer and they *need* thinning."

"But they aren't steak tartar. I love steak tartar."

"That herd's my living!" He threw the dishrag into the sink.

"It was only one."

"Yeah, one a month."

She looked at his feet. Being busted was so not her idea of fun. "I didn't mean to take all of them from you. I'm new to the area and wanted to eat. I thought it was from different ranchers."

Tom sighed and picked up the dishrag, which he shook at her, wet sprinkles emphasizing his words. "Promise me you won't do it again."

"Okay, I'll try. But I can't a hundred percent promise. You have no idea how good they taste off the bone."

"Try. Please. Go eat deer. I'll buy you steak tartar in a nice restaurant. Please." His green eyes beseeched her.

Who could resist that? "I'll try really hard."

****

Tom stared at Vonda. Unbelievable. *She* caused the thinning of his herd. Even so, even though he should still be pissed at her, he found her attractive. Her amber eyes gleamed with mischief and desire. Despite his failure last night, she wanted him. And he wanted her. More than he wanted his herd to live, he wanted this woman. What was it about Vonda that turned him on, that made him forget his anger?

"It's my sexy good looks." She smiled at him, wiggling her eyebrows.

"Are you reading my mind again?"

"You're broadcasting again. It's hard not to know what you're thinking."

He took a breath, wondering if she'd know the

answer to one question that plagued him all day. Or plagued him in those small moments when he wasn't contemplating what to do to Vonda's body.

"Did Margie say why, if I'm a genetically defective werewolf, I have telepathic abilities? Among other things."

"What other things?" Vonda stuck another plate in the rack.

"Did she or didn't she?"

"Maybe. What other things?"

"Are you always this stubborn?"

Vonda grinned. "On occasion."

He snorted. "Uh-huh. I'll go first. Sometimes I know what's going to happen before it happens. Now it's your turn."

"She might have mentioned something."

"Hey, no fair. I told you, the least you can do is return the favor."

"I will. But there are other things that have been on my mind all day concerning you and talking isn't one of them." Vonda raised her eyes to his, her amber irises glowing.

****

Ditto for him. So far this conversation was better than he thought it would be. "Yeah? Like what?" He couldn't help the grin that curled his lips.

She lightly slapped him on the upper arm. "Like what?"

Tom caught her wrist and pulled her toward him. "I can do better than last night if you'd like to try it."

Her hands slid up his chest, winding around the nape of his neck. "You have really good ideas tonight, mister."

"Glad you like them."

Warm lips touched his and the same spark shot through him that he felt yesterday when he shook her hand. Heat circulated through his body, his heart beginning a frantic beat. Muscles tightened as if he prepared for a race instead of a horizontal bed session. The scent of Vonda's skin pushed his desire to a new level, thickening his erection. If the damn thing got any bigger, it would unzip his pants on its own. Not that he was complaining; at least all parts were a go.

Vonda's body pressed against his as he deepened the kiss, stroking his tongue against hers. With one foot he closed the dishwasher door.

"Why don't we go in the bedroom?" He whispered in Vonda's ear.

She shivered. "What's wrong with the kitchen?"

"Elizabeth might not stay put."

"Oh, yeah. Bedroom it is."

She started walking in the direction of the bedroom, but he reached for her hand, turning her to face him. Lowering his head, he kissed her, not wanting to lose contact with her body even for the short distance to the bedroom. Vonda let out a little squeak when he wrapped his arms around her waist and lifted her off her feet.

Despite what studies showed about men, he could do two things at once, kissing and walking while holding Vonda. And with his erection straining against his zipper after four years of inactivity, he was so the man.

Despite his poor performance last night and the fact that Vonda would be the only woman since his wife died that he slept with, he felt an amazing lack of nerves. Being with Vonda felt right, as if his entire life happened to lead him to her.

The bedroom door shut with a resounding click when he nudged it with his foot, closing him in with his fate.

****

Vonda moaned as Tom's tongue swept against hers. His kisses made her legs weak. Thank goodness his arms were still around her waist, keeping her from falling. She tilted her head back as he kissed down her neck, nipping gently at her shoulder. The fire that shot through her veins burned hotter than anything she had felt before. Something about being around Tom made the mating heat stronger and yet his touch calmed her, as if curling up next to him would make everything in her life okay.

His mouth burned a trail of kisses from her shoulder across her skin to where her tank top began. When his arms loosened around her waist, she clutched at his shirt to remain on her feet. Tom slid his hands under her tank top, pulled it over her head, and dropped it on the floor in one movement. He traced a finger around the lace cups of her bra.

"Sexy." He winked at her and sprang the back clasp free.

Before he could remove it, she locked gazes with him and slowly lowered the straps down her arms, teasing him with small glimpses of her nipples, while she held the bra cups in place with one hand. His gaze left hers, fixated on her chest. Slowly, ever so slowly, she lowered the cups, the lace rasping against her sensitive nubs.

Tom licked his lips, glanced at her face and dropped his mouth to one nipple. With his tongue, he circled the bud, driving her crazy before finally drawing it into his mouth. She sighed as she ran her hands through his hair, holding him against her. The man had talented lips, fingers, tongue. Wonder if all parts of him were equally good?

Probably.

His mouth moved to her other nipple, while one warm finger circled the nub he had sucked, the contrast of warm finger and cold air causing chill bumps to form across her skin. She felt desire rushing through her blood, heating her, her core growing wet for him, because of him.

She wanted the feel of his skin against her. Needed it. Needed him. His shirt had to go. Now. Even if it meant breaking the connection of his mouth against her breast.

She yanked his tee-shirt out of his pants, shoving it up until it caught on his arms. Drat it.

"Eager, eh?" Tom grinned at her, male satisfaction gleaming in his eyes.

"You have no idea." She managed to yank the offending tee-shirt over his head and deposited it on the pile of clothes littering the floor. About time some article of his clothing joined the pile.

"I like you like this. Wanting me."

She smiled at him, pulling him close for a kiss. The mating heat might rule her hormones and cause her to need sex, but it didn't make her long for his touch. The longing was all Tom's doing. She had never wanted a man like this before.

She trailed kisses to his ear, while his fingers played with her nipples, circling, pinching.

"God, Tom, you make me want you. Now."

"Hmm. That's what I like to hear. But it's denied." He flicked a fingernail across her nipple, eliciting a groan from her. "You have to wait. I have a lot to make up for."

"Mmm. I like that idea. Unfortunately the sun sets soon, so unless you want a furry wolf in your bed, you need to get a move on."

"You have a point."

She reached for the button of his jeans. "Let's make you more comfortable."

His hands ran down her ribs, over her waist, stopping on the waistband of her low-rise jeans. "Ditto for you."

And then he kissed her and all thoughts except for getting that damned button undone left her mind. In a rush of hands, sweep of arms and some fancy footwork, they both managed to remove each other's jeans and underwear.

She felt the bed hit the back of her knees and she tumbled onto the patchwork quilt covering the mattress. Tom's weight fell on top of her, a delicious blanket of warmth and comfort.

She wrapped her legs around his waist as his hips rolled against hers, his cock rasping against her sensitive clit. He pulled back and thrust forward, teasing her, making her groan.

The fire built in her veins, centered in her core, as he continued teasing her clit, thrusting, pulling back, until she started convulsing. One big hand touched her mound.

"Not yet. I want to be in you when you come."

"Well then, hurry it up!"

Tom chuckled. Using his hand, he guided his huge erection to her entrance. Locking gazes with her, he thrust into her core, sinking to the hilt. She gasped as he filled her. For sure she'd be sore tomorrow. His thumb stroked her cheek, concern in his eyes.

"You okay? I'm a little big."

"A little? Feels good. Would feel better if you'd move." She tightened her legs, pushing his hips into hers.

Tom smiled and did as she wanted, pulling back and slamming into her, over and over again until she tightened around him, crying out. Two thrusts later and he joined her, spilling into her spasming channel.

Dropping her legs from his waist, she ran a hand through his hair and kissed his cheek. He raised himself onto his arms and tucked a strand of her hair behind her ear. A wrinkle appeared between his eyes, the anxiety bleeding into his gaze.

She smiled. "That was great. We'll have to do a repeat later. Like when I'm human again." Maybe

Margie didn't know what she was talking about. Everything looked to be normal. Oh, well. It had been an interesting theory.

The anxiety in his eyes vanished, replaced by joy. "We have a deal." He pulled out, the absence of his cock and weight leaving her feeling abandoned. Odd, that.

Since Margie was so obviously incorrect, she needed to clean up and mentally prep for the bone-wrenching pain of the change. After all these years of changing, she knew when the sun was about to set, when the magic of the change would overcome her, turning her into a wolf. Shouldn't be much longer now.

She made it halfway to the bathroom when she heard Tom cry out. She whirled around to see him kneeling by the bed, one hand bracing himself against it. Pain-filled eyes turned to her.

"God, Vonda, what's happening?" His voice broke, the ending of the last word coming out in a growl.

The skin on his back rippled and she had the oddest thought that the only time she'd seen another person change was when Margie forced it from Big G. And that had happened so quickly, she hadn't processed it. But this, this she processed. Did she look like that when she changed?

"Congrats. You're not genetically deficient after all."

He panted, gritting his teeth against the pain. "Huh?"

"You're changing." She knelt beside him, touching his shoulder. "Margie said it can happen if a half-breed who hasn't changed has sex with a full-breed. That's why she stuck around last night, to see if you'd changed. Guess she'll be surprised tomorrow. Shh, just relax, let it flow over you, don't fight it." Naturally, he fought it. She had too, all those years ago. Until she realized changing was much easier if she relaxed and let it happen.

"It hurts."

She ran her hand through his hair, wanting to take the pain from him. "I know. It will go away once the change is complete."

Tom opened his mouth as if to speak, but before he could, she saw the beast inside him win the fight. His face changed, growing longer, growing fur. He yelled, the sound turning into a howl as he changed. Fur rippled across his skin, brown fur tipped in black as if he were a calligraphy brush dipped in ink. His arms turned into legs and he collapsed on the floor.

Damn. Does it hurt like that all the time? His voice sounded in her head.

"Not quite that bad, but it's still painful."

Vonda felt the sun drop below the horizon, the magic in her veins pulling her beast out. Her skin rippled like Tom's had, flowing into fur as she dropped to all fours, shaking the pain from her muscles. Unlike Tom, she had grown used to the pain, or as used to pain as one could get.

Footsteps sounded at a fast pace, followed by a pounding on their door.

"Daddy! Are you okay? I heard yelling. Daddy?"

Elizabeth opened the door and burst into the room, coming to a halt as she stared at the two wolves. Fear crossed her eyes, but she held her ground.

"Vonda? Daddy?"

Don't be scared, honey. I seem to have changed.

It's okay, Elizabeth. Your Dad changed like me, Vonda said at the same time.

Elizabeth's eyes darted from one wolf to the other. "Oh, my gosh. Daddy changed into a wolf. How wicked cool!"

How wicked painful, Tom muttered.

Luckily Elizabeth didn't hear him. She ran over to him and threw her arms around his neck. Tom licked her face.

"Does this mean Margie isn't going to try to take me again? I like her, but I don't want to live with her."

No, sweetie, that's why Vonda's going to live with us, Margie isn't going to take you from me.

"But you're a wolf now."

I am, but Vonda is going to stay here and show us how to be wolves. Someone has to and I'd rather it be Vonda than Margie, wouldn't you?

Elizabeth looked at Vonda and then back at Tom. Vonda kept her mouth shut. She was staying, no way was she letting Tom go, but Tom needed to explain things to Elizabeth. If it wasn't for Tom's change, she'd have left the two of them alone to talk things out.

"Yeah, I like Vonda. She can stay."

Vonda gave her a toothy grin. Score, she was in with the kid. For now.

Tom, I'm going to run. You want to come with me? I promise I won't eat your cattle.

"She was eating on the herd?" Elizabeth's brows shook hands with her hairline.

They were tasty, but your dad made me promise not to eat on his herd. One of these days you'll understand the taste.

"Eww. I don't think so."

Honey, I'm going to go out with Vonda. You stay here. Keep the doors and windows shut and locked, we'll be back by morning. We'll be around the area if you need us. Okay?

Elizabeth shrugged. "No one's coming after me again, right?"

Right, honey. Will you be okay?

"Sure. Soon I can go out with you, too. Cool. I'm going to go read. Maybe I'll stay up all night reading since you won't be around to tell me otherwise."

Hey, now....

Elizabeth jumped up, kissed Tom's head and darted out the door.

She doesn't listen to me, Tom sighed.

Yeah? Get used to it. They tend to do that.

Are you happy with this? His paw gestured to her and back to him.

This?

Me. Like this. Or not like this. I mean, are you happy with this decision? It was forced on you and I appreciate you offering to stay with us so I could keep Elizabeth, but I want you to be happy with the decision.

Rambling. He was rambling. she smiled to herself. If a man rambles, well, that means he cares. And Tom caring enough about her to ramble made her heart sing.

I'm very happy. Ever since I met you, since I shook your hand, I've wanted you. And not just the sex thing. It's you. I've never felt about a man like I do you. I'm more than happy with this arrangement.

He walked over to her and licked her face.

It's a little hard to do what I want in this body. But once the sun comes up, don't run off. He waggled the hair sticking out above his eyes.

She licked him back. *Don't worry, I won't. Are you ready for the hunt?*

As long as you're with me, I'm ready for anything.

Anything? Her eyebrows waggled back at him.

Anything with you. Forever and always.

With Tom at her side and in her heart, the loneliness she'd experienced her entire life vanished, leaving only peace.

About the author...

By day, Karilyn works in the research department of an oncology clinic. By night, she tells the stories of her imaginary friends.

Karilyn and her most wonderful, ever patient husband share their home in the great state of Texas with two partially psycho dogs and a handful of colorful fish.

Thank you for purchasing
this Wild Rose Press publication.
For other wonderful stories of romance,
please visit our on-line bookstore at
www.thewildrosepress.com

For questions or more information,
contact us at
info@thewildrosepress.com

The Wild Rose Press
www.TheWildRosePress.com

LaVergne, TN USA
05 February 2010
172174LV00004B/1/P

9 781601 547095